Sookie Stackhouse attracted vampires, werewolves, and various otherworldly creatures. Even fellow authors fell in love with her and with Charlaine Harris's "magical and mysterious twist on traditional vampire stories" (*Houston Chronicle*). And though Sookie's story has come to an end, these tales of her and the characters who populated her world will give you a different perspective on the series you thought you knew . . .

In "Nobody's Business," Rachel Caine sends Kenya Jones and Kevin Pryor to Dallas on a search for a not-too-bright robbery/murder suspect—who just happens to be connected to a ring of criminals led by a dangerous vampire.

Witch Amelia Broadway decides to test a folk legend about witches being able to communicate with the winds, but she isn't prepared for the stormy consequences, in Seanan McGuire's "Knit a Sweater out of Sky."

While Sookie and Bill Compton are in Dallas, a Food Network crew unexpectedly shows up to shoot at Merlotte's, but what they're really cooking up is a deadly surprise for Bill, in Jeffrey J. Mariotte's "Taproot."

In "Widower's Walk" by MaryJanice Davidson, Eric Northman is passing through twenty-third-century Baton Rouge, which, for the first time in an age, doesn't have a vampire king but rather a shifter queen—from the famed and formidable Stackhouse-Merlotte clan . . .

"Blending action, romance, and comedy, Harris has created a fully functioning world so very close to our own, except, of course, for the vamps and other supernatural creatures" (*The Toronto Star*). And now fifteen of today's most popular authors have come along for the ride.

Ace Anthologies Edited by
Charlaine Harris and Toni L. P. Kelner

MANY BLOODY RETURNS

WOLFSBANE AND MISTLETOE

DEATH'S EXCELLENT VACATION

HOME IMPROVEMENT: UNDEAD EDITION

AN APPLE FOR THE CREATURE

GAMES CREATURES PLAY

DEAD BUT NOT FORGOTTEN

DEAD
BUT NOT
FORGOTTEN

Stories from the
World of Sookie Stackhouse

EDITED BY
CHARLAINE HARRIS
AND
TONI L. P. KELNER

ACE BOOKS, NEW YORK

THE BERKLEY PUBLISHING GROUP
Published by the Penguin Group
Penguin Group (USA) LLC
375 Hudson Street, New York, New York 10014

USA • Canada • UK • Ireland • Australia • New Zealand • India • South Africa • China

penguin.com

A Penguin Random House Company

This book is an original print publication of The Berkley Publishing Group.

DEAD BUT NOT FORGOTTEN

Ace Books are published by The Berkley Publishing Group.
ACE and the "A" design are trademarks of Penguin Group (USA) LLC.

ISBN: 978-0-425-27780-5

PUBLISHING HISTORY
Ace trade international edition / December 2014

PRINTED IN THE UNITED STATES OF AMERICA

10 9 8 7 6 5 4 3 2 1

Cover illustration by Lisa Desimini.
Cover design by Judith Lagerman.
Interior text design by Kristin del Rosario.

First published as an audio book by Audible.

The Edgar® name is a registered service mark of the Mystery Writers of America, Inc.

CONTENTS

INTRODUCTION

CHARLAINE HARRIS

I have to admit I was dubious about this project when Steve Feldberg at Audible first proposed it. I thought it would be strange to see my characters from someone else's viewpoint, and I thought it would be embarrassing to invite other writers to jump into my characters. But as I mulled the idea over for a few weeks, it occurred to me that I had already seen my characters from another viewpoint, on *True Blood*. Maybe seeing them through another prism would be just as interesting.

Gradually, I began to see how much fun this project might be, especially with Toni L. P. Kelner, friend and coeditor on so many anthologies, riding shotgun. We made up a list of writers who had let me know they'd enjoyed the books. To my pleasure, they all seemed excited at the idea.

I have been delighted with the stories we received. Each one has provided me with a sort of affectionate good-bye to the world where I lived for so long, and the people I created to populate that world.

NOBODY'S BUSINESS

RACHEL CAINE

Rachel Caine was enthralled by Kevin and Kenya, the Bon Temps police officers who appear in most of the Sookie books. She wanted to see more of their personal lives and to find out exactly how they came to realize they were really made for each other. Here's Rachel's version of their vampire-imperiled courtship, which also involves swamp water, addicts, and other assorted romantic shenanigans.

Hoo boy, it was hot. Though saying it was hot in Bon Temps, Louisiana, was a little like saying water was wet; even this late in the season, well into what probably felt like fall in other parts of the country, it was a sticky, steamy day. Like most other days.

Kevin Pryor reached for the controls of the air-conditioning on the police cruiser, but before he could get to them, his partner, Kenya Jones, was already there, expertly adjusting the knobs to get just the right mix of dry and cold. She also got out a thermos full of cold water, wetted a small washcloth, and handed it to him.

"Are you saying I stink?" he asked her, and made quick use of it, swabbing his filthy, sweaty face, neck, and hands. Not much he could do about the shirt; it was going to be one of those challenges that might be too big for regular laundry, and his mother would give him a lecture about taking better care of his things even though he was a grown-ass man.

Kenya didn't quite smile. "I wouldn't say that." Which was her way of saying that she was too polite. In fact, he smelled like rot and swamp, because he'd had to bend over and fish out the rotting suitcase from the green, stagnant pond and open it up to be sure there wasn't anything unpleasant in it, like body parts. There hadn't been. Just somebody's sad mess of clothes and some papers too rotted away to read.

They'd gotten the call about a suitcase floating in the pond just an hour ago, and both of them had, without discussion, decided to put it at the top of their to-do list. Bon Temps was a sleepy little backwoods place, but it still had its more-than-fair share of meth-heads, criminals, losers, and killers.

Some of their killers were vampires.

He didn't like to think *all* vampires were killers, because some of the ones he'd met, like Bill Compton, generally seemed to be good people, wanting to live whatever kind of life they had without trouble, but he understood that there was a spectrum in the undead, like there was in the living. Good and bad and shades between. One thing he'd learned early on as a cop: People were rarely on one side of the line or the other. Good people did bad things. Bad people did good things. You had to take it on a case-by-case basis.

"That was strange, wasn't it?" Kenya asked as she rewetted the washcloth and ran it over her exposed skin. He found himself watching that too closely, mind going blank, and had to blink and look away. Kenya was off-limits, obviously. First, she was his partner. Second, she was just about his polar opposite in every way—Amazon tall, rounded, built like Venus, if Venus could bench-press the weight of a grown man. And she was black, which didn't matter to him a hill of beans, but he knew it mattered in the landscape of Bon Temps society. Such as that was. It most certainly mattered to his mother. She didn't even like him riding with Kenya all day; after all, she was from a generation that had gotten all froth-mouthed over *those people* going to the same restrooms.

He loved his mother. He just didn't like her very much.

"You mean the suitcase?" he asked, dragging his mind back to the case—the *literal* case—they were working on. "Could have been some pissed-off boyfriend tossing his girl's clothes in the water during an argument. Or somebody's idea of recycling. No sign of foul play, at least. It's just junk."

Kenya nodded. She was frowning a little bit, but there hadn't been anything in the suitcase that either of them could point to as something that shouldn't have been tossed out. If there had been ID or a passport or cash or jewelry, that'd be one thing, but an old, scarred Samsonite with one good latch filled with threadbare clothes . . . "All right," she said. "I'll write it up in case something comes up on it. I checked missing persons. We got three, but none of them would fit the clothes in that bag."

The clothes had been for a generously sized woman without much sense of style. Generic stuff, sun-faded from flapping on a laundry line. Which, now that Kevin followed that train of thought along the tracks, didn't exactly support the theory of a spat with a girlfriend. Women of that age, and that particular style, didn't generally go in for fiery domestic arguments. When those kinds of women had fights, they were quiet, full of resentment, and the parties involved rarely threw things into stagnant ponds out of spite.

"Maybe we ought to head back," Kenya said, and cracked open the window. "I am not going to be friendly all day long with that shirt."

It did stink pretty bad, and he could feel the sticky chill of it now that the A/C was drying the fabric, slimy against his chest. In this job, you tended to get accustomed to bad smells; a couple of bodies rotting in the hot Louisiana summer adjusted your nose real fast. But this was different.

"Right," he said, and put the cruiser in gear. "Back to the barn."

Nothing in Bon Temps was a long drive, unless you went out into the fringe communities, and that was mostly about the quality of the roads, not the distance. So in under five minutes they were back on what passed for the main drag. They passed Merlotte's, which looked like it had a decent midday crowd going. He found himself craving lunch all of a sudden, and he caught Kenya's longing glance in that direction, too. Last thing he wanted was to wear swamp stink into a restaurant, though. Shower, fresh shirt, and then lunch.

Of course, it never happened.

They were a block away from the station when Marie Sandeman came running out in the street towing her ragged little boy along behind her and waved them down as if she were bringing in a jet for a landing.

"You're kidding," Kenya said, and glowered at the woman. Marie was none too stable at the best of times, and this didn't look like it was going to be one of her better days. She hadn't combed her hair, and she probably hadn't slept much, either, from the dark rings around her eyes and the pale, sweaty set of her face. Thin as a stick insect, so thin he could see her ribs under the crop top she was wearing. Her kid didn't look much cleaner, but at least he was better fed. Kevin sincerely hoped that the broad, dark smear on the boy's cheek was mud.

"You gotta help me!" Marie shouted, and pounded on the hood of the police car for emphasis.

"Oh hell, she did *not*," Kenya said, and had her door open before Kevin could turn off the engine. "Marie Sandeman! Take your hands off the car!"

Marie held up her hand in a trembling pledge to be good as she stepped back. Kenya fixed her with a blank, intimidating stare as Kevin exited the vehicle and came around to the front of the car near Marie. Kenya held back. It was the normal way they approached someone like Marie. He'd made his peace with the fact that in their partnership, he was the *less* intimidating one.

"You gotta help me," Marie repeated. Her little boy crumpled up a corner of his dirty, oversized Superman T-shirt and stuffed it in his mouth. His dark eyes were as wide as dinner plates. "He's in my house!"

That changed things, and Kevin heard it in the tone of his partner's voice as she said, "Who is, Marie?"

"My dealer—" Her brain must have caught up with her mouth, because she stopped midconfession (it would have been drugs) and looked sideways. Marie was a real bad liar. "His name's Quentin. He won't leave. He's tearin' shit up in there!"

"Is he high, Marie?" Kenya managed to sound warm and calm and strong all at the same time. Mostly, Kevin figured, it was for the boy's

benefit. They'd handled Marie so many times that kindness had generally gone out the window, along with Marie's self-respect.

"Probably . . . ?"

Kenya nodded to Kevin and got back into the cruiser. He delayed
long enough to say, "You go get yourself a soda or something, Marie.
Don't go home until we deal with this, all right?"

Marie might not be as smart as your average set of tools, but she
understood an opening when she saw one. "Ain't got no money," she
said, and took on a stubborn, defensive look. "Ain't my fault, I had to
run out of there so fast!"

Kenya didn't so much as blink. Kevin sighed, pulled out his wallet,
and gave Marie a five, which she snatched from his fingers with rabid
eagerness.

She looked down at her little boy as she stuffed the cash in her
pocket. "See? Cops ain't always bad. Just mostly."

Kevin shook his head and slammed the car door as Kenya flipped
on the lights. No need for the siren. Marie didn't live that far away, and
there wasn't any traffic to speak of between them and the destination.

"I already hate this day," Kenya said. "You know we have to go in
her house."

"I know," he said. "Bright side is, you won't notice how bad my
shirt stinks anymore."

Marie's screen door was pretty useless, with a half-busted top hinge and
most of the screen ripped into sharp-edged tatters. Old damage, rusty
at the ends. Behind it, the front door hung wide open.

"Don't look good," Kenya said. "Left or right?"

"Left," Kevin said. She nodded, made a silent three-count, and
eased into the darkness, going right. Kevin moved with her. They
clicked their lights on within a second of each other.

It wasn't better than the last time he'd seen the place. The floor was
choked with discarded clothes, broken toys, bottles . . . basically the
worst footing in the world if they had to move fast. Kevin swept the

corners with his flashlight, but there was no sign of an intruder, unless you counted the roaches scurrying to avoid the glare. The stench of old diapers and rotting trash made the swampy aroma from his shirt seem almost soothing.

It was also hotter than hell. He guessed Marie had forgotten to pay the electric bill again, or else couldn't afford to. What she *could* afford was meth, and he spotted some on the coffee table, right next to the open pack of fruit snacks her kid had probably been eating. Time to call social services again.

He heard the shuffling sound the same time Kenya did, and both their lights moved to pinpoint the doorway that led into the kitchen. Kenya moved like a tiger as she closed the distance from the other side, and despite the fact that this was damn dangerous, Kevin couldn't help admiring her. Moments like these, she was so beautiful it hurt. Not that he'd ever say so.

They paused on either side of the kitchen doorway, and Kenya gave him a nod, which was their sign that she'd let him go in first and low, while she covered high. They both moved their lights to converge, and pinned the intruder in place in the beams.

He wasn't exactly—right. Kevin took that in at a glance—the wide, wild, red-rimmed eyes; the matted long hair; the pallid face and red lips. Maybe he'd come to Marie's house looking to score.

He was holding a dead cat. That was why his lips were so red, and dripping.

"Jesus," Kenya said. She sounded disgusted. "Drop the cat and put your damn hands up."

He dropped the cat, all right, but it turned out that in his other hand he had a gun, and he used it. He shot wild; the bullet buried itself in the wall a good three feet to the right. Kevin fired back and heard Kenya do the same.

One of them must have hit him, because the junkie yelped and staggered back as he dropped his gun.

Kevin surged forward. "Down! Get down on the floor!" A fate worse than death, to lie on that floor, but his heart was ripping itself loose in adrenaline-fueled pounding, and he wasn't feeling particularly sympathetic.

The wild man bared stained teeth at him and knocked Kevin out of his way as easily as if he were a blow-up toy. It felt like being hit by a sledgehammer in the chest, and Kevin was aware of leaving the ground, a second of motion, and then a hard, rattling impact against the solid bulk of the refrigerator.

Kenya let out a wordless yell and fired, but the man was damn fast as well as damn strong, and she missed him as he smashed through the cloudy back window of the kitchen, launching himself out to the straggly grass of the lawn. He was already at a dead run when Kevin staggered forward to look. He couldn't seem to get his lungs to work, and for a panicked second or two he thought his chest had been crushed . . . and then his paralyzed solar plexus let go, and he whooped in a hungry breath.

Kenya was right there, holding him up while he got his legs under him again. "You all right?" she asked, and he nodded without speaking and motioned her on. She gave him a doubting look but kicked open the back door and sprinted after the intruder, who had already vaulted the back fence.

Get it together, Kevin told himself, and stumbled through the mess of the living room out to the front yard, then to the cruiser. Once inside, he caught his breath and turned the key. It was as if gunning the engine started something inside him, too, and he snapped back into focus with a vengeance. Still shaking, but this time it was with pure, white-hot rage.

You're not going anywhere, you fucker, he thought. He'd never say it out loud, because he'd been raised polite, but he meant every word.

He whipped the cruiser into a roaring turn and hit the sirens and lights, taking the next corner at a skid. Up ahead, Kenya was running hard and gaining on the intruder, who was just crossing the block up ahead. Kevin missed the man as he dodged and went sharply left up a narrow alley—too narrow for the cruiser. Kenya waved him on around, and he hit the gas again and took a left to run parallel with their fleeing cat-killer. It was a long block. His radio crackled as he took the turn to cut the man off, and he heard Kenya's voice say, "Kevin, he's got a truck, repeat, he's in a—"

Too late.

Kevin saw the truck in a blur as it headed straight for the front quarter panel of the cruiser. The next second he was spinning, and the impact knocked him sideways. The cruiser jerked hard right and tipped, but didn't quite topple over on its side, and then the truck pushed it out of the way and sped off, leaving a greasy smoke of burning tires behind it.

"Shit," Kevin gasped, and let go of the wheel. "Shit!" He tried to steer away from the curb he'd landed against, but the cruiser made a grinding metal groan, and he heard the left front tire shred and pop. "Shit!"

It hurt to slam his hands down on the wheel, but he did it anyway.

Kenya yanked his door open from the outside—it took three tries—and looked him in the face. "You're bleeding," she said. Her voice sounded flat and professional, but there was a look in her eyes that said something different. She popped the trunk and got the first-aid kit. "Here, put some pressure on it."

He didn't realize how much he was bleeding until he glanced in the rearview mirror. There was a wide cut on his left temple, probably from broken glass, and a swath of red down his cheek. It had already dripped onto his shirt collar. "Guess this shirt's done for sure," he said, which seemed an odd thing to say when he thought about it, but he was a little disconnected. Too much, too fast. And twinges of pain were starting to make themselves felt, like sparks flying up from a fire.

While he fumbled a gauze pack out of the first-aid kit, Kenya was calling in on her shoulder radio, rattling off pursuit information and requesting an ambulance. She'd gotten the plate number of the truck, which was a damn good thing; Kevin had been too busy spinning to manage it. "We need a new car," he said. "This one's not going anywhere."

"Only place you're going is the hospital," she told him. "Hush."

"Did you just tell me to hush?"

"Hush," she said again, and crouched down to eye level. She took the gauze from him and swabbed at the blood on his face. "Just hush."

He did.

He was still sitting on a table in the emergency room getting stitches when Kenya came back in with a fresh undershirt and uniform shirt she must have taken out of his locker. Once the doc had tied off all his knots and headed to the next crisis, Kevin stripped off the stained clothes and put on the new ones. Kenya watched him without comment. He could tell she was thinking of something else.

"Thanks," he told her. She nodded, but she looked tense and guarded and clearly was arguing with herself about something.

Finally, she said, "He ditched the pickup about fifteen minutes ago at a truck stop on the way to Shreveport."

"And?"

"And he killed a nineteen-year-old to steal his car. Word from the scene is he was headed west," she said. Her shoulders slumped a little. "Kid got torn apart, Kevin. We should have got him."

"Yeah," he said, and swallowed. "Not your fault."

"Not yours, either. I should have taken Marie more seriously from the get-go. We need to get her in a room and find out who he is, right now."

"Yep." Kevin slid off the table and tucked the crisp new uniform shirt into his pants. It still had sharp creases in it from his momma's ironing, and it smelled of some scent she'd started adding to the laundry. She'd started out with lavender, but he'd talked her out of that; who takes a lavender-scented cop seriously? Not that spring-fresh was much better.

Kenya sniffed him as he moved past her. "Better than swamp water," she said, and he laughed. Just a little. It died as Kenya's radio crackled and spat out their call number. She unhooked it and answered.

"It's Dearborn," the voice on the other end said. "Where you at?"

When Bud Dearborn got on the line personally, it was almost never good news. "Hospital, sir," Kenya said. "Kevin's getting stitched up."

"He okay?"

"Yes, sir, he's fine."

"Good. Alcee Beck questioned your witness, and he's got a name for your guy: Quentin Glick. He's got a good long record of assaults, possessions, robberies, the usual stuff. I'll send it to your e-mail along with his mug shots."

"Yes, sir," she repeated. There was a line grooving into her forehead between her slowly flattening eyebrows. "We're on our way in."

"No, you're not," he said. "I need you two to go up to that truck stop and talk with the detectives out there. Shreveport's none too happy that we sent them our problem, and they want everything you know."

Kenya opened her mouth, and Kevin knew she was about to protest, so he quickly grabbed the mike from her and said, "Yes, sir, on our way. Pryor out."

Dearborn didn't even bother to acknowledge. Yeah, he was pissed. Deserved to be, too.

Kevin pinned the mike back on Kenya's shoulder. "Let's go."

The truck stop was still a busy crime scene, and the arrival of their cruiser and uniforms only added to the circus. The news crews focused on them briefly before deciding they weren't as photogenic as the lumpy, bloody sheet under which the victim lay dead. Kevin and Kenya got looked over by the local detective and were ordered inside the truck stop Hardee's to wait. It was three more long, boring hours, and dark had fallen, before someone walked in, ordered his own drink, and sat down across from the two of them.

He nodded and took out a notebook. The cup beside him steamed vapor into the air, but it had a funny smell that wasn't coffee. That was when Kevin noticed that instead of the standard *REG* or *DECAF* boxes being checked on the side, someone had written in grease marker *B+*.

His gaze went back to the detective. Pale, thin, a coarse five-o'clock shadow. Long horsey face and big dark eyes under a mop of wavy black hair.

Not just pale after all. The detective was a vampire.

Kevin shot a look at his partner, but she'd already twigged to it, too; he saw it in the cautious, steady gaze she was leveling on the man.

"I'm Detective Wallace," the man said. He had a faint accent, something East Coast, maybe. "You're the ones who let him get away."

Kevin kept his silence. So did Kenya. If Wallace felt at all disconcerted by that, or their stares, he didn't show it, but then vampires weren't long on empathy. Kevin had always gotten along with Bon Temps's vampire celebrity, Bill Compton; he was a tolerant man by nature—live and let live. But there was something about Detective Wallace that raised the hackles on the back of his neck.

"What can you tell me about him?" Wallace asked. He tapped his pencil on the pad. It had chew marks. Kevin wondered if they were fang marks, technically.

"His name is Quentin Glick," Kenya said. "He's five eleven, about one fifty, greasy shoulder-length hair. He's on something."

"He's on a lot of things," Wallace said, "but in particular he's on vampire blood. The drainers must have got their hands on something special, and we're trying to track down everyone who bought it. This Glick's the last, as far as we know."

"We heard he tore somebody apart," Kevin said. "That wasn't literal, was it?"

Wallace shrugged, as if it weren't any nevermind to him. "One arm, one leg. Kid died of blood loss and shock."

The detective sounded disgusted by it, but Kevin had the feeling it wasn't because of the loss of the boy's life. More the waste of a good blood supply. "So this thing he's on, it makes him stronger." Kevin remembered the impact of what would have probably been a light shove from Glick that had sent him slamming into the refrigerator. He'd gotten off damn lucky.

"Faster, too," Kenya said. "He ran like he was heading for the gold medal. Junkie usually has no stamina to speak of."

That turned Kevin cold from the spine out, the idea that Kenya might have caught up with a man capable of ripping off limbs. He couldn't help but imagine it, and a sick feeling welled up inside him that he didn't want to properly identify.

"Do you know where he's heading?" Kevin asked. The detective hadn't taken any notes, and it looked to him as if the pencil and notebook were just props, there to make him look more normal. As the pencil's untouched eraser tapped the paper, Kevin found himself focusing on the letters on the side: *The Bat's Wing*. He'd never heard of it, but it sounded like the name of some vampire-themed bar, like Fangtasia in Shreveport.

"No idea," Wallace said. He sounded bland and bored, and he took a deep gulp of his not-likely-to-be-coffee. "You ever met this Glick before?"

Kevin shook his head, but Kenya said, "Once. I booked him for aggravated assault years back. Just another drunk, back then. He had the two-beer answer." Wallace gave her a questioning look. "Ask a drunk how much he's had, he'll always say two beers, even if he's falling down. That was Glick. Mr. Two Beers."

"He's hit the big time now," Wallace said. "What can you tell me about friends, associates, relatives?"

"Not too damn much. I looked into his files while we were waiting. He was pretty much a loner."

"You discovered him in the house of a local in Bon Temps. What was he doing there?"

"Eating a cat," Kevin said. "When he took the dead kid's car, which way was he heading?"

"My information is he was headed south. Why?" Wallace asked. His eyes met Kevin's, and there was something so darkly alien in them that it was hard not to break the stare. "Were you planning on going after him in hot pursuit?"

Yes, Kevin thought. "No, sir," he said. "Just curious. Wanted to make sure he wasn't going back to Bon Temps."

"Doesn't look like he is, so it's none of your business from this point on," Wallace said. "You can go. Thanks for the information."

He snapped the notebook shut, chugged down the rest of his blood, and left them with the empty cup sitting on the table as he headed out.

A few seconds later came another detective, overweight, tired, and in a terrible mood. He didn't bother to sit down, and he damn sure wasn't a vampire. He barked rapid-fire questions at them about Glick, and after the first three, Kenya held up her hand. "We already answered all this," she said. "Your Detective Wallace was in here first."

That got her a weary, cold stare. "I don't care who was in here or what you told him, you tell it again. Hell's bells, you're police, you understand how this works."

They did. Kevin controlled his own frustration, but while he filled in his own answers, he was busy turning over things in his mind. *I don't care who was in here.* That was a funny thing to say. The crime scene was busy, but not that busy.

When he started to ask a question, he got cut off by the Shreveport detective and told they could go. Again. Then the man was off, muttering under his breath.

Kenya let a few seconds go by before she said, "You get the feeling he and Wallace wanted us to turn around and go home?"

"I did."

"You want to turn around and go home?"

"I don't," Kevin said. "I don't even think Detective Wallace was police."

Kenya looked blank for a second, but he knew her mind was racing. It was a pleasure to watch. "That's why we just had to repeat everything," she said. "So who was he?"

"I think he was sent here to find out what we knew—and if we knew something they thought we shouldn't. Vampire business."

She slowly nodded, turned her head, and looked out the window. No sign of Detective Wallace. He'd completely vanished from the scene. "Damn," Kenya said softly. "I did not see that coming."

"The Bat's Wing," Kevin said. "Have you ever heard of it? That was the name on the pencil he was using."

"No."

He pulled out his cell phone and Googled, and it was right there, top result. It was a vampire bar in Dallas. Close to Shreveport, by virtually no coincidence at all.

He put his phone back. "How do you feel about a road trip to Dallas?"

Kenya gave him a slow, deliberate smile. "Better get a couple of burgers for the road, and change clothes. I don't expect we're making this official."

She'd switched their bags of civilian clothes, the ones they usually kept in the other (crashed) cruiser, into the new ride. That was what he liked best about Kenya, he thought.

Forward planning.

Kevin had been to Dallas before—he wasn't some hillbilly—but it was a shock coming out of the relative peace of Bon Temps, or even Shreveport. You could see the glow on the horizon long before the city itself materialized, as if it were permanently on fire. Once the buildings began appearing, it was the neon-clad ones first. There was some new downtown hotel with a moving-screen exterior; it was showing random screensaver patterns of pulses and colors, and it was mesmerizing as he took the downtown exit.

"Turn right up here," Kenya told him. If she was impressed by the lights and the traffic (which was considerable, though it was nearly midnight) she didn't say so. "Well, this looks like Hipster Central."

It did. The Bat's Wing was in one of those derelict chic neighborhoods that ten years ago would have been crack houses and gang graffiti and today was devoted to herbal shops, stores that specialized in fancy hats, tea rooms, and—just up ahead—a tattoo parlor that no self-respecting biker would ever walk into. Kevin expected it got a brisk trade from sorority girls and soccer moms. Maybe stockbrokers.

The Bat's Wing was two doors down from the tattoo place, which was probably ideal for them both. It had generous parking that was nevertheless completely full, so Kevin eased the cruiser into an illegal space, because cops never ticketed cruisers even if they were out of their own jurisdiction, and no business ever dared tow them.

The building itself was a windowless black-painted cube with a painting of a bat flight in red silhouettes that started small at one corner and exploded into huge wings at the upper diagonal. The neon sign just had a bat silhouette that flapped its wings. Kevin could hear the pump of music through the walls.

"Expensive crowd in there," Kenya said, nodding toward the cars; she was right, the lot was full of shine and polish, and every single vehicle cost at least three times their annual salary, probably more. Still, he thought she'd fit right in. Kenya's civilian clothes included a close-fitting pair of jeans that hugged her curves and a tight black shirt under a leather jacket. She looked hot and dangerous.

There were no clothes in the world that could make Kevin look buff and chiseled, but he'd done all right. As usual, all eyes would be on Kenya, and that was good. People tended to underestimate him, and it made it much easier to watch her back. He just blended into the woodwork in a place like this. He'd be lucky if people didn't try to order drinks from him.

"Kevin." Kenya's tone was calm and level, but it had some weight to it, and he blinked and focused on her. "You sure you want to do this?"

"That asshole back at Hardee's knew something," he said. "I figure it's something we ought to know if we plan to catch Glick before he does worse than he already did. I know it's not our jurisdiction . . ."

"He rammed you with a truck," she said calmly. "That makes it my jurisdiction. And you're right. I don't figure the Dallas police would put this at the top of their to-do list; they got plenty of bad stuff going on around here."

"It's weird. I can get past Glick killing a person. I just can't get past him killing that cat."

"You saw Marie's house. That cat could have died of embarrassment." She smiled, and looked ten years younger. He couldn't help but grin back. "If the vampires are trying to cover something up, then we're the only ones who know about it right now. Plus, we drove a long way for nothing if we don't at least get a drink."

He made a grand after-you gesture, and she straightened her jacket and headed on in.

It was probably wrong to admit, even to himself, that watching her back was purely a pleasure.

Kevin had been to the vampire bar Fangtasia before, but he hadn't liked the place much, and it had made him feel worse about vampires, too. Fangtasia had seemed like a cross between a cheap B-movie set and a butcher shop. He'd had the uncomfortable feeling that everybody in it with a pulse was looked on as cuts of meat. He hadn't stayed long, and he'd lied to his mother about where he'd been.

The Bat's Wing made Fangtasia look both better and worse. It was bigger, louder, glossier, and packed with people, but it seemed . . . soulless, in ways even the smaller vampire bar hadn't. If Fangtasia was a butcher shop, this place was a slaughterhouse, moving cows through with ruthless efficiency from farm to plate. Women dressed in skimpy, tight dresses tottered around on heels that ought to come with warning labels, and the men with them were either aging, balding, and wealthy, or gym-obsessed and cruising for a sugar momma.

And then there were the vampires.

They didn't mingle as much as the Fangtasia regulars did; a few glided through the crowd untouched, icy and perfect, but most were sitting in what was obviously a special section, roped off from the general public and guarded by two linebacker-sized human guards with experience in looking tough. More vampires there than he'd expected, but then Dallas was a big city. It only made sense that their community was just as big.

There was no mistaking who was in charge, although he wasn't at all what Kevin had expected. The man sitting in the concentric circle of vampires looked like a poster of a nerd, from the cheap sports shirt and khaki high-waisted pants to the tape fixing one side of his Buddy Holly glasses. It wasn't that the nerd sat higher than the others, but it just seemed that way; it might have been the way the others aligned themselves, half turned toward him, half away to watch the room. He was the hub at the center of the deadly, glittering wheel.

Kenya stopped at an empty stand-up table and signaled to a thinly dressed cocktail waitress; she ordered a Coke, and Kevin got a beer, because he felt like at least one of them ought to look as if they were here to party.

Then he felt like an idiot when Kenya openly ogled a passing vampire who must've been born of Asian heritage in his human life. The vampire noticed and gave her a bare nod, which was apparently how they expressed approval around here. Kevin heard jealous murmurs from a couple of women near him.

"What?" Kenya asked as their drinks were delivered, and he realized he was staring at her. "Got to fit in, right?"

"Right," he said, and looked around for a woman to admire. He couldn't find one who intrigued him half as much as the woman sipping her Coke across from him, dark eyes lively and darting from one threat to another around them.

He saw her fix on something behind him, and whatever it was, it got her unwavering attention. Her hand slid away from her drink and under her jacket, and he almost turned before she made a sign, just a little one, to stay where he was. She gave him a sudden, bright smile and leaned in close to whisper in his ear.

"Glick's here. He's right behind you."

"Shit," Kevin whispered back. "I should have brought my gun!" They'd discussed it but decided it was too big a risk to come strapped into a vampire club in a strange town. Vampires took their personal security damn seriously.

She nodded and laughed as if he'd said something hilarious, and *dammit* if he couldn't help but notice how warm her cheek was as it brushed against his, and how soft. "I've got my baton," she said. "Get in front of him and I'll take him down from behind."

He would have probably agreed to pretty much anything just then, and as he pushed away from the table and walked at an angle to cut across Glick's path, it occurred to him he was about to put himself empty-handed in front of a man who'd ripped the limbs off somebody just a few hours before.

He was also, coincidentally, heading straight for the guards who were blocking the entrance to the velvet-roped vampire section. They might have PhDs in flexing and intimidation, but they weren't stupid; he got their attention instantly. What was worse, though, was what was happening behind the rope . . . because all that vampire focus lasered right in on him. It was like being impaled on an icicle.

The nerd king's pale blue eyes suddenly glowed an even colder arctic green, and Kevin shuddered because however much the costume tried to make the vampire look human and inoffensive, those eyes gave him away. What was underneath was ancient and completely ruthless.

Spotting Glick coming for him was actually kind of a relief.

The greasy, blood-spotted wild man howled, though it was drowned out in the relentless sound of the techno song that started up; the beat hammered through Kevin's bones and made him feel as if he were about to shatter. Kenya was moving, but someone was in her way—a woman in skyscraper heels, made earthquake-unsteady by the drink in her hand.

Glick was almost on him. In the flash of the swirling lights, his eyes looked solid crimson, as if they were bleeding right out of his head.

Kevin swept a full champagne bottle out of a sweating ice bucket on a rich man's table, dumping cold water all over a woman's lap, and slammed it into Glick's temple like a wrecking ball. It should have put him down. Hell, it probably should have killed him.

All it did was set him back on his heels, dazed, and make him stumble.

That was enough time for Kenya to come up behind him, snap out her extendable riot baton, and deliver surgical strikes to the bends of his knees. Strong or not, Glick went down, and Kevin hit him again with the champagne bottle. He only realized once Glick was lying still that Dom Perignon was foaming out in jets all over him, and the rich man was yelling his guts out, and the woman was shrieking about her dress, and somehow over all that chaos the nerd stood up and said one soft, precise sentence.

"Close it."

There was an instant reaction, all over the bar—not from the patrons, who were still jerk-dancing and drinking their livers away, but from the vampires. They all stood up and *moved*—flowing over the velvet ropes as if gravity were just a suggestion. There were yelps of alarm from patrons, and suddenly the music cut off, leaving an aftermath of yelled, trailed-off conversations and confusion.

The vampires began shoving people toward the exits. There was resistance at first, and then willing flight, because one look at them showed that the vampires weren't playing.

Nobody laid a hand on Kevin, or Kenya, or the man lying between them. Kenya still held her baton but he knew she wouldn't use it; there wouldn't be any point. Fighting a vampire under those circumstances was an instant ticket to the morgue.

The Bat's Wing was cleared out in what seemed like seconds, and probably was; the humans were swept out like trash by the vampires' broom, and the doors slammed and locked behind them. Without the music, and with the harsh overheads flipped on, the place looked—as all bars did—cheap and pathetically stained. Tables were littered with glasses, full and empty. Some people had even left behind coats and purses. It reminded Kevin of a disaster area, as if a random shooter had come in to pop off a few rounds and the occupants had run for cover.

He even saw one of those seven-inch high-heel shoes lying abandoned on the floor. Add in some broken glass and blood and it could have been on the six o'clock news.

When he looked up, the nerd king was standing right in front of him, and Kevin had to work to control a flinch. The man moved without a sound, an eerie inhumanity that he either cultivated or just didn't mind displaying. Hard to say which one was worse.

"Name," the vampire said. He had his crew arranged around them now, though Kevin hadn't heard any orders given; maybe they communicated like ants, through some kind of chemicals. He and Kenya were really, really alone.

"Kenya Jones," Kenya said, and gave the vampire an unexpected smile as she collapsed her baton and put it away. "This is Kevin Pryor, my partner."

The cold stare—fading back to blue now, rather than green—transferred to her, and somehow she kept smiling. Kevin didn't imagine it was easy. "What makes you think you can come in here and do this?" Now that he'd spoken more than two words, it became clear he had a faint trace of an accent—something muted and lost in time. Whatever it was, it didn't fit his computer-geek disguise.

Kevin said, "We're with the Bon Temps Police Department, sir. In pursuit of a murder suspect." He pointed at the man on the carpet. "That's him."

There was an indefinable shift in the vampire, though Kevin couldn't have named what changed; maybe it was just a fraction of a rise in an eyebrow. "Bon Temps. Louisiana. Area Five. Did Sheriff Northman send you here?"

"Our boss is Sheriff Bud Dearborn, sir," Kenya said. "He knows where we are."

"Your pursuit of your murder suspect is curiously backward, since you preceded him to this club," the nerd king said. "My name is Stan Davis. I am the sheriff of Area Six. You are operating within my realm, and my establishment, without authorization from the sheriff of Area Five. I believe you would call that operating outside your jurisdiction." His gaze flicked down for a half second to the man lying between them. "Leave him."

"Can't do that, sir," Kenya said. "He's our prisoner."

"Do you doubt for a moment that you can all disappear?" said another vampire, a female one, bone white, with a feral light in her eyes. She licked her very red lips. "Let me take them."

"I don't want trouble with Area Five, Rachel," Davis said. "Police officers are easy to kill but hard to explain."

Though Rachel didn't actually pout—her features weren't expressive enough—Kevin got the sense of something like a toddler's tantrum, but bottled up tight and a whole lot more homicidal.

At their feet, Quentin Glick twitched and groaned. Kenya reached behind her back under her jacket—a move that made all the vampires tense up again—and came out with a pair of handcuffs that she clicked on the man's wrists to pin him facedown.

That was when Kevin spotted the vampire they'd talked to at Hardee's. He was standing off to the side, half-hidden in shadows, but he was clearly part of the group, or he wouldn't still be in the room. Stan Davis's agent?

Kevin nodded toward him. "He wanted to find out what we knew about Mr. Glick, here. Which means you wanted to know about him, Mr. Davis. Were you expecting him?"

Silence. Stan Davis's stare was unnervingly precise, like an ice pick. "You need to walk away now and leave him to me," he said.

"Sir, Glick needs to face justice," Kenya said. "He killed a boy in Louisiana."

Rachel laughed. It was a sound like hail on glass. "So?"

"There are matters you have no place in," Davis said. "Go home. I said dead police officers were hard to explain. Not impossible."

That was an order, and there didn't seem to be much of a way to argue about it. Glick had gone still, and maybe he'd actually passed out again. Hard to tell under that mess of stringy hair.

Kevin exchanged a look with Kenya—silent partner communication, the kind of calculations and responses they did in crisis situations when there wasn't time or strategic space to talk out loud. *Go?* he asked her, with a quirk of his eyebrows. He read the shift of her weight to her forward foot. *Stay.*

Well, crap.

Before he could start trying to negotiate their staying alive, the situation changed for all of them, because Quentin Glick wasn't unconscious after all.

It ought to have been impossible for anyone to snap those cuffs at that angle, but a single roll of Glick's shoulders and his hands were loose. Glick must have broken his own bones to pull his hands free of the restraints. Before Kevin could process that fact, the man was up, all teeth and crazy eyes and blood leaking down his face, and it was pretty clear that the sheriff of Area Six had decided that maybe the easiest way to handle this was to let Glick go mad-dog on them and then clear up the mess once it was over. The vampires were fast enough to have intervened, but none of them moved a muscle.

Kevin had one chance, and he took it, slamming his forehead hard into the man's nose. It slowed Glick down, at least, and Kevin backed out of the way, grabbing up his old friend the champagne bottle.

Glick whirled. A human couldn't move that fast, *shouldn't*, but he did, and before Kenya could finish snapping out her riot baton again, he had her clutched in both hands, one at her throat, one on the side of her head. Perfect leverage to snap her neck. Sickeningly, the broken bones in his hands were sticking out, one breaking the skin in a red-filmed white spear, but the pain wasn't stopping him.

Kenya went very still. Kevin came to a halt, bottle trembling in his hand and ice forming around his fast-beating heart. *No. No, no, no . . .* He carefully set the bottle down and spread his empty hands. "Let her go," he said. "Please."

"Don't you beg," Kenya said. "Don't do it, Kevin."

Glick snarled. If there was anything human left in him, anything rational, it was buried too deep to reach. Kevin felt a surge of rage and hopelessness, because there was nothing he could do, *nothing*; Kenya was going to die and he was going to have to watch it happen and he couldn't. He just couldn't.

Glick began backing away, dragging Kevin's partner with him. She was letting her weight sag, hoping to pull him off balance, but whatever was fueling him was letting him pull her along like she was a rag doll.

Kevin followed, keeping the distance constant between them. The vampires moved out of Glick's way as he backed toward the door.

"Open it," Stan Davis said. One of the vampires entered a code on the keypad next to the exit and hit the metal panic bar, and it sagged open to the night and a deserted parking lot; the patrons must have taken the hint to get *way* the hell out of Dodge. No sign of police, either.

Glick backed away through the door, grinning at Kevin through bloody teeth. It wasn't imagination; his eyes weren't just bloodshot, they were bloody. *Bleeding.* He was crying blood. He was hemorrhaging from his ears, too.

"My advice is to let him go," Davis said from behind them. None of the vampires had moved again, and Davis's tone seemed calm and disinterested. "Don't throw your life away, Mr. Pryor. She is a lost cause."

Fuck you, Kevin thought furiously. He hardly ever cursed, not out loud, but he wanted to yell it loud and rip the vampire's head off in that moment. Nice idea. Impossible, but nice.

He took another step as Glick dragged Kenya over the threshold and past the swing of the door.

"Now," Davis said, which seemed completely out of context, until the vampire who'd opened the door slammed it shut in Kevin's face and cut him off from Kenya and Glick. Kevin threw himself forward against the bar, but it gave only a little before a cold, inhumanly strong hand closed around the collar of his shirt and yanked him backward. Next thing he knew, he was pinned against a hard, chilly vampire body with an iron rod of a forearm across his throat to hold him still as Stan Davis glided up to face him.

"Son of a bitch," Kevin spat, and tried to slip free. He might as well have been trying to bend stone. "Let me go!"

"If I do that, you'll only needlessly sacrifice yourself," Davis said. "Calm yourself. If you want to see her alive again, you need to think before you act."

"Then *help me*!"

"I will," said the sheriff of Area Six. "For a price."

Once again, Kevin found himself sitting in a booth across from the vampire who called himself Detective Wallace. The difference this time was that next to Wallace was Stan Davis, and Stan's vampires were ranged around the room in easy striking distance.

"He's going to kill her," Kevin said. Every nerve in his body was on fire with the need to *do something*, to charge out that door and find Glick. "I'll give you what you want. Just help me get her back."

The silence stretched on. He might have been sitting across from two mannequins, except for the reaction in his gut to their presence. Finally, Wallace (if that was even his name) said, "You should have just let it alone. We knew he was heading for us. We'd have taken care of him."

"You know what's going on with him?"

Wallace shrugged. It was such a tiny gesture that it hardly even registered as a ripple, but it conveyed the exact level of disinterest he must have felt. "He got his hands on something he shouldn't have. We knew he'd come here for another hit when he started coming down."

"What the hell is it?"

Silence, again. Finally, Davis said, "I thought you wished to bargain for the woman."

As if he owned her. Kevin took a few seconds to calm himself before he said, "All right. What do you want?"

"A favor," Stan Davis said. "It would seem having eyes in Area Five might benefit me. I don't trust Sheriff Northman."

"You want me to spy on *vampires*? On Eric Northman? How am I supposed to do that?"

"How you accomplish it is not my concern. That is what I want, or your partner dies." There was something in Davis's cold eyes that might have been amusement. "I think you have some attachment to her beyond only professional loyalty."

Kevin hated that the vampires could see it in him. But he also knew that the seconds were ticking away, and he remembered Glick's bloody mouth, that limp cat in his hands. Remembered the dead teenager lying on the concrete of the dirty parking lot, covered with a sheet.

He hated that a whole lot more.

"All right," he said. "If I see something you need to know, I'll tell you."

"No," Davis said. "You will tell me everything. Everything that Sheriff Northman does. I expect monthly reports."

Kevin realized he was clenching his hands so hard that his fingernails were gouging half-moons in his palms. "Fine, I'll find a way," he said.

"One thing. If you promise and do not deliver, I will kill you and your partner. It will not be quick."

This time, he had to swallow a mouthful of bile to get the words out. "I said yes. Now *help me*."

Davis sat back and glanced at Wallace. That was apparently all the authority that was needed, because Wallace slid out of the booth, crooked a finger, and three vampires answered his summons. They headed for the door.

Kevin got up.

"Where do you think you're going?" This time, Davis definitely sounded amused. Cat-with-a-wounded-mouse amused.

"I'm going with them," he said. "If she dies, there's no deal, and I'll make it my personal mission in life to make you sorry." He meant it. It suddenly came into focus for him that what he felt for Kenya wasn't just a casual thing, wasn't just attraction or simple lust or infatuation. It was something strong, and whether she felt it didn't matter. He loved her, and he was going to see that she was all right.

He'd surprised Davis, just a little bit, which probably didn't happen too often. "All right," he said. "I'll expect my payment once we save her. Don't disappoint me, Officer Pryor."

Stan went back to sitting in silence, staring at nothing, surrounded by his vampires.

Kevin knew, with a sick feeling in his stomach, that he'd just made a deal with a devil, but he'd have dealt with Old Scratch himself to save Kenya. She might hate him for it.

He could live with that.

The area outside the club was silent except for the constant hum of traffic in the distance. Wallace was waiting in the parking lot, under the weak glow of a security light, and as Kevin came out, Wallace moved off, expecting him to follow. There was no sign of the other vampires who'd exited.

Kevin headed straight for the Bon Temps squad car, unlocked it, and strapped on his service weapon. He released the shotgun from its locked mount and took it, too. It felt better, being armed.

Kevin expected that they'd move toward the street, but he and Wallace went the opposite direction, behind the club where the rusting steel Dumpsters huddled in a row. They were up against a chain-link fence, which had been ripped open and wrenched aside. Kevin looked down. Hard to tell in the poor lighting, but he thought he saw a splash of fresh blood on the pavement. He supposed Glick would be easy to track for vampires, thanks to all the hemorrhaging.

"Is he dying?" Kevin asked. Wallace didn't seem to hear the question. "You said he got his hands on something he shouldn't. Was it a drug?"

"None of your business," Wallace said. "Quiet."

He slipped through the broken chain link like mist. Kevin had more trouble managing it and got himself scratched up in the process, but he wasn't concerned with a few dings. There were gouges in the ground on the other side of the fence, as if Kenya had fought to slow Glick down. He saw the impression of her heels.

More blood. It was still wet and glistening in the moonlight.

A dog barked somewhere in the distance, lonely and hopeless, and Wallace paused again, then set off to the east. This area was an urban jungle—twisted old live oaks, tangles of thorn bushes and trash trees. A possum, its grayish white fur matted with debris, peered at them blindly before ambling away. Kevin had no idea what kind of dangerous vermin Dallas might harbor; blundering around in the woods of Bon Temps was a sure way to get snake bit, or have a snapping turtle take a hunk out of you. He didn't imagine Wallace cared much, so he let the vampire break the trail, careful to follow exactly in his steps.

They broke through into another open area. It had once been some kind of brick building, but nature had long since shown it who was boss, and the remains were a couple of barely standing walls and a cracked concrete floor. Vandals had taken everything else and left a generous deposit of trash behind—condoms, needles, crack vials, bottles, fast-food bags.

In the corner between those two remaining walls stood Quentin

Glick. He had Kenya in a bone-breaking hold against him, and she was definitely the worse for wear; Kevin saw rips in her jacket and jeans from the fence, blood running down the side of her face, and she was holding one of her hands at an odd angle. But she was alive, and she was *angry*. It crackled off her in waves.

When she spotted Kevin, her eyes widened and then squeezed shut for a moment. When she opened them she said, "Damn you, Pryor. Get the hell out of here."

"Not happening," he said. "You hang in there."

"Got nothing else to do," she said, but there was something in her eyes, her face that made him go tense and still inside. *She's going to move,* he thought, and he dreaded it so hard it felt like a knife turning in his guts. She'd accepted her own death. She just wanted to make sure Glick got what was coming to him.

Jesus, he had no time. Wallace wasn't moving; there were other vampires here, too, crouched in the shadows, watching, but they weren't going in to save Kenya. It was as if they were waiting for some signal.

When it came, it was invisible to human eyes; maybe it was Stan Davis and his telepathy again. They all *moved,* white flashes in the starlight, vicious and deadly. Kenya was already twisting violently against Glick's broken hands, and the shotgun Kevin held wasn't going to work because she was in the line of the spread; before he even completed the thought, he was releasing the shotgun, and as it began to fall toward the ground, as the vampires closed in on Glick, as Kenya completed her turn, it felt as if everything ticked slower . . . slower . . . slower . . . except that his hand was moving in regular time, flashing toward the holster and closing and drawing with the same fluid motion he'd practiced all those hours at the range and *snap* the shot hit his senses at the same time the shock traveled up his arm and a black hole opened between Glick's bloody, rabid eyes.

By the time Wallace seized Glick, he was already dead, and Kenya was falling forward to the ground.

Kevin let out a wordless yell and lunged for her, went down on his

knees amid the crack vials and needles and condoms and didn't give a
good goddamn about any of that as he reached out to roll her over.
Don't be dead, don't be dead, don't be . . .

"Nice shot," Kenya said. She sounded almost normal, but he felt
the vibration under her skin, the tremors of adrenaline and the after-
shocks of terror.

He didn't even think about it. He just grabbed her and pulled her
into his arms. It didn't feel like embracing a partner. It felt more like
coming home.

"She's alive," Wallace said from behind them. "You owe Stan."

"The hell I do," Kevin said. "I shot him before you even touched
him. Stan owes *me.*"

There was a moment of silence, of chill and whispering danger, and
then Wallace shrugged. "I guess that would be between the two of you.
Good luck with that conversation."

The moment was over. Kenya's muscles were starting to tense, the
animal comfort of their embrace passing, and he let her go before she
had to reject him by pulling away. They didn't meet each other's eyes,
but he saw that she was smiling. It looked a little shaky, but genuine
enough that she felt like she needed to turn her head to hide it.

He didn't offer to help her up, and she wouldn't have accepted it.
They just climbed separately to their feet, and Kenya retrieved the shotgun from where he'd dropped it as he holstered his sidearm.

When he looked up, the vampires were gone. Glick was gone, too.
They'd carried his body off, and Kevin expected it wouldn't ever be
seen again. The official *Wanted* posters would go up in Shreveport, and
that dead young man's family would never have the comfort of closure,
but at least Glick was done.

He expected to feel something after shooting a man in the head, but
all he felt at the moment was a dull, ringing emptiness and a distant
relief.

"Kevin?" Kenya was watching him. "We need to get out of here."

It had been a hell of a long day, and the thought of getting the hell away from Dallas, from Stan Davis and the oppressive sense of being watched, made him say, "Let's get back home."

They spent the drive not talking, but also not really feeling the need to talk; he pulled over at a rest stop along the way and got out the first-aid kit to clean up her cuts so they wouldn't get infected. Her wrist wasn't broken, just sprained, and he wrapped it tight. She let him do it, a concession of vulnerability that wasn't like Kenya Jones at all. *As long as we don't say anything,* he thought. *As long as we don't face it, maybe it can seem like a real thing.* Because he knew it couldn't be. His family would never accept her. Hers would never accept him. And then there was the working-together problem. There were rules and all.

But he knew what he felt, and she knew, and when he put the last bandage on, he met her eyes and sat back on his heels. Held the stare.

She leaned forward and without a single word kissed him.

It was sweet and warm and made his heart stop with longing, and he knew he didn't respond the way he wanted but he was too shocked, and it was over too fast, and then Kenya was buckling herself back into her seat and staring straight ahead out the car window. All he could do was stand up, clear his throat, and put away the first-aid kit before climbing back behind the wheel of the cruiser.

The silence continued, but after a while, after another mile or two of asphalt burning away under the tires, he found he was holding her bandaged hand in his, and the pressure of her fingers, light and strong and constant, soothed some ache inside him he didn't know he had.

They made it into Bon Temps just as dawn was warming the horizon a light pink.

"You never did get to take a shower," Kenya said. "You still smell like swamp water."

"You rolled around in crack house trash," he said. "I'm not judging."

"Guess we need to check in at the station and report back to Bud about what happened."

"Do we?" He looked over at her, and her eyebrows rose. "What the hell are we going to say? That I shot a fugitive outside our jurisdiction?"

She didn't have an answer for that. She just put her head back against the headrest and sighed. "You know what the worst thing is?"

"I couldn't even guess."

"We still don't know who threw that damn suitcase in the swamp. I'm not going to sleep until I figure that out."

He laughed, and he couldn't stop laughing, and he had to pull the car over because it hurt so bad and so good, and for the first time in a long time he heard Kenya laughing without restraint, and she never let go of his hand. Never once.

What are we going to say?

Not a damn thing, he thought. *Not a damn thing. Because it's nobody's damn business.*

TYGER, TYGER

CHRISTOPHER GOLDEN

Christopher Golden's story "Tyger, Tyger" begins a few months after the final Sookie novel. Quinn, my favorite weretiger, is having a very bad day, which promises to get much, much worse.

Quinn watched the speedometer, kept the needle pinned at the limit, and tried to stop his hands from gripping the steering wheel too tightly. He had punched in a classical station on his satellite radio that played mostly baroque music, a secret pleasure. He liked all sorts of music but prided himself on maintaining an even temperament, and when stress or anger threatened to get the better of him, the beautiful strings of some of those baroque arrangements soothed him.

Soothed the savage, he thought, with an expression that was half snarl and half grin. If someone else had said that to him, he would've been offended, but he had to be honest with himself. He was a full-blooded weretiger, after all. In the right circumstances, he had savagery to spare.

His cell phone rang. He'd stuck it into the console between the seats but had forgotten that it was linked into the car via Bluetooth, and now the number showed up on the little screen at the center of the dashboard. Quinn made his living as an event planner and the caller was a client.

He tightened his fingers on the wheel, knuckles going white as he waited for the ringing to cease. When it had, he reached into the console and plucked out the phone, then tried gamely to keep his eyes on the road as he powered it off and tossed it onto the seat beside him. No clients today.

Quinn steadied himself, then glanced down to see that he'd let the car creep up to nearly eighty miles per hour when the speed limit was sixty-five. As he eased off the pedal and the speedometer needle dipped, he spotted the nose of a Louisiana state police car ahead, half-hidden behind the supporting column of an overpass.

"Stay right there, my friend," Quinn said as he drove past the police car, checking his speedometer again.

Sixty-eight miles per hour. The cop stayed on the side of the road. *Good for you*, Quinn thought. *Good for both of us.*

Not that he was in the habit of starting fights with police officers, but if there was ever going to be a day when it would be easy to rile the tiger in him, it would be today.

Ever since the world's shifters had revealed their existence to the public, things had changed. When vampires had done it, fear and curiosity had raged, but the typical human expected to be able to look at a vampire and notice that he or she was something other than ordinary. It wasn't that simple, but many humans comforted themselves with the idea that it could be. Now that the two-natured—beings who could shapeshift between a human form and that of an animal—had stepped into the light, human society was more unsettled than ever. There was virtually zero chance that your mailman could be a vampire . . . but could he turn into a wolf or a dog? A distinct possibility.

That unsettled the hell out of people.

Incidents of violence had begun on the first day. Though new laws protected his kind, Quinn had heard many stories of persecution. He didn't worry for himself, but for his mother and his sister, Frannie, not to mention his girlfriend, Tijgerin, and their baby. He comforted himself with the knowledge that it was easier for weres to live among humans than it was for vampires. Most people had at least one two-natured friend or relative and never even knew it.

Today, his mother was foremost on his mind. Unlike vampires,

Quinn's people suffered the tribulations of aging, and as they grew old and infirm they needed to be looked after in a safe environment. Once, it had been necessary to hide them, to keep their true nature a secret. Now aging and ailing shifters were kept apart from their human counterparts purely to ensure that they did not put themselves or anyone else in peril.

Vicki Quinn had spent a long time in nursing homes specifically for the two-natured. She suffered delusions and sometimes violent schizophrenic behavior stemming from psychological trauma, but recently her condition had deteriorated further. When she had begun to experience deepening dementia, the doctors at her previous residence had recommended a move to Evergreen Manor, a newer facility that offered treatments that might slow the progression of her illness.

Quinn turned off the highway and followed dimly remembered directions that, minutes later, brought him along a narrow, tree-lined street where a black wrought-iron fence guarded the grounds of Evergreen. For the sake of the residents, the facility's director would have said, to keep them from wandering off. But the fence was as much for the safety of the humans living near the property as for the patients. Either a werewolf with senile dementia or a pup going through the madness that sometimes gripped them during their teen years could do plenty of damage.

Tense and flushed with frustration, he gave his name to the guard at the booth and was waved through the gate. He said nothing to the guard about the circumstances of his visit but sensed the man's uneasiness. Would he call ahead and alert the administration that a big, bald, pissed-off were had arrived? Quinn thought he might.

The grounds were a lovely, rolling green, with flowers around the base of each tree and around the Roman fountain at the center of the lawn. Quinn inhaled the many rich scents of the place, and it calmed him a bit. He was here now. They could dodge him on the telephone but they couldn't ignore his physical presence. The time had come for his questions to be answered.

The home had a valet, but he ignored the service and parked the car himself. It tweeted as he thumbed the locking mechanism, and he headed for the ornate front steps without looking back.

"Good afternoon, sir," a well-groomed young man said as Quinn walked through the door. He sat behind a desk, pompous and proper, as if he were a concierge instead of an ordinary clerk. "Can I help you?"

Quinn glanced around the marble lobby with its churchlike vaulted ceilings and studied the residents being slowly escorted here and there. He examined the faces of doctors and nurses and physical therapists and recognized none of them, which wasn't a huge surprise, since he'd only visited his mother there twice before. To his knowledge, his sister, Frannie, who waited tables out in New Mexico, had never bothered.

"My name's John Quinn," he said. "I'm here to see my mother."

"Yes, sir," the clerk said with a broad smile. "And her name?"

"Quinn. You have a lot of Quinns here?"

The clerk—the little plastic tag on his chest identified him as Andrew—smiled more thinly. Even less convincingly than before.

"I don't know, sir. Let me just look her up for you," Andrew said, tapping away at his computer keyboard. After a moment, his eyes lit up. "Ah, yes, sir. According to her schedule she's in physical therapy at the moment. I'll call up and let them know you're here, if you'd just like to take a seat."

Quinn's pulse thundered at his temples. He breathed deeply, rising to his full six and a half feet, and glared at the clerk. Women always seemed to love the purple of his eyes, but when he was angry they grew darker, almost black.

"You know, most days I'm as polite as can be," he said, "but I won't be taking a seat today."

The clerk blinked nervously. "Sir?"

Quinn sniffed the air, breathed deeply again. He frowned as he glanced once more around the lobby. Then he stared at the desk clerk.

"You're human."

Andrew nodded vigorously. More blinking. "Yes, sir."

"The old place was staffed by two-natureds. When I was at Evergreen last, the same was true here. Now I smell humans all over the place. What is going on?"

The clerk gave a sheepish shrug. "It's becoming more and more common, Mr. Quinn. Ever since weres went public and piqued the curiosity of humans, we get volunteers. People are intrigued and want to help."

Quinn snarled. "Gawkers. That's what you're talking about."

"No, sir. Psychologists and nutritionists and orderlies and physician assistants, even a doctor or two."

Quinn waved him away. "I want to see my mother, and I want to see her now. I've been calling for days and am constantly told she's sleeping or in PT or in the bath or out on the grounds with her minders."

"Bad timing, I suppose," Andrew offered. "And again today, sir. But if you'll take a seat, I'll have my supervisor come down and speak with—"

Quinn brought his fist down on the desk hard enough that a cup of pens spilled over and the surface cracked, the sound echoing like a gunshot in the lobby.

"Bullshit!" he snapped. "I'm tired of the runaround. This is my mother we're talking about. You people have a lot of explaining to do, but you can't keep me from seeing her. You're going to take me to her—"

"Excuse me, sir," a voice said from behind him.

Quinn spun to see a young, broad-chested security guard approaching. The guy unsnapped the holster on his hip and drew out a Taser gun.

"Please step away from the desk and put your hands behind your head."

Quinn glared at him. "You must be joking. If you want to call the police, please do so. I'd like to speak with them myself. But I'm the wronged party here, kid, so you just stay where you are."

"Sir, I'm not going to ask a second time," the security guard said, coming toward him, ready for a fight, the Taser aimed at Quinn's chest. He thrust the Taser forward, about to pull the trigger. Quinn snarled, grabbed his wrist, and slammed him against the wall, shaking the Taser from his hand.

"Anyone else want to try keeping me from my mother?" he growled.

The *tick-tock* of high heels echoed off the linoleum and Quinn glanced over to see a tall, shapely woman approaching. She had ginger hair and wore a well-tailored skirt and jacket combination with old-fashioned horn-rimmed glasses.

"Not at all, Mr. Quinn," she said. "I'm Dr. Sondra Delisle, the new director of resident services. I'm sorry for the delay and I understand your frustration. Your mother's in our newly renovated dayroom with some of her friends. If you'd like to follow me, I'll take you to her."

"I thought she was in physical therapy," Quinn said, glancing at the clerk.

Dr. Delisle smiled thinly. "The therapist is out today. I'm sorry, Mr. Quinn, have we given you some reason to distrust us?"

Quinn stared at her, heart pounding, teeth still gritted but feeling foolish. He released the security guard, happy he hadn't broken the guy's wrist.

"I'm sorry," he said. "I'm usually in better control of my temper."

"Not at all," Dr. Delisle replied. "A man only has one mother. Come this way."

"Thank you," he said.

Quinn tried to give her his most charming smile but thought it must have come off as awkward. He shoved his hands into his pockets as if they were just as embarrassed by their actions as he was and accompanied her down a corridor, up a short set of steps, and then into another side corridor, where their footfalls echoed oddly off the walls. He frowned as he listened to their steps, surprised that he couldn't hear the voices of the residents in the dayroom yet.

"How far is the dayroom?" he asked.

"Just at the end of the hall and through a set of doors. Wait till you see it. The residents have all sorts of games, computers for their own use, a separate reading room . . . and the upgrades continue. We're putting in a new gym, specially tailored to the needs of our less able residents . . ."

Quinn inhaled, frowning deeply. He smelled something unpleasant.

In a nursing home, that in itself was far from strange, but this was something else. A musk. A pheromonal scent he hadn't expected to find here—true fear. Not the confusion of madness or the dark dread of illness and death, but something inching closer to terror.

As they reached the end of the hall, the double doors swung open. Quinn started to back away, but too late, as a man stepped through with a rifle aimed at him and pulled the trigger, firing three shots.

Quinn tried to throw himself out of the way, but the corridor left little room to move. He hit the wall and slid to the floor, twisting to look at the darts that stuck out of his side and leg.

Tranquilizers.

Quinn roared, lurching up at Dr. Delisle. "You bitch," he slurred. "Where's my mother?"

The man shot him with two more darts.

"You'll see her soon," Dr. Delisle said with a beatific smile, as blackness swam in at the edges of Quinn's vision.

Then he was out.

He did not dream.

Heavily sedated, his muddled thoughts buried under a thick blanket of drugs, Quinn sensed consciousness somewhere above him, as if his mind were a deep lake and he had begun to drown. Again and again he swam toward the surface of the lake, toward the world and reality, toward the tangible thing that meant *awake*. Time after time his fingers broke the surface and more than once he managed to get a sip of the air of awareness before being dragged down again into the gray, muzzy depths of numb nothingness. In those moments when he strove to wake, he felt panic and desperation and—beneath all of it, at the very bottom of the lake of his muffled thoughts—rage.

How long had he been out when his eyes fluttered open?

Quinn didn't know.

What he did know was hunger.

An IV drip hung by the bed, maybe keeping him sedated but also hydrated. He blinked and tried to move but his body felt as if it weighed twenty tons, and at the same time as if it weighed nothing and he might just float away.

"Hello, Mr. Quinn," a voice said, gentle and soothing as a caress.

His head lolled to one side, barely in his control. Dr. Delisle stood over him, smiling and lovely, her ginger hair framing her face. Quinn tried to reach for her, intent on breaking her neck, but his wrists were bound and he heard the clank of metal restraints. Normally he could have broken free, but the drugs sapped his strength just as they sapped rational thought.

His vision swam and faded for a moment, but he took a deep breath and stared at Dr. Delisle, forcing himself to see her clearly.

"You have the prettiest eyes," she said to him. "I've never seen that shade of purple before. But then, you're not just anyone, are you, Mr. Quinn?"

"Mmffhh," he said. All he could manage.

"I'll bet you're hungry. You must be. You've had a long couple of days."

Quinn's throat felt dry. His lips were chapped and he ached all over.

"My mother . . ." he managed to groan. "If . . . you . . ."

"Hush," Dr. Delisle said, and her smile vanished. She stepped back from his bed. "Your mother is an uncooperative bitch, Mr. Quinn. She has been unwilling to give us what we wanted, but that's all right. We knew that eventually you'd come to look in on her and we'd have a fresh opportunity."

Darkness pulsed at the edges of his vision, exhaustion and hunger and the drugs all dragging at his thoughts. He shook his head to clear it and saw the three men who were in the room with them. Two were big guys with guns, one scarred and bearded with the air of a hunter, and the other neatly groomed and hollow-eyed, a soldier or mercenary. Quinn had met his share of hunters and mercenaries before. The third man wore a brown suit with a yellow shirt and a green tie with a diamond stickpin. He had silver hair and smelled like money.

"Enough," said the man who smelled like money. "There's no value to mystery here, Dr. Delisle. Can he understand me?"

The man had a slow drawl Quinn thought hailed from Alabama, but what did he know? He was doped to the gills.

"I'm not sure how much he'll remember, but he'll understand what you're saying," Dr. Delisle said.

"Kill you," Quinn growled low in his chest.

"See?" Dr. Delisle observed, smiling. Pretty as a picture.

"Mr. Quinn," the man said, "I'll give it to you plainly. I represent a . . . consortium . . . of private military contractors who have been attempting to utilize the creatures referred to as 'the two-natured' for combat. Combat for hire, essentially."

Quinn's fingers opened and closed. He felt his skin bristle, felt his nails lengthen, and he snarled, thinking that he had begun to change. But when he ran his thick tongue over his teeth, vision blurry, he realized that he had not changed at all. Perhaps his teeth were a bit sharper, but he was still human. He could not focus enough to will himself to shift.

Go to hell, he thought, and tried to say. It came out a groan.

"There were two ways to go about it," the man went on. "We could recruit existing weres or try to create our own. Recruitment bore some fruit initially, werewolves and a handful of panthers, even two bears, but few of those who willingly signed on to our program had any prior military experience. Not good with authority outside their own packs.

"Creating our own two-natured has been more reliable in that we can draft volunteers from a pool of existing Special Forces military personnel, enlisting our recruited weres to bite the volunteers, passing on their nature. As you know, that process can be long and frustratingly unpredictable."

"My mother," Quinn managed, glaring at the man, thinking about the ways he might kill him if only he could clear his mind . . . and control his limbs.

He blinked, realizing that he had begun thinking a bit more clearly, that Dr. Delisle must have cut back on the sedatives feeding into his system. Quinn bared his teeth but purposefully did not focus on his visitor, this military contractor. He didn't want the man to know that he had begun to regain his focus.

"It might take being bitten three times for an ordinary human to become two-natured, or it might take considerably more," the man said with a thin, humorless smile. "But then, I don't have to tell you that, do I, Mr. Quinn?"

The were population was hardly plentiful. Only the first child born of a coupling between two full-blooded shapeshifters would be two-natured and able to shift at will. Any further offspring would be human, with maybe a little enhancement. One could become a shapeshifter by being bitten, but the bitten weres could not manage the full transformation from human to animal, only something in between, and could only change during the three nights of the full moon.

"Soldiers who've been bitten would be perfectly suitable for our needs," the man went on, "if their ability to change form weren't tied to the full moon. That's a bit of a handicap, don't you think? Yes, the bitten have their uses . . . but my employers are thinking more long term, planning for the next generation."

The man bent over and peered into Quinn's face. The smell of garlic and onions on his breath was wretched.

"In the meantime, though," the man said, "we'll have to make do."

"I want to . . . see my mother," he managed to rasp, his head lolling slightly. His heart thumped in his chest and he willed adrenaline to surge, anything to give him the power to kill this son of a bitch, but chemistry defeated him.

"And you will!" the man pronounced. "All we ask is for a bit of indulgence from you in the meantime."

"You want me to . . ." Quinn began, blinking and shaking his head, forcing his lips to form words. "Want me to go to *war* for you? Not a . . . not a chance."

Dr. Delisle tutted and came nearer to the bed. "We've done a thorough background on you, Mr. Quinn. We know you'd never be a willing recruit. But you're a weretiger, sir. You and your mother are the only weretigers we've encountered."

"You see," the garlic-breathed man said, "a small squad of soldiers who could transform themselves into tiger-men—even if only one night a month—would be invaluable to a mercenary force. Our clients would pay millions for the efficiency a kill team like that would achieve."

Dr. Delisle sat on the edge of the bed and put a hand on Quinn's leg, as gentle as a lover, but her smile might as well have been carved from ice.

"We have the trained mercenary volunteers, Mr. Quinn," she said. "All you have to do is bite them."

Quinn felt a terrible, dawning horror. "Where . . . where is my mother?"

The man gave him a lopsided smile. "Ah, the lovely Mrs. Quinn. You're wondering why we didn't just get her to do the job for us. The mad old thing's crazy, after all, so you'd think she'd be snapping away at every orderly, never mind people we'd actually want her to bite. She had a history of nipping at the staff at her last residence, so you'd assume, wouldn't you?"

His smile turned to a sneer. "But no. She flatly refused. No matter what we did to her."

Quinn roared, straining against his bonds, and the man jerked back a step. Dr. Delisle stayed where she had seated herself, stroking his leg.

"What did you—?"

"She'd already lost many of her teeth," the man said. "It shocked us all when she smashed the ceramic edge off her bathroom sink and used it to break the rest. Just to thwart us. She's mentally unstable, your mother . . . but she's still got enough of her wits about her to be quite the bitch when she—"

Quinn roared again. This time he could feel his teeth elongating and the familiar ripple on his skin as fur began to sprout.

Dr. Delisle jumped from the bed. "Let me adjust that," she said nervously, rushing toward the IV.

"Not yet!" the man snapped. He crossed to the door, opened it, and stuck his head out. "Bring her in!"

Heart full of fear and worry for his mother, who had already endured so much cruelty in her life, Quinn strained at his bonds, trying to see out into the corridor.

The man leaned over and whispered into his ear.

"She's no good to us now, you understand," the man said. "Except as leverage."

Quinn heard his mother yelp in the hallway, then heard her roar, crying out without words. Savage and desperate. The door banged open fully and three men dragged the tigress in, each using a control pole that ended with a noose around her neck. The fur of her muzzle was matted with blood and her shoulder had an open gash. They surrounded her, forcing her through the door and into the room.

"Let her go!" Quinn cried.

When the tiger heard his voice she swung her big head around and stared at him, just for a moment giving up her fight against her keepers. All the breath seemed to go out of her and she changed before his eyes, slowly and painfully, bones shifting and fur withdrawing . . . and then she was just his mom, covering her naked body with her arms as the three men glared at her, using the control poles to make certain she couldn't attack them.

"Baby boy," she breathed.

Quinn slumped against the bed, no longer struggling against his restraints. An abyss of despair opened up within him. He turned toward the man, tongue still thick, thoughts still blurred. *I'm going to kill you,* he thought. But those weren't the words that came out of his mouth.

Instead, what he said was, "Tell me . . . what you want me to do."

The next time he woke, he was in chains. Better safe than sorry, they told him. The man with the garlic breath had a name, as it turned out—Bartholomew Teague—but Quinn saw him only rarely. Teague and Dr. Delisle kept him drugged despite his acquiescence, and the days blurred into nights. Doctors came and went, some with their faces hidden behind masks. They took blood and tissue samples. Orderlies brought him food, gave his chains just enough drag so that he could feed himself, and changed his bedpan. On the first day, when a nurse woke him by roughly inserting a catheter, he clawed her arm purely by accident. He didn't see that nurse again.

There were five volunteers—four men and a woman, each of them dead-eyed, stone-faced soldiers whom Quinn wanted to hate. Instead, he marveled at their courage. To put out their arms or bare their shoulders and willingly allow him—half man and half tiger in those moments—to bite into their flesh, knowing that he could have shifted further and snapped his jaws shut, taking the limb or the shoulder completely off . . . that was impressive. Not that he respected them. Those four men and that one woman knew that he was a captive, that whatever he did was done under duress, but they cared nothing for the distinction. He admired their courage and wished them dead, all at the same time.

For his mother's sake, he would not harm them any more than Teague wanted them harmed.

Almost constantly, Quinn pondered the question of how long it would take before his half sister, Frannie, or his girlfriend, Tijgerin, would wonder why they had not heard from him. Frannie had started a new and busy life with her husband in New Mexico and Tij was in seclusion, as was the custom of weretiger women when they had recently given birth. Tij intended to raise their son in secrecy, and though it hurt his heart not to see his child, Quinn had acceded to Tijgerin's wishes out of love for her and for the sake of the baby.

His clients would have noticed his absence fairly quickly, but when he did not return their calls or appear for events, they would be more likely to contact the parent company of Extreme(ly Elegant) Events than the police.

A prisoner, he slept. Sometimes the supply of drugs they were feeding him would run thin and his thoughts would crystallize enough for him to put his will into devising an escape, but he could not conceive of one that did not leave either himself or his mother—or both of them—dead.

So Quinn obeyed. It killed him to do it, made him strain against his bonds and roar at the ceiling in the middle of the night, but he obeyed. The drugs made it seem almost acceptable, blunted the edges of his hatred enough that submission began to seem a strategy instead of a defeat. Other times he screamed his throat raw demanding to see his mother, but they would never bring her back to visit him.

He bit the soldiers on Teague's command and they bled, and then he ate and he slept, trying not to wonder where they would be sent when his bites transformed them. Whom they might kill, these children of his violation.

The irony was not lost on him. It sickened him. Once, many years before, his mother had been raped by a group of men and she had lost her mind. His mom had never been the same again. Now dementia had crept in to add insult to that injury, and a new group of tormentors had torn down all the reassurances she had built up over the years to persuade herself that those terrible men were not still out there, waiting for her.

Quinn would endure whatever torture, perform whatever task was asked of him, if only to protect his mother from any further pain or indignity.

One morning, after he had lost track of the days, the clank of the door latch made him open his eyes. His mind had gone sluggish, just like his limbs. It felt like thoughts and muscles were both trapped deep in thick mud. His mouth hung open and he felt drool on his stubbled cheek and for the first time since his captivity, instead of fury, he felt shame.

"Mr. Quinn," Teague said, "you've been holding out on us."

Quinn wished he could kill him with a glance. He stared hate at Teague, thinking the man would smile and cajole and make light of that hatred, as he always did. But there were no smiles from Teague today.

"Did you hurt her?" Quinn asked, his voice a rasp, his lips curling back as he thought about how deeply his teeth would bite into Teague's flesh and bone if he could only get the man close enough.

Teague arched an eyebrow. "Your dear old mama? Her condition is unchanged. But she has been chatty lately, the old dear. Her mind drifts, as you know. This morning she mistook me for some old acquaintance or another. Maybe the accent triggered some precious memory. All she wanted to do was boast about her children, about her beautiful daughter and her handsome son, the successful entrepreneur."

Quinn blinked, trying to make sense of Teague's demeanor.

"I told you we were thinking long term, Quinn," the man said slowly. "About the next generation. I told you that full-bloods were more useful to us. That mother of yours might be a few clowns short of a circus, but her little episode this morning has more than made it worth my while to keep her breathing."

In the deep mud of Quinn's brain, a thought began to form. A terrible, terrible thought.

"No," he rasped.

Now Teague smiled. "Oh, yes. Congratulations, Mr. Quinn. Mama told us you're a new daddy."

The smile slid away, vanishing slowly until Teague looked feral.

"You will tell me where to find this infant, Mr. Quinn. In return, I will not order my people to torture your mother. I will not order them to kill her. I will not order them to torture you. Your son will be raised well, if strictly, and he will grow to be a great warrior—in the service of the highest bidder."

Quinn stared death at him.

"Tell me, and you will all live," Teague said. "Even your son and his mother."

"You would have to kill me," Quinn snarled. "And you would have to kill his mother."

"You drive a hard bargain, but okay. We'll kill you and we'll kill your wife, or whatever she is. But your mother will live."

"No, I . . ." he mumbled, fighting the effects of the drugs. "You think I . . . No. You will never touch my child. Never see my child. Even I do not know where he is."

Thank you, Tij, he thought. *Thank you so much for your insistence upon tradition.*

Teague actually laughed. "Do you really expect me to believe that?"

"It doesn't matter."

For several seconds they only glared at each other, and then Teague threw up his hands in frustration.

"All right. Honestly, I hoped it could be done simply, but it isn't as if I expected you to just tell me, even with all the ugly things my people will do to your mother."

"Don't—"

Teague shook his head. "Be serious, Quinn. I have a job to do. You haven't left me any choice."

They made no attempt to torture Quinn himself—at least not physically. Teague had to know that no amount of physical agony would have persuaded him to willingly surrender his infant son. Instead, the man in charge was as cruel as his word. That afternoon, they tapered off the sedative drip just enough so that he could clear many of the cobwebs from his mind. He still couldn't focus enough to make a full transformation, but he could watch as they brought his mother into the room with the same control poles. They humiliated her, spat on her, and kicked her. She was not as sedated as he had been during his weeklong haze, but they had drugged her enough that she could not fight back as they cut her skin.

Quinn roared at first. In time, he wept. When Teague brought in an electric branding iron of the sort ranchers used for cattle, he hurled himself against his bonds. The chains clanked and strained and he heard the creak of metal stressed to its limit, and one of Teague's men chambered a shotgun round and aimed at his mother's face.

"Sit back, Mr. Quinn," Teague said. "Sit back or her life ends now."

"Do it, then!" his mother roared, whipping her head up to face the shotgun.

Quinn held his breath, staring, the little boy he had once been crying out inside at the sight of his mother tormented . . . again. Images cascaded through his mind of the night years ago when she had been beaten and raped . . . the night he'd killed the men who had done that to her. He had vowed then never to allow her to come to harm again.

"Mom," he said.

Perhaps she heard a hint of surrender in his voice. Quinn didn't know where his girlfriend and their baby were living, but he had his suspicions. He could tell Teague what he knew just to stop his mother's anguish and then wait for an opportunity. Figuring out where Tij was and actually finding her were two different things. Speaking now would spare his mother and buy him time. He could escape somehow, kill Teague . . .

"Stop!" he shouted.

His mother whipped her head up and met his gaze. Despite whatever sedatives they had given her, the fog of madness and growing dementia had cleared. Her eyes were vivid purple, almost like his own, and brightly alert. Perhaps pain had given her clarity.

"Not a word, boy," she told him. "I'll suffer any pain to keep that baby safe. Death for me now would be victory. Don't take that from me."

Quinn's blood ran cold and he felt his heart go still. He exhaled and eased back down onto the bed, giving his chains a rest as warm blood ran from his wrists and ankles where he had strained against the metal.

Teague saw the moment pass between them. As mother and son made peace with whatever came next, the man screamed out his own rage, so much more savage than Quinn had ever been. He knew now that he would never get what he wanted from them.

"Enough!" Teague snapped. He turned on his men. "Take the bitch out of here."

Quinn watched him in silence. No taunts. No threats. No pleas.

"You *will* give me what I want," Teague told him before he followed the torturers out, not waiting for a reply.

When he was alone again, Quinn kept working at his bonds. The blood from his wounds lubricated the shackles, and he thought that might be enough to help him slip free. But then an orderly came in and turned up the flow of drugs into his IV. He thrashed, attempting to tear the needle loose, but in seconds he had drifted into darkness again.

When he was allowed to emerge from the narcotic fog, the torturers had returned. There were no control poles this time. No nooses. Such measures were not necessary for an ordinary human, a defenseless woman.

Like his sister, Frannie.

Wide-eyed with terror, Frannie had fresh bruises on her face and neck. The left side of her mouth was swollen and her lip had been split. Blood trickled from a cut just above her eyebrow on the same side. They had her on her knees, these men, one with a shotgun aimed at her head and the others only waiting.

"John?" she whispered.

His little sister, now a grown woman, happily married and living her peaceful human life. Until now.

Hatred seethed in Quinn's heart. The tiger awoke.

Teague waited nearly ten minutes before entering the room, perhaps purposely giving him that time to contemplate what came next.

"You don't need to say a word," Quinn told him. "Just listen. I have an idea."

"I'm sorry I got you into this," Frannie said unhappily, staring at him with the sad eyes that had always been able to change his mind and heart.

The thrum of the airplane's engines created a constant white noise around them, and the pressurized air in the cabin made his ears feel as if they were about to pop. Quinn sat in his seat, shackles on his wrists. They were overkill—the men with the guns knew he wouldn't try anything as long as his sister's life was in peril. That was why they had brought Frannie with them in the first place.

The private jet had eight rows with a single seat on either side of the central aisle. Quinn sat about halfway down the left side of the plane with his sister in the seat in front of him. Across the aisle were three gun thugs, one adjacent to each of the Quinn siblings and a third one row up, just for good measure—three killers in a row.

"Do you really think this is somehow your fault?" he asked, frowning. "You didn't get me into this, Fran. You're here because of me."

The man sitting across from Quinn raised the gun from his lap and aimed it at him. "Shut up."

Frannie had been half turned so she could talk quietly with her brother, but now she slid around to face straight ahead, like a schoolgirl who'd been scolded.

Quinn forced himself to exhale his rage, to stay calm. Even in shackles, he could have killed the man in seconds, gun or no gun. Perhaps he would be shot, but he thought the odds were with him. Trouble was, the two guys who were covering Frannie would shoot her instantly. He'd never be able to disarm them all before they killed her.

Quinn glanced at the man to his right, at the gun resting on his lap.

"You know," he said, "you're going to have to take these cuffs off when we get there. No point in keeping me like this."

The man gave him a sidelong glance, almost a sneer. "I've got my orders, man. Just like you. We'll both follow them and maybe everyone comes out of this alive."

Quinn grunted. "Maybe."

The guard in Frannie's row turned to stare back at Quinn. "You gonna make a move? Are you that stupid?"

"I won't endanger my sister's life."

The man smiled thinly. The one guarding Quinn seemed all business, but this one took sadistic pleasure in their circumstances. The urge to twist his head off was strong. Quinn inhaled again and caught the scent of fear. Remarkably it came not from Frannie but from the final guard, the man in the row ahead of Frannie's. He glanced back nervously, clearly terrified of being in an enclosed space with a weretiger.

You're the smartest one, Quinn thought.

"I really *am* sorry," Frannie said quietly.

The guards all glanced over at her. The one across the aisle from Quinn seemed about to object, but then he settled down, perhaps deciding that he no longer cared, that conversation between brother and sister would not change the outcome.

"You didn't put me here," Quinn said, his voice a low growl. "That bastard Teague did this."

"Teague forced your hand," Frannie agreed, "but you suggested this setup to protect Mama and me, and the baby."

Quinn said nothing. He would never blame Frannie or his mother for the cruelty, greed, and savagery of other people. Faced with the threat of harm to his family, or the nightmare of his boy being enslaved to murderous combat like some ancient gladiatorial beast, he had made a different offer to Teague—Quinn would become the weapon they sought. They didn't have to wait twenty years for his son to be their tiger-warrior; he would serve them now, go anywhere and kill anyone as long as they abandoned any effort to take and use his son, and as long as they left his mother and sister alone.

They had kept him in a cell for more than another week, only lightly drugged and with the threat that if he attempted to escape, Frannie and his mother would die. As the days passed, he had realized that they were waiting for the full moon, thinking that he would be stronger then, and that he would be less able to control his own ferocity. On those counts, they had been correct.

Quinn glanced out the window of the plane. The sky had begun to darken as they hurtled toward the horizon, the clouds sifting away below them. Soon they would fly into nightfall and the moon would shine.

"I don't even know where you're taking me," he said.

"A place where the people won't obey, and the tyrant who rules wants to set an example. The company is being paid very well for your services."

Frannie had been brought along as a reminder of what would happen if he did not fulfill his promise. Teague's employers had not tried to recruit Quinn initially because they did not believe they could count on his cooperation even if he agreed, but that was before they had learned of the existence of his son. This assignment would be a test run. If he made one wrong move, disobeyed a single order, they would kill Frannie on the spot and begin anew the search for Tij and the baby. The guard in the row ahead of Frannie's had a massive tranquilizer gun—they would kill his sister but keep Quinn alive, drugged and enslaved.

"In the future," Teague had said, "I don't think we'll need your sister to go along. But this first time, having her with us might help you focus."

The future, Quinn thought, jaw tight as he hung his head and clenched his fists. *I am their killer, forever.* He studied the curls of his sister's hair that stuck out beside her seat.

So be it, he thought, sighing deeply. *Whatever it takes.*

"John?" Frannie said quietly, turning again in her seat so she could see him.

The guards all glanced warily at her. The one across from Quinn kept watching, but the other two looked away.

"It's getting dark," Frannie rasped. It sounded as if her voice were full of emotion. "Whatever they're going to have you do, it'll be soon."

"I guess."

"There's something I need to tell you."

Quinn frowned. "I'm not going to die tonight, Fran. I'll be back. Tell me then."

"It has to be now. There's a reason I haven't visited Mama in a while. A reason I haven't seen you in months. Something I've been dealing with."

The guard across from Quinn glanced away, apparently sensing a moment of intimacy between brother and sister. It seemed he had decided to allow it.

"Go on," he said.

"Her mind . . . You know how she gets," Frannie said, an angry furrow on her brow. Her chest rose and fell and she gritted her teeth as she tried to keep that anger in. "I tried to visit her regularly, tried to lift her spirits, but sometimes she would barely know me. She'd be lost in some awful memory or just confused, and if I tried to touch her, she'd lash out."

"I'm sorry," Quinn said thoughtfully, studying her, wondering at the source of the anger he saw. "I know I should have visited more. It's been a complicated year."

Her left hand gripped the side of her seat as she peered back at him. Her hair hung down, veiling part of her face, but her eyes glinted with dark light.

"You saw that she'd knocked out some of her teeth?" Frannie rasped, voice hitching, lowering her gaze.

Quinn frowned. They had told him that Mama had knocked out the rest of her teeth, but that she'd been missing many of them before that.

"Yes."

"She started that because when she was lucid, when the madness and the growing dementia retreated, she would realize what she'd done."

"What *had* she done?"

Frannie's upper lip curled back and she practically snarled the next sentence.

"Sometimes," his sister said, "Mama would bite me."

Quinn went cold. His breath caught in his chest. "How many times did this happen?"

Outside the plane, it had grown dark. The full moon shone brightly through the oval windows.

His sister glanced up at him with tiger's eyes.

"Enough," she growled, as her teeth began to lengthen and sharpen and elegantly striped fur began to push slowly through her skin.

The thug in Quinn's row noticed first.

"Son of a bitch," he muttered, raising his gun as his eyes went wide.

He aimed at Frannie, and that was his mistake—taking his focus off the man he was supposed to be guarding.

Quinn lunged across the aisle at superhuman speed, shattering his handcuffs as he slammed the gunman against the inner wall of the plane, gripped him with hands beginning to sprout their own fur, and broke his neck. In a death twitch, the man's finger pulled the trigger on his gun but the dart punched into the floor and lodged there.

By the time Quinn twisted around to go after the others, still only beginning to change, Frannie had killed the man with the cruel smile. She lifted her head—half human and half tiger, only able to achieve that partial transformation, like other bitten weres—and her muzzle was soaked with the gunman's blood.

The third man—the frightened one—threw his gun on the seat cushion and raised his hands in surrender, backing up the aisle toward the pilot's cabin.

"I'll do whatever you want," he said, voice quavering. "Please, just don't—"

Brother and sister roared in unison and a jet of urine streamed down the man's leg, soaking his pants.

In the thrall of the full moon, Frannie had no control over her rage. She killed him there, in the aisle, blood soaking into the thin airplane carpeting.

Quinn halted his transformation and willed himself to revert to human. He felt the full moon's sway but had spent his life mastering it.

"Frannie," he said.

She glanced up from the dead man, chunks of his flesh in her jaws, tiger eyes gleaming in the moonlight.

"Stay here," Quinn said, moving past her, stepping over the dead man. "Do you hear me? Stay here while I go and talk to the pilot."

He thought of Teague and Dr. Delisle and of the things they had done to his mother—the things they had threatened to do to his wife and son.

Just before he banged on the cockpit door, Quinn glanced back at Frannie. He had never wanted this for her, never wished this life upon her, and he knew that it had never been her desire. Yet he could not help feeling a deeper love for her now. They had always been brother and sister, but now they were a different kind of kin, connected not only by their own blood but by the moon, and the blood they had spilled.

"We're going back," Quinn promised.

His sister, her lovely orange and black fur dappled with blood, purred contentedly and went back to her meal.

THE REAL SANTA CLAUS

LEIGH PERRY

My friend Leigh Perry's favorite character is Diantha, the half-demon niece of the mostly demon lawyer Desmond Cataliades. In *After Dead*, I say that Mr. Cataliades drops in on Sookie just before Christmas every year. In this story, set while Sookie is pregnant with her third child, the lawyer's pre-Christmas visit reveals that things aren't merry in Sookie's household, and Mr. C tasks Diantha with finding out why.

"Maybehesanelf," I said.

"More slowly, please."

"Talkingordriving?"

"Both, I think."

"Suresuresure. I mean, sure."

My uncle, Desmond Cataliades, was in the backseat of his new black Lexus while I drove at a fraction of the speed I should have been going. I like working for Uncle Desmond, but he's got rules. One of them is for me to try to avoid getting more speeding tickets.

"Anyway, Santa Claus," I said. "Maybe he's an elf. I read that story—'The Night Before Christmas'—and it says he was a right jolly old elf."

Uncle Desmond said, "Indeed?" which was what he said when he wasn't really listening. He's way polite. He says manners help him control his demon-ness, which is important because he's mostly demon. I'm only half demon, so I don't need to be that polite.

Even though he wasn't listening, I kept talking because driving that gorgeous hunk of car at the speed limit was putting me to sleep. "The thing is, I've seen an elf or two and they didn't look anything like Santa Claus. Their ears were funny looking, their hair looked like fur instead of hair, and they weren't fat. Plus they both had these pointy teeth that I thought were kinda hot, but they'd freak out any human kid who tried to sit in their laps."

"Almost certainly." He kept tapping away at his laptop, working even though it was Christmas Eve.

Not that demons really go in for celebrating the birth-of-Christ thing, but a lot of the people Uncle Desmond does business with do, so we non-human-American types take the time off and have our own parties. After all, who doesn't like getting presents?

I said, "I bet the guy who wrote that story never even saw an elf."

"I suspect you're right, Diantha. Elves rarely leave survivors."

"Besides, all the elves have gone back to Faery, and kids keep getting presents, so . . . he can't be an elf."

"Well reasoned, my dear."

"That lets out most of the rest of the fae, too—the really powerful ones are gone and the part-fae like Sookie don't have the juice to pull it off."

"Indeed," he said again.

"Maybe a vampire. He only comes out at night, and hanging a stocking or putting up a sign that says *Santa Stop Here* is kinda like an invitation into the house, and nothing hides bloodstains like a red suit. Those sugarplums dancing in the kids' heads? Vampire whammy power."

"Mmmmm."

"Of course, you almost never see a fat vampire, but hey, what would a vampire look like after gorging on sleeping kids all over the world? He'd get bloated, right? There's still the reindeer, but maybe they're were. Did you ever hear of a werereindeer?"

"I don't believe I have."

"Shifter Sam could change into a reindeer."

"I must remind you not to call Sookie's husband Shifter Sam. When one speaks rapidly, as you frequently do, that sounds uncomfortably like Shifty Sam, which Sookie would certainly take amiss."

"Suresuresure." I didn't do it on purpose. Sam didn't always like it when we came to visit, but he wasn't shifty. "Maybe Santa is a shifter like Sam—he could shift into something small like a cockroach to get into the houses and have other shifters around to turn into reindeer." I liked the idea of a cockroach Santa but had to say, "Nah, a bug wouldn't be able to carry presents down the chimney, and the reindeer would need a talisman or something for flying. No, wait!" I snapped my fingers.

"Both hands on the wheel, my dear."

"Suresuresure." It wasn't like I didn't have fast reflexes, especially when we were going so slooooow. "What about a witch? A spell to teleport into the house, a magic hold-a-bunch-of-stuff bag for the toys, and either bespelled reindeer or an illusion. It would have to be a powerful witch, but it could happen."

"It's within the realm of possibility."

"But why would a witch have anything to do with Christmas? They've got their own holidays. And why give away all that stuff? Witches charge through the nose for every little spell."

"When have you done business with a witch?"

Burningcrap, I'd finally gotten his full attention. "Not me, a friend of mine. A were I met. From Albany."

"I see."

I could feel him staring at the back of my neck, which is scary. I work for him, and we're family, and he likes me, but still. Mostly demon. Finally he started back tapping on his laptop and I relaxed.

I hadn't bought the hex anyway. It cost too much just to play a trick on Uncle Desmond's daughters even though Eudokia, Kallistrae, and Myrrine deserved it. They were such asshats.

I spent the rest of the drive to Bon Temps going through the supe roll call trying to figure out what Santa really is. A maenad would have parents doing a lot more than kissing under the mistletoe; ghosts wouldn't be able to make toys; goblins don't care about humans and don't have the right look anyway; Britlingens are all about fighting; and whatever Dr. Ludwig is, she's definitely not Santa Claus.

When we finally made it to Sookie's house, which is in the middle of nowhere, even for Bon Temps, I jumped out and ran around the car a couple of times to get the kinks out before opening the back door for Uncle Desmond. While he was still climbing out, I got the trunk open and grabbed a bunch of wrapped presents, making sure to only get the ones for Sookie and her family. The packages for my cousins and their kids had to be bigger and fancier because one time they'd noticed that Sookie's presents looked as good as theirs.

"Careful, Diantha," Uncle Desmond warned. "Some of the gifts are fragile."

"Suresuresure." I keep telling Uncle Desmond that it would be faster to buy gift cards, but he says that lacks the personal touch. At least he doesn't make me do his shopping since that time I got into a hurry at Macy's and broke some things. I don't like waiting in line.

I do like going to Sookie's house because I like Sookie. She's human but treats me nicer than a trio of cousins I could name. I particularly like going at Christmastime because her house isn't so dull then. Sookie and Sam put up colored lights outside and decorate inside the house, too, with a big Christmas tree and garland all over. It's still not as colorful as my place, but it's a lot better than it usually is.

Only when I looked at the house, there were no lights. Of course, it was still daytime, so I wasn't expecting them to be flashing, but they should have been up. There was a wreath on the door, but it was solid green. Dull.

As soon as Uncle Desmond got most of the way to the front door, I went knock-knock-knock-knock-knock-knock. And waited. I was thinking Sookie wasn't there because it took forever for her to open up, but when I saw her I understood why she was going so slowly. She was as big as a whale!

"You're having another baby?" I said. Sookie and Sam the shifter had two kids already, which seemed like plenty.

"Well, hey, Diantha," she said, sounding kind of exasperated. Probably because of being so big. "You guessed it—I'm pregnant." She looked over my shoulder. "Hey there, Mr. Cataliades."

"The warmest of seasons' greetings, Sookie," he said, with a little half bow.

Uncle Desmond is Sookie's sponsor, which is like a godfather only with no god involved. Another reason I like Sookie is because my cousins hate their father being around her worse than they hate him working with me. At least I'm half demon. Sookie's mostly human. Uncle Desmond gave her telepathy when she was born, which would be cool to have, but I like having speed better. Besides, she can't read supe minds, and why would I want to waste time reading human minds?

Sookie said, "My, you're looking festive today, Diantha."

"ThanksgoingtoapartyandIwantedtogetintheholidaymood." I took a breath and said, "Thanks. I'm going to a party and I wanted to get in the holiday mood." I wear short skirts and leggings because they don't get in my way while I run. These leggings were green and red striped and my skirt was red with white polka dots. I couldn't find a red or green shirt so I wore a purple tank top under a white faux-fur vest. My hair was more orange than the red I'd meant to dye it, but it didn't show much because I had on a Santa Claus hat with leopard-pattern trim and green and gold sequins. My sneakers were plain silver sparkly hightops, which are blander than I like, but they go with everything.

"Well, you sure nailed it," Sookie said. "Would y'all like to come in?"

Uncle Desmond bowed again while I went on inside.

"Sookie, you want me to put this stuff under the tree?" I looked around. "Where's the tree?" Not only was there no great big Christmas tree, but none of the other decorations I was used to were up, either. No tinsel in sight.

"Sam hasn't— We haven't had time to put it up yet."

"Isn't Christmas Eve, like, now?"

Sookie's smile was looking kinda forced, but she said, "There's still time. You can just leave those on the table."

"Sure thing."

"You're looking radiant, my dear," Uncle Desmond said, which was a lie. She had bags under her eyes, and her hair was hanging like something dead. "I was so pleased to hear about the new addition to the family. Diantha, you recall me telling you and the rest of the family the good news at Thanksgiving?"

"Suresuresure." I was lying, too. He'd given a long drawn-out speech or toast or something, but I'd been busy eating.

A minute later, I heard what sounded like a crowd slamming down the stairs, so I jumped in front of Uncle Desmond. Not that I thought Sookie would have hellhounds in her house, but better safe than sorry. But it was just Sookie's kids, Neal and Jennings. Neal knew me well enough to give me a fist bump, but little Jennings would only look at me. I think he was trying to read my mind—Uncle Desmond had given him telepathy, too—but it wouldn't work on me and the kid was confused.

"Jennings," Sookie said in the tone Uncle Desmond uses on me a lot, and he stopped trying. "You probably don't remember, but this is Mr. Cataliades and this is his niece, Diantha."

"Pleasedtomeetya!" I said, and stuck out my fist. He thought about it a long time, but he gave me a quick bump in return.

"Would y'all like something to drink?" Sookie asked, and when Uncle Desmond said something polite, she said something polite back.

Uncle Desmond and I sat on the couch, Neal followed after his mother, and Jennings stood and stared at us. I stared back until I got bored. By then Sookie was back with apple cider and cookies. Sookie makes great Christmas cookies, but these were Oreos. Not even the winter ones with red stuff in the middle—just plain old Oreos. Of course Uncle Desmond ate them as if they were petit fours or something like that.

"How have you been, Sookie?" he asked.

"Oh, fine," she said brightly, but even I could tell she was lying.

Uncle Desmond raised one eyebrow, which was his way of reminding her that he could read her mind, even if she couldn't read his.

She got kind of red in the face. "Boys, why don't y'all go upstairs and play while we grown-ups talk."

They did, but Jennings kept staring at me as long as he could. I stuck out my tongue at him 'cause I was a grown-up and he wasn't.

Sookie said, "I should know better than to pretend with you, Mr. Cataliades. To tell the truth, it's been a rough month."

"Vampires attacking?" I asked. "Weres? Fae coming out of that portal in your backyard?"

"What? No! Just normal things. Normal human things, anyway. Sam's had a bad cold since Thanksgiving that he can't seem to shake, and the doctor doesn't want me working this late in my pregnancy so we had to hire a new waitress, and business at Merlotte's has been slow. We usually do well around the holidays, but not this year. Sam has been working extra hours even though he ought to be resting, and so a few things have slid." She kind of shook herself. "But here I am whining on Christmas Eve when I ought to be thinking about how lucky I am. The boys are doing great, and soon we'll have a new baby." She lowered her voice to a whisper. "It's a girl. I'm going to name her after Gran."

"And the pregnancy is going well?" Uncle Desmond said.

"Just the usual swollen feet, and being tired a lot."

Just then the front door opened and Sookie's husband, Sam, came in. "Sookie? Is somebody here?"

Sam looked even worse than Sookie did, but where she was big he looked like he'd lost weight. His hair is always reddish, but this time his nose was, too, and he sounded stuffed up. That explained why he hadn't known it was Uncle Desmond and me—normally he'd have scented us as soon as he got out of his pickup.

"Hey," he said, sounding about as welcoming as my cousins did when I came over. He's not overly fond of us, but usually he fakes it better. "I brought some food for y'all to have for lunch—figured the boys could use something other than a sandwich for a change." He held up a paper bag that said *Merlotte's.*

Sookie looked like he'd slapped her and said, "I was going to make them some soup."

"Now you can save that for later," he said, maybe sounding kind of sorry. "I didn't know we had company or I'd have brought more food."

"That's very kind of you," Uncle Desmond said, "but as a matter of fact Diantha and I were just leaving. We just stopped by to drop off some presents, but I'm afraid we have to be on our way. Christmas is such a bustling time."

"Too bad," Sam lied. He put the bag on the table and said, "I gotta get back to work."

"Can't you stay long enough to eat with us?" Sookie asked. "I thought you and the boys could go out in the woods after lunch and pick out a tree."

It sounded pathetic, and Sookie isn't like that usually. It made me mad, and from the way Uncle Desmond's jaw tightened, it made him even madder.

But Sam just said, "I can't—we're short a waitress for the lunch rush." And off he went, not even kissing Sookie good-bye.

I knew Sookie was trying not to cry, so Uncle Desmond and I left so she could be alone.

As we went out to the car, I said, "I could go find a tree and chop it down if you'll tell me what to look for. Wouldn't take long."

"No, there's more wrong here than a missing Christmas tree." Uncle Desmond was quiet in the car, not even opening up his laptop. When we were in what passes for downtown Bon Temps, he said, "Diantha, pull into that McDonald's parking lot."

"Since when do you like McDonald's? Whoever calls it fast food is totally lying."

"I'm not interested in the menu. I'm concerned about Sookie."

"Being so big?"

"Her size is normal for her stage of gestation. It's her marriage that concerns me. Sam working long hours, not having the time to assist her in the decoration of her house, the monetary shortfall. I fear that he may be straying."

"You mean screwing around?"

He nodded. "Normally, of course, Sookie would detect any such activities, even with the unusual thought patterns of a shifter, but while she's pregnant, her powers are not up to their usual level. Sam could easily be concealing a paramour."

"Then he really is Shifty Sam."

"We don't know that, but if he is, steps will have to be taken. As Sookie's sponsor, I would be remiss in allowing such disrespect." Uncle Desmond may be polite, but that doesn't stop him from taking people apart. Literally. "Were it any other time, I would investigate the situation personally, but Eudokia is expecting me at their holiday ball tonight and I would rather not disappoint her. Would you be willing to stay in Bon Temps overnight and see what you can find out?"

"Suresuresure."

"It would mean missing the ball."

"Great! Your daughters are asshats and Eudokia's parties suck."

"I fear that you may be right, but family comes with certain obligations."

Since I wasn't going to be at the sucky party, Uncle Desmond gave me my present early. It was a leather messenger bag made up of a zillion different-colored pieces, and stuffed with all kinds of things that might come in handy while I was delivering messages and doing the other kinds of work I did for him. Demons aren't big on hugging or fist bumps, so I slugged him on the shoulder to thank him.

Then he gave me a bunch of money and a credit card for expenses, told me to call him as soon as I knew anything, and climbed into the front seat.

My first stop was Merlotte's, the bar that Sookie and Sam owned. Uncle Desmond had offered to drop me off on his way out of town, but I said I'd rather run. The weather was perfect for running—dry and a little chilly—and I could get there faster on foot anyway.

The bar's parking lot was mostly empty—so much for the lunch rush Sam was talking about. The lot itself looked bad, too—it had potholes and the lines that showed the parking places needed to be repainted. The employee lot was even worse, with grass coming up between the gravel. I could have ripped out all the weeds in ten minutes, five if I went really fast, but Uncle Desmond had said I should be discreet.

I found a tree that would give me a good view of the front window and climbed up. My fab messenger bag had been stocked with a pair of binoculars—sturdy in case I dropped them—so I could do the discreet thing. I could see okay, but not as well as I should have been able to. The window was dirty, and the inside of the restaurant looked grubby.

A couple of parties came in, and the waitress was painfully slow to talk to them—not just by my standards, but by human Southerner standards. When they got their food, both parties called the waitress back over. I couldn't hear what they were saying, but they didn't look happy. One table took four trips back and forth to get their order right. No wonder Sam wasn't making any money.

But he was there, not climbing into the wrong bed. I could see him the whole time: drawing drinks behind the bar, bringing out food, answering the phone, wiping tables. Poor guy looked dog tired, too. No wonder he hadn't wanted to go tromping in the woods to cut down a tree. I kept watch for a couple of hours, and Sam kept on working. He didn't make any calls, text any pictures of his parts, or do anything else like a man getting some on the side would.

Something was weird.

I thought about calling Uncle Desmond, but he was probably still on the road because he goes like a glacier, and he didn't like to talk on the phone while driving. Besides, I didn't have enough to tell him. What I needed to do was to get inside Merlotte's without Sam knowing it was me.

I put away my binoculars, slipped down the tree, and ran toward town, looking for what I needed. Or rather for *who* I needed.

There! A car with North Carolina plates had just pulled into the Grabbit Kwik for gas, and I saw a curvy redheaded woman in tight jeans, high-heeled boots, and a short leather jacket scooting for the restroom like she'd been holding it in for hours. I waited a minute before following her in, and was standing at the mirror messing with my hair when she came out of the stall and gave me a sideways look that reminded me of my cousins. I stared her down in the mirror, which made her nervous, and while she was edging out of the restroom, I snatched a couple of her hairs so quick she didn't even notice.

I went out of the bathroom long enough to make sure she was gone, then went back to lock myself in a stall while I held the hairs in my hand and said the right words. When I came out again, I looked just like the woman who'd needed to pee so bad. The humans at the Grabbit Kwik didn't even notice that "I" had already left the building once.

Since I looked like I was wearing stupidly high heels even though I was really still in sneakers, I tried to keep it to a normal pace until I was sure nobody was watching, then zipped back to Merlotte's. Sam looked up when I came in the door, but his stuffy nose kept him from recognizing my scent, which the magic hadn't changed.

"Just have a seat wherever you like, ma'am."

"Suresuresure."

He gave me a look.

"I sure will," I said, trying to sound like Sookie. I must have been good enough—he went back to wiping whatever it was he'd been wiping and I sat at the bar where I could keep an eye on him. He gave me a menu but his smile was a professional bartender smile, not a come-hither smile. That was one point for Sam.

I ordered a cheeseburger, fries, and a Coke, and while I was waiting, I tried to flirt with Sam. Okay, I'm not the biggest flirt around, but I can stick my chest out, make suggestive comments, and give eye-sex. But not only did Sam not respond appreciatively, he seemed too sick to even notice.

Another point for Sam.

At least I was going to get some good food—I've eaten at Merlotte's before. Only when the food came, the fries were cold and greasy, the burger was dry, the lettuce on top was wilted, and I spotted a lipstick stain on my glass. I ate it anyway—I am half demon—but in between bites, I did a little figuring. I couldn't speak for how long that lettuce had been hanging around, but I'd heard the burger hitting the griddle and smelled the fries while they were cooking. The meat hadn't cooked long enough to get that hard and dry, and the fries should still have been hot enough to scorch my tongue.

Something was really, really weird. Plus I was catching the scent of something wrong.

I stuck around for a while and kept trying to flirt, but mostly just watched other customers come in and listened to them complain about food that couldn't have gotten that cold that quick. Not one customer was completely satisfied. One party refused to pay, and Sam didn't even seem to have the energy to argue with them. Those who did pay left lousy tips.

I also saw the waitress on duty drop two glasses that she had a firm grip on, spill more salt than she managed to get into the shakers she was refilling, and wipe tables that were stickier after than before she wiped.

Around five o'clock, the last party grumbled its way through their meal, and Sam sent the waitress and cook home early for Christmas Eve, even though the place was supposed to be open until six. He gave me a hopeful look, too, but I just asked for another refill on my Coke.

As soon as his back was turned, I ran to lock the door and put up the *CLOSED* sign. Then I hopped back on my bar stool and whipped off my vest and tank top. Or maybe it was the leather jacket and shirt worn by the woman whose appearance I was using. Magic is weird. The important thing was that when Sam turned around, he wasn't going to see my boobs, which aren't that big anyway. He was about to see the boobs of that other woman.

That doesn't make much sense, but magic is like the Internet—I don't have to understand how it works to use it.

So Sam turned around, blinked, and backed away with his hands held up as if I was aiming something a lot more lethal than a pair of C cups. "Ma'am, I think you should leave now."

"Seriously? I'm nearly naked and you've got something better to do than jump my bones?"

"I'm a married man, ma'am. Now, why don't you put your top on and head home?"

"You sure? I'm not looking for a commitment. You give me a quick ride and I'll be on my way, no questions asked."

"I've got a wife and two kids at home, and they're waiting on me to come put up our Christmas tree. I'm not interested in any quick rides."

"Oh. Okaythen. MerryChristmas." I grabbed my stuff off the floor and headed for the door. "Wait, I haven't paid my check."

"That's okay," he said. "It's on me."

"No, no, you've got that wife and kids." I reached into my pocket to pull out a couple of twenties and put them on the bar. It was Uncle Desmond's money anyway.

"Ma'am?" Sam said as I was unlocking the door.

"You change your mind?"

"No, I just thought you might want to get dressed before you go outside."

"Yeah, good idea."

As soon as I was out the door, I zoomed off and ducked behind a tree before Sam could notice that I didn't have a car in the parking lot. He locked the door pretty emphatically, and a few minutes later, I saw him come around the back, look around nervously, then get into his truck and drive away. I didn't bother to follow him to make sure he was going home.

Before I put the rest of my clothes back on, I'd caught a glimpse of my reflection in the window—or rather that other woman's reflection—and I looked pretty damned good. If Sam didn't want a piece of that, then Sookie didn't have anything to worry about.

But something was still hinky at Merlotte's. I broke my spell so I would look like myself again and started sniffing around the parking lot. Uncle Desmond says my sense of smell is better than most weres, which can be good or bad depending on what's around to smell.

The edges of the parking lot were okay other than a couple of spots where drunks had decided to pee before they got into their cars, but the closer I got to the building, the worse it smelled. There were whole layers of stinky, but it wasn't just the garbage in the Dumpster.

Somebody had cast a curse on Merlotte's. Worse! They'd cast a crap-load of curses.

I moved away before I barfed up that burger and started counting out the number of curses I thought had to be in effect. First up was something to make food go bad quick. Another must have made clean surfaces sticky even after cleaning. There was also either a clumsiness spell, or a spell to make waitresses tired enough to be clumsy. Maybe something to make people cranky, too, but that could have been a side effect of the other spells. Plus I spotted a colony of rats living around the foundations of Merlotte's that hadn't been there when I'd visited before, and I didn't think it was just because of the bad food. Finally, something was keeping Sam sick enough that he couldn't smell the curses or the rats.

That was somewhere between five and seven curses, and there might be more I hadn't caught. It would have taken days for a witch to cast all those spells, which was bad luck for her. It meant she would have left her scent around. I cast around for a while but with weather and normal outdoor smells, it was too diffuse outside. I was hoping I'd have better luck inside, and fortunately for Sam's windows, one of the other presents in my Christmas bag was a set of lock picks that were better than my old ones and maybe a little enchanted. It didn't take me any time at all to get inside the back door, and I was glad to see I'd flustered Sam so much he'd forgotten to set the alarm.

It took over half an hour of sniffing to finally isolate the scent of a person who'd been around a lot but that didn't match any of the stuff in the employee lockers. On the good side, it gave me the chance to catch a couple of overconfident rats. It had been a long time since lunch.

Once I had the scent clear in my head, it was time to go hunting. If the witch hadn't been local, I'd have been out of luck, but I was betting that any witch who came to Merlotte's over and over again had to be in Bon Temps. So I ran up and down all the streets in town, one by one. It was nearly ten by the time I caught the scent in a cheesy split-level house with yellow vinyl siding at the end of a cul-de-sac.

The name was on the mailbox, so I used my smartphone to access Uncle Desmond's private database of info about supes. It gave me everything I needed to know about Ms. Marietta Singleton.

There were no lights on in the house, but I rang the doorbell until I heard somebody stomping down the stairs. I'd have picked the lock, but I figured a witch might have house protection spells so nobody could screw her the way she'd screwed Sam. Marietta opened the door only as wide as the door chain allowed. "Who's there?"

"I need a witch."

She cursed under her breath, but it was the four-letter-word kind, not the turn-me-into-a-toad kind. "It's Christmas Eve."

"I know—I want to buy somebody a spell for Christmas."

"Right now?"

"Well, duh. Santa Claus comes tonight."

"It's going to cost double."

"So?" I said, as if I didn't care. Which I didn't, since it was Uncle Desmond's money.

She started to unhook the chain. "Just so you know, I've got protection spells that'll blast you to dust if you so much as pull my hair."

"Understood."

Marietta was dinky, but that didn't mean she didn't pack a nasty punch, spellwise. According to the database she was in her thirties, but she looked younger in the cutesy-poo flannel sleep pants with kitty cats on them and an oversized T-shirt with still more kitty cats.

"Come into my consulting room," she said.

She'd converted a spare bedroom into what looked like a low-rent doctor's office, complete with flimsy wood paneling and beige shag carpeting. Beige! It was a good thing she had those spells to protect it all—I wanted to rip it up to keep from having to walk on it.

She handed me a pen and a clipboard with a piece of paper already on it. "If you'll just fill out this form."

"Are you shitting me?"

"This is how I work. Take it or leave it."

"Fine." I grabbed the thing, read the form, and in the section that said *Service required—be specific and use back of form if needed*, I wrote, *TAKE ALL THE CURSES OFF OF MERLOTTE'S NOW.* Then I handed it back to her.

As soon as she saw that, I could feel her starting to pull magic to herself. So I said, "I work for Desmond Cataliades."

She knew the name, and she paused, but started up again.

"I'm his niece." And I smiled. My teeth aren't as sharp as an elf's, but they're sharp enough to show which side of the family I'm on.

That stopped her. For one, everybody who knows anything about Uncle Desmond knows that he takes vengeance very seriously, and for another, spells don't always work right on demons.

"I didn't know Merlotte's was under Cataliades's protection," she whined.

"Now you know. I want every single spell, hex, curse, or hidden talisman taken off. Tonight."

"It's not that simple. I signed a contract to keep those spells maintained for six months. A blood contract."

"Then I'll get the contract canceled. Who's the client?"

She looked prissy. "I guarantee confidentiality."

I reached into my bag and pulled out a knife with a serrated edge that Uncle Desmond had given me and smiled again.

"I can't tell you," she stammered. "Confidentiality is part of the contract."

Crapcrapandmorecrap. Even if I tortured her, she wouldn't be able to tell me. I could have called Uncle Desmond and asked him what to do, but when he gives me an assignment, he expects me to carry it out. He doesn't get mad often, but when he does . . . Hoo boy.

Who had it in for Sam, anyway? Sure, there'd been trouble when the shifters and weres first came out, but that was old news. Besides, if it had been any kind of human motive, Sookie would have winkled it out with her telepathy. That made it a supe, but then what? I knew for a fact Sam wasn't in the local were pack, but he had good connections with it. The local vampires left him alone because Sheriff Ravenscroft had told them to. Another witch would have cast the spells herself and not hired Marietta. Who did that leave, and how could I get any more information out of the witch when she was bound by a blood contract?

Blood contracts were powerful—both parties had to sign in blood and the penalties for breaking them usually meant a lot more blood. The only way to break a blood contract was for both parties to agree or for both of them to die. I didn't have a big problem with killing Marietta after eating that awful cheeseburger, but I wasn't sure I could work around all her protection spells and I didn't know who the other party was. But I had an idea.

"Hey, a blood contract can't be done over the phone or the web, can it?"

"Of course not."

"So that means your client came here?"

She nodded slowly, as if she weren't sure if the contract would stop her.

"Into this office."

She nodded again.

"Then don't move, don't cast any spells, don't call anybody, don't text anybody." Then, because it was Christmas Eve, I said, "You can take a nap if you want." I didn't expect her to take me up on it, but at least I'd made the gesture.

Sookie had said Sam got sick around Thanksgiving, which meant Marietta's client been at that house less than a month earlier. So I was hoping that the witch wasn't a very good housekeeper and that she hadn't had a holiday rush of clients needing spells. I started sniffing my way through the office, starting with the guest chairs, then going down the hall to the front door and even onto the front stoop. There was something, something kinda familiar, but I couldn't get enough to ID it.

I went back to the office and saw that Marietta hadn't moved, which was a good thing for her front teeth. I was trying to think of a question she'd be able to answer when she asked me one. "Do you need to go to the bathroom? I keep one just for clients. It's the first door on the right."

"Marietta, you are officially forgiven for this carpet. And the sleep pants, too." I went to a door I'd gone past before and went into the bathroom. The first thing I noticed was that I'd forgiven her a minute too soon. The bathroom was in beige—even the toilet was beige. The second was a scent that was entirely too familiar.

I grinned and went back to the office. "I'm going to go now and make a phone call. A little while after that, you're going to get a call from your client, and she is going to tell you to cancel your blood contract. You can do that part over the phone, right?"

She nodded.

"Good. As soon as that contract is canceled, I want you to go to Merlotte's and wipe all those curses clean. And throw in a heavy-duty protection spell while you're at it."

"I have to have you here for a blood contract."

"Don't need it, and don't need this kept confidential. In fact, I want every supe around to know that Desmond Cataliades is paying for this. You send him a bill and it'll be taken care of. Got it?"

She nodded.

I thought about offering a fist bump to seal the deal but didn't think she'd take it the right way. "I don't think it's going to take long for your client to call, so you better get dressed so you can get right to work." I let myself out because she still hadn't moved from her chair.

I called Uncle Desmond while I ran back to Merlotte's, and even though his voice didn't change exactly, I could tell he was so mad I wouldn't have been surprised if my phone had caught fire. What I should have figured out as soon as I found all those spells is that there aren't many people who can afford to pay for that much magic. Of course Uncle Desmond could—he's rich. And so are Eudokia, Kallistrae, and Myrrine.

His daughters, who bitch about him spending time with Sookie and hate him buying her and her family presents. And right around Thanksgiving, when they were starting to plan their ball, they must have started thinking about how Uncle Desmond was going to be shopping for the Stackhouses again and they'd probably been paying attention when he'd told them Sookie was having another baby.

They'd known they couldn't do anything to Sookie directly, and Uncle Desmond would have spotted any curses put on her house the next time he went to visit. But they could sure hurt her indirectly by messing with Merlotte's. Uncle Desmond never goes there because Sam doesn't like him much.

The low-rent part was that it wasn't like the curses would kill Sam, they'd just ruin his business. They'd spent all that money just to make Sookie miserable. If it made Sam and the kids unhappy, too, all the better.

What asshats! There were a couple of choice items in my bag that I'd have loved to try out on them, but I figured Uncle Desmond would take care of that. It didn't take long, either.

I got back to my tree at Merlotte's and had only played Angry Birds for half an hour when Marietta drove up in a Honda—beige, of course. She went right to work saying words, waving stuff around, blowing smoke around. She was in the middle of a chant when I sneaked up behind her, and I waited until she was done to say, "Did you get them all?"

She screeched and jumped, which was what I'd been going for.

"That was the last," she gasped.

"Cool. Stay here while I check." I zipped around the building a couple of times, then picked the lock again so I could check inside. No bad smells, no sticky tables, not even a stray rat, though that was kind of disappointing.

Even though Marietta was watching for me, I got another jump-and-screech out of her when I went back. "It's clear—you're good to go." She hopped in her car and gunned it out of there without wishing me a merry Christmas or blessed be or anything.

Uncle Desmond had told me to head for a good hotel when I was done and charge it to him, but the night was clear and the streets were empty, so I decided I'd take another shot at making a sonic boom while I had a chance.

But on the way out of town, I zipped past Sookie's house and crept up so I could peek in the window. Breaking the everlasting mild cold spell on Sam meant he already looked healthier, and Sookie and Sam were making out on the couch. They hadn't gotten all the decorations out, but they'd gotten their tree up and had it covered with shiny balls and tinsel and stuff. As for the outside lights, they were so busy with each other that they never heard a thing while I picked the lock of the shed behind the house, pulled out the lights, and got them put on the house. I plugged them in and then ran for it before they could come and see what had happened.

I was halfway home when I realized what I should have realized all along. I knew what Santa Claus had to be. That kind of power, that kind of speed, being able to figure out what people wanted.

The real Santa Claus was obviously a demon.

TAPROOT

JEFFREY J. MARIOTTE

Jeff Mariotte contributed "Taproot," which takes place shortly after the events that open *Living Dead in Dallas*. If you remember, Sookie has to call Andy's sister, Portia, to pick up Andy, who's had too much alcohol to drive. When Andy comes to pick up his car the next day, there's a nasty surprise inside. With Sookie and Bill out of town, it's up to Andy to figure out what's going on in Bon Temps.

Like most Louisiana police detectives, Andy Bellefleur made occasional trips to the Louisiana State Penitentiary at Angola. One of those, two autumns back, had coincided with the annual prison rodeo. The warden insisted that Andy take advantage of the timing and gave him a behind-the-scenes tour of the arena.

There, Andy had seen a bull called Bust-'em-up, a battle-scarred veteran the approximate color of fresh blacktop. Somewhere along the way, Bust-'em-up had lost the tip of its right horn and acquired a reputation for meanness. The enormous creature could barely move in the chute; frustrated, it smashed into the sides, almost dislodging from their perches the cowboys trying to help the unfortunate rider who had drawn it get settled on the animal's back. The bull stamped and snorted and kicked up clouds of dust, eyes rolling wildly in its head. The beast's only need at that moment was release: to be let into the open space of the arena, to buck the offending weight off its back, to *move*. If it happened to crush a few ribs or break a leg or tear open somebody's scalp, well, that was gravy. Mostly, it wanted to be free.

Andy felt the same way.

He was not a small man. He liked to think of his muscular heft as a professional advantage, that he came across as a solid citizen, someone the townsfolk could count on. The Honda Civic his sister, Portia, had provided—borrowed from a longtime client of her law firm, who would never have the resources to pay everything she owed—was okay for a short while, but nothing he'd want to use for long. He liked being able to stretch his legs. Belted into the small car, with the door closed, he felt more than a little claustrophobic.

Like Bust-'em-up, he just wanted out. In Andy's case, not into a rodeo arena, but into the parking lot of Merlotte's Bar and Grill.

The Honda was painted a vibrating orange color that made Andy's teeth hurt. But it was cheaper than a rental, and until his Buick was released from impound—taken because Lafayette Reynold had been found inside it, murdered, in the parking lot at Merlotte's—it would have to do.

Officially, Andy couldn't work the case. When a homicide victim turns up in your car, it doesn't matter who you are, you sit near the top of the list of suspects. He was on desk duty for the moment, which meant he was not expected to catch cases but to spend his days twiddling his thumbs in a cubicle where the air conditioner was almost as weak as the coffee. Anyway, Merlotte's was on Renard Parish turf, not inside town limits, so the Bon Temps PD wasn't directly involved in the investigation.

But unofficially, there was no way Andy was staying out of it. He was a regular at Merlotte's, where Lafayette had worked as a cook. And everyone in Bon Temps knew Lafayette. A flamboyantly gay African American man in a small northern Louisiana town might as well have been carrying around a neon sign with an arrow pointing at you and the words *LOOK AT ME* emblazoned across it every time he left his house.

Somebody had broken Lafayette's neck and sexually assaulted him. Andy knew *he* hadn't murdered anyone, and he sure hadn't messed with him, but that was all he knew. As far as he was concerned, the list of nonsuspects was one person long, and the suspect pool contained everybody else. And the fact that the body had been dumped in his car made the whole thing sort of personal.

He found some shade by a big pine, determinedly not parking in what had been his usual spot but never would be again, and disentangled himself from the car's seat belt. He was passing through the front door when three luxury SUVs and a white van pulled into the lot.

Sam Merlotte stood at the bar, enveloped by the yeasty fragrance of beer on tap. Andy usually liked the smell, but now it reminded him of the night Lafayette had died, when he had kept putting them away until they'd put him away. "Might want to raise your prices, Sam," he said. "Some high-end vehicles parking outside."

Sam glanced at the door. "I'll leave 'em low," he said. "Maybe they'll tip better. In my experience, the more well-heeled someone is, the worse he tips." He gave Andy a searching look. "How you doing, Andy?"

"Oh, you know," Andy answered, wanting to dodge any questions about the other night before they were asked. "I'm lookin' for Sookie. She here?"

"She's off for a few days," Sam said.

"Off? She at home?"

Sam's gaze shifted toward the front door. Maybe he was waiting for the people from those SUVs. Or maybe he was trying to avoid Andy's gaze. Andy found the latter explanation more likely. "No, she's . . . out of town. With Bill."

Andy didn't have much patience with vampires, as a general rule, and he particularly didn't like Bill Compton. "Well, you were here that night. The night . . . you know."

"Yeah."

"I was just hopin' someone could tell me who all was in here that night. You know, were there any strangers around, anybody who looked nervous, anyone who just came in for a few minutes and left again? Like that."

"I was here," Sam said. "But I—" The front door banged open, and something like relief passed across Sam's face. "Hello," he called out. "Welcome to Merlotte's."

"I'm looking for Sam Merlotte," the man at the front of the pack said. He was dressed in a cream-colored shirt that looked like silk, with French cuffs and big gold cuff links. Over that he had on a navy blue blazer. His jeans were the overpriced kind that mimicked the look you could get by buying a pair of Wranglers off the rack and dragging them behind your truck for a couple of days.

Others streamed in behind him, not quite as overdressed, but clearly not folks who bought their clothes at Tara's Togs or the Bon Temps Walmart.

"That's me," Sam said.

"Marvelous." The man crossed the plank floor in a few long strides, his right hand held out before him. He looked vaguely familiar. He had piercing blue eyes under a curly mop of coppery hair. His facial features appeared small, or maybe his head was just big. Mostly, Andy saw two slabs of deeply tanned cheek, blocking in a finely chiseled nose and a mouth overstocked with bright white teeth. Although the combination of parts was strange, somehow it came together in a way that wasn't unpleasant to look at.

The man had reached the bar and gripped Sam's hand by the time Andy realized who it was. "Hey," he said. "You're—"

"Tristan Kowel, Mr. Merlotte," the man said, ignoring Andy. "*Delighted* to meet you. You've got a lot of fans on the coast. A *lot* of fans."

"Portia watches your show," Andy said. "My sister. Portia."

"I'm sorry, Mr. . . . Kowel, is it?" Sam said. "Fans?"

"He's got a show," Andy said. "On the Food Network. *Burgers and Beer*, isn't that it?"

"Triple B," Kowel said. "*Burgers, Beer, and Bar-B-Q*. We spotlight the best bar-and-grill establishments from coast to coast."

"Portia loves it."

"I'm still not clear on—" Sam began.

"We're *thrilled* that you've given us approval to shoot here," Kowel said. He didn't seem like a guy who listened much. If at all.

"I don't remember giving anybody—"

"You'll hardly know we're here." Kowel executed a spin that Andy thought might be most accurately labeled a pirouette. "Of course, we'll touch the place up some. Charmingly rustic, isn't it?"

"Touch the place—?" Sam began.

"What do you think, Bradley?" Kowel asked. "Bradley Millham is our set decorator. He's a big fan, Mr. Merlotte. Sam. I can call you Sam, right? It's like I've known you forever."

"Sure," Sam said. "Everybody calls me Sam. But I—"

"Bradley?" Kowel said. He swept an arm toward the back bar. "What do you think? Does it all have to go, or can you work with it?"

Kowel's voice filled the cavernous interior of Merlotte's, almost empty in the hours between the breakfast and lunch rushes. Bradley, on the other hand, was so quiet Andy had to strain to hear.

"I think . . ." he said. "I think some of it isn't too awful. You know, considering."

"Considering what?" Sam asked.

"You know, the point of the series isn't to present stylish bistros. We like our featured locations to be rough around the edges. We'll have to do some work, to establish some sense of realism, but—"

"What do you mean, realism?" Sam said. "My place is plenty real!"

"It's *real*," Kowel assured him. "But it's not *reality* real." Sam sputtered something, but Kowel just kept talking. "Don't worry, Bradley is the best there is. You'll love what he comes up with."

"Listen," Sam said. "I'm not sure I want this place—"

Kowel raised a hand to silence him. To Andy's surprise, it worked. "Trust us, Sam. We do this all the time. The publicity value alone will be enormous—you literally cannot buy this kind of advertising. And our location fee should help you overcome any minor qualms."

"Location fee?"

"It was covered in the agreement we sent you. Casey-Lynn?"

A female voice called out from the throng milling near the doorway, and Andy's head spun around as if mounted on ball bearings. "Yes, Tris?" she said.

"You did cover Mr. Merlotte's location fee in the agreement, cor-
recto?"

"I'm sure I did." Casey-Lynn stepped toward him.

Andy couldn't hold his mouth closed. "Casey-Lynn Jennings?"

"Why, Andrew Bellefleur," she said, stopping short. "It really is
you, isn't it?"

"I think so. I mean, it was last I looked. Oh, hell, that don't make
any sense."

"Then it's you, all right."

Casey-Lynn moved into Andy's arms, which he hadn't even realized
he had spread. She wrapped her considerably more slender arms around
him and squeezed. Her grip was tighter than the Honda's, and far more
pleasant.

"Casey-Lynn," Kowel said, stretching out the *nn* until it was its
own syllable.

"He sounds impatient," Andy said. His arms had closed around
her, and he didn't feel inclined to let go.

"Always," Casey-Lynn whispered. She eased herself from Andy's
grasp, one hand lingering on his arm. "Yes, Tris, we covered that." She
took her hand away, though Andy could still feel its warmth, and dug
into a cloth bag hanging from her shoulder. "I have a copy of the agreement right here," she said, withdrawing a pink file folder.

As she carried it to the bar, Andy found himself wondering if it was
actually a pink manila folder, or if "manila" was the color. Manila was a
city in the Philippines, he knew, but that didn't help. He was, he realized,
thinking absurd thoughts to keep from staring at her behind as she leaned
on the bar. That behind was a little fuller than it had been in high school,
but no less shapely for that. Which was the last time Andy had seen
Casey-Lynn Jennings, though not the last time he'd thought about her.

A girl like her—a woman, now—didn't come into a guy's life every
day. She could disappear in a flash, he had learned, but that didn't mean
she was easily forgotten.

While he stood there, his mind reeling with Casey-Lynn's sudden, unannounced reappearance in Bon Temps, the rest of Kowel's crew got busy. Most were young, all lean and polished, and even the ones wearing T-shirts and ragged jeans wore obviously high-priced T-shirts and ragged jeans. Men and women bustled around Merlotte's, bringing in what looked like enough gear to build a bar from scratch if they'd wanted to. A couple went into the kitchen, where days earlier Lafayette might have been working. Today Andy's cousin Terry objected loudly to the intrusion. One bearded guy with rectangular, heavy-framed glasses held his hands in front of his face and peered through the square hole they made. Another guy, with a heavier beard but thinner glasses, was counting electrical outlets and handling power cords as if he could intuit from the weight what events might have occurred in their vicinity in the past.

If he could, that might be a better trick than Sookie Stackhouse's.

A gentle hand on his shoulder let him know that Casey-Lynn was finished with Sam. "I'll be in town a few days, Andy," she said. She had lost all but a trace of her Louisiana accent. "Busy, but I should have some time to myself. I hope we can get together. You know, talk about old times."

"Yeah. Uhh, yeah, okay, sure." Andy fumbled a business card from his pocket and handed it to her. "My numbers are on there. Call whenever."

"You're a cop," she said. "Isn't that precious? I'll call soon as I can get a free minute. Got to run, now." She gave him a peck on the cheek, letting her lips rest there a long moment before pulling away. Then she was rushing toward the kitchen door, where Tristan Kowel stood, arms folded over his chest, waiting with what must have been his trademark impatience.

Andy looked around for Sam, who never had answered his questions about that night. When he finally spotted him, Sam was deep in conversation with Bradley and one of the bearded guys. Andy, it seemed, would just have to wait.

Casey-Lynn Jennings. How about that? At first he couldn't wait to tell Portia he had seen her, but by the time he was belted into the torture-Honda, he had changed his mind. Portia had never liked her. When Casey-Lynn had broken up with him, Portia had said—and these words had been blazed into his soul ever since—"Good. That scrawny bitch doesn't deserve you anyway."

Even that was selective memory. Truth was, she never had broken up with him, really. She had stopped answering his letters and stopped coming to the phone when he called after her family had moved to Arizona. Then the number he had was disconnected and he'd never heard from her again.

He never would have taken her for a Hollywood type. But years had passed since he'd known Casey-Lynn. A lot of them.

Bon Temps was small enough that everybody in the high school more or less knew one another. You saw the same people every day for four years—most of them people you'd known in grade school and junior high—and every face became pretty familiar. But there were people you socialized with and those you didn't, and even though Andy had thought Casey-Lynn Jennings attractive, he had never believed they had anything in common.

He played football and hung out with jocks. Friday nights, after the season ended, were for drinking beers and maybe plinking at cans out in the woods. Casey-Lynn hung out in the library, wrote poetry, and was friends with the drama club people. If they had been drawn into a human Venn diagram, they would barely have intersected.

Until midway through the season during his junior year, when a rough tackle had left Andy sidelined with a torn rotator cuff. He had still suited up for practice, and for the first couple of weeks he sat on the bench cheering on his teammates. But when the pressure of an upcoming midterm in his World History class had caught up with him, he'd started cracking his books instead of watching drills and practice scrimmages.

That was when Casey-Lynn entered his life. Andy was sitting in the shade of the bleachers, near the chain-link fence surrounding the stadium, and had a couple of books spread out on the ground as he scribbled in a spiral notebook.

"What're you working on?" a voice asked from the other side of the fence. Andy looked up and saw Casey-Lynn there, fingers laced through the chain link. The late-afternoon sun was in her face, and her big green eyes were squinting, her nose crinkled. She had long blond hair that caught the sunlight and seemed to magnify it, and he thought, in that moment, that he had never seen a prettier girl.

"History," he said. "I have to know the causes of World War One, and I'm trying to keep these names straight. Archduke Ferdinand, Gavrilo Princip, Kaiser Wilhelm, and the rest of those guys."

"Ferdinand's assassination was the immediate catalyst, but don't forget about the spread of European nationalism. And the Pig War."

"Pig War?" Andy echoed.

When Casey-Lynn released the fence and sat, her crossed legs transformed her long, floral-print skirt into rolling meadowlands. "It was really a customs blockade of Serbian pork," she explained. "But it's symptomatic, and it did play a direct role."

"No shi—no kidding?" He hadn't heard anything in class about a Pig War. But Casey-Lynn sounded like she knew what she was talking about. When she launched into a detailed description of the events that pushed the world toward war, she made it both more entertaining and easier to follow than Mr. Ludlow, Andy's history teacher, had ever managed to do.

By the end of the lecture, he'd asked her out.

Casey-Lynn declined.

She also said no the second time, and the third through ninth.

But somehow she never made him feel rejected or demeaned. It almost turned into a game between them, and their friendship deepened to the point that at school they spent most of their time together, except when class schedules interfered. Finally, the tenth time Andy asked, she agreed to accompany him to the school's Christmas dance, though she insisted on meeting him there.

That night was as close to magic as anything Andy had ever known.

He arrived at school to find her waiting outside. It was cold enough that every exhalation produced a puff of steam, but she was wearing a red sateen dress that left her arms and shoulders bare. If she'd come in a coat, she had already ditched it. As Andy approached, she dashed into his arms and welcomed him with a kiss that seemed like it would never end, and at the same time was over far too soon.

They danced together to every song—Andy had never been much of a dancer, except for that night—and during slow ones, they held each other as if they would never let go. Once in a while, she tilted her head up and found his lips with hers, for kisses that went on until, on one occasion, Assistant Principal Duckworth warned them that if they did it again, they'd be escorted from the premises.

After, in Andy's car, the kisses were faster and more frantic, and accompanied by groping and heavy breathing that curtained the windows with steam. Later, Andy couldn't say when the pickup truck had stopped beside his car in the now-empty school lot, or how long it had sat, engine rumbling, before he and Casey-Lynn noticed.

"Shit!" she said when she finally peered outside. "It's my brother. I have to go, baby."

"I could take you home in a while." She had never invited him to her house or introduced him to her family. He was curious about the brother, but fogged windows and the truck cab's height blocked his view.

"No, it's okay. I'll get in trouble if I don't go with him."

"But, Casey-Lynn . . ."

She pushed his hands away from her. "Seriously, Andy. I have to go."

"Can I see you tomorrow? Or over break?"

"We'll see. I'll call you."

And she had, from a gas station pay phone in Houston. The family, she told him, was moving west. She apologized for not being able to see him before they left, but she would let him know where she landed. Then she said, "Someone's coming, I gotta run," and hung up.

She had written, for a while, and taken his calls for a while.

Then nothing.

Until now.

She called at eleven the next morning and asked if Andy could meet her at Merlotte's for lunch. He was off that day, not even exercising his thumbs at his desk. He had already showered and shaved, but he did so again, then got in the hated Honda and drove over.

Sam's parking lot was full of booth benches and tables and bar stools and chairs and kitchen equipment, stacks of dishes and glassware, pots and pans, trays of utensils, and all the miscellaneous stuff Sam used inside. A carpentry crew had set up sawhorses and acquired lumber and was hard at work on some object Andy couldn't identify. The sounds of power saws and hammering filled the air, as did scents of sawdust and paint. Plastic sheeting trailed from the front door, and a paint-spattered guy was carrying two five-gallon cans inside.

Sam Merlotte stood at a remove from it all, watching and scratching the top of his head.

"What's goin' on?" Andy asked him.

"I don't really know anymore."

"Lot of activity. Looks like they're tearing the place apart."

Sam glanced at him. "They are, pretty much."

"That okay with you?"

"Apparently I signed a contract saying it was. I don't actually remember doing that, but it's my signature."

"Could it be a forgery?"

Sam showed him a wry grin. "One thing I've learned in Bon Temps, Andy. Anything could be anything."

"Guess that's true."

"Count on it."

"Listen, Sam," Andy said. "About that night—"

"I've been trying to remember, Andy. Lafayette was my friend as well as my chef. But I really can't say that anyone came in that night who was at all out of the ordinary. Anyway, I doubt anyone would have dumped his body while we were open. There are always people coming and going, and they couldn't have known you'd get a ride home, until you did. I figure the body was put in your car after hours, when it was the only car left in the lot. They might not even have known it was yours."

"Could be," Andy agreed. He had thought of that. In the couple of days since, he had considered just about every possible angle.

Still, he had to be missing something, because he hadn't yet figured out who had done it.

"Sorry, Andy," Sam said. "I—"

"Yeah," Andy interrupted. Casey-Lynn had appeared in the doorway and was looking outside, shading her eyes against the sun. "If you think of anything else, let me know."

She spotted Andy and burst from the door. He broke away from Sam and met her halfway. They embraced, not quite with the passion of that evening outside the Christmas dance, but it was, Andy thought, a better hug than most he'd had since then.

"You ready for some lunch?" she asked.

Andy gestured toward the restaurant furnishings clotting the parking lot. "Is it open?"

"Only to crew," Casey-Lynn said. "But Terry's on the grill. He can whip up anything you want."

"I know that. He's my cousin."

"Of course he is, silly."

She took him by the hand and led him inside. Emptied out, the place seemed huge. The crew had set up lights on stands and suspended more from the ceiling. Against one wall, workers were installing a kind of wooden latticework with indentations that almost looked like the insides of egg cartons, except with hollow centers. Soundproofing, Andy guessed. Others were refinishing the bar with a high-gloss, almost metallic finish, and yet more were painting the kitchen. Andy wondered how Terry was managing to cook anything, with what seemed to be all the kitchenware outside and a crew of painters underfoot.

Casey-Lynn led Andy through the interior and out the back door. A handful of tables had been set up between the restaurant and Sam's trailer, and various crew members occupied a couple of them. Tristan Kowel sat by himself, at a table with a single chair and a big umbrella covering it. He gazed on the scene before him with what looked like barely restrained revulsion.

"Guy's kind of a jerk, ain't he?" Andy said softly.

"Tristan? He's okay. He knows he's the show. Without him, it's just footage of a bunch of greasy spoons nobody would want to go into."

"Sam's place isn't bad."

"I don't mean Merlotte's," Casey-Lynn said quickly. "But most of them. *This* is like coming home."

"It wasn't here when you were."

"I mean Bon Temps. You. Being here again, after so long."

"It has been a while."

She took his hand, held it. The years had etched tiny lines in her face: around her eyes, at the corners of her mouth. He liked them. Her hair was a shade or two darker than it had been, and cut short, even with her jawline. She had put on a little weight, and he liked that, too. He wondered what the transition had been like, from the smart, pretty girl he had known to the accomplished woman she was today.

"I guess I owe you an apology, don't I?" she said.

"For what?"

"Disappearing like that."

He chuckled. "It was kind of abrupt."

"You didn't know my parents."

"You never let me."

"There was a reason for that." She let go of his hand, and her gaze wandered around the back parking area. Andy followed it. Fall was starting to set in; leaves were beginning to brown, and some had already dropped, dry and curled, onto the ground. Nobody had told the mosquitoes yet, but they would get the message soon enough. "I guess we didn't use the word *dysfunctional* in those days, but that's what they were. *We* were. My daddy was never any good, Andy. He was a petty criminal, as lazy as the day is long, always looking for the easiest way to do anything. Mama wasn't much better, and that's how they reared up us kids. When one of them would come home and say, 'Time to pack up and move,' we packed up and moved. It usually meant there was a sheriff on the way."

"You wrote me back for a while. You answered when I called."

"Until they told me I couldn't. If anybody figured out I was talking to you, they could find us through you. So I had to stop, and I couldn't say why. I'm so sorry, Andy." She met his gaze again, her eyes liquid, her lower lip trembling. He hoped she wouldn't cry. He never had liked it when women cried. A cop saw too much of that. "I'm really, really sorry."

"I can't say I wasn't hurt," he said. "But that was a long time ago. I'm over it now."

She managed a smile, though it looked a little pained. "I'm glad to hear that. When I knew we were coming here, I hoped I'd be able to see you. I admit, I looked you up online, saw that you and Portia were still here. I even knew you were a cop before you gave me your card, even though I pretended to be surprised. And I saw some pictures of you, so I knew how handsome you'd become."

Andy felt heat rising into his cheeks. "Not half as handsome as you are pretty, Casey-Lynn."

"Oh, stop." She waved her fingers at him. "I'm practically haggard."

"You're crazy. You look beautiful."

"Obviously the years have affected your eyesight, but I'll take it."

A production assistant came over with a legal pad and took lunch orders. A little while later, they were eating burgers and fries that weren't half-bad and hardly tasted like paint. Casey-Lynn told him how she'd wound up in the television business, and Andy tried to bring her up to speed on events in Bon Temps. To the extent that he could, anyway; as he talked, he realized that a lot of people around Bon Temps seemed to have secrets they wanted to protect. That was probably true everywhere, but it seemed especially pronounced here. He stopped short of telling her what he knew of Sookie's abilities, but he did bring her name up after she got him talking about Vampire Bill. He couldn't tell if she was more fascinated by the fact that Bon Temps now harbored an out vampire, or that Sookie was dating him.

"I would love to see Sookie," Casey-Lynn said. "I never knew her that well, but I always thought she was cool. And I wouldn't mind a look at that vampire. When do they get back?"

"Sam's not sure," Andy replied. "Couple of days, maybe."

"Okay, good. I mean, we should still be here."

"I meant to ask you something, Casey-Lynn. Sam says he doesn't remember signing any contracts. How did you approach him in the first place?"

She let her gaze fall to her plate and tapped her fingernails on its edge. "E-mail, I think. It might have been a phone call, though, then e-mail. I do whatever I can to line up the places Tristan wants to visit."

"How did he hear about Merlotte's?"

"I told him about it."

"But you'd never been here."

"Andy, I spend my life studying up on bar and grills, roadside cafés, that kind of thing. When I heard about it, that it was in Bon Temps, of course I was intrigued. I did some more research and it sounded like it was right up Tris's alley. So I got in touch with Sam and made the arrangements."

"Which he forgot all about. He sure wasn't expecting you yesterday."

Her eyes narrowed. "Are you trying to say something here?"

"I'm just curious about how y'all do things in Hollywood," Andy said. "Sam was genuinely surprised."

"We usually call a few days before we show up. Somebody might have dropped the ball on that. Or else not been able to reach him. I hear there was quite a stir over here the other day."

Andy had wondered when that would come up, and how. He told her what had happened that night, admitting that he'd been emotionally ravaged by a pedophilia case and gotten much drunker than he'd intended. Talking about the case, even in the most general terms, twisted his guts into knots.

When he was finished telling Casey-Lynn about that, and the aftermath—Sookie finding the murdered Lafayette in his car—she was holding his hands, trying to quell their trembling. He swallowed, hard, and knew the blood had drained from his face. Casey-Lynn regarded him as if trying to decide whether she should dial 911.

"I'm so sorry, Andy," she said. "That's truly awful, start to finish. I'm sorry you had to go through it, but I'm glad you're strong enough to stand up for people who can't stand up for themselves."

"I guess," Andy said. He'd never been great at accepting praise. "Thanks."

"How did Sookie handle it?"

"She's pretty tough, I guess. She's okay."

"When did you say she and Bill Compton are getting back into town? I'd hate to miss her."

"I'm not sure," Andy said again. "Shouldn't be too long."

Kowel had gone inside while they ate, but now he came to the back door. "Casey-Lynn, I need you," he said.

She gave Andy's hands a final squeeze. "Duty calls, babe. I'll let you know when I can get free again."

"Okay, Casey-Lynn," he said. "See you later."

She went inside. He waited a few minutes longer, not sure his legs would support him yet. His own story had affected him, as he had known it would. He was more surprised by the impact of hers. He had thought there was something off about her family, about their disappearance. Who just picks up and vanishes like that? For years, he had woven fanciful tales of intrigue in his mind. Thinking about it now, he suspected that taste of mystery might have been one of the factors that had driven him to become a detective.

When he felt stronger, he pushed back his chair, rose, and headed through the restaurant. The crew had finished putting up the strange egg-carton construction on the west wall. Now one of the clean-shaven guys stood on a ladder, inserting what looked like six-inch wooden dowels into the holes in the center of each depression. Andy wasn't sure what the point was, but he was impressed by the crew's thoroughness. He even saw one of the female crew members spraying something onto a cloth from an unmarked bottle—some cleaning solution, he guessed— and wiping out the inside of each glass.

Driving home, he couldn't get the lunchtime conversation out of his mind. Casey-Lynn hadn't quite been all over him, but she had been more physically affectionate than he'd expected. Did she want to pick up where they left off, all those years ago? That was impossible, wasn't it? Too much had happened—and, he had to admit, he had been really hurt. He wasn't sure he had entirely forgiven her. He'd thought he had, but her showing up again had peeled away the emotional scar tissue, exposing the original wound again.

He was glad to see her, and the attraction was still strong. But he felt there was something she wanted, and he couldn't figure out what it was.

He was a smart guy. He was a detective, a good one, who solved real crimes. So why couldn't he figure out Casey-Lynn? If she had an angle, it was opaque to him. If she wanted to rekindle something long since buried, what was the purpose? She wasn't likely to stick around in Bon Temps, and he had no interest in going to Hollywood. And she was still beautiful, but he would never have anything like movie-star looks.

So it wasn't that. There was something else going on. But he didn't know what it was, and that fact wouldn't stop gnawing at him.

He woke shortly after two in the morning and sat up in bed, eyes wide.

He sat there for a few minutes, trying to talk himself down. What he was thinking just couldn't be.

But he couldn't make it *not* make sense.

He dressed and left the house quietly, so he wouldn't wake his sister or grandmother, and got into the Honda. He followed the twin cones of its headlights down Magnolia Creek Road to Parish Road 34, then turned onto Hummingbird Road and took that to Merlotte's. The restaurant was dark. Andy drove around it and parked outside Sam's trailer, feeling a little guilty about what he had to do.

He pounded on the trailer door until lights blinked on. Sam opened the door a minute later, wearing boxer shorts and holding a shirt closed over a chest furred with tightly coiled, golden hairs. Andy looked away. "Sorry if I woke you, Sam," he said.

"*If?* Of course you woke me. Those Hollywood people ran me ragged all day. What is it?"

"How do you organize your e-mails?"

"What?"

Andy repeated the question, though it had seemed straightforward enough the first time.

Sam blinked a couple of times. "Organize? I run a bar and grill. I'd be surprised if I get ten e-mails a day, if you don't count groups asking for money and junk mail about growing a bigger—"

"I get those, too," Andy said, cutting him off. "Not that I need 'em."

"Anyway, I don't organize my e-mails. I just leave them in the order they come in, except for the ones I trash. Why?"

"Your computer in here or in the restaurant? Or both?"

"In there. When I'm here, I want to be away from the business."

"Can't blame you for that."

"What's this all about, Andy?"

"Open the place up and I'll tell you."

"You're not drunk again, are you?"

"Hell no, Sam. I might be seeing clearly for the first time in days."

"Okay, hang on." Sam let the door swing closed. When he emerged a minute later, he had shoved his feet into some shoes, pulled on a pair of jeans, and fastened a few of the pearl snaps on his shirt. "Wish you'd tell me what this is about."

"It's about what those people are doing in your place," Andy said.

"What people? Tris? The crew? They're getting ready to shoot a TV show. This could really put Merlotte's on the map."

"You sure you want to be on the map?" Andy asked as they crossed the parking area to the restaurant's back door. "Seems like for some of the people working here, being put on display in front of the whole world might not be their most favorite thing."

"Maybe. What's that got to do with e-mail?"

"Nothing," Andy replied. "I'm just saying."

Sam stuck his key in the lock, turned it, hit some light switches on the way in. "Andy, you're not making much sense."

"Just find me the e-mail Casey-Lynn sent you when she asked if they could film here. Hell, doesn't even have to be the first one. Find the one where she sent you a contract, the one where she offered you money. Anything."

Sam stopped, halfway toward his office, and turned slowly. He looked at Andy, something like comprehension beginning to glimmer in his eyes. "You know? I'm not sure I can."

"That's what I'm thinking."

"What, though? This is all some kind of setup? For what?"

"I don't know yet. That's what I want to find out."

"Yeah, okay. I'll check my e-mail. I really don't remember any, but she and Tris said they'd been in touch. They knew so much about the place, I believed them. And you know, things have been a little crazy around here, these last couple months. I could've been distracted."

Sam went into his office, and Andy wandered around the restaurant. It looked like a different place. The crew had remodeled and repainted and refinished. The furniture had been brought back inside, but it looked new. Polished glassware was arrayed behind the bar, and there was a new mirrored back bar with tiny spotlights illuminating the bottles of liquor and artificial blood, creating an elegant effect.

"This looks great!" Andy called. "They did a hell of a job!"

"They did, didn't they?"

"I thought the point was to show the world the places they found, though, not to turn them into something else."

"Andy, it's TV. Nothing's real on TV."

"I wouldn't know."

Sam emerged from his office, looking glum. "I can't find them. Not a single e-mail."

"I'm not surprised."

"What the hell is going on?"

"I don't know, Sam. But I got a feeling Casey-Lynn Jennings is right in the middle of it. Do you know when they'll be here?"

"They're shooting tomorrow. Today, I guess. She said around six."

"Know where they're staying?"

"They have some fancy tour buses over at Don's trailer park. They need the hookups, Bradley said."

"So we got, what, almost four hours? That should give us time."

Sam was wide-awake now, but confused. "Time for what?"

"To figure out what they're up to." Andy glanced toward the egg-carton construction. "What's that thing?"

"Bradley called it a decorative accent."

"I think it's a lot more than that," Andy said. He dragged a table and a chair over beside the wall, then stepped up into the chair and onto the table.

"Careful."

"Don't worry," Andy said. He reached inside the little hole at the back of the indentation with two fingers, and withdrew what he had thought were dowels.

They weren't.

The crew showed up a few minutes after six. Andy and Sam and Bud Dearborn and Alcee Beck were waiting inside, sitting around a table with coffee cups and a mostly empty pot on top of it. Bud was the Renard Parish sheriff, Alcee one of his detectives.

For the past hour, Andy had felt a growing kinship with that old bull Bust-'em-up. The nearer six o'clock came, the more he felt trapped in a narrow space, when all he wanted to do was get out, get away, run. *Move.*

But he stayed and drank coffee and traded stories with the Renard Parish cops, even though he'd heard theirs before and they'd heard his. When the door opened and Tristan Kowel looked in, Andy sat with his hands on the tabletop, trying to look as if he hadn't a care.

"Sam?" Kowel said. "Ready for the big day?"

"Come on in, Tris," Sam said. "Everybody with you?"

"The whole crew."

Kowel entered, and the others trailed behind him, each looking at the men around the table with some measure of curiosity and surprise. When Casey-Lynn came in, she started toward Andy, then hesitated. The pause was brief; some people might have missed it, but Andy didn't. Then she was walking toward him again, her steps a little more determined. Also more forced, as was her smile.

"I didn't expect to see you here so early, Andy," she said. She put her arms around him, gave him a quick hug. He returned it without enthusiasm. "Something wrong?" she asked.

"You tell me."

"I don't— What are you talking about?"

"It's Bill, isn't it?" he said.

"What do you mean?"

Andy pointed to the egg-carton wall. "Wooden stakes, loaded into spring-fired launchers, enough to blanket the whole dining area. Silver nitrate coating the inside of every glass in the place—barely enough to be noticeable, maybe enough to make some humans sick. But probably enough to make a vampire dead. Electric current in the bar, wired separately for each position, probably controlled remotely. I don't know what else—we only had a few hours, so we haven't completely torn the place apart."

"Andy, baby, I—"

"When I told you about him, I called him 'Vampire Bill.' You knew he was Bill Compton, even though I never said his last name. And you acted surprised when I mentioned that there was an out vampire livin' here—but how could it be a surprise if you already knew his name?"

As he spoke, something changed in her face. It was almost like she'd been standing in a light that had been switched off. She closed up, looked away from him, pressed her lips together. For a long moment, she didn't speak.

Then she touched his arm, a glancing pass, and dropped her hand to her side. "Okay, yes. I told you about my family, Andy. How none of them—none of *us*—have ever been any good. That's true, much as I hate to admit it. And that kind of thing has deep roots."

"What's that got to do with Bill?"

"Bill's the taproot," she said. "The one from which all the rest emerged. He murdered my great-grandfather. It's family legend. Everybody in my family knows Bill Compton's name, and everybody knows that after his death, Enoch's wife, Clara, went a little nuts. More than a little."

"So you're trying to kill Bill—and endangering everybody else in Merlotte's in the bargain—because of something you think he did decades ago?"

"Longer than that. And we *know* he did it. That's never been at issue. Some don't think that's the only reason the family fell apart, but I believe it is. The hatred, the bitterness, the thirst for vengeance—that's as hereditary as hair color or high cholesterol, and it got passed down to all of us. Bill Compton's an abomination, and I hate him. But not *just* him—I hate *all* bloodsuckers. That's why I joined the Fellowship of the Sun—because their goals match those I've had for so long. And if some vamp-loving people get hurt, too, well, that'll just make a bigger statement, won't it?"

"You're a member of that cu—"

"Don't say 'cult,' Andy. It's a church. We *believe*."

"I thought churches believed in forgiveness. You might try that sometime."

"Some things aren't so easily forgiven," she said.

"Tell me about it." Even as he spoke, he knew he hadn't truly forgiven, either. If he had, he might not have been so quick to suspect her. "So, what, is the whole crew in on this?"

"Just a few. Fellowship folks got me the job in the first place. When I told them what I had in mind—what a splash it would make—they were on board. Not Tristan, though, so don't blame him. He never knew. I was the instigator." She raised the hand to his arm again, and this time clutched it tight. "I'm sorry, Andy. About . . . you know, everything. The way I was raised. The way I left you. Lying to you."

"I'm sorry, too, Casey-Lynn. I don't like vampires, either, but the law's the law. And Bill's never done anything to hurt me, or anyone else I know. You'll have to go with Bud—with Sheriff Dearborn, there. What happens after that is out of my hands."

She swallowed, eyes glistening, but then she hardened again, dropped her hand, looked him straight in the eye. "It was a hell of a plan, Andy. And this doesn't change anything. The Fellowship's work—the Lord's work—goes on, with or without me."

She turned away and went toward Dearborn, hands out, wrists together. "I take it you'd like to handcuff me?" she said.

Bud talked quietly with Casey-Lynn for a few minutes, and she pointed out the four Fellowship members who had helped her. Some looked like they wanted to run, but Alcee was blocking the door, and nobody wanted to tangle with him.

While Bud and Casey-Lynn talked, Sam and Tristan Kowel were deep in conversation. Then Dearborn and Alcee led the conspirators away, and Kowel turned to those left behind. "We're going to put it back, people."

"Back?" someone asked.

"Merlotte's. Back to what it was when we came."

"But it looks so much *better* now," Bradley complained.

"*Back*," Sam said.

"Back," Kowel echoed.

As the crew debated how to proceed, Andy walked out the front door and watched Bud and Alcee divide the detained into two vehicles. Bud took Casey-Lynn, though she had to sit in his front seat.

She craned her head as Bud drove out of the lot. When she met Andy's gaze, her lips curled into a smile. It wasn't a smile of victory, or even one acknowledging an old friend. He thought perhaps it was the smile of the faithful, of someone who could afford to take the long view. It lasted for only an instant, and then the smile was gone and she looked straight ahead, through the windshield, as if ready to face whatever came next.

Andy watched her leave him again. He'd thought the last time was for keeps, but he knew this one was. Even if she was convicted and incarcerated locally, he wouldn't visit. He would testify at the trial, but that was all. He wouldn't be drawn into her life again. That was a trap, as surely as a rodeo chute to a bull, and he wasn't dumb enough to enter it a third time.

When both sheriff's vehicles were out of sight, Andy started back into Merlotte's, but he stopped himself as he reached for the door. He needed some sleep, a clear head.

Bill was safe, for now, but Lafayette's killer was still out there.

Andy stood there a moment longer. The early-morning sun picked out the needles on the big pines, defining each one distinctly and surrounding it with a halo of light. The smell of the trees hung heavy in the morning air and high clouds dotted the sky, and somewhere a bird chittered, and he heard the whine of a mosquito, and he knew that Bon Temps was waking up.

Bon Temps. *His* town.

He got into the Honda, but instead of going home and closing his eyes, he drove to Caddo Road, made a right on Court Street, and cruised slowly through downtown, then the side streets leading away. He didn't have Casey-Lynn, or anyone like her. But he had someplace he knew he belonged, and she'd never had that. Maybe that made a difference. All the difference.

Anyway, it did to him.

KNIT A SWEATER OUT OF SKY

SEANAN MCGUIRE

Seanan McGuire has always found Amelia fascinating. The witch has crossed paths with Sookie time and again, but her true home is New Orleans, a city that needs its witches more than ever after the last few years. Luckily for Amelia, she has her boyfriend, Bob, to keep her from biting off more than she can chew . . . most of the time.

—————————

The cherry tree on my dining room table was growing steadily. According to my notes, it was likely maturing about a day every two seconds, giving me a respectable "one minute equals one month" benchmark to use for judging its age. It had been a seed when I'd dropped it into the pot filled with rich bayou soil and started the stopwatch. In the fifteen minutes since then, it had reached and passed a year's growth, putting out branches and stretching eagerly toward the ceiling. If Wikipedia was correct, I'd be seeing the first pale cherry blossoms within the next three-minute "season," even though I couldn't expect fruit until the tree reached its fourth year.

The trouble with witchcraft is that, for the most part, the only people practicing it are witches. That's sort of like taking an entire field of engineering and only letting it be used by Boy Scouts, or handing obstetric medicine off to bird-watchers. You'll still get bridges built and babies born, but it'll come with a lot of weird bric-a-brac around the edges, like the tolls have to be paid with merit badges, and you can't go into labor until someone's spotted a blue-winged blackbird or something. Witches enjoy tinkering with the subtle fabric of the universe. It's how we're made. We're the sort of people who see a loose thread and think, "I should yank on that to see what happens," and it doesn't much matter whether it's a thread on a sweater or a weather pattern. Yank the wrong thread on a sweater and the whole thing unravels. Yank the wrong thread on a heat wave and you're having a snowstorm in New Orleans in July. Half the bizarre weather in the South can be blamed on witchcraft gone stupid—only half, thankfully. No one who grows up in hurricane territory goes playing with *those* threads, because there's just too much chance that your try at a Hail Mary pass will cause another Katrina. We don't mess with big weather, but no witch born has ever been able to resist the little threads—and sometimes little threads can be more effective than big ones. Which brought us back to the cherry tree, spreading branches as big around as my wrist and laying in the infrastructure that would eventually be used to support a healthy crop of delicious fruit.

Witching isn't like shapeshifting or being a telepathic fairy lady that all the vampires want to cozy up to; it's big and it's versatile and it's dangerous as all hell. But that's also what makes it so much fun.

The cherry tree was brushing the ceiling, and I was no longer confident in my ability to get it out of the apartment. I glanced at the stopwatch. The tree was entering its fourth year and should be reaching its private summer in another eighteen seconds. I watched intently as petals fell down like confetti, blanketing the room in pink and white, and small green fruit began to appear.

There were footsteps behind me. Bob was back from the store. The footsteps stopped abruptly, and he said, sounding bemused, "Amelia, there's a tree in the dining room."

"I know," I said, not taking my eyes off the rapidly swelling fruits of my labor. "It's a modification on that stasis spell I used right after Sookie's cousin got killed. I was thinking if I could use it to freeze time for a while, maybe turning it on its ear would make it so I could speed time up within a certain limited sphere. I started it on the cherry seed, didn't enchant the dirt or the pot I planted it in, and look—it's working."

Bob didn't say anything. That wasn't a surprise, although it was something of a disappointment. Then again, we'd been together for both more and less time than the calendar would admit; we'd been dating as humans for less than a month when I'd accidentally turned him into a cat by trying something outside my witchy weight class. He'd lived with me throughout his "feline period," been turned back by someone who wasn't me, tried to kill me, dumped me, taken me back, and, finally, taken me to Paris. It had been a weird relationship progression at best, and a really problematic one at worst. But he was a witch, too. He understood what it was like to see a thread and want to yank on it just to find out what would happen.

That didn't make him comfortable with me being the one doing the yanking.

"Can you get a bowl from the kitchen?" I asked. The fruit was ripening with glorious speed, and that meant I needed to focus on suspending the spell. The last thing I wanted was to cover my entire dining room with rotten cherries.

"Sure," said Bob. The footsteps started again, followed by the sound of a cabinet swinging open. I kept my attention focused on the cherry tree, where the cherries were about two seconds away from the peak of ripeness.

Witchcraft is a funny thing. All the really *good* spells are in Greek or Latin or something that sounds like Greek or Latin, but is probably as made up as Klingon or Pig Latin. It doesn't make sense. Either only people in Europe ever figured out how magic worked—and I know that's not true—or magic didn't exist until some point after the rise of the Roman Empire, and that doesn't make sense, either. We have stories about vampires and weres and fairies that go back way earlier than the Caesars, so why should witchcraft be any different? Answer is, it shouldn't be. Our insistence on dead languages is all in our heads.

It's all in our heads, but I still didn't want a dining room full of rotten cherries. I rattled off the syllables of the break spell, making the modified hand gesture I'd concocted to go with them, and was gratified when the cherries stopped swelling. The tree rustled once before settling in its pot with a faint but audible *thump* that knocked the first few cherries off their branches. Most of them hit the table. I managed to catch one and looked at it admiringly before I popped it into my mouth, where it burst in a sweet rush of cherry juice against my tongue.

"Well?"

I turned to face Bob, grinning with cherry-flavored lips, before spitting the cherry seed into my palm. I tucked it into my pocket for luck and said, "I'm baking a pie tonight."

The nice thing about being a witch in a committed if complicated relationship with another witch is not needing to explain things like, "Where did you get twenty pounds of fresh cherries?" Bob wouldn't have bothered to ask even if he hadn't seen the tree. Instead, he went for the practical side of things, asking, "What are we going to do with a cherry tree?"

I paused in the act of pitting a bowlful of cherries, looking past him to the dining room where our cherry tree, branches still laden with fruit, waited for its fate to be decided. "I don't know. I think it makes a nice centerpiece, don't you? Plus we can trigger another harvest anytime we feel like a fresh slice of cherry pie."

Bob looked at me dubiously. I beamed at him. That only seemed to intensify his dubiousness, returning him to what I sometimes thought of as his factory setting: the funereal, almost dour man who'd managed to catch my full attention just by seeming like the last person in the world who'd have any interest in the arcane. "And you don't think anyone will notice the buckets of cherry seeds? Or were you planning to bribe all the neighbors into silence with cherry pies?"

"Now that you suggest it . . ." I batted my eyelashes. Bob scowled. Laughing, I went back to pitting cherries.

"Amelia." Bob sounded perfectly calm, which didn't really tell me much; Bob almost always sounded perfectly calm. Bob was one of those men who could have looked a charging *T. rex* in the face and said, "I thought you were extinct," while the rest of us were working up a good head of running and screaming. That was part of his appeal, if I was being honest with myself. He kept me calm. "I know you well enough to know that you didn't just start experimenting with cherry stones because you wanted a pie. What were you trying to accomplish here? What was the goal?"

I focused a little more tightly on the bowl of pitted cherries in front of me. It was starting to look disturbingly like a bowl of organs, making me wonder whether haruspicy would work if you read fruit instead of a sliced-open dove. "I want to try something," I said quietly.

"What was that?"

"I said, I want to try something." I raised my head. "I haven't really been stretching myself since that whole thing with Sookie and the blood bond, and I can't really say that using a ritual someone else created to sever an artificial connection to a dead man is 'stretching myself.' The universe doesn't want to connect living things to dead ones. Breaking them apart doesn't really upset the natural order of things. Good for me if I don't want the magic going strange, but not so good if what I'm looking for is a learning experience."

"As someone who's been on the receiving end of a 'learning experience,' can I just say that I'm not really that excited when you go looking for them?"

I flicked a cherry at him. It bounced off his shirt, leaving a little red mark behind, like a lipstick stain or a wound. Bob looked at it, sighed, and murmured a word with too many vowels. The stain lifted off his shirt and flapped, like a molecule-thin butterfly, to hover in the air above the garbage. Once there, it burst, sending cherry juice raining down on the coffee grounds and used paper towels.

"Very mature," he said.

"I'm not going to turn you into a cat again," I said. "I know what I did wrong that time, and besides, it's not like the spell I want to try would be directed at you. I've learned my lesson about using magic on my boyfriend."

"It's a miracle," said Bob dryly. "So what, exactly, do you want to attempt that would somehow be made easier by being able to magically generate a cherry crop in our dining room?"

I smiled hopefully. "Help me get our pie in the oven and I'll explain?"

Bob sighed and reached for the spare cherry pitter.

"Lots of cultures have stories about witches who've bound a wind to their service somehow," I said, taking another bite of cherry pie. It had come out perfectly, with a flaky golden crust and just the right amount of sugar to make the cherry juice that oozed out of the pastry taste like a little bit of heaven. "Winds are supposed to be like puppies. If you do the right things and say the right words, they'll come when you call, heel, sit, stay, the whole nine yards. Doesn't that sound like about the best thing you've ever heard? Who needs the SPCA when you can have a pet weather pattern?"

"Since I was the last 'pet' you had, this isn't really selling me on the idea," said Bob blandly. "I have two major reservations. First, where does this wind come from? Are you stealing something from the local troposphere? Because we don't have the most stable weather in the world here in New Orleans, and I don't want the next hurricane to have your name on it."

His words stung, and rightly so. Living between the Mississippi and the haunted waters of Lake Pontchartrain meant that we were always at risk of a flood or storm, and the scars from Katrina were still all over the city for anyone with eyes to see. This was the last place for someone to be fooling around with weather magic—which was exactly why I planned to start fooling around with weather magic. If we could just find a way to make the storms a little less severe, either by making friends with the local winds or by taming breezes that could interfere when things started to get bad, we might be able to keep things from being quite so bad in the future.

"You know that new girl, Minda? The one who thinks she's better at witching than anyone?"

Bob nodded, looking perplexed.

I stabbed my fork into my pie. "I mentioned I was researching this ritual, and she said . . ." I swallowed. "She said, 'Too little, too late,' like the storms we've been having were *my* fault somehow. Like I should have been wrestling with the wind years ago. I asked her what she meant by that, and she said I knew what she meant. That if I wanted to sit around like some little old lady, knitting and gossiping while the world fell down, that was my lookout. It got under my skin, Bob. I won't pretend it didn't. I want to be able to do something the next time a storm blows up."

This time, Bob's nod was slower, and he looked almost understanding. "You didn't answer my questions," he said. "Start there."

"I think you call the wind in from elsewhere; at least that's how it tends to work in the old stories," I said carefully. "Winds that live where you send out the call are more like, I don't know, feral cats. They aren't interested in being tamed. I don't know why foreign winds would be any different, but everything I can find says that they are."

"This is sounding more and more sketchy," said Bob. "What does Octavia have to say about this?"

I bristled. "Nothing," I said. "She's not my sponsor anymore, and I don't *need* her permission to try new things. I'd consult her if I thought I needed her. I don't."

"And I would still be a cat if not for her, so you'll forgive me for being a little cautious," said Bob. "Which takes us to my other concern: What happens if this goes wrong? What happens if you attract a nice little wind and it comes with a not-so-nice big hurricane? I don't want you to be the reason this city finally washes away."

"I'm getting a little annoyed about all the little 'Amelia can't control her magic' comments tonight, okay? I'll head out to the river before I try anything, and I've modified the stasis spell enough that it should be able to stop anything that I start before it snowballs out of control." I forked off another bite of pie. "I won't say it's perfectly safe—magic is never *perfectly* safe—but I think it's worth the risk, and I don't think that the chances of it going wrong are high enough that it's not worth doing." I canted my chin down a bit and looked up at him through my eyelashes before playing my hole card: "I was really hoping you'd be there to check my ritual circle and make sure that I'm not missing any steps."

Bob sighed, the long, pained sound that meant I'd just won the argument. "Do you *promise* not to flood the state?" he asked.

I grinned.

Weather witchery is difficult for a lot of reasons. There's the whole "weather is a big, complex thing" to be considered, as well as the potential for property damage if it's done wrong, but mostly the problem is in the intricacy of the rituals involved. I normally wouldn't have attempted something like this without at least three witches, preferably four or five. But with most of the practitioners in the city still focusing on cleaning up their own neighborhoods, it was just me and Bob setting up the circle down by the riverbank. Lightning bugs flickered in and out of view, and a soft breeze was blowing out of the west, smelling like fresh flowers and somebody's home-baked muffins. It was making me hungry.

"I'm still not sure this is a good idea," said Bob.

"Never know until you try it," I said, and held out a hand. "Can I get the jasmine?" Bob solemnly handed me a Tupperware bowl full of dried flowers, and I commenced to scattering them around the lines of salt, iron ball bearings, and cedar ash that I had already drawn. Something this size required more effort than a slap-and-tickle "runes and salt and prayer" design. This was the kind of ritual where I needed to cast it like I meant it.

"Let's just go over things one more time," Bob said.

"I know what that means," I said. "That means 'Let me explain why this is a bad idea one more time, because I'm sure this is the time you'll mysteriously decide to listen.' Well, I'm not going to listen, and I'm not going to change my mind, so how about we skip that part and move straight to me getting down to business?"

Bob smiled in that slow way that always made me want to tear his clothes off with my teeth. "It's a good thing I like it when you're impulsive," he said, and took a step back from my circle. "I'm here if you need me."

"All right." I sank to the ground, sitting cross-legged to minimize the risk that I'd somehow blur one of the lines I'd spent so much time and care to draw. Resting my hands on my knees, I thought back to the words I'd translated from the books of folklore that first led me down this possibly foolish road. There were so many different variations, and so many possibilities, all of them leading to either success or failure.

I'm not a girl who likes to fail.

What I *am* is a girl who likes to get things right the first time. I'd spent so long staring at the slips of paper with my translations written on them that when I closed my eyes, I could see the strings of cursive unspooling against my eyelids like a map waiting to be followed. The first word came to my tongue like a promise. The second followed like a prayer, and then it was just words upon words, spilling out into the cool night air with all the force of a vow that had been yearning to be heard. Magic is a thing that lends itself to metaphor, because there's nothing in this world or any other that can be said to be exactly like it; magic is what magic is, and all our descriptions have to call upon other things, or make no sense at all.

I could feel Bob standing behind me, his love and support mingling with a healthy dose of wariness and concern. It wasn't like mind reading—I couldn't tell if he was wondering whether he'd left the oven on or admiring my ass—but it was a sort of temporary empathy, his magic resonating back on mine in a form of complicated sonar. I could feel the moths in the air and the frogs in the mud and the gators in the water around me the same way, although they were mostly just presence and not personality. That was all right by me. I've never much felt the need to get up close and personal with any part of an alligator, and that includes its feelings.

The ritual was long enough to be exhausting and short enough to be achievable. I gasped out the last of the words and felt the air around me go suddenly and impossibly still, as if I had—without moving—stepped into the eye of a storm. Bob cleared his throat nervously. I opened my eyes.

Nothing hovered in the still air in front of me; nothing twitched its ephemeral tail back and forth like an anxious puppy, waiting for me to notice it and remark on how clever it was. My eyes went wide. "Bob?" I squeaked. "Do you, uh . . . I guess 'see' isn't the best word here, is it? Do you perceive what I'm perceiving?"

"Do you mean, 'Can I tell that there is a breeze of some sort hanging a foot from your face'? Because if that's what you mean, then yes, I can." Bob sounded rattled. I wasn't sure if that was because he hadn't had faith in my magical abilities, or because this whole situation was more than a little unnerving. I was going with the latter, since _I_ was pretty rattled, and I had absolute faith in my own magical abilities. Besides, that way I didn't have to be mad at him, and I was going to want some celebratory sex as soon as we got back to the apartment.

Slowly, I began to grin. "It worked," I said. "I put together a ritual based on research and logic, and it worked. I am the _man_."

"Point of order," said Bob.

"I am the _woman_," I amended. Cautiously, I reached for the stationary wind. "Hi, little fella. I'm Amelia. I'm the one who called you here. It's nice to meet you. I hope we're going to be friends."

"Do winds make friends?"

"Shush. Having a moment of deep mystic import here," I said, and continued reaching my hand toward the nothing I could sense hovering just outside the boundaries of my ritual circle. Something brushed my fingertips, something insubstantial as air that nonetheless tingled like an electrical storm. My eyes widened in wonder and delight—

—and just like that, my little bit of tamed nothing was gone, vanishing back into the night. I jolted backward, feeling as if I'd just been stung by a swarm of hornets.

"What just happened?" I demanded. "Where'd my wind go?"

"Where did _all_ the winds go?" Bob sounded more frightened than dismayed. I twisted without getting out of my ritual circle, frowning at him. He frowned right back, gesturing wildly with his hands. "The air is completely still. How often have you been this close to the water and not felt any wind at all? They stopped right before yours showed up. I thought it was part of your spell."

"I didn't cast anything that should have interfered with the wind outside of the one I was calling," I protested. I climbed to my feet, the pins and needles in my calves telling me that I should probably have done that a few minutes earlier. "I'm serious, Bob, I know what I did and didn't do, and I didn't do anything as big as that."

Bob frowned slowly. "Who did you tell that you were going to try this?"

"Not much of anyone, really . . ." I said. His frown deepened. I sighed. "All right, I may have told a few of the other witches. Just to get their perspective on things."

"Did you share your notes?"

I didn't answer. I didn't have to.

Bob picked up a handful of salt and flower petals from the edge of the ritual circle, holding his hand flat and blowing on the mess as hard as he could. It drifted out as an improbable cloud before falling to the mud, forming a rough arrow that pointed east.

"I love magic," I said, and grabbed the ritual supplies before taking off at a run.

Without wind, the surface of the river was perfectly still, more like a sheet of glass than an actual body of water. The fireflies had disappeared. They probably didn't know how to fly in air that wasn't moving at all. I ran, and Bob paced me, both of us watching for anything out of the ordinary. I don't know what I was expecting, really; a circle like mine, maybe, or someone holding up a sign that read, *I am the source of all your problems.*

Honestly, the woman standing on the surface of the water about eight feet out from shore was overkill where the "unusual sights" department was concerned.

I slid to a stop, the slick mud beneath my feet making the gesture graceless, although the rapid pinwheeling of my arms did at least keep me from eating riverbank. Bob was wearing slightly more sensible shoes and had an easier time of it than I did, although my pride was reassured by the fact that he had to do some pinwheeling of his own to keep from tipping over.

The woman on the water turned to face us, and smiled. "Hello, Amelia. And Bob, too. It's a surprise to see you out on the river tonight. I genuinely didn't think she'd be able to talk you into this."

Bob reached up and adjusted his glasses. He didn't say anything. He just scowled.

Sadly, my daddy raised me a little more polite than that, even when I'm talking to someone who's clearly decided that the laws of nature don't apply to her. "Evening, Minda," I said, folding my hands behind my back in a vain attempt to look nonchalant. "What are you doing out here?"

"Isn't it obvious? I'm showing the world what a two-bit charlatan you are." She was holding a censer in one hand. As she spoke, she inscribed a wide arc with her hand, leaving a trail of smoke behind her. It didn't move at all. One more sign of the absence of wind. "One little breeze? Really, Amelia? What's the value in that?"

"Well, it was sort of a 'proof of concept' order, with a little bit of 'not upsetting the local weather systems so much that we all get washed out to sea' as a bonus," I said carefully. "You didn't live here when the hurricane hit. You don't know how bad things got." How bad things still were, in certain parts of the city. It was difficult to overstate what Katrina had done to our beautiful city. There was a reason most of the local witches wouldn't even have attempted weather magic. It was the same reason that I was being so careful.

Minda snorted. "I've seen storms. That wasn't the hurricane's fault."

I felt, rather than saw, Bob drawing himself up beside me. He'd missed Katrina completely, on account of his having been a cat at the time, but he'd still seen its marks. "Are you suggesting that it was the city's fault somehow?"

"No, I'm outright stating that it was *your* fault. All you lame-ass witches who couldn't bother to figure out the spells you needed to keep the weather under control. You deserved what you got." She made another lazy circle with her censer. Another ring of smoke formed and hung preserved around her. "You're weak. You've been living in the Big

Easy so long that you've started to think life should be all sunshine and games. Well, there's a new witch in town, and I am going to show you how it's *done*."

There was something about those preserved loops of smoke that bothered me almost as much as the motionless air. I took a step forward, my shoes squelching in the mud. "Minda, let's talk about this. I don't think you really understand how delicate the systems are here. Make one mistake and we're all going to wind up paying for it." I sounded like Bob. There was something almost poetic about that: I hadn't listened to his warnings, and now it looked as if Minda wasn't going to listen to mine.

I hadn't listened to his warnings . . . My eyes widened as I looked at Minda's loops of smoke in a new light. Viewed from the side, they were random, overlapping with one another to form an almost chaotic series of squiggles. But viewed from above . . . viewed from above, they would form a series of broken concentric circles. She was sketching a ritual circle, using water instead of earth and smoke instead of salt. It was brilliant. It was audacious.

It was going to get us all killed.

"Minda, you have to stop."

"No, I don't," she said smugly. "All I *had* to do was wait until I felt you start your spell, so that I could be ready to call you here to witness my greatest triumph. Now sit back, Miss Broadway, and get ready to see a *real* show."

She flung her censer into the air, and the sky exploded.

The thing about magic is that it doesn't really care about right or wrong or maintaining the balance of things; magic finds its own balance if you give it long enough. What magic cares about is respect. Do you respect what you're doing? Do you understand it well enough to do it properly, or are you just a kid fooling around in your mama's closet and making a mess out of things? Magic isn't forgiving. It doesn't treat nicely with people who don't treat respectfully with it. But sadly, that doesn't mean the people who *are* respectful are immune from getting hurt.

Minda's frozen circle remained exactly where it was as the water around her kicked into windblown life, suddenly ripped into waves two and three feet high. It was the sort of water that normally accompanies a bad storm—and from the black clouds that were racing into view on the horizon, that was exactly what we were about to get. I tried to take another step toward the water, only to find myself pushed backward by a fierce wind that roared out of nowhere and knocked me into Bob.

He caught me before I could go sprawling, his strong hands gripping my shoulders as he leaned close and shouted against the wind, "She's going to blow us away!"

"Not just us!" I shouted back. Clouds of that size weren't going to be happy with three witches and a stretch of riverbank. They were going to keep on gathering until they found themselves a bigger target. "We need to stop her!"

"How do you suggest we do that? Throw rocks at her until she feels bad about herself and stops trying to kill us?"

"Not quite! Do you trust me?"

There was a brief pause. Bob didn't have to say anything for me to know how loaded a question that was, especially coming from me to him. Finally, without taking his hands off my shoulders, he shouted back, "Yes! Yes, Amelia, I trust you!"

"Good! Then hold on tight, because I'm going to need you keeping me grounded!" I plunged my hand into my pocket, digging through the lint and small debris of daily life until I found the thing that I was looking for: a cherry stone.

"This better work," I murmured, and pulled it out of my pocket, chucking it into the onrushing wind as I began to chant.

The ritual I'd used to call my small, quickly stolen breeze had been based on the idea of calmness and respect in the face of something that was never meant to be commanded. I could recognize echoes of that ritual in Minda's chant, but where I had politely asked, she was ordering, and where I had offered, she was demanding. It was a harsh contrast that made me question my own motives a bit. Had I really been trying to push my understanding of magic, or had I been showing off?

Maybe a little bit of both, if I was being honest, and yet neither one was going to be as much of a stretch as what I was trying now. The wind was forming into a funnel around Minda, racing around and around in the classic cone shape that always made my heart feel like it was going to stop. She didn't seem to realize just how much danger she was putting herself in with that positioning. She kept chanting, and her chained winds carried my cherry stone—taken from a fruit that had grown on my magical cherry tree—once, twice, three times around her, all clockwise, sketching out the idea of a ritual circle in the air.

Circles don't need to be drawn with concrete materials. If I'd forgotten that, Minda's circle of smoke would have reminded me. She drew my circle for me, etching it around hers, and when she was done, I began to do something that was, if not impossible, at the very least difficult, and dangerous, and very, very ill-advised: I began casting multiple spells at the same time, a part of one and then a part of another and then a part of a third, all as I pulled on the world around me and tried to weave them together like a rope made of nothing but will and wind.

"Standing stasis, catch and hold—come to me, oh wind of Aeolus, master of—faster, faster, spin the wheel—keep the lines as drawn forever, heeding neither time nor—" On and on it went, the three spells chasing one another like a dog chasing its own tail, until I no longer knew for sure where one ended and the next began. Bob was still behind me, his hands on my shoulders, lending his strength to my casting. If not for the twin solidities of his body and his will, I might have gone straight over into the mud and let Minda have this impromptu wizards' duel.

Won't Octavia be proud of me for getting my butt kicked in such a traditional way, I thought dizzily, and kept on chanting. I could feel the winds starting to waver. Some of them were bowing to my insistent command that they heel, sit, and stay. Down, boys, down.

Maybe talking to forces of nature as if they were dogs wasn't the most respectful way to go about things, but I didn't have the time or energy for respect, given the circumstances. Minda was shrieking indignantly from her place on the water, and when her shrieks gave way to high, angry chanting in a language I didn't understand, I knew that the real fight was just beginning. I dug my heels into the mud.

The force of Minda's pocket storm slammed into me like a freight train only a few seconds later.

The thing about magic is that it hurts like hell when it punches you in the face. I managed to keep on chanting, but it was close. Bob held on more tightly as I reached into the storm with both hands, the triplicate spells of stasis and speed and binding spilling out of me and into the storm-torn winds, confusing them as much as they were confusing my own magic. Casting something to speed the world up and something to stop it at the same time seemed counterproductive, as if I would be canceling out my own magic rather than strengthening it. That was sort of the idea.

Minda had whipped these winds into a killing frenzy. I was all right with keeping them there—that was what my stasis was for, intended to prevent her from pulling her own magic out of the equation, no matter how much she might want to. And she was *going* to want to, if I had my way, because no one with half a brain would stay in the spell once she realized what I was doing. Assuming that what I was doing didn't backfire and age me into dust in a matter of seconds.

Belatedly, I realized that if the spell backfired in that specific way, Bob might well be within the blast radius, at least enough to catch a decade or two that he hadn't asked for and probably wouldn't want. *Sorry, sweetie,* I thought, and kept casting. My throat was starting to ache from the strain of shouting against Minda's storm. It seemed like a small price to pay, all things considered. The little reprobate had used *my* research, *my* ambition to set herself up to be Queen of the Storm. Well, if anybody was going to profit irresponsibly from my research, it was going to be *me*.

Stasis, to keep her storm from dissipating. Binding, to transfer it to me if she let it go. And finally, speed, to wear it out and wear it down to nothing before it could move beyond this empty little stretch of river. The gators and frogs that lived here wouldn't be happy about having their habitat churned to gumbo, but everyone else would live untroubled and unaware of how terribly wrong things had very nearly gone. That was enough for me.

Minda was pouring everything she had into the storm, whipping it to greater and greater heights. I just kept pushing and pulling at the same time, the motion reminding me of a spinning wheel twisting and turning the fiber into thread—or maybe Rumpelstiltskin's fabled wheel, turning straw to gold. I kept that image as central in my mind as I could, trying to use it to motivate myself. *Chase the impossible, Amelia. Do whatever it takes, but chase the impossible, and don't let it out of your sight.*

The first length of fiber to spool down from the storm was surprising enough that I almost dropped the spell. It was rough and resisted being pulled; it burned my palms. I pulled it harder, starting to wind it around my arm the way I'd seen older witches work when they were unwinding store-bought yarn to turn it into a usable ball. And it kept coming, length after length of gray and blue and white fiber that was so much like wool as to make no difference, all of it spinning down out of the sky.

I kept pulling. Bob's hands tightened on my shoulders, holding me in place and giving me his strength. We were both nearly exhausted. I didn't know how I was doing what I was doing—that would be something to worry about later, when we weren't fighting for our lives against a crazed witch with a storm the size of Louisiana ready to chuck at anyone who riled her up.

But it wasn't really all that big anymore, was it? The storm that had seemed poised to take on the whole state was now barely big enough to cover the river, and it wasn't breaking free of that arbitrary boundary. Minda screamed again, sounding more frightened than angry this time, and there was a splash that didn't sound like raindrops or jumping frogs; somebody's "walk on water" spell had just gone the way of my patience, shattering into a million pieces and dropping her into the troubled, alligator-filled water beneath her feet.

I kept on pulling. Minda might be out of play, but her spell wasn't, not quite; there was still enough magic in the air to keep those clouds spinning, and that meant I had to keep doing my own sort of spinning, chanting my triplicate spells and ripping impossible yarn out of the troubled sky.

I don't know how long that went on. I just know that the last length of yarn dropped into my hands as the final storm cloud wisped away into nothingness, and I collapsed backward into Bob, who seemed like the most solid thing left in a half-faded world, and he caught me before I hit the mud, and my eyes closed. Then my spell was cast, and there was nothing else for me to do but pass out in the least ladylike way possible.

I woke up lying on the grass in front of our car, which was a serious improvement on the muddy bank where I'd lost consciousness. Bob had piled his Windbreaker up under my head as a sort of pillow, and I appreciated the gesture more than I could say. Bob himself was sitting a few feet away, cross-legged, winding what looked like lengths of storm-colored yarn into balls.

"Is that it?" I sat up, blinking. "Is that the stuff I pulled down out of the storm?"

"It is," he replied. "Care to explain how you did it?"

"I haven't the faintest clue, but won't we have a nice time figuring it all out?" I beamed at him. I was exhausted down to the bone, but I was also damned proud of myself. I'd done something completely new. Something even better than calling a single wind. Which reminded me . . . "Where's Minda?"

"I didn't see her come out of the water."

"Good," I said viciously. "Maybe the gators got a treat."

"Could be," said Bob.

I leaned forward, plucking at one of the trailing pieces of yarn. "I'm going to need to learn how to knit."

Bob's eyebrows raised. "Why's that?" he asked.

"Well, I figure it says something nice about my skill as a witch if I knit myself a sweater out of sky, don't you?"

Bob blinked. And then, to my relief and delight, he began to laugh.

"Come on," I said, picking myself up and offering him my hand. "Let's go home. I want a slice of cherry pie."

LOVE STORY

JEANNE C. STEIN

Most of the readers of the Sookie novels were shocked to find out
that Sookie's beloved and revered Gran had conceived her two children out of wedlock. How did this out-of-character union come
about? In Jeanne Stein's story, we find out.

AUTHOR'S NOTE:

Adele Hale Stackhouse, Sookie's loving Gran, had a secret she carried with
her to the grave. It wasn't until after her death that Sookie found a letter
among her grandmother's things and the secret became known.

Sookie's real grandfather was a fairy.

The letter was scant in detail. Adele admitted she'd been unfaithful to
her husband, Mitchell, with a beautiful, part-human fairy named Fintan,
who walked out of the woods around her home one day and not only swept
a storm-downed tree out of her driveway, but swept Adele off her feet as
well. They made love, more than once, resulting in the birth of Sookie's
father, Corbett, and two years later, in the birth of his sister, Linda.

In her letter to Sookie, Adele is vague about her relationship with Fintan. She was apologetic about deceiving her husband, Mitchell, but tells us
that after five childless years, she and Mitchell were desperate for a baby. She
told us why she had an affair, but until now, the details of that fateful meeting with Fintan were lost. Certainly, Sookie never imagined learning more.
It's possible she didn't want to. It wasn't easy for Sookie to accept that her
grandmother had been unfaithful, even though she and Jason were the prod-

ucts of that infidelity. It may even be that Sookie didn't want to believe the story was true.

Until fate stepped in.

Fate came in the form of a journal, found when Sookie and Sam were performing the spring cleaning ritual—a rite raised to an art form in the South. Sam found the journal while chasing a dust bunny under an old dressing table, Adele's dressing table, in an upstairs bedroom. He had shoved it away from the wall when a loose board fell off the back. When he went to push the board back into place, he saw the journal stuffed in the space between two drawers. Opening it, he quickly recognized what it contained. His first reaction was to keep it from Sookie. Her life was just beginning to come together, she was happy, her future bright, her faith in her family secure. But he also knew that Sookie was never one to run from the truth. She had a right to the journal. What she did with it—read it, burn it, or put it back in its hiding place—had to be her decision.

And so the journal of Adele Hale Stackhouse was placed in the hands of her granddaughter. How I ended up with it, I choose not to reveal at this time. I will say, however, that I have Sookie's permission to present an abridged version of what it contained. I have faithfully reproduced Adele's thoughts about the events that occurred. The entire journal covers nine months, from the day Fintan appeared to the birth of Adele's son. I am presenting here only the first few days—days that changed her life forever. That she transcribed details of their conversations, that her emotions were so thoroughly and wonderfully depicted, made my job easy. Perhaps one day, the entire journal can be made public.

Some may see this as a story of betrayal and infidelity. Others, a story of a good woman beguiled against her will by a beautiful creature. Sookie never told me how she felt about it. I suspect, knowing her as I do, that she might see it as I do . . .

A love story.

SUNDAY, JUNE 27, 194—

I've never been one to write down my thoughts, to keep a diary or journal. I don't know why I feel the need to do it now. No, that's not entirely
true. I think this is my way of being sure I'm not losing my sanity. If I
record the events as they happened, maybe I can make sense of it all.

It began two days ago.

Mitchell had left for Baton Rouge during a terrible thunderstorm
early Friday morning to pick up work supplies. I was alone, sitting on
the porch, watching lightning bounce from treetop to treetop in the
woods, wondering if he would turn around and come back. Hoping
that he would. Our fifth anniversary had just passed and instead of
marking the date with cake and candles, we marked it as another
reminder that we were still childless. Oh, not in words. Rather as a
weight we try our best to ignore though it bears down on us more and
more. It colors everything we do in a pale wash and makes us hesitant
to express our love the way a married couple should.

So I sat alone, feeling lonely and depressed. Normally, I love the
rain, even when it pounded like it did that morning, stripping leaves off
the apple trees and making miniature lakes on the dusty ground of a
dry spring. Life quickened as I watched, reviving, grass and flowers lifting their faces to capture the moisture like a child opening his mouth to
catch a snowflake. Something loosened in me, too. I was spellbound by
nature's majesty.

A flash of lightning split the sky, followed immediately by a roar of
thunder . . . then another sound. I watched as a huge pine failed, shud-
dering, creaking, screaming as it crashed to the ground, its thirty-foot
length blocking the road onto our property.

My first thought: Mitchell couldn't get back to the house now even
if he had a mind to.

My second thought: However was I going to move that tree?

Even as these ideas formed, the rain stopped. As abruptly as it
started. The clouds parted so quickly and the sun returned so blind-
ingly that steam rose from the ground like smoke. I pulled on mud

boots and walked out to survey the fallen tree. We had no close neighbors except the snooty Comptons across the graveyard, and no telephone to call them even if I thought they would come to help. Seemed to me my only choice was to hack away the middle, leaving a path a car's width. Mitchell could clear the rest when he returned, but I faced a monumental chore. The tree was green and at least three feet across. With a sigh, I went to the toolshed to fetch a saw.

Mitchell was the handyman. I looked around stupidly to decide which of the two or three saws hanging in his workshop would do. I chose the biggest one and hauled it back to the tree.

It was slow going. It seemed as if I had been sawing for hours and I had just barely cut into the tree's girth. My shoulders and arms ached. I finally decided to take a break and go back to the house for a cold drink. I had hung laundry out back before the storm hit and knew it would be hopelessly drenched, so I thought I might as well bring it back inside. Another rinse in the tub, another crank through the wringer, and maybe there would still be enough time to let it dry in the sun.

All these little details are so sharp in my mind. As if leading up to what happened next made them important. I took down the laundry and put it back in the tub.

But somehow I knew I couldn't put off the real chore any longer. I had to get back to that tree.

Back in the yard, that's when I saw him. No, that's not quite right. I felt him first. A tingling on the back of my neck. Not like when you're frightened. More like when you anticipate something happening. Something you know is going to change your life. Something you want.

Then there was a scent on the air. Like the earth. Rich, fertile, full of the flowers of spring. Feminine yet darkly masculine, too. Musk. I'd never experienced anything like it.

He appeared out of the woods. He was mist, then fog, then fully formed. I should have been frightened—I knew about ghosts and spirits said to populate the forest and graveyard—but he was so beautiful. And he was smiling. At me. I had to resist the urge to run to him. I held my ground and watched him as he approached. I didn't realize I'd been holding my breath until he spoke to me and, like a spell had been broken, I felt my chest heave.

He held out a hand. "Are you all right?"

I clasped my hands to my chest and nodded. It was all I was capable of doing.

His smile widened. "You need help with this," he said, gesturing to the tree. "Let me take care of it."

I stepped back, still too brain numb to form words. He took off his jacket and laid it on the ground, and I thought he would reach for the saw embedded in the tree trunk. Well, he did, but only to pull it free and place it on the ground beside his jacket. Then he put both hands close to the tree trunk and, with no effort at all, raised the tree and moved it with nothing more than sheer force of will. The entire tree slid back into the forest to the point where it had fallen. It just moved, as if pulled by an invisible truck. After the first shock of watching the tree, I studied the man.

He was tall and broad-shouldered, slim at the waist and muscled where the cloth of his shirt pulled against his chest. His face and body looked human, but after watching him materialize as he did from the forest and then move the tree, I knew he couldn't be—at least not completely. And his eyes. He had eyelashes women covet: long, dark, curled at the tips, framing the bluest blue eyes I'd ever seen. His mouth was full, his lips . . . Well, I wanted to kiss those lips, heaven help me.

"Adele?"

When he spoke my name for the first time, I realized I was staring at his face, at those lips, and the smile on his face made my cheeks flame with embarrassment. He seemed to know what I was feeling, what I wanted, and while his smile wasn't exactly smug, it was perceptive. I didn't even think to ask how he knew my name. After watching him move a tree, it didn't seem too important.

I got hold of myself long enough to remember my manners. "Thank you," I said, regretting the words as soon as they left my mouth. What a stupid thing to say to this otherworldly creature! I should be asking who he was, what he was. Then I asked the second stupid question. "Do you have a name?"

He laughed and the sound was musical. "Of course. It's Fintan."

He held out his hand for the second time and I took it. His grasp was warm and firm, and electricity sparked from his fingertips to mine. Startled, I pulled back, but he held on.

His eyes locked on mine and I found myself stammering, "Would you like something? A drink of water?"

He nodded, continuing to hold my hand as I drew him toward the house. I wasn't scared. I didn't even question the wisdom of bringing a stranger into my house. It felt as natural as rain to be with him. And more than that, it felt natural to want to be with him.

In the kitchen, he released my hand. I fetched a glass of water from the tap and held it out to him. Once again, when his fingertips brushed mine, it sent a current rushing through me, a burst of energy that traveled up my arm and sent heat to parts of my body—it embarrasses me even now to think about it. (If Mitchell ever finds this journal, I will be mortified. I love him. More than anything. But God help me, his touch never evoked such passion in me. My mind can deny it was desire, but my body knew the truth.)

I turned quickly away from Fintan and went back to the sink. I got myself a drink of water even though I wasn't really thirsty. I just wanted to put distance between myself and this stranger who seemed able to evoke emotions in me so powerful I was afraid of losing control.

I felt Fintan watching me. He had taken a seat at the kitchen table. My hands were shaking. My head spun with feelings of guilt. For what? I'd done nothing. Yet. Oh, but I knew. I knew. Whatever happened next, no matter the provocation, my life was about to change.

I wanted it to.

My back was still to Fintan. His chair scraped against the linoleum. I didn't turn around. When he placed his hands on my shoulders, the glass slipped from my hands and shattered in the sink. Neither of us moved.

Then Fintan spoke. "Adele. You have nothing to fear from me."

"I'm not afraid." In spite of how my heart was pounding, I was proud of the steadiness in my voice. I lifted my chin. "Should I be?"

His grip tightened ever so slightly so he could turn me toward him.

"No. I have come today because I know your heart's desire. I have watched you from the forest."

That was the first thing he'd said that sparked a tiny flame of protest. "You've been spying on us?"

He shook his head. "Not spying. And not on Mitchell."

A burst of fear made my shoulders jump. Illogically, I hadn't questioned that he knew my name, but that he would know Mitchell's somehow alarmed me. "How do you know my husband's name?"

Again, he shook his head, smiling gently. "I mean your husband no harm. Mitchell is a good man. He treats you well. You are content when you are with him. But he cannot give you what you want most. He cannot complete you."

"What are you saying?"

He took a step closer to me, so close I could see the tiny laugh lines that radiated from his eyes, so close I could breathe in his intoxicating fragrance. I closed my eyes. Was this what being under a spell felt like?

"No."

My eyes flew open.

"You are not under a spell, although I could certainly influence you if I chose."

I drew in a breath. "What are you?"

"Human. Partly." He glanced toward the forest outside the open kitchen window. "Partly supernatural being. You have lived in Bon Temps for a long time. You know there are others who walk among you. In the world, but not necessarily of it."

I found myself nodding. Still, I'd always believed those "others" were to be feared. I searched his eyes. "Why am I not afraid?"

"Because you know me. You've felt my presence before. Think about it."

I turned away from him then, to scour my memory. There had been times in the past when I felt a presence. Especially growing up. I told my mother about it at first, but she'd wave it off, tell me I had an active imagination. Still, a cloud would pass over her face and she'd quickly change the subject.

"You've been watching me since I was a little girl?" I asked.

"You know I have."

I faced him again. "Why have you chosen to show yourself now?"

His hand brushed my cheek. "Because it is time."

"Time?" But even as I said the word, I knew instinctively what he meant.

Time.

I bent my head. I was in the middle of my monthly cycle. Five years without a child. Mitchell's face, so understanding when my menses arrived, yet the disappointment in his eyes . . . He'd wanted five or six children—a big brood to match the big love in his heart.

Still.

I couldn't fool myself into thinking what I'd be doing was all for Mitchell. I wanted a child, yes. But I wanted this stranger, too. I was raised a churchgoing Christian. What would my pastor think if he knew what was going through my head? Could I live with the guilt?

Why was I so sure making love with Fintan would result in a child? And, more important, what kind of child would it be?

Fintan had been standing quietly. He hadn't once intruded on my thoughts to reply, though I knew now he could have. But at the question of what kind of child might we have, he answered.

"The child would be born of love. Yours and mine. He would be normal in every way. I promise you that."

I believed him. God help me.

"Mitchell." I half whispered, half choked my husband's name. "What do I tell Mitchell?"

Fintan stroked my cheek, a butterfly touch that made me shiver. "Whatever you think is right," he answered. "My only request is that you wait until the child is born. Watch his face when he holds the baby for the first time. Then decide."

"What happens now?"

He put his arms around me and pulled me against his chest. He tilted my head up to meet my eyes. "This, my sweet Adele."

Then he kissed me and my heart soared.

MONDAY, JUNE 28

I stopped writing yesterday. Too overcome with emotion to continue. But I don't want to forget anything that happened these last forty-eight hours. Even the feeling of emptiness when I awoke Saturday morning and found Fintan gone.

Only his scent remained behind, and the hollow in Mitchell's pillow where his head had rested. I rolled over in our bed and buried my face in the pillow.

I can't explain the feelings that washed over me. All that we did, Fintan and me, came back like a dream, and for a moment, I thought maybe it had been. That I'd imagined the storm and the tree and the mysterious figure appearing out of the forest. The feeling of Fintan's hands on me and the sweet way he'd made love to me first downstairs, then up here in my bed.

In Mitchell's bed.

I turned over and stared at the ceiling.

It wasn't a dream. My body still tingled where Fintan's hands had touched me. And like the grass and flowers during the thunderstorm, there was a blossoming in me now, too.

I got up and slipped into a robe. Mitchell wouldn't be home for another day. I stripped the bed. Reluctantly. I would have loved to keep that pillowcase, even for one more day, to have Fintan's essence to breathe in once in a while. But Mitchell . . . what if he came home early? He might pick up on the unfamiliar scent and I would never want to hurt him like that.

I grimaced at the irony.

I carried the bedclothes downstairs. The tub was still filled with yesterday's laundry. I went about my morning chores in a kind of trance, wringing the first load to prepare to take to the clothesline, refilling the tub for the bedclothes, hanging everything in the still spring air when it was done. I avoided looking toward the forest. I hadn't asked Fintan if I would see him again. I was sure I wouldn't. He came to me yesterday for a reason. And that reason is growing inside me.

What happens next?

I'm downstairs now, writing this at the table. The sun beams in, coloring the kitchen in shades of golden warmth. I have to make myself think clearly. I have to make plans. When Mitchell returns, we'll make love. We hadn't before he left, the night of our anniversary. Or for days before. We had pretended to be too tired, or too busy (I was to host the next Descendants of the Glorious Dead meeting, and there is always baking to do in preparation) while the real truth was, we couldn't face another disappointment. If we didn't try to make a baby, we couldn't fail.

But this minute, I'm filled with eager anticipation. This will be an act of love. This time, there will be no disappointment. There will be a baby, a baby that will be ours, Mitchell's and mine.

I cannot explain why I have such faith in an act that I should be ashamed of. The guilt may come. Maybe one day, I'll look back on this and be overcome with loathing. I'll curse Fintan's name. Curse myself for succumbing.

Maybe.

But please, God, let there be a child. If there is a child . . .

My life will be perfect.

I—we—have so much to look forward to. Already, I'm envisioning the bedroom upstairs we'll prepare as a nursery. And I remembered a wallpaper I saw at the hardware store just last week—fairy-tale characters on a background of pale yellow. My hands clasp softly over my still-flat abdomen. This is a boy. Mitchell would never understand how I can be so sure so it's going to be a boy. I don't understand it myself. But I *know*.

What will we call him? We'll have to pick out two names, of course. One for a girl, one for a boy.

How long will I have to wait before I tell Mitchell I'm pregnant?

My period is due in two weeks and when I'm two or three days late, I'll tell him. I can't wait to see the expression on his wonderful, handsome face! Course, I'll also insist we not spread the word until we're sure. Just to be on the safe side.

For the first time, I feel a little swell of uncertainty. What if I'm wrong? What if I've been tricked by Fintan into giving myself to him for no other reason than to satisfy his otherworldly lust? Has he tricked other women this way? Did I betray Mitchell because I was lonely and weak? Because I blame Mitchell for our being childless?

And what of the child? What if Fintan lied about that, too, and I give birth to a monster?

Panic washes over me. *What have I done?*

God, forgive me. Please, please, don't let Mitchell ever find out. Please, if there really is a child, make him normal and I promise, I'll love him with every fiber of my being. I will bring him up to be a good Christian. I will never stray again. I will honor my marriage vows and make Mitchell the best wife ever.

As recrimination heaps coals of fire on my head, a breath of air wafts in through the window, carrying with it Fintan's scent. I rush to the door and fling it open. I will make him answer my questions, make him tell me the truth.

There's no one on the back porch. The yard yawns empty before me. I close the kitchen door, return to the table, and pick up my pen.

Disappointment is like a dash of cold water. Fintan hasn't come back, but the realization brings clarity. I hadn't expected that he would, had I? Why would I want him to?

Why am I racking myself with guilt?

I will not see Fintan again. If he has planted a seed inside me, he has done it to give me a gift. To give Mitchell and me a gift. Isn't that what I've been asking God for? Didn't I just think that a child would make our life perfect?

And doesn't God answer prayers?

TUESDAY, JUNE 29

Mitchell came home today. He was surprised when I made him drop his bag at the door and didn't even ask him how the trip had gone before I led him upstairs. I'm not usually the aggressor in our love life. But after the shock wore off on him, I guess he didn't mind. We spent the afternoon in bed.

Then I went downstairs to fix dinner and he went outside to unload the truck. He looks so happy.

I'm going to continue to keep this journal. I'll have to be careful. Mitchell mustn't ever find it, but I'm glad I started it. I don't know what the future holds, but I'm more confident now than ever before that it will be good.

I hear Mitchell on the porch. I have to find a place to hide this.

I can hardly wait to tell him he's going to be a father . . .

SECOND AUTHOR'S NOTE:

So began the journal Adele kept for almost a year. Most of the days are filled with the trivia of daily life, but nine months to the day after Fintan appeared out of the forest, she gave birth to a baby boy. It wasn't the end of the story, of course. Fintan reappeared in her life two years later to father a daughter.

At the birth of Adele's children, Corbett and Linda, Mr. Cataliades, a man she called a kind of "godfather," appeared to see them. He returned twice again—once after her granddaughter Sookie was born and at grandson Jason's birth. He told Adele that he had given each of her grandchildren a gift. He wasn't specific then, but clearly in Sookie he saw something, "an essential spark," and because of that he bestowed upon her telepathic abilities. Jason, unlike his father and aunt, who seemed not to benefit at all in their father's legacy, was given the powers of seduction and attraction, the ability to attract lovers. As Jason was to learn, not always a good thing.

Later, when Mr. Cataliades appeared one more time, it was to Adele to pass along the cluviel dor Sookie eventually inherited. Adele was afraid to ask the question, but Cataliades's words that Fintan had given it to him to bring to her if Fintan died first said it all. Fintan was indeed dead. Adele greeted the news with a mixture of sadness and relief. Sadness because if the words of the stranger were true, Fintan's "gift" meant he really had loved her. Relief because although she loved her children and grandchildren more than life itself, guilt from keeping such a huge secret from Mitchell had taken its toll.

In all the time to follow, Mitchell never questioned the paternity of two children he loved as his own, just as Adele would never regret giving life to

Corbett and Linda. Watching Mitchell with the children, seeing the love on his face when he held his babies for the first time, she knew Fintan had been wise to advise her not to be hasty to tell him about how those babies came about. Mitchell deserved to be happy, and regardless of whatever moral questions arise over what Adele did to ensure that happiness, the results cannot be denied.

And so I conclude where I began. Was this a story of betrayal and infidelity? Was Adele beguiled against her will by a beautiful creature?

Arguments can be made for both. But the greater question is does God hear and answer our prayers? And if yes, who are we to question his ways? So, I propose again that this is a love story. A love story between two people who loved each other as much as they loved the two children and later, the three grandchildren who came into their lives. Two people who asked God for children and had their prayers answered.

This is the love story between Adele and Mitchell Stackhouse.

THE MILLION-DOLLAR HUNT

JONATHAN MABERRY

Jonathan Maberry decided to write about Mustapha, my ex-con lone wolf. To make enough money to give his lover a better life, Mustapha agrees to take part in a reality game show where weres of all stripes hunt one another for nonlethal sports entertainment. But there's a much darker game running. The real game is an absolute killer.

-1-

The trick was to remember that this was a game.

Hard to do when you're dying.

Hard to do when they're hunting you.

Hard to do when you are absolutely sure you're going to die.

A game.

Yeah, sure.

Just not *his* game.

-2-

Mustapha Khan moved through the forest as silently as possible, doing his best to avoid the cameras mounted high on trees.

Sometimes he ran on two legs.

Sometimes on four.

Different advantages to each.

Different vulnerabilities.

The werewolf could move faster than the man.

But when he was human, the drugs didn't seem to knock the world sideways as much. Whatever was on those damn claws was clearly designed to disorient the wolf, not the man.

Weird science.

Or, just weird.

He didn't care.

Besides, at the moment, he needed two legs and two hands. One hand to pull himself up the slope of the ravine—grasping slender sapling trunks and gritty root tangles—the other to keep his wadded-up T-shirt pressed tightly against his wound.

Wounds, really.

Four long, deep cuts. Mustapha didn't know how bad they were. The pain was less than he expected. Probably shock. And if it *was* shock, there would be one tossed-bone of a benefit. Shock slows bleeding. Put that in the win column. Kind of.

He smiled weakly at the thought of that "benefit." It was the kind of good luck he usually had. The universe was always being so damn kind to him.

Shit.

He looked up at the side of the ravine and could swear it was twice as high.

"Come on, goddamn it," he growled. Not sure if he was mad at the world, mad at himself, or just mad. As in batshit crazy.

A purple-brown root curled out of the slope like a loop of intestine.

He reached for it, closed his fingers around it, took a breath, pulled. Pain seemed to explode in every molecule of his body.

"Fuck you," he told the pain, the root, the slope, the drugs in his blood, and the son of a bitch who'd cut him. Bitterness was something he could grind his teeth on as he climbed, so he snarled with anger and pulled himself another foot upward. And another.

Late yesterday afternoon, when he'd come this way, the ravine was nothing. A twenty-five-degree decline on one side, maybe thirty on the other. Nothing he couldn't manage in human form without working up a sweat. Now that slope felt like a sheer cliff. He fought for every inch upward.

Twice he slipped and slid all the way to the ravine floor. Thirty-five feet of hidden rocks, sticker bushes, rotted vegetation, and wormy dirt. This was his third try.

Sweat ran in crooked lines down his skin. The rags of his clothes were soaked with it, and with blood. A small fragment of consolation came from the knowledge—the red memory—that some of it was *his*.

His.

The bastard who'd clawed him.

At least he could bleed.

At least that son of a bitch wasn't as invulnerable as he wanted everyone to think. Close, yeah, sure. Real close. But if he could bleed, then . . .

Mustapha took a breath, snaked his hand out for a maple sapling. His fingers closed around it but immediately began to slip, gravity and weakness prying his hand open.

"No!" he shouted.

No.

But the day said yes.

And he fell.

He hit every goddamn rock and stone and root on the slope. He bounced twice and rolled over off the edge of an outcrop of limestone. From there it was a straight drop to the ravine floor.

He landed badly.

Far above him was a camera, but its red eye was pointed elsewhere. Maybe it hadn't seen him. Maybe it was still looking for him.

Or maybe a man bleeding to death in a ravine made for bad television.

As his life leaked out of him he found that he no longer cared.

Mustapha's grip on consciousness slipped as easily and completely as had his hand.

"No . . ." he said once more, very weakly. The canopy of trees above him lost its form, the leaves smearing into a dark canvas on which was painted absolutely nothing.

-3-

Dreams offered no rest for him. They did not let him forget.

As Mustapha lay in a rag-doll sprawl at the bottom of the ravine, his mind rewound the last few days as if it were all recorded on videotape. Be kind, rewind. Except it was no kindness.

The tape seemed to be damaged. Splotchy. The memories came in chunks, pieces, with scenes unfinished and missing dialogue. As he fell deeper and deeper into the black well, he watched it as if it all belonged to someone else's life. To a life that could not possibly be his.

Sitting at the Hair of the Dog, drinking unsweetened iced tea from a sweating glass, thinking about the Long Tooth pack. Join, don't join. Over and over again, looking at it from all sides. And in the middle of that come two guys in city suits. Big white guy, medium-sized black guy. Gray suits. Hand-sewn Italian shoes. Oakleys that they never took off. Big smiles with lots of white teeth. Gold rings and Rolexes. Money, even from a distance. As they come in, Mustapha sees the Lexus LX 570 sitting outside.

Without preamble the black guy says, "KeShawn Johnson?"

Mustapha gave him the look. *The* look. The one that says *Go away while you can still walk* in any language you want.

The white guy says, "Our pardon. Mustapha Khan?"

"Who's asking?" Mustapha replies.

The white guy produces a business card, holds it out, and when it isn't taken he places it faceup on the tabletop.

Real Adventure Productions

Expensive card. Embossed.

Name on the lower left is Ronald Hawes. The address is in Hollywood.

"I'm Hawes," Hawes says, then nods to his companion. "This is Mr. Bell."

Mustapha still gives them the look, though he changes the frequency to include a clear "so what" vibe. But he doesn't say anything. Lets them do the work.

"We would like to talk to you about *The Million-Dollar Hunt*."

"What the hell is that?"

Hawes and Bell smile their whitest smiles. "It's how you become a rich and famous man."

"Not much interested in becoming famous," says Mustapha.

"What about becoming rich?" asks Bell.

Mustapha takes a breath. "Yeah. We can talk about that."

And then only fragments of the conversation that followed. Snatches of sentences.

". . . whole new kind of reality show . . ."

". . . like *Survivor* or *The Great Race* but with a real edge . . ."

". . . two players . . ."

". . . like, not prerecorded . . ."

". . . subscription only . . ."

After that, it was murkier for his dreaming mind. A flight to Los Angeles to meet with producers and a director. And lawyers. Papers to sign. Checks to deposit. Photos to be taken. Interviews timed for the rollout of the show.

The show.

The Million-Dollar Hunt.

That's what it was called.

A new spin on *The Most Dangerous Game*, except that it wasn't men hunting other men.

It was were hunting were.

Players go into the woods wearing only the clothes on their backs. They live off the land and follow scent markers to find equipment, weapons, and food. The weapons are mock—rubber knives, paintball guns, water-balloon grenades. No killing weapons.

Even in his delirium Mustapha thought, *Yeah, right.*

The rules were simple.

In round one, it's all about surviving dummy booby traps. That part was easy, even a little fun. With the tree-mounted cameras recording it all for all the pay-per-view couch potatoes out there, and the possibility of residuals from DVD sales down the road. Maybe even a book deal for the winner.

Then there was round two.

Round two was about weres fighting one another with fake weapons. Each weapon rigged with a little built-in sensor to record wounding blows and killing blows, like in fencing matches. Touch a throat and earn a beep.

And earn a bonus.

Starting pay before Mustapha set one foot into the forest was ten thousand dollars. Serious bank.

Escaping or disarming booby traps earned cash ranging from two hundred dollars to a grand.

Battles with rubber weapons were scaled, too. Disabling injury—a touch to bicep or thigh—was low pay. Getting a beep from touching a throat, a heart, a groin, an artery, was bigger bucks.

All in fun.

The fat slobs in their La-Z-Boys watching from the comfort of their homes would be getting boners imagining that it was them out there. Fighting with skill, fighting with ferocity.

Mustapha still liked that part of it.

Then there was round three.

Round three was what it was all about.

That was were fighting were for real.

No rubber knives.

No splashy water balloons.

Round three was claws and teeth.

Even so, it was supposed to be simulated. A fight with no more reality than the brawling in the Ultimate Fighting Championship. Some bruises, sure. A little blood? Why not? It looks great on a flat-screen TV. But at the end of the day, the losers go home with a short count on their paychecks and the winner cashes a check for one million dollars.

His dreaming mind sneered.

Even drugged and bleeding, he knew the difference between a Hollywood truth and a brutal reality.

This was either a scam of the most dangerous kind or a runaway train that was off the rails.

In either case, Mustapha was losing the game.

He lay there, sprawled in the dirt at the bottom of a gash in the earth. Four ragged lines torn in his flesh leaked blood into the soil.

-4-

The memory of the fight replayed over and over as he lay there.

Mustapha had just won a mock fight with rubber hatchets. He and the werefox he'd beaten had stayed in human form for the whole fight. That was the rule for that round. They had to prove themselves as human warriors.

The fox was a tall, wiry Texan with bright red hair and a dozen piercings on his face. Sunlight struck sparks from earlobes, lips, eyebrow, nose, and on the diamond stud drilled through the bridge of the man's nose.

Little bastard could fight, though.

He and Mustapha had feinted and dueled for almost a full minute—which is a long damn time in a fight. In the movies and on TV a fight can spill out for minutes, but when it's real—really real, not two guys measuring their junk in a bar—it was all over in seconds.

Mustapha and the fox—he never did learn the man's name—both knew how to handle blades, and the other guy had the kind of moves you only ever learn in a prison yard. Okay, not hatchets per se, but the dart-and-dodge body movements that kept a blade fighter alive while he deconstructed the other guy. The kind of fighting cons doing hard time pretty much hold a patent on.

It was the prison thing—and all the memories that came with it—that made Mustapha want to win that fight. He did, too. He let the fox guy get close enough to land a solid elbow shot to the short ribs, which was part of a well-known combination to deliver a follow-up close-range shank. Mustapha took the elbow hit, but he was already moving to counter the follow-up. He pushed himself into the hit, taking it too soon, jamming the fox guy's pivot, spun him around, and wrapped one muscular arm around his throat from behind, kneed him in the coccyx, and reached around to chop him in the crotch with the rubber hammer.

Still hurt, though.

Still hurt like a son of a bitch. Just not as bad as what he'd done to the fox.

Fox guy dropped to his knees, vomited, and collapsed sideways, clutching his balls and turning a nice shade of puce.

That was the first in round two. Each round doubled the number of encounters, and that one wasn't two guys bashing each other with rubber weapons. It was were against were, and in this case, a werepuma.

That one was quick. Probably too quick for good ratings, and definitely too quick for a top bonus, but it was a win. Mustapha had trapped the puma on the edge of a bluff and when it reared to slash him, Mustapha had simply run into it. The puma went right over the edge and into the water. By the time he climbed out, the current had taken him too far downstream for Mustapha to bother. It wasn't a simulated big-ticket kill, but it was a win.

Mustapha figured that getting to the end of the game and snatching that big prize was going to do him a lot more good than getting scuffed up in a bunch of piddling duels. Especially if he had an opponent waiting for him who was going to be real trouble. Like a werelion or weretiger.

Or werebear.

Oh, my.

Forty minutes after dunking the puma he ran into a bear.

Son of a bitch.

The bear.

Buoyed by his win, and already counting the bonus money, Musta-pha shifted to four legs and ran through the woods, burning off nervous energy, letting the adrenaline dilute as it passed through his racing blood.

He ran up and down hills, delighting in the mental rush of power that came from winning. Even though there was no kill. Even though this was not fighting for inclusion in a pack. A win was a win was a win.

Put it in the bank.

He never saw the bear.

He smelled it, though, about a half second too late.

It was waiting for him. Patient, the way *good* hunters are. Silent. Snugged down in a tangle of fallen pine boughs that were clumped beside a well-worn game trail. Hiding amid all of those other scents. Deer and elk and raccoon. Invisible for that extra half second. Cameras in the trees recording it all.

Mustapha was in midstride, his senses just beginning to alert him to a wrongness in the air. Then there was a blur of movement. Brown fur, white fangs, and yellow claws.

The impact was terrible.

Mustapha was a powerful wolf. Lean and muscular.

The werebear was bigger.

Much, much bigger.

And it was in full motion when it blindsided him.

The impact knocked him sideways and they rolled over and over together, both of them growling and snapping, claws reaching for flesh. They struck a pine tree and broke apart, landing on either side of it. Mustapha whipped around and hunched down, showing his teeth.

The bear got to its feet without haste.

As if it knew this was a kill, not a fight.

They stared at each other from fifteen feet apart, with only the torn bark of the pine between them.

The rules of the Hunt had been clear.

You can bite to break skin.

You can cut only skin deep.

No kills.

No muscle-deep wounds.

Blood was fine.

Nobody dies.

Those were the rules.

But as he crouched there, Mustapha could feel his stomach begin to burn. He dared not take his eyes off the bear to look. But he could smell his own blood.

Too much of it.

Too much.

Too deep.

The bear had nearly gutted him.

The brute's mouth was open. Hungry. Waiting to bite.

Dark brown eyes stared at him.

Three things happened in the next moment.

They changed the game. They cracked the world open.

The first thing was that Mustapha *knew* those eyes. He knew them in bear form. And he knew them in human form.

His wolf mouth was not constructed for human speech; otherwise he would have blurted the name. He would have spat it out as a statement, a question, an accusation of betrayal. The name burned in his mind, though.

Gundersen.

Gundersen?

The big werebear was from his days before Shreveport. They were from his prison days. This was Dutch Gundersen. A guard on his cell block. Not exactly a friend, but not an enemy. Gundersen had treated him fairly. He wasn't the kind of screw to vent his problems on prisoners. He was tough, but he was always stand-up. He wasn't the kind to do this. The game, maybe. But not to break the rules.

The second thing that happened in that same fractured moment was that Mustapha saw something on the side of the bear's muscular neck. Two somethings.

They looked almost like hummingbirds. Bulbous bodies with brightly colored feathers. Mustapha had only seen the things on nature shows. When field biologists or zookeepers have to subdue a large and dangerous animal.

Tranquilizer darts.

Two of them, their needles buried so deep in the bear's neck that they hadn't torn loose during the attack.

The third thing—the last thing that moment could afford to tell him—was that Gundersen's eyes were filled with all of the wrong emotions. There was hate. There was bloodlust. But there was also absolutely no sign of recognition.

And over those burning eyes was a narcotic glaze.

The bear was *drugged.*

While he slept and bled and remembered, Mustapha knew that the drugs were now in him, too. Through bite and spit and claws, whatever had been in the bear's bloodstream was now in his.

He feared it as much as he feared the bear and the broken rules of the game and the wounds in his body.

He dreamed of the rest of the fight. Of how he had torn and slashed at the bear, wounding it in turn. Of how they had fought to the edge of a drop-off. How they'd chased each other through a sudden downpour. And how Mustapha broke away and ran for his life during the heaviest of the rain.

The dream played over and over again. Each time the fear was worse. Like the hoofbeats of something approaching.

Fear pushed him down deeper into the dreams.

Fear was the claw that tore at him while he lay there.

-5-

Saying a name out loud woke him.

"Warren."

His lover was not in Mustapha's dream, but it was a reason to come back to the light. To open his eyes.

To be alive.

He lay there and looked up at the canopy of trees as if he could see Warren hiding among the boughs and leaves.

"Warren . . ." he murmured.

There was no answer.

Of course there wasn't.

Warren was hundreds of miles away. Back in Shreveport. Maybe watching all of this on TV. Watching *him* die out here in the woods.

Mustapha briefly closed his eyes, embarrassed and ashamed of his weakness. Of his defeat. Of letting Warren down.

The money from this gig was supposed to be their out. Their exit strategy from all the games in town. The packs and all of that. It was supposed to be a million-dollar ticket to the quiet life far away. Maybe down in Florida. Or way, way out in California.

Not up here.

Not in the endless forests of Washington State.

This was a million damn miles from anywhere.

A million miles from Warren.

And Mustapha could feel his exit door swinging shut.

In his mind's eye—in that cruel lens through which he could always see the trail of mistakes and small failures that led him from who he had been to what he was now—he thought he saw Warren. The slim, small man with the killer's eyes and the gentlest hands. Warren was there, standing on the far side of the exit, and as it closed he made no move to keep the door open. Lines of sadness were carved onto his face. His eyes were wet with disappointment.

"Warren . . . ?"

The door closed and so did Mustapha's eyes.

Once more the world went away.

This time, however, he did not dream.

Instead he lay unmoving, his chest barely rising, as night slowly closed its fist around him.

-6-

Mustapha did not wake up.

The wolf did.

-7-

In wolf form he rose.

The pain was there. The wounds were still there.

The wolf didn't care.

The man was submerged. Deeper than he had ever been. So deep that the thing that climbed slowly up the side of the ravine wasn't a werewolf at all. In wolfshape Mustapha was still Mustapha. His mind, his will.

Not now.

Now he was nearly all wolf.

The commingled aspects of man and monster were disconnected, victims of the drug and blood loss and exhaustion. Now it was the wolf that clambered over the edge of the ravine and stood trembling at its edge. The forest was filled with shadows, but darkness was no veil to him. Not anymore. His eyes seemed sharper. Far more acute. Seeing this forest with a different spectrum. Its eyes could track the wavering flight of a moth through the densest shadows. Its ears could track the fall of a leaf from a tree half a mile away. And stripped of human thoughts, this wolf's mind was simpler, more pure, less confused by distractions. The clarity was a powerful thing.

For a moment it stood there, reveling in these new senses. The inrush of sensory information was incredible and yet the wolf's mind could process it. On some level, down where Mustapha still dreamed, he knew this was wrong. Wolves are not able to do this. Their senses are sharp, but not this sharp. Not anywhere near this sharp. This was wrong.

Wrong.

But it felt so incredibly right.

It felt correct.

As if this was how it was supposed to be before . . .

Before what?

His dreaming mind could not answer the question. The wolf did not want to. It accepted.

The wolf began walking away from the ravine, slowly at first, listening to what was happening inside. Tasting pain to understand damage.

When Mustapha changed from man to wolf, that wolf had the same mass and weight. It was larger than ordinary wolves. It was no different now. He was the same size wolf—but this wolf was not the wolf he had always known. The muscles felt different. Leaner in parts, bulkier in parts. And his jaws and throat were heavier. Whatever was happening to him had created a new matrix, a new kind of wolf.

But what was it?

Mustapha knew the answer, though it made no sense.

Canis dirus.

That came to him from all the reading he'd done on wolves. On their nature, their physiology. Their history.

Canis dirus.

Something older than gray wolves.

A proto wolf.

A dire wolf.

Stronger and faster than the wolves that lived and hunted today. With sharper senses and a much more powerful . . .

Bite.

But that was impossible. The dire wolf was gone. Extinct. Lost ten thousand years ago.

Except that it wasn't.

Somewhere, locked inside the DNA of all wolves, was that code. That potential.

What did it mean? Why, after all these years as a werewolf, had this new and much older aspect of the wolf emerged?

The answer leaped at him.

The bear. Its claws.

Whatever was on those claws had done something. Sparked something.

Something so wrong.

Something that felt so right.

These thoughts swirled in the dreaming mind. They were fueled by the instincts of the werewolf. And man and werewolf were still qualities in this animal, but it was pure dire wolf mind that governed it as it moved deeper into the forest. Exultant in its power. Newfound or reclaimed? That was an impossible question. Healing with every step. Sniffing its own backtrail to follow the blood scent to where the fight had taken place, to the point where it had received those wounds.

To the place where the thing that delivered those injuries had last been.

It took an hour to find it.

The wheel of night turned, dragging cold stars across the sky.

The moon—a white face in the silky blackness—stared down at the wolf, and in her glow the wolf felt powerful again.

The wounds barely ached now.

It reached the clearing where the werewolf had fought the werebear. The ground was torn. There was blood that smelled of chemicals. There were claw marks on ground and trees. There was the smell.

The big animal was still out there. Still hunting. It, too, would be healed by now. Or near enough.

For the wolf, it was a simple choice that required no thought. Be hunted or go hunting.

The scent was strong on the air and in the ground. Stronger still in the trail of blood.

The wolf bent and sniffed the blood. The richer, more exotic blood of a bear.

The wolf lifted its head and uttered a long howl. It sounded lonely and lost.

But it was not.

The cry was filled with promise.

The wolf lowered its nose to the ground to reclaim the scent, and then it ran. All memory of injury and fear forgotten.

It ran in the direction of the wounded bear.

-8-

Mustapha wasn't sure when he came back to himself.

It all felt like a dream.

He knew it was probably the drug.

Maybe.

Or something else. Some quality of his Were nature that he didn't understand. There were always new things to know. Always surprises because it seemed to him that reality was hardly real.

He was a werewolf.

He worked for a vampire.

There were faeries and telepaths and other things in the world.

As gruff and stoic as he tried to be, as cool and casual about it all as he pretended, he was constantly amazed by the world.

And now this.

The last thing he remembered was thinking about how his death here in these vast woods would disappoint and hurt Warren.

The next thing he knew he was in wolf form, running free and wild in the woods. Not really werewolf anymore. Not in any way Mustapha understood. It almost felt like the wolf owned this flesh and that he was an unwelcome stowaway. He never felt that way when he ran as a werewolf. The werewolf and the man were the same person, the same being.

This was different.

Then it hit him in a moment of insight and clarity.

This was what a *wolf* felt like.

Not a werewolf.

A wolf.

There was a simplicity to it. A purity that he had never known as either man or werewolf. Nor was it anything he perceived among the stronger or older members of the pack he was considering joining.

This was . . . *different.*

This was such an ancient feeling.

And . . . a healing one.

Mustapha rode along in the body that was his and not his, feeling the muscles work, appreciating an efficiency and economy of movement that was different even though the body was the same. His body. But with a different hand at the controls.

The wolf ran, picking up speed as it followed a strengthening and freshening scene. The bear was close now.

So . . . why wasn't the wolf afraid?

He certainly was. Man and werewolf. Definitely afraid.

Not the wolf, though.

Not the wolf.

Not the *wolf.*

-9-

It was there.

On the other side of the hill.

The wolf moved around the base of the hill to keep its own scent off the wind.

It could smell the bear.

The wolf sniffed the air.

Definitely a bear, but not currently a bear.

The change happened so fast that Mustapha wasn't aware he was going to change.

One moment he was the wolf. Sturdy, strong, four-legged. Then there was a blur as if he were going blind and deaf all at once.

Suddenly he was Mustapha again, kneeling on the ground, trying to see what a wolf sees but with merely human eyes. The night sounds changed, smeared out, just as the shadows were smearing. Becoming blander, confused, less precise.

He stayed there, breathing, almost gasping, from the speed of the change.

There was no pain. Just the disorienting shift from the pinnacle of perception to the blandness of what human senses could take in.

And yet . . .

As he rose to his feet he realized that this was not entirely true. The darkness should have been far darker than it was. The night sounds should be meaningless beyond the pulse of crickets. The smells should be a nonsensical olio without depth.

That was not the way it was.

Somehow, something of the wolf remained with him. It shouldn't have, but it did.

His senses were not human senses.

They were not the wolf's superb perceptions, nor were they the hunting senses of the werewolf. But they were not entirely human, either.

He stood in the darkness and tried to absorb it all. Process it.

He was seeing with human eyes, smelling with a human nose, hearing with human ears. And yet . . .

How had all of this happened? What drug was it on the bear's claws? It seemed to have driven Gundersen into a mindless rage state, but that wasn't how it was affecting Mustapha. Had its passage through Gundersen's bloodstream changed it? Was the effect different for bears and wolves? Mustapha was a long way from being a science geek. He could remember less than half of the basic chemistry he'd learned in school.

Besides, this could be something new. A designer drug.

Or an ordinary drug whose effects were warped by combination with were blood.

So many questions.

No fucking answers at all.

He sniffed the air and could smell the bear. Sweat and piss and blood on the air as separate smells.

Was this an anticipated side effect of the drug? Did whoever shot Gundersen with those darts know it would do this? Had that been the goal? Or . . .

Or was this all something coming at everyone from the blue? Even the asshole with the dart gun?

Mustapha couldn't tell.

Then he had a crooked thought.

What if this was part of the game? What if that drug was introduced to make the players stronger in order for them to play a more dangerous game?

That sounded possible in his head, but felt wrong in his gut.

What, then, was this?

Why had he become a wolf instead of a werewolf? How was that even possible? And why was his human aspect not quite . . .

Human?

In a moment of panic he touched his face, afraid that he would encounter an alien shape. Something primitive and wrong, like the sloping brow of a Neanderthal.

His face was his face. Normal. Wrinkled with concern, but his.

He hadn't realized he was holding his breath until he felt how long and hot the exhale was that burst from his chest.

Then he froze.

It had been too loud.

Loud as a whisper and whispers were like shouts to the were.

"It's okay," said a voice from over the top of the hill. "I already knew you were there."

A voice.

Gundersen.

Damn it.

Mustapha held his breath. He'd come to kill. Not to fight, not to talk. He wanted to cut that backstabbing bastard to pieces. Eat his heart. Claim his power, drugs or no.

"It's Mustapha, right?" called the voice.

Shit.

"Gundersen?"

"Yup."

"Shit."

"Yeah. Come down here."

"And walk into another ambush. No thanks."

"Is that what happened?"

"You know it is."

"Actually . . . I don't. Come on over," said Gundersen. "I'll explain." There was a heavy pause and what sounded like a soft groan of pain, then Gundersen spoke again. "Believe me . . . you'll want to hear this."

-10-

Mustapha moved very carefully. The wolf was just beneath his skin the whole time. The werewolf, too. It gave him a strange new feeling of confidence to have both aspects, the old and the new, riding shotgun with him.

When he reached the top of the crest he shifted to one side and crouched, peering between a couple of low shrubs, cautious, ready to bolt if the bear was ready to pounce. Mustapha had no illusions about how a second fight with this brute would turn out. It's no accident that there are no wolf packs in areas where bears roam free. If there were bears in Africa, even lions wouldn't be king of the jungle.

Mustapha was tough, but one of the keys to survival was to know the exact dimensions of your personal power. Without self-deception. No sane person lets his ego write a check his ass can't cash.

He bent low and peered through the shadows.

He saw Gundersen.

He also saw a lot of blood. Smelled it, too. A delicious smell.

Slowly, slowly, Mustapha stood up.

He let out a slow breath, and then walked down the hill.

-11-

"You're a damn mess," he said.

Gundersen smiled. Even his teeth were bloody.

"Yeah, well, life's a mess," he said.

"What happened to you?" asked Mustapha as he crossed his legs and lowered himself to the ground. "I didn't do all that."

"You wish," laughed Gundersen, and then his face twisted as first a spasm of pain and then a string of ragged wet coughs tore through him. It took a long time for the coughing fit to pass and when it was done, Gundersen settled back, pale and sweating. His chest, stomach, and left hip were soaked with blood, and Mustapha could see torn flesh through the dried blood and dirt caked on the man's naked skin. Some of the wounds had begun to scab over—evidence that the were genes were still firing, still working overtime to try to repair damage at speeds no human physiology could match. However, other, deeper wounds still gaped. From the scuffed nature of the ground and the layered smears of blood on the tree trunk against which Gundersen sat, it was evident he'd been here for a while. Hours.

Gundersen nodded to Mustapha's own wounds. "Aren't we a pair?"

"What happened?" Mustapha repeated.

"The jackals, what else?"

"Jackals? What jackals?"

"You telling me you didn't see them?"

"Since the game started all I've seen was that little fox guy, a pussy of a werepuma, and you."

Gundersen grunted. "Which explains why you're still walking."

"Tell me."

"Not sure where to start."

"What came first, the darts or the jackals?"

"The darts."

"Okay, start there."

"It's the game. It's how it's played," said Gundersen. "You know it's rigged, right?"

"I figured. But how? By who? And why?"

"Like I said . . . the jackals."

"You're not making sense, man."

Gundersen nodded. "Probably not. My head's all scrambled. Those damn darts. God only knows what was in them. At first I thought it was a tranquilizer. Something to knock me down a peg. You know—werebear and all. Odds were pretty much in my favor from the jump."

"Really?" said Mustapha dryly. "I'd have never figured that one out."

"So when I got hit I thought it was that. Something to level the playing field."

"But it wasn't?"

"Nope. Got a needle stick from ketamine once a while back. One of the convicts smuggled it onto the block. This was before your time. They were running K as a party drug."

"Heard about that shit."

"People call it a horse tranquilizer, but it's used for all sorts of things. Point is, when I got hit the symptoms came on the same way, so there's probably some K in there. Maybe as a base. But there was something else, too. LSD, maybe. Something like that."

"So, basically, I had my ass handed to me by a *stoned* bear?"

Gundersen grinned. "Life is a complete bitch, isn't it?"

"Testify."

"Anyway, the drugs kick in and suddenly I'm Timothy Leary the Bear. Can't see straight, can't think worth a damn, but at the same time I felt my *were* self in a different way."

"Stronger, right?"

"Not just stronger," agreed Gundersen. "It was something else, too."

Mustapha hesitated for a moment, then nodded. "I know. I felt it. Or, maybe *feel* it. When I changed . . . I became a wolf, you dig? Not a werewolf. A wolf. Like I was sharing headspace with an actual animal. Some weird-ass shit."

Gundersen closed his eyes. "God, yes. That's it exactly. For a while there I was a bear. Kind of a . . . What do you call it? Not just a real bear, it's more of a . . ."

He fished for a word until Mustapha provided it.

"A *primal* bear."

"That's it. It felt weird. It felt *older,* if that makes any sense."

"It does. But what I want to know is why they'd put something like that in the drug? I mean, I can see dialing you down to make the fights more even. These assholes are gamblers. People are getting rich betting on us. There's somebody out there now taking bets on what we're going to say or do to each other right now."

Gundersen shook his head and gestured weakly to the edge of his clearing. Three video cameras lay there, each of them comprehensively smashed. "No one's listening. Mind you, they might come and fix that, but for now, it's just us."

"Good to know," said Mustapha, then he prompted, "Jackals."

"Right, right," said Gundersen, wincing at a spasm of pain. "After we beat the shit out of each other, I limped off to lick my wounds. For real, which is something I wouldn't ever admit to someone who wasn't like us."

"Yup."

"I tried changing back and forth, you know? To see if I could clear my head? Seemed like the drug effect got worse when I was a bear. When I was human I could think better, but the injuries were worse. I had to risk it, though, 'cause I needed to think this through. Understand it. I drifted around, trying to spot and dodge the cameras. Avoided a couple of fights, too. There's another werewolf—some clown from Arkansas, and there was a werewarthog, which is something I never even heard of before."

"A werewarthog? Jesus."

"I know, right? Anyway, I was just starting to get my act together. Wounds were healing well enough for me to make some good time. I wanted to get to the end zone."

"I thought they wouldn't let us go there unless we wanted to opt out of the game."

"What the hell you think I was trying to do? I was going to opt out and then get to the first phone I could find and call the cops. Maybe the FBI. If this game is as rigged as it seems, then soliciting us from all over the country—and following that up with interstate phone calls and e-mails—makes this a federal conspiracy to commit. I mean, this whole game couldn't be legal. I did a pretty thorough net search and there's nothing about this for TV. There's no preorder pay-per-view website. Nothing in the cable guide. No production company listed on the Internet Movie Database. These guys aren't legit. I figure this whole thing is really about the blood fights, the were-versus-were stuff. And it's probably subscriber-only, going to a very select clientele. People will pay big bucks if they think someone's going to get maimed. Or die. There was something like this with vampires over in Thailand. Anderson Cooper did a story. Even had some human assholes climbing into the ring against vamps on the odd chance of winning a big purse. Lot of people died. So . . . sure, this was crooked from the jump."

"Which makes me wonder why you're even here, Gundersen. Upstanding prison guard and all that shit."

"Yeah," said Gundersen with a sigh. "Everybody makes mistakes. You know that much."

"What was your mistake?"

Despite his wounds, Gundersen colored. "Doesn't matter," he mumbled.

"Come on, man. Out with it."

"You're going to laugh at me."

"I probably am."

Another long sigh. "Shit. Online poker."

"*What?*"

"Ran up a tab. Big tab. Nine thousand. No way I could pay it off, and the interest was insane. I could have lost my house."

Mustapha didn't laugh. "I can understand it. I did it to get me and Warren the hell out of Dodge. For good."

"Warren—?"

Mustapha hesitated. He'd kept his sexual orientation under wraps while in prison. A gay man could quickly become everybody's punch in the joint, and he didn't want to do all his time on his knees. And he didn't really feel like baring his soul to Gundersen. On the other hand . . . fuck it. What could this man do with that knowledge? Not a goddamn thing.

"He's my partner," he said.

Gundersen didn't even blink. "Cool. He a good guy?"

"The best."

"Cool," the guard said again. "Good to have something worth fighting for. Someone to go home to."

"What about you?"

"Wife left me, took the kids. But I get them on weekends and every other Christmas. I wanted to get clear of my debts so I could . . . I don't know . . . so I could be the dad they think I am."

They looked at each other, nodded at the way the world spins.

"Jackals," Mustapha said again.

"Jackals. So I'm making my way to the end zone when half a dozen guys step out of the woods. Pretty nice ambush. I'm so into my own pain and still half in the bag from the drug and suddenly there they are. None of them that big, but there's six of them, you know?"

"Sure. What happened?"

"Exactly what you think happened. They shifted into a pack of jackals and went for me."

"Damn, son. How'd you get away? Six to one, why ain't you dead?"

Gundersen gave him a small shrug. "Still a bear."

"There's that."

"Jackals versus bear. If I hadn't been hurt, there'd be six dead god-damn jackals and me on the phone to the feds."

"But—?"

"But I *was* hurt and I *was* still whacked out on the drug. So now there's one jackal dead and five jackals who didn't have the kind of afternoon they wanted."

Mustapha grinned. "I'd have paid to see that."

"Somebody probably did. There were plenty of cameras in the trees. That's probably why they chose that spot. Lots of coverage. Must have looked great on TV."

"Unless you were betting on the jackals."

"Yeah, well, I can't claim to have won every fight I've been in, but I never went down without a fight."

"Heard that."

"So, I got out of there. I had enough strength left to run, and I guess maybe I scared them bad enough so they didn't follow. At least not right away. Getting here, though, that took some doing. I'd spotted this place earlier today. The cameras don't really have a good view here, and I kind of nudged the ones around here to give me a bigger blind spot. Not something so obvious they'd send someone out to fix. I needed to rest up. The jackals, though, they cowboyed up after a while and came hunting. The five survivors and a few more. Maybe eight in all."

"That many?"

"Yeah. But there could be more."

Mustapha grunted.

"What?" asked Gundersen.

"You know, man," said Mustapha slowly, "maybe this is something more than a handful of these jackal jerkoffs messing with us out here."

"What do you mean?"

"Maybe this is their game. Maybe the deal is that they get the rest of us to beat the shit out of each other, kind of take the edge off. Maybe they film that, maybe they don't. Then they wait until one of us comes along—tired, weaker, maybe hurt—and then they attack. If you're a jackal—and let's face it, they're smaller, and one-on-one they're not worth a wet fart—and you're on camera taking down a werebear? Or a werewolf? Even if you have buddies helping you, that's status. That's going to get you laid by some jackal honey or some were groupie. If you're doing it on some kind of pay-per-view murder channel, it's going to get you laid *and* rich. Who knows how many werejackals there are around the world with cable access and a PayPal account."

Gundersen thought about it. "Shit," he said.

"That's what I think's happening. And I think you killing one of them isn't going to help ratings." Then Mustapha corrected himself. "No. I'm wrong. It's going to jack up the betting 'cause this shit's real now. You killing one of them made this a real life-or-death show."

"Balls."

"Kind of sucks that you just made the game better for them. Worse for us."

"Goddamn it."

They sat in silence for a few minutes, chewing on the facts. The night deepened around them and the moon was moving toward the mountains. Soon it would be pitch-black. Gundersen flexed his legs.

"Cuts are healing. Hurts like a bastard, but better all the time."

"Faster than usual?"

"Much faster. I think I could walk again soon."

"Same thing with me. Those slashes you gave me should have put me down for the night, or maybe down for good. But now . . . all they do is itch."

"That's weird."

"It's weird I don't mind," said Mustapha. "Don't understand it, but I don't mind, that's for damn sure."

"You think it'll last?"

"I don't know," said Mustapha. "But I doubt it. It's a drug. It'll pass through us. I think we got this for now, but not for long. So we'd better use it."

Gundersen nodded.

An owl inquired of whatever passed in the night.

After a moment, Gundersen said, "You think they used the drug on anyone else?"

Mustapha chewed his lip for a moment. "Maybe. That werepuma I fought. Much as I'd like to take credit for kicking his ass so easy, I think maybe he was whacked out. He fought sloppy and I took him out like he was nothing. But, shit, man, he was a puma."

"So he was drugged?"

"Don't know, but I'd bet he was. Maybe there was some asshole sitting in the bushes with a blowgun."

"Pretty sure they use rifles."

"Not the point. I think they wanted to amp all of us weres up. Make us go crazy and beat the shit out of each other. Then maybe they'd hunt the winner."

"That would be risky for them, though."

"Would it? If we're all doped up and going ass-wild on each other, what are the odds any of us would be in perfect shape afterward? Shit, look at what we did to each other. If the jackals had caught up with me a few hours ago they'd have been able to bitch-slap me all over this forest. Maybe they already took down the puma and whoever else. The people watching TV wouldn't know the jackals were fighting a doped were. All they'd see is jackal versus puma, or jackal versus wolf. That'd be some big shit on a high-def TV."

Gundersen ground his teeth. Then he cocked his head to one side and said, "If that's true, then I think that proves they don't know about the side effects. About what that stuff did to you and me. Amping up the primal versions of what we are."

Mustapha nodded. "Yeah. You're right."

"You think anyone else's figured it out? Any of the other poor dumb schmucks like us?"

Mustapha grinned. "Be kind of fun to find out."

"Fun? How the hell would that be any fun?"

"How could it not be, man? You think any of them are going to be happy about what those jackal dickheads are doing to us?"

"No, but . . . it still leaves us six miles up shit creek. The jackals are holding all the cards right now."

"Maybe not. Maybe they done stuck their dicks in a doorjamb."

"How so?"

"Because I think I just figured out how to win this game."

-12-

The jackals moved in a pack.

Gundersen had been wrong about the size of the pack. There were twelve of them. All average-sized men. Maybe on the smaller side of average. Five-seven, five-eight. One-sixty or thereabouts. Individually, nothing. In a pack?

Deadly.

Mustapha watched them from beneath a pile of pine boughs he'd torn down. They moved along a firebreak cut into the vastness of the big forest. One of them walking bold as balls down the center, the others split into two smaller subpacks that ranged forward just inside the forest walls. One pack, nicely placed for an ambush.

Twelve of them.

Mustapha cursed under his breath.

He was bone tired and bleary-eyed. It had been a long damn night. First the fight, then the ravine, then Gundersen. After that . . .

A long night.

Now the red eye of morning was opening. It was one of those mornings where the sun seemed to light a match to the streamers of clouds. The sky looked as if it were too hot to touch.

Mustapha took a deep breath, mouthed a silent promise to Warren, and stood up. The pine boughs fell away as he rose and the bloody sunlight painted him crimson from head to toe.

He took another breath, then bolted across the width of the firebreak, running as fast as two human legs could carry him. Even tired and recovering from wounds, Mustapha was fast.

"There's one!" came the cry from the jackal walking point. "He's making a break for it."

Mustapha cut a look over his shoulder and saw them all freeze and turn their eyes his way. Twelve men. Naked, painted in camouflage military greasepaint to let them blend in with the forest.

Bet they think it looks great on TV, thought Mustapha. He thought they looked like a pack of damn fools.

And then the men were gone.

The air around them shimmered as if heat were rising from the ground.

The men changed. The features of each man seemed to melt and run. Painted skin stretched over bones that were reshaping. One by one they dropped to all fours. Skin ruptured with a wet *glop* and bristled along their sides and shoulders and legs. Tails stretched out, ears elongated.

Mustapha staggered to a stop to watch, his chest heaving, body aching.

Twelve men had been there.

Now a pack of jackals faced him.

And with a chorus of mocking cries, they charged.

"Shit," he breathed. He whirled and ran as fast as he could.

There was a winding trail that spurred off from the firebreak and snaked its way through the forest. Mustapha reached the trail one hundred fifty paces in front of the pack.

One hundred fifty paces was no distance at all.

The jackals were fast. Damn fast. In bursts they could run thirty-five to forty miles an hour, and they could run at ten miles per hour all damn day.

"Catch me if you can, assholes," growled Mustapha as he crumpled to the ground, his bones grinding within him as he changed. His mouth opened to scream, but that sound changed as the shape of his throat and jaw, neck and teeth changed. The colors of the day changed, the visible spectrum broadening as man became werewolf and werewolf became *dire wolf*. It happened fast. So much faster than ever before. Maybe, if these drugs were going to pass through him, this was the fastest it would ever be for him. If so, what a rush. His hands became paws as they struck the ground.

The jackals were almost on him.

If he could have laughed, he would have as the wolf launched itself forward.

His speed increased. Forty-five miles an hour.

Fifty.

The jackals howled as they fought to catch up.

The wolf ran on, delighting in its own power, however temporary. Drawing on resources Mustapha could not even guess at. The dire wolf tore through the forest, miles burning away beneath its feet.

The jackals barked and cried as they struggled to keep their prey in sight. They knew—as the wolf knew—that if they caught up, their numbers would matter more than speed or purity of nature.

In the end it was always numbers.

The wolf ran on.

Above the forest, the rays of the sun slashed at the clouds, soaking the morning with blood.

Then the wolf began to slow.

As it ran up the side of a steep mountain, it slowed.

Its mass and speed warred against gravity, and lost. And it slowed.

Exhaustion that was too deep, too comprehensive for even its power dragged at it, and it slowed.

And the jackals caught up.

The wolf staggered into a clearing that was already splashed with blood. A man lay sprawled against a fallen log, his body crusted with dried gore.

The wolf finally stopped, sides heaving, spit flecking the corners of its mouth.

With howls of delight the jackals burst into the clearing and raced toward the two weak and spent victims.

High on a tree above them, a camera saw it all.

That should have been the first warning.

The camera should not have been there.

The camera belonged to a different tree in a different part of the woods.

It was here now, though. Watching. Recording. Transmitting. Everything.

The man.

The wolf.

The pack of jackals.

The microphone mounted on the camera could capture every yip and gasp and grunt and hunting cry as the jackals closed in for the kill.

Just as it captured—with excellent clarity—the words spoken by the man as he, despite apparent injuries, suddenly rose to his feet. The words were spoken in the split second before man became werebear and werebear became primal bear.

The words were spoken with deliberate clarity and projection. The man wanted each word recorded.

"Payback's a bitch," he said. "Take 'em, boys."

The woods suddenly burst apart in a fury of snapping branches and torn leaves as body after body lunged out.

Fox and puma.

Warthog and coyote.

And bear and wolf.

The camera captured it all with its unblinking eye.

The screams. The blood. The pieces that flew everywhere.

The camera missed nothing.

Around the world, on big-screen TVs, on tablets and laptops, and in a private theater belonging to the leader of this pack of jackals and the humans who clung to them and followed them, the video feed played with high-definition clarity and perfect audio.

It was not the show they had paid for.

It was not the show they wanted to see.

But, damn if it didn't make for an exciting fifteen seconds of reality TV.

Worth every penny of that million dollars.

Mustapha hoped the sons of bitches enjoyed it.

He sure as hell did.

And he was damn sure going to collect every single penny owed to him.

Yes, indeed. Even if he had to bring *his* pack along to make sure those jackal sons of bitches paid up. Not the Long Tooth pack.

This pack. Temporary, sure. Strange and unlikely, absolutely. But for now, this was his pack.

He let thoughts of money drift inside his head as the wolf howled out its killing cry and joined in the slaughter.

BORDERLINE DEAD

NICOLE PEELER

Nicole Peeler became interested in Desiree Dumas, whom I introduced in *Living Dead in Dallas* through the memories of her friend
Bethany Rogers. Bethany and Desiree were roommates and col-
leagues at the Bat's Wing, a vampire bar in Dallas. In this story,
Desiree attempts to escape that life and the person it made her.

——————

As if trying to commit suicide by Chevy, a giant, hairy shape hurled itself
out of the darkness directly in front of my truck and collapsed. I stomped
on the brakes, squealing to a stop inches from the twitching body.

Taking a deep breath, I tasted burning rubber and the old-Dorito
tang of my own fear.

"Goddamn it!" I shouted, unsure whether to be angry or scared.
After a second, I decided I was angry. Hella angry. "What the fuck?"

Peering over my hood, unsure of what I'd nearly hit, I was relieved
to see fur—lots and lots of tan fur.

Not a person.

But also not moving. I waited another minute, my eyes never leaving the bits of animal illuminated by my headlights. When it didn't
budge, I shifted my battered pickup into reverse just enough to see the
thing fully.

"You have got to be shitting me," I said, to no one in particular. For
the creature on the pavement still shimmering-hot from an Arizona day
was a coyote, but larger than any I'd seen. It was the size of a small

bear, although unmistakably a coyote with its lean legs, tan and gray pelt, and long, sharp features.

It was also absolutely beat to shit.

Savage cuts marred its flanks and neck, as did deep bite marks. Something had given tearing out the animal's throat the good old college try, and had damned near succeeded. Down south, a huge hunk of flesh was missing from its haunch, and one hind paw looked mangled.

I knew what I had to do when I saw the coyote's bleeding sides rise once and then again in breaths full of pain. My cranky Cajun father had taught me everything I knew about the wild and about survival. And since, except for the odd Sunday church service his momma had dragged him to by the hair, he'd grown up as undomesticated as one of those feral children, his knowledge was considerable. One of his first lessons had been about never leaving an animal in pain when a body had the power to end its misery.

"Sometimes killing is a mercy," I heard my daddy say, his voice as clear as if he were sitting in my cab with me rather than lying in a crypt perched atop his beloved Louisiana bayou. Grabbing my shotgun from the gun rack behind my head, I opened my glove box to take out the box of regular ammo I kept stashed alongside the silver shot. Kicking out the expensive silver shells for regular, I cracked open my door. When the coyote didn't stir, I hopped down from the cab, shotgun trained on it.

I raised the gun, fitting it to me as casual and comfy as if I were scooching in under a lover's arm.

The coyote opened one golden eye, filmy with pain. It fixed on me just as my finger found the trigger.

And then the fucking thing shimmered, leaving in its place a naked man. One whom I recognized.

"Desiree?" he croaked in accented English through bloodied lips, before passing out cold.

I considered shooting Enrique Garcia anyway, for a number of reasons. One, for scaring the shit out of me. Two, for nearly fucking up my truck by running into it. And three, for forgetting ever to mention he was a motherfucking shapeshifter.

Instead, I loaded Ricky's bloody, unconscious body into the back of my truck, swearing at him the whole time. It took forever, what with him being so heavy, bloody, and naked. It was like wrestling a lubricated gator.

I really hated supernaturals.

That morning, Ricky had looked a lot prettier. As usual, he was waiting for me when I pulled in to the Super Gas-n-Go catty corner from the Mission. It didn't say much for our Arizona town of Milagro, so small it was known by locals as Migas, that our entire main street consisted of the Mission where Ricky lived, the gas station and convenience store at which I'd worked for the past year, and a small cafeteria that had closed about ten years before.

"Desiree Dumas," Ricky greeted me in his lilting English, pronouncing my full name as he did every morning. He'd told me once he liked the shape of it in his mouth, to which I'd responded with an eye roll, air-jacking an imaginary penis at him.

While my daddy had been a fine teacher when it came to survivalism, I'd missed out on the whole Miss Manners debutante thing.

But Ricky only laughed at the rude gesture, the tanned skin at the corners of his coffee-brown eyes crinkling in amusement.

That morning I'd pushed past Ricky to unlock the Gas-n-Go's door, surprised as I always was at the heat of him where he brushed against my arm. Another thing I'd had to get used to in the desert was how cool the nights were, despite the redonkulous temperatures of the day. But Ricky never seemed cold.

"I bring you *chaqueta*," he said, "for tonight."

I narrowed my eyes at his offer of a jacket. "You don't have to," I said. "I'll be fine."

He smiled, that wide wolf's grin of pleasure I saw in my dreams nowadays, more often than not. He had the teeth of a hunter, and it made the little girl-rabbit in my heart want to run so he would chase me all the way to bed. Not that I'd ever let him know I had a thing for boys with sharp teeth.

That had already gotten me in hella trouble, after all.

"I bring you *chaqueta*," he insisted. "I'll see you later." The last sentence was said carefully, Ricky practicing one of the new English phrases he'd picked up. He gave me another sharp smile before walking back to the Mission.

And I'd refused to feel any guilt as my eyes roamed down to his muscular ass, perfectly framed in a pair of tight jeans. A girl could look even if she had no intention of touching.

I put thoughts of Ricky aside as I made the coffee and unwrapped the shitty pastries we sold at the counter, placing them in the warming case that never got them very hot even as it managed to dry them to dust. I made sure there was toilet paper and soap in the bathrooms, turned on the television sets, did some light cleaning, and stocked the few shelves still empty from yesterday. Finally, I unlocked the door, flipping the *Closed* sign to *Open* before taking my place behind the counter.

Then I waited. And once again, my thoughts turned to Ricky.

Not getting involved, I reminded myself, after dwelling on his damned hands. They were huge—disproportionately large, like Hulk hands. I remembered them disturbingly well.

You're moving on again as soon as you have the money, I reminded myself.

But those hands, whimpered my ever-traitorous lady business.

Keeping my thoughts of Ricky from veering into X-rated, our usual morning customers finally made an appearance. Most were locals, picking up a pint of milk and a newspaper or a pack of smokes. They nodded at me but didn't take too much time to chitchat. Milagro, like many border towns, was a place of transience.

"Morning, Desiree," said Father Bryan McMahon, one of my favorite early visitors. He always came in to buy the paper and a chocolate milk, a little indulgence I appreciated in the otherwise straitlaced priest.

I rang up his purchases, looking up in surprise when he swore lightly.

"Damn vampires," he said.

I followed his gaze behind me to one of the televisions mounted in the corner. It showed the beautiful, undead countenance of Grace Ortega, the Arizona representative for the Bureau of Vampire Affairs, speaking animatedly into the camera. A few taps on the remote control taped to the counter beside the register and we could hear her cool, slightly accented voice explaining the BVA's newest endeavor.

". . . America's borders are our borders, Steve. We're citizens of this great nation, just like you and your viewers. We want to help the U.S. *stay* American, in accordance with our laws and the will of our fine people."

The camera cut to a lean blond man with a shark's smile and shiny Ken-doll hair.

"But what can a vampire do patrolling our nation's borders that a human patrolman can't?" Suddenly Grace and Steve were in split screen, indicating that now was the time on Fox News when someone had a showdown.

But instead Grace laughed, a preternatural tinkling that raised the hairs on my arms. "Oh, Steve," she said, as if he were the most charming creature she'd ever encountered. "Vampires can see in the dark, without needing any expensive night vision equipment. We are swift and silent, as you know. But we are not perfect. We can't work a day shift." Grace leaned forward coquettishly, and Steve, in his own studio millions of miles away, leaned forward as well.

Who can resist a vampire?

"We would never seek to take anyone's job, or to burden our government. Instead, we are offering our services free of charge to the American people, as a thank-you to our country that has welcomed and accepted us. Let us help our great nation keep her borders safe."

In his split-screen box, Steve's face had slowly morphed from tight-lipped and narrow-eyed to smiling and nodding. Grace had him hooked. Not so much Father Bryan.

"Those assholes," he muttered. I nodded my agreement, but he was on a roll. "What garbage logic is that? You've been welcomed into a society so you'll help cut off others? That's bullshit!"

"Easy, Father. This is on the house," I said, passing him a Danish. He blinked at it. "You know the vamps don't give a shit about the borders. They're just courting the Righties. Elections are coming up."

"Strange bedfellows," Father Bryan said, biting savagely into the Danish.

"There ain't nothing like hate to bring people together," I said. "And the vampires know the only thing almost as hated as them by the Righties are illegals. So the real bogeymen promise to keep out the imagined. It's sorta genius, really."

Father Bryan chewed through his Danish with the grim face of a soldier eating an MRE, watching me thoughtfully. Then he took a long pull from his chocolate milk, probably wishing it were something stronger.

"I didn't know you were interested in politics, Desiree. That was a very astute analysis."

"Yeah, well, I've got layers, Father. Like an onion. But I try to smell better." I knew I should probably be offended at Father Bryan's surprise that I wasn't a complete idiot, but being underestimated wasn't a bad thing. Especially when it came to getting one over on a man, or surprising an enemy, or running away from the insane vampire king who owned the bar in Texas where you'd been employed.

Father Bryan raised his chocolate milk in a toast. "You definitely don't smell like an onion. More like gasoline and coffee." I shook my fist at him in mock anger, and he grinned. "Not to change the subject, but Lupe would like you to come to dinner tomorrow night. She's making enchiladas."

My mouth watered. Ricky's younger half sister made the best enchiladas I'd ever tasted. She also knew I was less likely to tell her no than I was her brother. I liked Lupe. She was shy and sweet, and very obviously lonely.

"Sure," I said. "I can fix that sink while I'm there, too."

Father Bryan smiled gratefully. "You're a good lass, Desiree."

"Not really," I said, feeling Father Bryan's compliments like a cut, as I always did. "But I can fix your sink. Tell Lupe I'll be there."

Father Bryan said good-bye and walked back to his Mission. For the next few hours, I told myself I was only looking forward to Lupe's enchiladas and finally getting that sink fixed, not spending time with Ricky.

That had been this morning. But damned if I wasn't disappointed, despite telling myself I shouldn't care, when, for the first time since I'd met Ricky, I had closed the gas station alone. That evening he forgot to bring me his jacket.

Apparently, Ricky had also forgotten to mention he was a supe, which was a whole 'nother crawdad to boil. I only hoped I'd get the chance to put him in a little hot water, as I drove his broken body back to Father Bryan and the Mission they both called home.

Father Bryan answered the door after only a few minutes of my knocking, a pistol clenched in his white-knuckled grip.

"Delivery," I said, indicating the open flatbed behind me.

"Ricky?" Father Bryan ran to the young man. The Mission's two young Korean nuns, known by their Anglicized names of Maggie and Kate, stood in the doorway.

"What happened?" asked Sister Maggie, her English clipped but clear.

"He ran out in front of my truck, but I didn't hit him. He was like this already."

Father Bryan assessed Ricky with careful blue eyes, his once-red hair—now mostly silver—standing up like the quills of a put-upon porcupine. He was wearing pajamas under his buttoned-up black coat, a priest's collar working its way loose from underneath the lapels.

I grabbed my shotgun, already reloaded with silver shot, as Father Bryan and the nuns hauled Ricky out of my truck. Sister Maggie and

Sister Kate weren't squeamish at all around the naked, blood-encrusted body. Of course, having spent so much time with vampires, neither was I.

To my surprise, when we carried him into the well-lit chapel that was the first building of the Mission I saw that he didn't look nearly as bad as he had when I'd loaded him up.

He's not human, I reminded myself. *Shifters heal fast.*

As we carried him out the back door of the chapel and through the small courtyard that separated the Mission's public house of prayer from its private living quarters, one of the handful of children who had arrived last Friday night peered around a corner at us. An older woman pulled him back, and they soundlessly disappeared into the Mission's anterior rooms.

Not for the first time, I wondered who these rotating groups of people coming in and out of the Mission were, exactly. Now I had a hint, having seen Ricky change from coyote to human. A coyote was someone who helped illegal immigrants cross the border, and Ricky had always enjoyed a good pun, whether in English or Spanish.

"Was Lupe with him?" Father Bryan asked, disturbing my thoughts as we carried Ricky through the Mission house's big foyer and into the kitchen and dumped him on the wide trestle table. Sister Maggie went to the refrigerator, dragging from atop it a large red bag stitched with a white cross.

"I didn't see her." I watched the nun pull medical supplies from the bag. "Should I have?"

Father Bryan looked grim. "She went out with her brother tonight."

"Well, I didn't see anyone besides Ricky. Except . . ." I stopped, suddenly realizing that, if Lupe was a shapeshifter like her half brother, she could have been a bat sitting on a cactus for all I knew. But did Father Bryan know about Ricky? Shapeshifters had come out only recently, and maybe Ricky was still on the furry down-low.

Father Bryan's eyes went all squinty as he thought about his next words. "Was Ricky naked like this when you found him?"

Father Bryan was being as cagey as I was, and the question was leading enough that I decided to take a risk. "Less naked and more hairy. Possibly with paws."

Sister Kate looked up at us with inscrutable black eyes as she neatly threaded a needle. I looked quickly away.

"So you did see him." Father Bryan took a deep breath, studying my face. "Okay, well, as you now know, both Lupe and Ricky are shapeshifters." When I grimaced, his finger wagged under my nose. "But other than that, everything you know of them is true."

"It sure seems I don't know all that much, Father." I shivered, the words leaving me cold.

"You've known Ricky for months," Father Bryan said. "Lupe, too. They're the same people they always were."

I ignored his emphasis on the word *people*. "Ricky visited me sometimes. We were hardly besties."

That was untrue, of course. Ricky came around all the time, and he'd always been a real gentleman. He'd carry stuff for me or bring me lunch and bunches of wild desert flowers. And I'd liked his attention. Despite myself, I *had* wanted to know him better. I'd certainly wanted to know that strong body better, not to mention that golden skin and that hawklike Indian nose, prominent under straight black brows and eyes the deep brown of my *grand-mère*'s famed roux.

Now that I knew Ricky was a shifter, I wasn't sure how I felt about him.

"Sister," Father Bryan said to Maggie, "run and look for Lupe. Maybe she's returned. If she hasn't . . ." His words trailed off, his face stricken.

I swore for him, taking one for the team. I'd forgotten about Lupe in all the drama. I prayed she'd gotten away from whatever had hurt them. And, after seeing Ricky's wounds up close with him in human form, I had a pretty good idea of what he'd tangled with.

"I'm guessing there's a reason Ricky was a giant coyote? Maybe something to do with all your houseguests?"

Father Bryan's shoulders twitched.

"Ricky and Lupe were helping people," he said. "Their parents were killed by unscrupulous coyotes—the kind that get people over the border only to rob them. If the kids hadn't been able to shift and get away, they'd have been sold as slaves. All their parents wanted was a better life for their children, and they died for their pains."

"Wow, really? Both of them murdered?" I felt that information like a punch, right in the gut. I knew what it was like to lose your parents.

"Yes. Well, Ricky's mom passed away when he was a baby. But he was raised by his stepmom, Lupe's mother, who died that night alongside their father, both killed giving the children time to escape. That's why Ricky and Lupe do what they do."

Putting Ricky and Lupe's childhood suffering to the back of my mind to process later, I raised my hands. "Hey, I get it. I've lived here long enough to know that shit is complicated. But working as a coyote—shapeshifting coyote or human coyote or whatever—isn't exactly safe, especially considering the current political climate."

"Damned vampires," Father Bryan spat, for the second time that day.

I approached the patient on the table, keeping my eyes away from where Sister Kate was industriously sewing up Ricky's side. Examining the ugly wound at his neck, already neatly stitched, I pointed to the telltale marks.

"Looks like Ricky already got bit by the new Border Patrol," I said.

"Vampire did this?" asked Sister Kate in her lightly accented English, crossing herself when I nodded.

Father Bryan said, "After all the prejudice vamps have suffered, I can't see how they'd get in bed with the devil like this."

"Father, they're vampires. They *are* the devil."

It was his turn to cross himself. "But I don't understand why they'd attack Ricky."

"But wasn't he working as a coyote? Exactly the people the vampires are supposed to stop."

Father Bryan shook his head. "You don't understand. Ricky and Lupe liked the joke of shifting into coyotes, but they weren't bringing people over themselves. They were only helping people who had already crossed."

"Helping?"

"Yes. Ricky and Lupe would investigate rumors of coyotes selling their customers to slavers or robbing them. If the rumors were true, they'd rescue the people and bring them here."

"So the people always hanging around the Mission . . . ?"

"Are immigrants rescued by Lupe or Ricky, but always people already on this side of the border."

"Still, maybe the vamps who attacked Ricky and Lupe didn't get their little joke and mistook them for the real deal," I said.

"So where's Lupe?"

"*La raptaron,*" we heard whispered from the head of the table. Ricky, his eyes bright with pain, was struggling onto his elbows.

"*La raptaron,*" he repeated. Then, in English, "They have her."

"Who?" asked Father Bryan.

"*Los vampiros.*"

I swore, stroking my shotgun for comfort.

"They arrested her?" Father Bryan asked.

Ricky looked confused. "Arrest? No. Not *policía*. No uniforms."

I frowned. In order to be as in-your-face as possible, the Arizona vampires working the border wore the familiar Border Patrol uniforms, only done in smoky gray and black with large American flag patches on the left *and* right biceps. They were out to prove they were all-American vamps fighting for American values, even if some of them were older than the country itself.

At that point, I realized I needed to go. It didn't matter that I liked Ricky or his shy sister with her large doe eyes and small smile.

I stood up. "I've got to get something from my truck," I lied. "You, um, take care of Ricky." Father Bryan raised an eyebrow, but he didn't call me out.

"We will," he said. "Go with God."

Sister Kate didn't look up from where she was setting bones in Ricky's right foot, but the priest watched me with his piercing blue eyes as I turned on my heel, clutching my shotgun.

Sister Maggie burst back into the kitchen as I was leaving. "Lupe not here," she said. "She missing." I paused, hearing that, but lowered my head and kept walking.

I couldn't get involved. Not with vampires. Not again.

I got into my truck but didn't start the engine. Instead, my forehead flopped forward onto my steering wheel as I took a long, deep breath.

I'm making the right decision. I can't get involved.

To fortify myself, I plucked my old cell phone out of its holder on my dashboard. Then I did something I hadn't done since I left Texas over a year ago.

I opened up my photos.

The old Desiree grinned at me, fangs blazing in the flash of the camera. They were fake fangs, of course, but the two men flanking me in the photo sported the real deal.

Nicholas and Trey, my former lovers, and the former me.

Inspecting the photo, I had to admit I'd been hot. I'd always been a bit plump, but mostly in the right places. So my body seemed made for the corset cinching my waist, making my breasts sit like treats on a platter, ready to be tasted. My hair was bleached and long, rather than the natural honey brown it was now, cut much shorter to get the last of the blond off.

And those boys. I was as in love with Nicholas and his gorgeous protégé as any idiot in a made-for-TV movie. Trey, a newly turned vamp from Dallas, wasn't much older than I was, while Nicholas was as old as dirt. I'd thought the two of them loved me back, because I was just twenty-two and stupid as shit. Needless to say, stupid as shit and old as dirt made for a dangerous combination.

Meanwhile, my two Romeos were happy to take my blood and make me the ham in their hot man sandwich—memories of which still made my lady business flutter a bit, despite everything. But they never loved me.

I was food. Pretty, fun-loving food, but food nonetheless.

Scrolling through my photos, I remembered the triumph of getting that job at the Bat's Wing, one of the hottest vampire bars in Dallas—me, a girl from the bayou, whose daddy had taught her to cheat at poker, skin squirrels, make moonshine, and not much else. A daddy who'd died choking drunkenly on his own vomit, leaving her nothing. Despite all that, beautiful, immortal vampires had given me a glamorous job working the gift shop at their nightclub, and I'd been everybody's favorite.

Then I'd met Nicholas one night when I was helping out behind the bar, after another girl called in sick. I'd looked down to wipe a glass and when I'd looked up, he was there. "What is your name, *ma chère*?"

I was so proud of myself for not flinching at his sudden appearance. I'd thought I was getting used to vampires.

"Desiree, sir," I'd said, standing straighter, spine arching under his crazy-beautiful eyes. "And what can I get you?"

He'd ignored my question. "Your outfit becomes you." Tawny eyes swept over me, lingering at hips, waist, breasts. Cool approval shone on his face and my heart skipped a Disney beat, my own eyes tracing the curve of his lips, his patrician nose, the mop of golden curls that my fingers itched to touch.

Another vampire, a huge man with black hair who looked like a football player, ambled over to take a seat next to the blond. The blond's long white fingers touched those of the big man.

"I am Nicholas and this is my child, Trey. Trey, this is Desiree." Nicholas pronounced my name like a caress. My knees wobbled.

"Ma'am," said Trey, giving me an open, honest grin, the last vestige of the good country boy he'd been until quite recently.

They'd had me at hello.

I pushed aside those memories as my fingers numbly swept across the screen of my phone. So many photos of me with the two vamps. I stopped at one of the last, near the time I'd left.

The difference in my appearance was shocking. The plump girl was almost gone, my body working overtime to supply blood to two hungry vamps. My arms encircling the trim waists of Nick and Trey were much thinner, as was my neck, covered in scabrous bites that now looked barbaric to me, but of which I'd been so disgustingly proud.

Nick liked to leave his mark on me, he'd said, and I'd been so happy to be his.

And yet it wasn't the sight of my neck that got me; it was the girl in the background of the photo, carrying a tray loaded with bottles of TrueBlood: Bethany Rogers, my coworker and roommate, who would die the night that photo was taken.

It had been Bethany's death that got to me, finally. Of all the shit I'd seen—humans coming out of the john with no memory of when they'd gone in, vampires talking about us as if we were cattle, human boyfriends or girlfriends disappearing to visit mystery aunts or uncles and never returning—at Bethany's death I saw through the veil.

I guess that's called growing up. That moment when you see yourself for real, as opposed to how you think you are. When they found Bethany's body in that Dumpster, I suddenly realized I was about five minutes from my own ignominious death. That the missing men and women weren't visiting long-distance relatives, that vampires were killers, and that I was letting two beautiful demons drain me dry.

By that point, of course, I knew better than to up and quit. How many times had I seen human employees stomp into the manager's office, only to wander out, dazed? They'd appear the next night pleased as punch to work the job they'd sworn they were quitting the previous evening.

Why kill us, when we could be made to forget we were unhappy?

So for damned near three months I smiled, sold Bat's Wing T-shirts, and made love to Nick and Trey until the dawn broke when I'd saved just enough money to pack up my truck with a single suitcase of clothes and drive as far as I could that day, and the day after, and the day after that, until my money ran out. That had been over a year ago, and here I was. Ready to run again.

And I wasn't even sure why, really. There'd been no attempt to follow me. I'd heard through various channels that the vampire community in Texas had some serious trouble, and quite a few vamps died in a shooting. Maybe Nicholas and Trey were dead; they certainly hadn't come after me. So I wasn't sure whom, exactly, I thought I had to run from.

Except maybe that blond girl in the picture, looking so happy in the embrace of two lovers who could have killed her and not given a single solitary shit.

That Desiree was a rotten layer of my onion I sure hoped I'd carved out.

I turned off the phone and leaned back in my seat, brushing angrily at the tears that had formed in my eyes. I flipped my visor down to check my mascara in the mirror there, swore, and flipped it back up.

The desert was never dark when the moon had any heft to it, and tonight the landscape was lit like a strip mall parking lot so I could clearly see the puffs of sand kicking up quite a distance away.

Something was coming toward the Mission, and I doubted it was anything good.

I started the truck. If I left now and got right on the highway, I would be well away before the vamps arrived.

This isn't my fight, I reminded myself. *I've escaped all this shit.*

Ricky, Father Bryan, and Lupe be damned.

The puffs of sand kept coming, closer and closer. I made my decision and threw my truck into drive.

Father Bryan jumped when I kicked open the door that led from the foyer into the kitchen. Sister Kate didn't look up from where she was bandaging Ricky's foot, but Sister Maggie gave me a small, fierce smile.

I held the duffel bag in my right hand out to her, my movement limited by the shotgun cradled in my left. She came to take the bag, wincing at its weight.

"Company's coming. How's the patient?" Ricky moved his head at the sound of my voice but didn't open his eyes.

"Already healing, but he has a way to go," said Father Bryan, blanching as I began unpacking the duffel I normally kept hidden in a lockable hidey-hole above my wheel well. "Do you really think we'll need all that?"

I loaded the two service revolvers with silver bullets. "If we're dealing with vampires, yes. These won't kill them but it'll hurt a whole hell of a lot. Do you have silver for that gun I saw earlier?"

"No."

"Then take one of these." I passed him one of the guns. "Sisters, can you shoot?" The women shook their heads, so I threw each a can of silver aerosol, sticking the other revolver and my last can of silver mace into my belt.

Then I lifted the final item contained in the black duffel. It was my pride and joy, my baby, my most beloved possession.

She was a Stryker Strykezone compact crossbow. Her name was Lolita and she was powerful enough to bring down any wicked old wolf a nice young lady might meet in the woods.

But she was loaded with wooden bolts, all the better to kill a vampire with.

"You ever have vampire guests, Father?" I asked.

He was staring at the crossbow in horror, undoubtedly wondering who the hell I was, really. I felt that acute pang in my conscience that I often developed in his presence. I'd never told him about being a fang-banger, and I hated the idea of having to admit the truth once this was over.

Then again, we might all be dead in a few hours, so I couldn't worry about that now.

"Yes, once," he said, answering my question about vampire visitors. "Members of the new patrol coming to introduce themselves."

"Where were they able to enter? Think carefully, this is important."

"They came through the chapel, into the courtyard. Then they knocked on the main door." Father Bryan waved at the set of big double doors that led from the big entry room just off the kitchen into the courtyard.

"Did you have to invite them inside?"

He frowned. "I don't know if they came in at all . . . I'm sorry, I think they just stayed in the courtyard."

"Crap. Well, you've got a conundrum, here. The Mission is partially public, but it's also your home. So I'm not sure if the whole invite-only thing works for this place or not. Clearly the chapel and the courtyard are fair game, but hopefully they can't get into the main living area."

"Is house of God," Sister Maggie said, clutching the large crucifix at her neck. I shrugged.

"Doesn't matter, unless they're baby vamps. If they could come into the chapel, they can come in here. I've parked my pickup across the chapel doors. They'll have to move it before they can come in . . ."

Suddenly, from outside, we heard a huge crash, as if someone had flipped over, say, a junky, if reliable, Chevy truck. I grimaced and picked up Lolita, after passing the shotgun to Father Bryan.

"Your truck," said Sister Maggie, white faced.

"Fucking vampires," I swore, channeling Father Bryan. "Father, let me do the talking. Sister Kate, come with us. Sister Maggie, you stay with Ricky. I imagine it's him they want. Spray anyone you don't recognize, you hear me?" Sister Maggie nodded, clutching the aerosol can.

"No," said Ricky groggily. He struggled to sit upright, reopening the wound in his side. Setting down my crossbow, I rushed to push Ricky back down.

"Ricky, you gotta stay here. You're beat to shit."

"No," he said. *Mi hermana . . .*"

"I know, honey. And I'm'a do my best to get her back, okay? But you can't help. I know you want to . . ."

Ricky tried to sit up again and got pretty far with his supe strength, despite my pushing on both his shoulders. "Desiree, I help you, please."

I managed to shove hard enough to get him back on the table. "Ricky, you can't walk." I pointed down at his mangled foot. "Let us handle this. But you can protect Sister Maggie." I passed him the silver mace from my belt.

He glared at me. Sister Maggie took over for me, holding him down.

"Come out!" yelled a male voice from the courtyard. "Come out, come out, wherever you are!"

"I gotta go. We'll be fine and I'll get Lupe back." For a split second I let my hand rest against his cheek, forgetting he was a supe, remembering only the sweet boy who took the trash out for me every night.

And who had such killer cheekbones.

With a sigh I pulled myself away. I picked up Lolita, motioning for

Father Bryan and Sister Kate to follow. Together, we left the kitchen, closing the door behind us to walk toward the big main doors of the Mission's house. There, I pulled open the right-hand door's speakeasy-style grille and peered out cautiously. About fifty feet away, two vampires held a battered Lupe between them. Her clothes were dirty but intact, her hair falling over her eyes where she hung limply in her captors' arms.

"Howdy!"

I jumped back, looking away to keep from getting glamoured as a large gray eye popped up in the grille. The eye backed away, revealing a scruffy, pale face. I kept my gaze trained carefully on its chin.

"Don't look in his eyes," I warned my friends. "Anywhere you can shoot is fair game, but avoid the eyes."

"We found one of your shifters," the vampire said, indicating Lupe. "Which is perfect, as you seem to have some property that belongs to the man who hired us."

I looked over at Father Bryan, who shook his head in confusion.

"Lupe, you all right?" I called. The girl didn't move.

"She's kinda out of it," the vamp said. "We had to tranq her. Y'all understand—couldn't have her going all hairy on us."

"If you've touched her inappropriately, I will cut off your man parts and feed them to you," I said.

He laughed. "She's fine. We kept your property in fine fiddle, just like we know y'all did our boss's. To make our exchange real tidy-like."

"He must be talking about the group Ricky brought in last," Father Bryan whispered before I could tell him to shut up. Suddenly, the vampire's obscenely pink mouth was framed in the door's grille.

"Exactly. They don't belong to y'all. Or to us, actually. We're just doing a job, see, so nobody needs to get hurt." The vamp moved back from the door again.

I was pretty sure that, like most vamps, they weren't armed. And they obviously couldn't come into this part of the Mission without invitation, or they wouldn't be out here chattin'. They'd have ripped our throats out and called it a day.

Now that I could see the other players and had some inkling as to the cards they held, I made my decision.

Ready to turn and get this game started, I heard a noise from the kitchen that gave me pause.

"Fuck," I said. Assuming we'd been wrong and that the vamps had gotten into the house, I nearly shot Ricky when he hopped on one foot through the kitchen door into the foyer, Sister Maggie clinging to his waist and pleading with him to stop.

He wore only an apron and carried a jacket.

"*Hace frio*," he said, holding it out to me, his face set stubborn as an old mule's. Or a Cajun's. I knew I'd lost this battle.

"Thanks, Ricky," I said, moving to take the jacket from him. But instead of giving it to me, he held it open, helping me into it. He turned me around, zipping it with trembling fingers.

"Is my sister," he said, his pale face stricken. Before I could assure him I wouldn't let Lupe come to any harm, he cupped my jaw with one of those big hands I'd been dreaming about earlier.

"Is you," he said, his voice rough.

Hot tears pricked my vision. No one had cared if I got hurt for quite a while, and certainly no man.

"You sit here," I said, pushing him back to the low bench that sat next to the kitchen wall. "Keep your mace." I took it out of the apron pocket where he'd tucked it, wrapping his fingers around it. Looking deep into his pain-filled eyes, I told him the truth. "We need to talk when this is over, but we will. 'Cause it will be over and we'll both be fine. So will Lupe. You need to trust me, though. Okay?"

After a second, Ricky leaned his forehead against mine. Warm breath puffed against my lips as he spoke. "*Sí*, Desiree Dumas. Okay."

I nearly kissed him right then and there, but Daddy always said there was a time and place. He'd been talking about displaying taxidermy, but it was still good general advice.

"Good. Now, everyone back up and get ready," I said, straightening abruptly and moving to the big doors. My fingers felt clumsy as I unlocked them, swinging them open and backing up, all the while keeping a firm grip on my crossbow.

"There you are! I was getting worried y'all had forgotten about us!" the vamp shouted. In full view, he looked even shabbier. Ripped-up fatigues and an army-green shirt strained over his chubby belly and thighs, and his compadres weren't much better. They also looked rough, in old denim and faded tees.

"You're not Border Patrol," I said, starting to get a handle on the situation.

"Hell no, we ain't," said the leader, whom I deemed Fatty. "Like I said, we're just here to do a job. Your shifters have been giving my boss a hell of a time—taking his merch, messing up his deals. He's tired of it. But I'm a patient guy." He spit a pink gob into the sand at his feet. "And I get that we all gotta make a living. So I tell you what, you give us the group we're missing and we'll give you the girl. *If*"—he paused, picking at one long fang with a dirty fingernail—"y'all promise to stop interfering."

"We can't give them anyone," Father Bryan said, before I could stop him. Of course the vamps heard.

"Now, that would be unfortunate," said the fat vamp. "Because I'd hate to have Chip back there hurt your friend. Shifter blood is strong, though, so he'd not require too much encouragement." Fatty laughed and Chip grinned, pulling Lupe's head back by her hair to trail a finger down the girl's throat.

My eyes narrowed. "Unbunch your panties and don't touch her, ya hear? Now, you're telling me that all y'all want is your merch back, and a promise that we'll back off, and y'all will give us Lupe *and* leave both Lupe and Ricky alone?"

"Sure," Fatty said magnanimously. "It's a win/win situation I'm offering, girl."

"And how can I believe you?"

Fatty threw back his head and laughed. "You can't! But like I said—this is just a job. I ain't gonna risk my neck for a job."

Funny, that's the realization I'd had all that time ago at the Bat's Wing. And "risking my neck" had been just as literal then as it was now.

Father Bryan fidgeted beside me and I glanced at him. "Calm down, Father. And don't you dare go out there."

"But we can't give those people to them," he said. "They need to understand that. They need to listen. We're not . . ."

Chip's fingernails dug into Lupe's neck and she came around enough to let out a low whine. My grip on Lolita tightened and Father Bryan gasped. Then he handed the shotgun to Sister Kate and moved forward before I could stop him.

"Now, son," said the priest, stepping out of the Mission and into the moonlit courtyard.

"No," I howled, but it was too late. Fatty had Father Bryan by the throat, grinning at him with those horrible fangs gleaming.

"It seems you're not taking negotiations seriously," said Fatty. "But, despite my appearance, I am a serious person. Maybe you need a reminder of that?"

Father Bryan's shrill scream of pain was cut short by the fangs in his throat. Blood gushed red down his neck, soaking the white of his priest's collar. His eyes rolled in their sockets, wild with fear, finally settling on me, begging.

I heard my daddy's voice again that night, telling me just what I had to do. Raising the crossbow on my forearm, I sighted and fired.

Chip, having stepped away from Lupe just a fraction in anticipation of Fatty's strike, crumbled into dust. Before I could get another bolt loaded, the other vamp was holding Lupe, using her as a shield but otherwise unsure of what to do as I trained the reloaded crossbow on Fatty. He hissed at me over Father Bryan's bloody neck.

"You're going to stop drinking and put that priest down, you hear me?" I said. "Then you're going to heal his wounds, take your remaining minion, and get the fuck off my lawn."

Lawn was hardly an appropriate term for the patch of desert that was the Mission's courtyard, but it worked. Fatty raised his mouth from Father Bryan's neck, keeping the priest in front of him to fuck up my aim.

"And why would we do that?" Fatty asked. "Especially now that you've killed Chip. I think that means we should commence raping the shit out of you, until we decide to kill you."

I shook my head. "That's no way for a gentleman to behave, first of all. But you're not going to rape or kill me. Wanna hear why?"

Fatty cocked his head, as if indulging a slow child.

"Because if you make a move toward us, Lolita here'll kill at least one of you. Either you or your little cockroach over there. And Sister Kate here might not have wood in her gun, but she has silver, and anybody can hit the broad side of a barn with a shotgun. Since you're about as big as a barn, that much silver is gonna hurt mighty bad. Who knows, it might even kill you.

"So one of you is gonna die tonight, maybe both of you. And I believe you when you said y'all were just hired guns. Are you really gonna die for a job?"

"It's about more than money now, honey," said Fatty, licking obscenely at Father Bryan's dripping neck. "It's about reputation, and honor. A man has to able to look himself in the mirror when he shaves, you know?"

"Vampires don't shave," I clarified primly. "And even if you're not scared of me, I'm thinking that the Bureau of Vampire Affairs won't be happy y'all are hiring yourselves out to human traffickers when they're trying to make themselves look good for the upcoming elections."

Fatty laughed. "And who the fuck are you that the Bureau will know about our little operation?"

My daddy always taught me that if you played the ace in your sleeve and you got caught, then you only had one other option. Flip the fucking table over and start punching.

I flipped my fucking table over, knowing that by doing so, I'd be revealing my sordid, fangbanger past to all and sundry in attendance. But it couldn't be helped.

Forgive me my sins, Ricky, I thought. I knew at least Father Bryan and the nuns would have to, as forgiveness was part of their job description. But what would Ricky think of me when all this was over?

"Oh," I said, "I am *totally* nobody . . . except for one thing. I'm the favorite pet of Nicholas Le Grange, le Comte du Rhône. Nicholas *is* someone, I'm afraid. And he's real close to Stan Davis. You know Stan Davis?"

Fatty's pudgy face managed to get even whiter, a feat I appreciated. He did know Stan Davis, it seemed, and I was glad of that. Because I sure as hell didn't know Stan Davis well enough to call on him, and neither did Nick, not really. I'd been a mere human servant at Stan's bar, and Nick a problematic vampire nestmate with a penchant for turning underage high school quarterbacks. Also, I think the "Comte du Rhône" thing was something I read on a wine bottle.

But Fatty didn't have to know that.

"So, just to clarify, all I have to do is pull my phone out and make a call. Then this *nobody* will tell the BVA exactly what you fuckers are doing. I've heard vampire justice is swift and thorough. I'm sure y'all will enjoy it immensely."

Fatty glared at me. I never lowered my crossbow.

"Phone's in my back pocket, Sister Kate," I lied. It was in my truck, or what was left of it.

The nun's hand snaked toward my hip, keeping her eyes carefully on the ground to avoid Fatty's.

"Stop! Fine," he shouted. "This ain't fucking worth it." With a savage movement, he bit into his own wrist, rubbing it roughly over Father Bryan's throat. Then he dropped the priest, signaling the other vampire to do the same to Lupe. The girl fell to her knees, catching herself as her shifter blood finally began to metabolize the tranquilizer.

"Watch your back, girlie," said Fatty to me. "Because one night . . ."

"One night, if I disappear, y'all will find your name and description delivered directly to the bureau and to the human media, along with a thorough recounting of tonight's events. So I suggest y'all forget about me, forget about this Mission, and find a new line of work. Maybe in a new state, in case I decide to send those descriptions anyway, just to be on the safe side."

Fatty swore, spitting again. Then the two bloodsuckers were gone, ducking out with vampire speed.

I pulled Sister Kate back before she could run to Father Bryan.

"Go get us stools from the kitchen," I said to the nun. "He'll be fine. And we're going to sit here till sunrise, or until either Lupe or the good Father can drag the other's ass inside. In the meantime, we shoot anything that gets close to 'em, you hear me?"

Sister Kate nodded, wide-eyed. She'd obviously been surprised to hit the violent layer of my onion.

A lot of people were.

After Sister got me a chair, I risked a glimpse back at Ricky. He was slumped against the wall, asleep, his face ashen but peaceful.

Turning to guard my friends, I pulled his jacket close around me. I could smell him in the collar—soap and cologne and man—and it sure was cozy.

It was true that I didn't need it, I realized, keeping my crossbow trained into the darkness as Lupe and Father Bryan finally pulled themselves, together, over the Mission house's threshold.

But it was nice to have something keeping me warm on a cold desert night.

Creeping through darkened corridors, I bit back a squeal when a heavy hand fell on my shoulder.

"Taking advantage of a wounded man," said Father Bryan. "You should be ashamed of yourself."

"Don't sneak up on me like that!" I hissed.

"You owe me a confession or two, it seems. As does Ricky."

I blushed hotly, grateful the priest couldn't see me in the dark. "We're adults," I began, but he cut me off.

"And if you choose to spend the night playing Scrabble, it's none of my business. But maybe you can move your game-playing to your apartment when Ricky recovers fully."

"Got it," I said, wondering how a priest still had the power to make even a lapsed Catholic die of shame.

"I heard your truck's fixed," the priest said, backing up toward the window so I could see him in the moonlight. He was physically healed from the vampire attack, only a lot more silver hairs indicating his recent adventure.

"Yep," I said.

"Will you be moving on?"

I shrugged. "The truck was expensive, even with your help. I'll need to earn some more money."

"So you're just waiting on money?"

"Yes. Although maybe Milagro ain't so bad . . ."

Father Bryan smiled. "I thought it might be growing on you. Well, I'll leave you to the patient. Don't overtire him . . . playing chess, or whatever."

"Roger that," I said, pushing Ricky's door open.

I could hear his quiet breathing, deep and slow. He was asleep.

Stripping silently in the dark, I took my now-familiar place at his side. Without fully waking, he curled protectively around me. I sighed at the heat of his skin, so delightfully warm.

After a few very long talks, in which he told me the truth about himself, and I told him the truth about me, we'd forgiven each other. And then we'd made out like teenagers in a dark closet playing Seven Minutes in Heaven, but for, like, forever.

I hadn't spent a night alone in a few days now, which I appreciated.

"Desiree Dumas," he murmured in my ear, apparently more awake than I'd thought. Much more awake, I realized, as something extra hot and hard prodded at my hip. He snuffled at my hair, a shifter ritual I enjoyed now that I'd gotten used to it.

"Desiree Dumas," I affirmed, enjoying the roll of my name on my own tongue.

For at some point in the last week, helping Ricky, Lupe, and Father

Bryan recover from the attacks and guarding them in case the vamps returned, I'd learned a good lesson.

That if anything came after me—say a beautiful French vampire who'd discovered where his pet had got off to—I knew I needn't run.

After all, I had the fixin's of a truly Cajun happy endin': a good man, a crossbow named Lolita, and enough wooden bolts to protect myself and the people I loved.

Daddy would be proud.

EXTREME MAKEOVER VAMP EDITION

LEIGH EVANS

Leigh Evans's fancy was caught by Todd Seabrook and Bev Leveto, the vampire hosts of a reality show mentioned in *Dead and Gone*. The two fashionistas have never met their makeover match, until the night Eric Northman sends them to deal with the recluse of Vicksburg. Best friends Todd and Bev have their work cut out for them.

"You lead." Bev's gaze traveled over the outline of the old two-story house, taking in the broken slats of the shutters, the buildup of brush around the foundation.

Todd extended his hand to test the light Louisiana rain. "Why do I always have to go first?"

"Sweetie, what have I always told you?"

"Always moisturize before dawn?"

"Not that."

"Never have a midnight snack who's eaten lasagna?"

"No, silly." She gave him a hearty shove out of their custom-painted RV in the general direction of the front door. "Always lead with your best asset."

Todd streaked across the weed-choked yard at full speed—a long blur of dark hair and cream cashmere. Once he'd gained the relative shelter of the leaking porch, he twisted himself to stare at her. "Now what?"

Five years ago, maybe even three, she would have shaken her head in irritation at his constant need for direction. Now she simply mimed knocking.

"I wish we'd brought the camera crew," he said, after giving the warped wooden door an enthusiastic pounding. "I know this makeover is pro-boner but I don't see why we couldn't have brought them."

"Pro bono," Bev corrected. "And a vamp marriage ceremony is not for public consumption." *Though we would have killed in the ratings. The living love schmaltz.* She extended a manicured nail toward the gray hive hanging from the corner of the porch's roof. "Besides, there *are* cameras, Toddy. There's a small one hidden inside that wasp's nest."

She'd noticed the first one when they turned onto the dirt road. Admittedly, her powers of observation had been dulled by the languor of her self-induced starvation (a short-term deprivation due to the fact that they'd just finished a shoot and she'd met her mortal end smack-dab in the middle of her monthly period bloat). Malnourished or not, Bev's survival instincts had kicked in once she'd noticed the presence of a surveillance camera in the fork of the old oak tree. As a rule, a dere-lict house and a few acres of scrub didn't warrant the cost of security cameras. She'd quietly searched for others as her co-host painstakingly steered their RV around the worst of the driveway's potholes. By her count, the camera in the wasp's nest made four.

"It's a camera? Really?" Todd spun around, completely intrigued.

That was both the downside and joy of Toddy. Since he had the attention span of a teenager with a remote control and a thousand channels, he greeted each new experience without the been-there, done-that ennui of most vamps his age. Agreed, it was a virtue set by default. His long-term memory was full of holes; thus most things *were* new to Toddy.

His maker had never bothered to perform an intelligence test before he turned the handsome farm boy with the dimples and flashing teeth into an immortal.

"See the red recording light?" Bev asked.

Todd strained on his toes to get a better look. "Peaches, it *is* a camera!"

he said with delight. For the benefit of the device—Toddy loved *any* camera—he bestowed upon it one of his widest smiles. "Hello, Liara Giacona! I'm Todd Seabrook and this is Bev Leveto." Then he paused (because she'd drilled into him that timing was everything) before delivering what they called the "Come to Vlad" kicker. "And we're from the hit show *The Best Dressed Vamp*. We're here to uncover your true beauty!"

Dead silence from the house.

"I don't think she's home," Todd whispered.

"Oh, she's home."

"How do you know?"

"Our bride-to-be is a recluse." Bev crossed her arms, mentally recalculating their timetable. "Where else would she be but inside? Reclusing?"

For the seventh time since they'd left Shreveport, Todd said, "I wonder who the groom is. It has to be someone well connected for Eric to call in such a big favor."

Bev set her expression to "squash"—dark eyes narrowed until her thick lashes almost tangled, thin cheeks sucked in until the soft inside brushed against the hard plastic of her flipper. It was askew again. She willed her left fang to retract, then nudged her dental device back in its proper place with the tip of her tongue. Hunger and flippers, two things that constantly worked against each other.

Beauty never came cheap.

"Toddy," she said for the eighth time since they left Shreveport, "remember that nothing matters beyond the makeover. That's what we do. We make ugly people beautiful. Everything else is a detail. And we don't—"

"Like details," finished Toddy.

She was giving him the atta-boy nod when something fluttered in her peripheral vision.

"Toddy," she whispered. "There's something behind you. Don't kill it, okay?"

Ever since "the incident"—or as Toddy called it, "when that psycho bitch tried to kill me"—her co-host had been a trifle twitchy.

Three things happened next. Toddy spun around, the porch lights flickered on and off, and Bev felt the first stirring of real curiosity since the moment Eric had summoned them to Louisiana to perform a hasty makeover on the recluse of Vicksburg.

Showmanship. Now, that was something Bev admired.

A semitransparent figure was doing the dance of the seven veils in one of the downstairs dark windows. As visions of Gothic horror go, it was a humdinger: female, Medusa hair, wearing what looked like a cat-shredded muumuu.

"Goooooo awaaaaaaay," the thing moaned. "Gooooooo now!"

Todd's eyes bugged. "Our makeover's a ghost?"

"Now, what would be the point of that?" Bev reached for her box of tricks. "Sweetie, the woman lives alone and has no one to watch her back. She has to have some sort of alarm system to keep the squatters out of her place during the daylight hours. It's nothing more than an illusion, probably done with mirrors."

"Go awaaaaay!" howled the apparition.

"Not going to happen, Liara!" Careful of her heels, Bev picked her way across the soggy ground.

"I already don't like her," Todd muttered when she joined him on the porch.

"Eyes on the prize, Toddy." Bev set her case down. She'd come loaded for bear, filling her sturdy tool kit with fourteen shades of blush, two dozen bottles of thick foundation, every conceivable shade of eye shadow, superglue, latex, and several types of tape. You never knew who needed a rib or two broken to fit into the perfect dress.

"Liara Giacona," she said, in a clear, firm—*always be firm*—voice. "Before sunrise, you will be brought to Fangtasia. You will arrive there begowned and bedazzled. Your makeup will be divine, your imperfections well camouflaged, and your booty—should it require help—will be as high and round as the best shapewear can make it. When you meet your groom, I can promise you that you will look absolutely radiant, even if we need to glue a smile to your lips."

"Leaaaaave here," intoned the apparition.

"You wish." Bev unzipped her shoulder purse to extract a sealed envelope. "Since you've chosen to ignore his e-mails, Eric has directed me to hand you this communiqué reminding you of your debt to him."

"All debts are paaaaaid."

"Well, brace yourself, cookie. Now that Felipe de Castro's made his move, old debts are being shifted between vamps faster than a Vegas cardsharp shuffling aces into the pack. Eric's called in all of our markers and here we are."

"Told you we shouldn't have taken his money for the flipper start-up," said Todd.

"Not in front of the makeover candidate," she murmured, her lips barely moving. Though now that the question was raised, Bev found herself briefly wondering what possible political benefit Eric could earn by connecting a Louisiana recluse to one of Felipe's new boys.

A moth fluttered toward the wasp's nest, drawn to the camera's red eye. *Details.* Bev gave herself an internal shake and went back to business. "Liara, we're here to make you pretty."

"Go awaa—"

"Oh, for Pete's sake." Bev passed the envelope to Todd. "Open it and hold the letter up to the camera so she can read it."

"I wish you'd let me kill the spook," said Todd, removing the sheet of paper. Lips set in a snarl that in no way diminished his beauty, he held Eric's missive up to the wasp's nest.

The window's ghostly apparition winked out.

And stayed out. Bev checked her watch. Eight hours until dawn. "Heads will roll if we don't get this done in time," she muttered.

Either Liara was an achingly slow reader, or she was choking over the contents of Eric's missive. Curiosity tugging again, Bev edged sideways to read the letter over Todd's shoulder. *Dear Liara*, it began, prosaically enough. It wasn't until paragraph two that Bev's gut plummeted.

Him? Liara was to be Anton Van D.'s consort? Bev's brain—the one part of her that was demonstrably still alive—hiccupped. *Not him.* She read it again. Yes. There it was in black and white. Anton Van D. was to wed the recluse of Vicksburg.

Bev's path hadn't crossed his since Hoover's party. When was that? Before or after Kennedy? She couldn't remember but it didn't matter. She could recall the room, the dresses, the pool of people circulating the room—minnows unaware of the very hungry shark. She'd been leaning against the wall, debating the wisdom of informing J. Edgar that the rigid girdle under that sateen horror of a dress had been a terrible mistake, when she'd heard Anton's laugh.

Light. Mocking.

She'd left right away. True, she'd stopped to snag a diplomat as a consolation prize before she sailed through J. Edgar's door, but still— she'd left without pausing to acknowledge Van D.'s existence with so much as a polite nod.

And now, Eric had tasked her with prettying *his* bride.

Oh, the irony.

Todd glanced at the paper, then asked casually, "Whose head will roll?"

"Ours," she said faintly.

"Oh hell no." The paper fluttered to the porch as Todd spun on his heel. One hard kick and the rickety door was reduced to splinters. He skipped over the debris littering the threshold while Bev bent to retrieve Eric's note.

The moth followed, fluttering into the hallway to strike up a flirtation with the single, bare lightbulb.

"You listen here, missy!" Todd put his hands on his hips. "I have not lived through five centuries of war, plagues, and stake-happy villagers just to lose it all over a vamp who's too dumb to take advantage of my fashion sense! We can transform you! We *will* transform you!"

Her co-host's spiel was delivered to the moth, a mouse quivering under the floorboard, and not a great deal more. The living room appeared deserted, as was the attached dining room and Formica-proud kitchen. All three rooms were fastidiously clean.

And empty of one Liara Giacona.

"I'll find her," Todd promised.

Bev's nod was at best abstract. She smoothed Eric's letter carefully before folding it into a precise square. Maybe she'd use it for target practice later. After she'd made a fashion-backward recluse into a bride worthy of Anton Van D.'s appreciation.

Toddy did his best. No cupboard was left unopened, no bed left unturned. Shoulders slumped, he descended the stairs. "Well, I got nothing. I can't find her anywhere."

Reminding herself that *everything else was a detail*, Bev stepped into the hall and inhaled. The stale air carried the faintly dry smell of an old female vampire, but it was missing one vital tooth-taunting scent.

Her co-host sampled the air, too, his brow crumpled. "What's wrong?"

"I can't smell any fresh blood," she said. Old vamps usually preferred their meals warm and organic. But the only scent of nourishment present in this house was the chemical hint of TrueBlood. The aroma was the most pungent in the old-fashioned parlor, over by the back wall, near the easy chair that sulked under the flimsy weight of a truly ugly antimacassar.

Bev removed the crocheted dust catcher with a grimace.

This was where Liara spent her nights? This lumpy chair positioned to face an old portable TV? How did she stand the quiet? The lack of lights and company? The set was on, its screen streaming a surveillance video feed of the backyard. A remote rested on the side table beside a deck of cards.

"This place reminds me of somewhere." Bev turned to reexamine the fireplace mantel with its matching brass candlesticks, the standing lamp with its bobble-trimmed shade, the spindle-legged dining table. Incongruous were the other, far less obvious details—the little pinhole projector over the window, the motion detector alarm, the water sprinklers in all of the rooms.

"What about that nursing home in Miami?" Todd said, after a deep think. "All those scotch mints and menthol anti-inflammatory creams?"

Bev nodded, though she thought he was wrong. The place felt more

like a movie set. *Arsenic and Old Lace* or some thirties B film. Its hom-
iness felt staged.

Toddy picked up the TV's clicker and began testing how well the
power button worked. On. Off. On. Off.

"Sweetie," she murmured, holding out her hand.

He dropped it into her palm and she turned to place it back on the
table. That was when she noticed a thick tome jammed between the
chair's cushions. It was both expensive and heavy: an art book filled
with images of jewel-toned Renaissance paintings. She picked it up and
had to work hard to suppress a shudder when the book automatically
fell open to a page of belly-rolled nudes.

"Ew," said Toddy, peering over her shoulder.

"Double ew," she agreed, flicking past pages and pages of women
with apple-sized breasts and meaty thighs.

"Maybe she's a lesbian," said Toddy. "That's her porn and she
doesn't want to be debutched for any guy."

"And maybe she likes art. Or she's agoraphobic. Or maybe she
thinks she's Helen of Troy and she doesn't need our help." Bev dropped
the book to the floor. "I don't care. All I want to do is finish this job
and head back to New York."

Liara's home decorating efforts were getting on Bev's nerves. The
only thing remotely tasteful in the place was the long rectangular mirror mounted on the wall behind her favorite chair.

As was her habit, Bev checked her reflection.

Damn.

Humidity was trying to restore her blond hair to its original,
crimped permanent wave. Excellent. She was going to stink like a sales-
clerk from Target for the rest of the night because Toddy had emptied
the last can of unscented hair spray on yesterday's makeover. Maybe
she should hit it now with another layer of lacquer before it became
unmanageable? Her gaze started to slide toward the doorway, then
stalled. There was a mess of fingerprints on the mirror's beveled edge. A
line of them, as if someone habitually grabbed one side of the mirror's

ornate metal frame. Oddly placed, those grubby marks. The rest of the glass was clean, except for that cluster of smudges at approximately hip level. Now, why would someone . . .

This Liara woman is devious.

"Toddy, I think this mirror is a two-way." She tested her theory by tugging on the edge of the frame. A piece of wood splintered off, but the mirror didn't so much as shiver on its mooring. "Yes, it is. She's hiding behind a false wall."

Todd floated over. "You're kidding."

"Not this time." Bev tucked the offending lock of hair behind her ear. Perfection nearly reinstated, she scratched the polished glass with her sharp nail. "Come out, come out, wherever you are."

"I don't think so," Liara replied from the other side of the wall.

"Yours is not to think." Bev turned, searching for the source of the voice, and finding it in a small speaker that she'd dismissed as an air grate. "Yours is just to do. In this case, hold perfectly still while we throw some curlers in your hair and take a hedge trimmer to your eyebrows."

"Why would I want to do that?"

"Because I've seen your picture." A small fabrication. The image in question had been a frustratingly unfocused shot taken at a gathering of Louisiana vamps. Eric had tapped his finger on a dark-haired woman, half-hidden behind two very large males, and said, "That's her in the sweats."

Yes, *sweats.*

Try as she might, Bev hadn't been able to pick out one distinguishing feature that could turn the toadstool into the temptress. Did Liara have great hair? Fine eyes? Who could tell from that blurred photo? Liara's hair had been scraped back, and her face was a pale blur, save for a pair of thick, dark brows. "Darling, it's time to shuck you out of your sweats and let your inner goddess shine."

"Why don't you buzz off? I have no intention of coming out."

Toddy pulled his lips back to show all his teeth.

In her line of work, Bev had run into a few reluctant vampire brides and grooms. But eventually, they all came around to going through the rites of the ceremony in relatively good grace because they knew marriages between their kind weren't always love matches. All too frequently, they were the results of credits owed and debits balanced.

But this vampire was saying no. Flat out. Not only to her obligations to Eric, but to Van D.—the same misbegotten son of a bitch who'd dallied with a chorus girl named Bev through an entire off-Broadway season of *Kiss Me, Kate*.

"You want me to break down the wall?" asked Toddy.

"Not yet," she replied.

Serves you right, Van D.

Five months they'd had together. Anton had taught her lots—like how to test a pearl for quality and how to hone her personal taste until it was sharp as a stiletto. And mostly, they'd had fun and naughty times until the night he'd returned home with takeout and her refusal to eat (she had an audition the next day) had culminated in an absurd and final argument about how it was all in her mind; she didn't look any thinner when she starved herself. She'd snapped back, and he'd huffed off. Leaving Bev to deal with the next month's rent, a dead human, and the curious feeling that she somehow hadn't measured up.

"Stand back," said Todd. "I'll break the mirror."

"Not this time." Bev made a fist, then punched the wall with all the anger she'd kept locked inside her since the night she lost that part to Bernadette Peters. Perhaps with a little too much force. On impact, plaster pulverized.

"Peaches!" Toddy exclaimed.

Teeth clenched, she cradled her throbbing hand while her bones knitted back together and visibility was restored. When the dust settled into a ground-level haze, Bev inhaled in shock.

"What is it?" inquired Todd. "Did you ruin your manicure?"

Her assault had left a large jagged hole in the plaster, exposing a wall behind a wall. The latter was gray, smooth, and metallic.

"That's not a false wall," she said. "It's a *safe* room."

Todd had done as Todd was prone to do—act first, think last. Diverted by the thought of a secret room, he'd forgotten about the splendor of his attire and attacked the rest of the wall with all the enthusiasm of a sunburned kid peeling off a layer of dead skin.

He stepped away, dusting his hands. "That's a big safe room."

That's an understatement, Bev thought, her gaze moving along the sixteen feet of exposed steel wall. She opened the window and leaned out to see how far back it went. The building extended another ten feet, maybe eight.

"It must have cost a fortune," she said, as much to herself as to Toddy.

"Forty grand and the lives of the three mortals who knew of its existence," crowed Liara through her speaker.

Bev eased herself back into the room. "Well, bless your heart. It must be nice to be so rich."

"Four words," said Liara. "Buy low. Sell high."

Todd fussed with his cuticle while Bev prowled the length of the wall. She gave it an experimental slap. "There's always a way in. Like a button or something."

Eyes gleaming, her production partner pivoted. "Like a secret switch? A book or a . . ." He zipped over to the fireplace mantel. The candlestick on the left end was briefly examined, then tossed. Likewise the taper on the right. Once set on a task, Toddy was gratifyingly OCD. Ever helpful, he picked up everything in the room that could be possibly lifted and tweaked anything that could be possibly tweaked.

"Stop messing up my house," Liara shouted through the speaker.

While her roommate explored, Bev eased aside the panel of polyester drapes flanking the window near the mirror. As she'd suspected, the lock to Liara's lair was hidden behind them. Mounted at hip height, it was surprisingly small—she'd anticipated a keypad or maybe a big fat red panic button. But there were no buttons, just a small, card-sized, flat touch screen.

"Shoot," she said. "She has a fingerprint scanner."

Todd dropped the vase he was on the point of shattering against the wall. "This is like a Bond movie," he cried, thoroughly charmed. He zipped across the room, then leaned over her shoulder to press his thumb on the pressure pad.

Nothing happened.

"I'll go get my Glock."

"This is not a mailbox, Toddy. Destroying it will only jam the door lock."

Her friend worried his lip between his teeth. Except for the copier that sat on the counter in the RV—he liked to take imprints of his face and other parts of his anatomy—Toddy was a trifle intimidated by electronics. "Maybe I'll go look around the house. See if I can find anything that will help."

"You do that." She dusted off the chair's arm before she lowered herself to it and crossed her legs. Neatly, on an angle, so as best to display their length. Then she focused on the pressure pad, thinking hard. There's always a way in; you just have to find the right lever.

Liara spoke. "I'm perfectly comfortable in here."

"I know that."

"And those walls aren't steel," called Liara. "Tell your gun-happy dimwit that they're Kevlar." Then she chuckled nastily. "You're never getting me out of here."

Bev was formulating a perfectly wonderful reply when she caught the smell of burning kerosene. "Toddy, nooooooo!"

"What?" Todd skidded back into the room, carrying high his version of the Olympic flame—a kitchen broom, well wrapped with kerosene-doused rags, that he'd set alight.

"Put it out!" Bev shouted.

He cocked his beautiful, empty head. "Why?"

"Because of that!"

It was almost like the water sprinkler had been waiting to be introduced. No sooner had she jabbed a finger at it than it stuttered to life.

Water whipped—horizontal, vertical, *everywhere*—from its nozzle head. She could have counted each elongated drop of nasty wetness had she not been so busy screaming directions. "Cut the power!"

"How?" he shouted.

"Go outside and find the electrical box!"

Todd and his smoking Olympic flame fled the room. "Box, box, box," she heard him dither before the lights went off and the deluge from hell abruptly ceased.

He skulked back into the room. "Peaches?"

Bev stared at the puddle by her knee for a moment, working up some calm. Then she lowered the seat cushion she'd used as a shield and asked a stupid question. "What were you thinking?"

"That we'd burn her out." Toddy lifted a tense shoulder. "You know. Like the old days . . . Burn him! Burn him!" He chewed on the inside of his cheek for a moment of deep reflection. "You're really wet, Bev."

She didn't have to glance down to confirm that, though she did. Her merino wool skirt, bought with the aim of outlining her taut thighs, clung like stretched cling wrap. She touched her hair, relieved to discover that its roots were mostly dry.

A small grace, because Liara's *heh-heh-heh*s were eating through her spine.

Bev eyed Todd fretting over a scorch on the edge of his sleeve. "It wasn't a terrible idea, Toddy. But what we really need is something like a blowtorch. Why don't you go get us one? Some farmer has to have one in his shed." She waved her hand vaguely, hoping that he'd have to fly all the way back to that welding shop they'd passed in Natchitoches to find one. "Off you go."

"That's a great idea," said Todd with relief.

"I'm just full of them." Once he'd left on the mission that would hopefully keep him out of her hair for the next hour, she went into the hall to retrieve her tool kit. When she returned, her teeth were set as tightly as a Vegas showgirl balancing sixty pounds of feathers on top of her head.

"Your spray tan is running," snickered the recluse of Vicksburg.

Refusing to flinch (though good golly, she wanted to), Bev placed her box of magic on the side table. "Yuk it up, Liara. The full replacement cost of my Stella McCartney jacket is going on the expense account. And if I know Eric, he'll expect you to reimburse him for every penny we have to spend on your transformation."

"Hah," said Liara.

Bev lifted the top tier up and out until all four trays were splayed open like a stretched accordion. "If I were you, I'd be more worried about angering Eric. He's facing a lot of pressure from the King of Nevada. He's using every connection he has to survive, and he's not going to tolerate you digging in your heels."

Liara's speakers really were top notch. Bev could hear her unscrew something with a twist top as acutely as if she were standing beside her.

"Eric's got people, but I've got better people," the woman replied. "And my people like what my investment advice does to their portfolios." From the speaker came the distinct sound of something thick and viscous being poured into a glass. "In the end, you'll find that money talks louder than his old-world connections. Besides, I covered the short in Eric's account yesterday. If he'd looked, he would have seen that. I don't owe him a penny, so he's got nothing on me. You go back and tell him I'm not going to jump just because he snapped his fingers."

Bev's fangs ached to extend. She removed her flipper and placed it inside one of the trays. One only needs to consume enough blood to survive, she reminded herself. A mouthful or two, every other day.

"So," said Liara, in a voice that was suddenly flat and hard. "Why don't you take your pretty boy and your fancy RV and just go? I've lived under siege before. I've got enough TrueBlood in here to outlast the next presidency."

Resolutely, Bev turned to the mirror. Droplets of water beaded it. Deadpanned—as if the sight of her rat-tailed hair didn't pain her—she inhaled until her empty lungs were filled and her cheeks were hollow. Then, pursing her rouged lips, she blew a thin stream of cold, dead air.

Right where a line of fingerprints marred the mirror's finish.

"You going to huff and puff until these Kevlar walls blow down?"

Liara chuckled and then took a deliberately noisy, long swallow of her drink.

Bev silently cursed the quality of the sound system as her fangs extended with a slick *snick*. But she kept going—blowing on that polished glass as if her sharp canines hadn't just pierced her bottom lip—expelling air until its surface was as dry as her throat and all that came from her puckered mouth was a pitiful whistle.

Her tongue nipped out to tidy her mouth as she studied the mirror. Bev smiled. Amid the smear of prints was one perfect thumbprint.

"You're going to discover that I don't give up easily," she lisped, turning back to her box of tricks. "By the time we leave here, you're going to be beautiful."

"What if I'm already beautiful?" Liara asked after a few seconds of silence.

"I'll be the final decision on that."

"Who crowned you Fashion Queen?"

"The former queen, of course." Once dumped by Van D., Bev had set upon refining her personal sense of style with a vengeance. She'd studied, she'd sacrificed. For crying out loud, she'd endured nine months as Joan Crawford's dresser, just to get close to Edith Head. Every single night had been a terrible ordeal, during which she'd silently suffered, clamping down on the acute temptation to drain the opinionated actress drier than the Mojave Desert. But in the end, her self-discipline had proven to be worth it. Edith had become an acquaintance and then a mentor.

Now Bev knew style.

No—now Bev *was* style.

She selected a pot of eye shadow. "Fortunately for you, I have learned from the best." She deftly loaded the sable end of her fattest blush brush with a light measure of Dior's finest taupe. "Unlike you, who wouldn't know what to do with a tube of lipstick if one were thrust into your hand."

"That's not true. They make wonderful markers." Somewhere inside the bunker, Liara placed her glass on a table with enough force for Bev to recognize the chink of crystal. "So tell me about this dude that Eric and his king want me to marry."

"He's a vampire of discerning taste."

"So, you know him?"

"I've met him once or twice."

"A Swede like Eric? Tall and blond?"

"No, he's dark and short." In fact, by modern standards, he was Lilliputian. But if one had looked—and Bev had gazed long and hard at him before his roguish eyes had turned in her direction—his lack of vertical inches was a minor issue. His body was well made, lightly muscled, well proportioned. Tousled hair with auburn highlights. A carefully tended goatee that drew the eye to his wicked lips.

He'd been the good thing that came in a small package.

Until he wasn't.

Bev bent forward to delicately tap the powder-loaded brush onto the thumbprint.

"Well, now I'm all a-quiver to meet him." Liara poured another measure into her glass. *Glug, glug, glug.* "So, give me more details. What type of man is he?"

"He's elegance personified." Though, when she'd known him, he'd had a weakness for velvet. Which, on reflection, now seemed a tad outré. What would Edith have said about his velvet-trimmed collars?

"No. What's he like as a person?"

He's alive. The thought slipped in so quickly, she didn't have time to edit it. That was what had drawn Bev to him. Despite his age—Anton had seen the Renaissance period—he still had the smallest flicker of life inside him when she'd met him in the middle of the last century. She hadn't read ennui on his face, only curiosity and a restless need to move. Through his eyes, she'd seen things. Like, for instance, the perfection of a well-drawn line.

Toddy reminded her of him, in a way. Toddy didn't care much for art—at least not the type that hung in galleries—but his whole body would tighten when he spied a well-executed design. Come fashion week, he'd study the runway photos with the fixed concentration of a nuclear physicist teasing apart a problem of relativity. And let's not forget the tears—sudden and touching—that had welled in Toddy's blue eyes the day she'd presented him with tickets for the Alexander McQueen retrospective. Yes, her Toddy understood art.

Bev carefully blew the excess dust off of the glass. "Anton Van D. is an old vampire," she said, sidestepping Liara's question. "Need I say I more?"

"You wouldn't have made a dime selling shoes."

Bev found the tape, cut a length, then considered just how to position it over the dusted print.

"That doofus you hang around with is a lot of work. Letting some vamp slash his neck on prime-time television? He made you look bad. You should have handed him his paycheck that night and called it quits."

Ignorant, ugly, *stupid* woman. Bev slapped the tape down. "He's got great taste."

"He's dumb."

"He's useful." And he was. In his own way. Come morning, when the faint pink of a new dawn rimmed the horizon, Bev was confident that she'd be sitting cross-legged on her bed in the RV, watching Toddy clean their makeup brushes. And when her lids could no longer stay open, she knew Toddy would say, "Bedtime, Peaches." Then he'd seal the door and activate the metal shutters, and lie down beside her. They'd talk. About where hemlines should go, or whether they should improve on their test flippers or just give up on that venture and invent a brand-new tooth paint that would successfully whiten some of those old vamps' yellow teeth. They'd talk until she mumbled. Then Toddy would twine his pinkie around hers, and she'd feel safe to close her eyes.

And she'd sleep.

Without dreaming of stage lights, or men with cruel smiles.

"What are you doing?" Liara asked with an edge.

"Getting ready to lift your prints."

"You're presuming that getting that door open is all you need to do to pry me out of this room."

"There is no such thing as an impenetrable defense." Bev teased the tape's edge with her nail. "All you have to do is keep rooting around until you find the right leverage."

"What's yours?"

Fear of being alone. She'd never thought of her Achilles' heel as being leverage, but she supposed it was. It was the sharp-pointed triangle on which her life balanced.

The motion detectors went off again and light flooded the back garden. Bev flicked a hurried glance to the window. Todd was floating outside, his teeth flashing. He lifted his burden so that she could see it. "Isn't it great?" he said. "I got it from the neighbor's garage."

"It's marvelous," she said, intent on the job.

"I got the key to this sardine can," Toddy hooted. With a flash of teeth, her friend pulled the rip cord and the chain saw buzzed to life. He whooshed upward. A moment later metal teeth began to chew through the second floor.

Machine tools and Toddy. Another poor combination.

"Just another second," she murmured to herself.

The tape lifted, thumbprint intact, at precisely the point of catastrophe.

From Bev's point of view, there was no real warning. She'd lived through natural disasters; she knew to duck for cover when the joists creaked over her head. But who could hear anything over the buzz of a chain saw?

The ceiling collapsed on top of her in a shower of wallboard, dirt, and splintered aged wood. It didn't hurt. It wasn't a fraction as painful as the time she got cornered by the small mob in that one-horse town in the Midwest.

But she was covered with ceiling stuff. Hunks of broken wallboard and a hundred years of accumulated dust. Grit—dry as a dead vampire's ashes—coated her fangs. Once again, Bev waited for the cloud of dust to settle, then looked upward. Todd floated above her, a horrified look on his face. She drew her finger across her throat.

The chain saw cut out. It would have been silent—it *should* have been silent—except Liara's guffaws seemed to fill the room.

"You okay, Peaches?" Todd asked in a small voice.

She didn't reply, as she was intent on pulling a strand of ash-coated hair from the corner of her mouth.

"I thought it would—"

"Shh!" she hissed. She toed aside the desiccated corpse of a long-dead squirrel, then picked her way carefully across the minefield of broken timbers. Using the sleeve of her $2,500 jacket, she wiped the glass clean and gave in to the inclination to rest her forearm against the glass. A moment later, her head drooped to the crook of her elbow.

"Did your maker ever talk to you before he made you into his child?" she asked over Liara's cackles. "Did he spend any time getting to know you?"

"None."

"I thought so. If he'd any inkling into what type of stubborn witch you were, he'd never have made you immortal."

"That's what I thought. But he was another dickhead who only saw the surface of things. He saw me, he wanted me, he took me. He got his, though. The jerk never made it past the French Revolution. Did he have enough smarts to ditch the powdered wig? No, he kept walking up and down the Versailles Hall of Mirrors, thinking he could glamour a crowd of peasants hoisting hoes. I learned a lot from him. Either blend in or hide."

Bev's fist tightened on the piece of tape. "When did you stop trying to blend in?"

"When it got too hard. When I got too tired of feeling like I was running in a marathon that had no winner's tape. A girl needs to be . . ."

Appreciated, thought Bev.

"A girl needs to claim herself. Be real," said Liara. "At some point or another she has got to stop apologizing to the world for being who she is."

"What a marvelous sentiment." Bev, the ex–chorus girl, straightened. "Too bad it's left you living in the boonies, hiding behind a steel wall."

"Peaches?" Todd floated down through the hole in the ceiling, arms slightly canted from his sides. A dusty fallen angel, clad in cashmere and penitence. "Can we go back to the RV? This isn't fun anymore." His tongue played with the sharp edge of his fang. "Besides, I'm really hungry."

"We can't do that, Toddy." She wiped her mouth with the back of her hand, then firmed her jaw. "We live on our reputation for success. We're only as good as the next makeover."

"We've got ratings."

"And I've been in stage productions that got gushing reviews and still folded. We can't take anything for granted. Do you want to go back to those days where you had to cadge closet space from guys who just wanted to . . ."

Pain in his eyes.

She lifted a shoulder, one survivor to another. "You know what they say, Toddy."

"There's no business like show business?"

"You're only as good as your last hit." She took out one of those white papers they used to blot oil and pressed the cellulose with Liara's prints sticky side down. "Take this to the RV and make a photocopy of it, okay? You can grab a couple of bottles of TrueBlood and bring them back."

"Okay." He started to float toward the door, then turned in a graceful arc, a puzzled expression on his lovely face. "Why do you want me to photocopy her prints?"

He needed her. He *truly* needed her. "Because a copy of them will fake out the fingerprint sensor, sweetie," she told him in her gentle voice.

"Are you sure?"

"I saw it on *MythBusters*."

Case closed as far as Todd was concerned. He heaved a sigh. "All right, but this is a lot of work for a wanker like Anthony van Dyck. The guy's so . . ."

While Bev waited for him to find the right word, she mentally finished the statement with some of her own: *fascinating, demanding, artistic,* and *sexy.*

Her best friend lifted his shoulders. "He's a tool, Peaches, and he's got no class. Not like you and me. When I knew him, his lace used to drip from his wrists." The horror of the recollection clearly sickened Toddy, and he rubbed his flat stomach as if to soothe it. "In my time, two lengths of pearls was perfection. Three lengths and you may have well carried a sign saying, *Buddy, I got no taste.* Do you know that he wore five strands every day?"

She pulled her brows together. "Five?"

Encouraged, Toddy continued. "You know what else? He reeked of linseed oil and turpentine. And after he became one of us, he was the worst whiner." Todd raised his voice into an uncanny mimicry of Anton's voice. "They'll recognize my brushstrokes. You've cursed me for eternity! I can never paint again!"

Bev smiled, just faintly.

The coffee table book had not fared well. Its glossy pages were gummed together; a layer of dust and debris coated its shiny cover. She flipped it open to the index and ran her nail down the staggering line of print until she found *van Dyck, Anthony.*

She stroked the words. "I always felt small around him."

"He made you feel thin?"

"No, he made me feel like a loser."

"But you're no loser," spluttered Todd. "You're Bev."

"Toddy," she murmured softly, shaking her head.

"Bev Leveto is a star." Toddy touched her shoulder, his fingers featherlight. "I knew that the second I saw you giving Madonna a smackdown. You shine, Peaches."

And there it was—the one thing that Toddy did better than anyone else. A feeling of warmth spread over her. She knew it for what it was— a phantom; a sense memory derived from the living part of her. But still, she felt contentment.

Sweet, soft, safe.

Toddy opened his mouth to add another comment, but whatever he was going to say to that was lost in the double click of a heavy metal lock turning. A moment later, the mirrored door swung open to reveal the interior of Liara's safe room. Bev's eyebrows rose as she took in the magnificence of the intended bride's hidey-hole. Color, color, everywhere—the walls of the vault had been swagged with rich fabrics, and the result was an orgy of rich jewel tones.

Then, without the drum roll and requisite clash of cymbals, the recluse of Vicksburg stepped out of her sanctuary.

Bev heard Toddy's sharp inhale of shock. And part of her wanted to chastise him—breathing was for breathers and they were so above that. But how could she? Her own mouth was gaping wider than a country hick's at a girlie show.

"Are you telling me that my intended is Anthony van Dyck?" Liara demanded. "The famous Flemish artist?"

She wasn't ugly, though her clothing choices were heinous—cheap sneakers and baggy sweats. There was material there that could be worked with. Her long hair was parted in the middle and fell in untamed ripples down her back. Her chin was childishly rounded, and her cheeks baby-smooth. Good skin's hard to find.

Though in Liara's case, there was a staggering abundance of it.

"We're going to need a bigger pair of Spanx," whispered Toddy. "She's got to be a size sixteen."

Bev shook her head. "Fourteen, petite."

For a corpulent shrimp, Liara moved fast. She swarmed over to where Bev stood frozen, ripped the art book from her hand, then thumbed it open to a well-worn page. She turned the heavy book outward, holding it propped open in her arms. "You're saying that Eric Northman has arranged for me to marry the man who painted *this*?"

Bev's gaze slowly traveled from Anton's chubby betrothed to the book and the image of a poorly coiffed, almost naked fat woman.

Toddy inched forward to read the small print. "*The Penitent Magdalene*?" He stepped back with a grimace. "At least it's not another one of van Dyck's self-portraits," he said to Bev. "That guy knew Photoshop before there was Photoshop."

Bev hardly heard him. With one painting, her world had tilted, stopped, and then reset. A score of Anton's comments, insults delivered so delicately that the result was a vague feeling of self-dissatisfaction, had been explained. *That's what he'd wanted.* She tore her gaze from the picture and moved it to Liara, where it lingered, her artist's eye seeing the hourglass shape beneath the vamp's clothing, the appeal of a face that belonged in a Renaissance portrait.

Change her? Liara Giacona was every curve-loving, Baroque artist's wet dream.

"One century's pinup girl is another's poster child for obesity," she said in a bemused tone.

"Pooh," said Toddy firmly.

"Anton never really saw me," she said, feeling her way. "Not really. All he saw was a blank canvas, waiting for him to add layers of paint to it." Had she been that needy? That open to manipulation? Bev thought back, then shook her head, and the tight feeling inside her eased. "I'm *nobody's* blank canvas. I'm my own work of art." She waved her manicured finger in a dismissive circle at the page. "And I don't *ever* want to be that girl."

"Who in their right mind would?" Toddy exclaimed.

She wanted to laugh. She wanted to do her high kick—the one that made Flo Ziegfeld stroke the corner of his mouth. But she didn't. Because *she* was a professional who'd learned from the best.

"If you want to look like the woman in that painting, we can do it," she told the vamp holding the art book as if it were last month's *Vogue*. "Or we can make you look like yourself, but better. Which do you prefer?"

"What do you think, genius?" said the vamp, combative to the end.

A real smile curved Bev's lips.

"Aw, Peaches, must we?" asked Todd, warming up to a whine.

Bev slanted her head. "We didn't bring the right wardrobe for her." At last, a flutter of anticipation. "The cut and the fabric is all wrong. What we really need is something that resonates with the Renaissance. High waisted and full skirted." She licked her lip, her creative hunger rising. "With a train."

"Pearls, two layers short, two layers long," murmured Todd.

"The dress should be made of a rich fabric . . ."

"Like velvet."

"Yeah, but—" She broke off, surprised by her colleague's not-so-gentle shoulder bump.

Toddy's teeth gleamed in the dark night, very white, very bright. "Like the stuff she's got on the walls of her safe room?"

"How fast can you sew, Toddy?"

"Faster than a June bride sprinting for the spring sales racks at Kleinfeld's."

They'd found a place to park the RV upwind of the Dumpster behind Fangtasia. Toddy had celebrated by bringing home dinner. After partaking of a Bear and a Goth, they'd settled down to an evening of quiet.

Another tradition.

Postmakeover, you ate, you cleaned up the house, you watched the sky lighten, and then you put a half a pound of deep conditioner on your head.

Toddy wiped his fingers. "Which shower cap, Peaches?"

"Mmm," she said drowsily. "Maybe the one with the sunflowers on it. I'm in the mood for some van Gogh."

She tilted her head to the side so that he could tuck all the soaked tendrils of her hair inside the cap. "We did good, Toddy."

"I wish you'd have let me talk her into the Spanx."

"No, it was better this way. Did you get a load of his expression?"

"Like a man seeing his first pair of Salvatore Ferragamos."

Funny how thinking of Anton didn't sting anymore. Bev pulled down the covers on her side and slipped into bed. "She never said a word, other than, 'Uhm,' 'Yes,' and 'I do.'"

"Starstruck," he said, sliding in beside her.

"That will change." Though in the meantime, Eric was going to look like he'd finessed a marriage made in heaven for one of Felipe's vamps.

Politics. Give Bev fashion anytime.

She stifled a yawn. "When do you think he'll meet the real her?"

"I'd say a week." Toddy smoothed the lavender sheets so they were a perfect flat border across both their chests. With a sigh, he settled into his pillow. His shower cap crinkled in protest as he turned to gaze at her.

"We did good," she repeated, and she moved her arm so that it lay against the long cool length of his. Her stomach was full and her lids felt heavy.

"We always do." He twined his pinkie around hers. "Night, Peaches."

"Night, Toddy."

DON'T BE CRUEL

BILL CRIDER

Bill Crider has always been a fan of the King. The hapless enter-
tainer, whose change into a vampire didn't go very well, has been a
recurring character in Sookie's story. Do you remember the time he
almost got crucified as entertainment for Russell Edgington and his
friends? You can bet that Bubba does. And it all started with a cat.

-1-

Bubba felt right proud of himself. He'd scoped out the territory around
Russell Edgington's mansion and located Bill Compton just like Mr. Eric
and Miss Sookie had asked him to. Bill wasn't in very good shape, but
at least he was alive, and Bubba could tell that Miss Sookie was sure
relieved to hear that last part. The vampires had him in an old garage
that might have once been a stable but had now been converted into a
series of rooms. Getting Bill loose and away from where the other vampires had him was going to be a problem, but Bubba didn't have to worry
about that. He could take orders just fine, but he wasn't real good at
planning things. His part in the rescue was over.

He did have one contribution to make to the discussion of what to
do about Bill, however. "Miss Sookie, they'll put werewolves to guarding him during the day."

Miss Sookie was real interested in hearing that, and after she and
Mr. Eric talked it over, they seemed to have come up with a plan to
rescue Bill the next day.

Bubba didn't understand most of it, so he just said, "You'll do great, Miss Sookie." Then he looked at Mr. Eric, waiting for him to tell him what to do.

Something had gone wrong when Bubba had been brought over, or maybe it was all the drugs in his system at the time. At any rate, his mind didn't work exactly right. He was good at doing what he was told, though, and the other vampires who knew his story tried to take care of him and keep him out of trouble. Sometimes he wandered off and people caught sight of him, after which there'd be articles in the paper and on the news, but Bubba didn't pay them any mind. He didn't read the papers, and he hardly ever watched TV, though he seemed to remember that he'd once enjoyed it.

"You need to get off this estate and go to ground, Bubba," Mr. Eric said. "We don't want anybody to know you've been here. Can you do that?"

"Sure can," Bubba said.

Going to ground was another thing he was good at. He was thinking about where he might go when someone knocked at the door of the bedroom they were in. Nobody had to tell Bubba what to do in that situation. He was out the window and gone in an instant.

Getting off the estate wouldn't be a problem. Bubba wasn't brilliant, but he had a certain shrewdness. He'd gotten over the wall that surrounded the place, after all, and he'd found Bill. He wasn't worried about getting caught.

Bubba dropped lightly down to the ground beneath the window and looked up at the big house that was lit up like some kind of party was going on. Bubba didn't like the house. He couldn't say exactly why, except that it reminded him of some other place, somewhere he used to live, he thought. He couldn't remember much about that old life, and reminders of it tended to agitate him. So he turned his back on the house and started off through the shadows toward the wall.

The wall didn't worry Bubba. It wouldn't give him any trouble. It was solid and high, built to keep out humans, but it didn't mean a thing to Bubba or any other vampire. In less than a minute, he'd be out of there.

And he would've been if it hadn't been for the cat.

Bubba couldn't figure out where the cat came from. Vampires weren't generally fond of pets, so the cat didn't belong there.

Bubba, on the other hand, while he wasn't fond of pets, was mighty fond of cats. Not because he liked to hear them purr when he stroked them or because he thought they were cute when they hid in paper bags. He had other, more practical reasons for liking cats. Unlike other vampires, Bubba wasn't much interested in human blood, but cats were another story. This one was a brindle, and Bubba particularly liked brindles. Their blood had a special tang.

Bubba knew he should ignore the cat. He knew he should do what Eric had told him. He almost always did what he was told when he could, but impulse control wasn't one of Bubba's better qualities. He took off after the cat.

Sensing trouble, the cat bristled, bushed its tail, and ran for the trees that grew near the garage where Bill was being kept. Bubba was very quick, but the cat managed to get up a tree just as Bubba made a grab for it. It scrambled up nearly to the top branches before it turned back to look down. It sat there hissing, growling, and howling.

"Dadgum noisy cat," Bubba said, looking up at it.

All Bubba had to do was jump up there, something he was perfectly capable of, and grab the critter, but it was probably too late for that. The vampires guarding Bill would be wondering what all the fuss was about, and one of them might come out to check on things. Bubba sighed. He sure wanted that cat. To heck with somebody checking on things. Wouldn't take but a second to get the cat. Bubba jumped.

So did the cat, as soon as Bubba reached it. It jumped right at Bubba's face and landed just right, stretching out its front legs so that its body completely covered Bubba's eyes and reaching the legs all the way around Bubba's head to sink its claws into the skin of his neck.

Momentarily blinded, Bubba fell backward, crashing down through a couple of limbs before hitting the ground. He wasn't bothered much by the fall, and he grabbed the cat by the scruff of its neck, jerking it from his face.

"You ought not've done that, kitty cat," Bubba said. He'd forgotten all potential danger now. He couldn't think about anything but the cat. "I'm gonna have you for supper."

The cat writhed and howled, but Bubba held it fast. He grabbed hold of its hind legs with his left hand and flipped it backward. It clawed at him with its front legs, but Bubba just snatched them in his right hand.

"Now then, you brindle scoundrel," Bubba said, as his fangs extruded.

Then there was a lot of hissing and howling, but it didn't come from the cat, which was free and running faster than it ever had before. It disappeared into the trees.

The hissing and howling came from Bubba, who writhed on the ground and tore at the silver mesh that had been flung around him. He gave it up after a minute or two and looked up at the two vampires who'd captured him.

"What the hell was he about to do?" asked one of them.

"Looked like he was gonna drain that cat," said the other.

"Ewwwww."

"Yeah. What kind of animal drains cats? It don't seem right."

"I guess we need to get him secured a little better," the shorter one said, pulling another silver net from a backpack with heavily gloved hands.

"Ummbitch," Bubba said, his voice muffled by the net.

"Now, don't you go cussin' us. You're the one trespassin' on the estate of the King of Mississippi. Mr. Edgington don't like trespassers, 'specially not when he's got other guests."

"You know something, Earl?" the taller vampire said.

"I know plenty, Oscar. I got a high school education, you know."

"That ain't what I mean." Oscar pointed at Bubba. "Don't he look like somebody?"

"Ever'body looks like somebody."

"No, I mean like somebody famous. Some singer, maybe."

Earl though it over. "Maybe." He paused. "Robert Goulet?"

Bubba started to scream and writhe, tearing at the mesh with his teeth.

"Nah, that ain't it," Oscar said. "It'll come to me. Let's get him put away."

"We better not put him in with the other one," Earl said.

"We got other rooms. Let's go."

They reached for Bubba's legs.

"Wait a second," Oscar said. "I know who he looks like, it's—" He said a name that Bubba didn't like to hear.

"Naw," Earl said, bending over to peer at Bubba's face. "Couldn't be. Just one of them impersonators. This'un would have a hard time of it in that line of work, though. Don't look much like him at all to me."

"I guess you're right," Oscar said.

They grabbed Bubba's legs and dragged him to the garage, where they put him in a room well away from the one where Bill was kept.

"I'll go tell Mr. Edgington," Oscar said when they had Bubba well tied down.

"You just want to get the credit for catchin' a trespasser," Earl said.

"We can't both go. Somebody's gotta watch him."

"Hell, you go, then. I don't give a damn."

Oscar left, but he was back within a few minutes, along with Russell Edgington himself.

"So this is the trespasser," Edgington said, running his hand through his thick red hair. His Southern accent was even more pronounced than that of the guards. "He looks somewhat familiar."

"That's what I thought," Oscar said. "But Earl don't agree. What're you gonna do with him?"

"I think I might use him for entertainment purposes," Edgington said. "And give him and everybody else a little lesson about what happens to trespassers."

Oscar looked at Earl, who gave a barely perceptible shrug. Whatever Edgington had in mind, it wouldn't be pleasant for the trespasser.

"Just keep him here for the rest of the night," Edgington said. He looked around the room. The one small window had been boarded up long ago. "Tomorrow night, bring him up to the main house as soon as he wakes up. We'll have something prepared for him."

"Yes, sir," Oscar said.

Edgington nodded and left.

"I wouldn't want to be in that fella's shoes," Earl said when Edgington had been gone for a few minutes. "Remember what happened the last time we caught somebody?"

"Yeah," Oscar said with a nod toward Bubba. "You think they'll stake him?"

"Oh, *hell* no," Earl said. "That's too quick. Whatever they do, it'll be a lot worse than that."

-2-

The first thing that Russell Edgington learned when he awoke after sunset the next day was that Bill Compton had escaped. Not only that, Edgington's hired Weres hadn't followed his orders, which facilitated the escape, not to mention the guards having caught a prowler on the estate. To top it off, Lorena, the two-hundred-year-old vampire who'd turned Bill and lured him into Edgington's trap in the first place, was missing. Edgington hadn't taken this news well. He raged up and down the hallways of his mansion, and nobody dared to come near him, not even Talbot, his favorite companion.

Betty Joe Pickard came into the room. Edgington looked up. Before he could open his mouth, Betty Joe said, "Don't you dare raise your voice to me."

No one but Betty Joe would've dared say that, and even she was on shaky ground. Edgington snarled and started to stand.

Betty Joe held up a white-gloved hand. She was always dressed to the nines, June Cleaver style. "Hear me out. Don't you have someone you can vent your feelings on? The one they caught last night? Maybe he even helped Bill escape."

Edgington leaned forward, started to speak, then leaned back.

When he spoke, his voice was almost calm. "You might have a point. It might cheer me up, and it would certainly be entertaining for my guests."

Betty Joe smiled. "You see? You're feeling better already."

"For now," Edgington said. "Let's get ready to have a party."

"What will the entertainment be?"

Edgington smiled. It wasn't a nice smile. "You suggested that I had someone to vent my feelings on, so our prowler will be the honored guest. I think a crucifixion is in order."

"A crucifixion?" Betty Joe said. "That might prove fatal."

"And your point is?"

"You might want to question him first."

"I'll question him during," Edgington said. "If he knows anything, he'll tell me."

"Maybe," Betty Joe said.

Edgington was looking downright jovial by this time. "Oh, he'll tell me, all right. You don't have to worry about that."

"No," Betty Joe said, "I don't suppose I do."

-3-

Bubba had woken up exactly at sunset, as he'd been doing ever since he'd been brought over. He didn't really notice that much difference, since he'd spent most of his life before crossing over sleeping during the day and waking up to enjoy the nightlife.

Tonight was different, however. He was trussed up in silver mesh, and for a couple of minutes, he couldn't quite figure out what was going on. Then the pain flushed through him, and everything came back to him. He kicked and strained against the mesh, trying to break free, but that just made the pain worse. He lay still and silently cussed the brindle cat and wished for sunrise so that he could lapse into unconsciousness again.

Earl and Oscar came in after a while, and Oscar asked how Bubba was doing.

Bubba could tell he didn't really give a damn, so he just glared at him.

"You might's well be civil to us," Oscar said. "Not our fault you came sneakin' around here and got caught. Now you gotta take what's coming to you."

Bubba didn't like the sound of that. He'd heard what they said the previous night, though he wished he hadn't.

Oscar and Earl didn't say anything else to him. They went over to a card table, sat down, and started to play some game or other. Bubba didn't care for card games. He twisted around in an attempt to get some relief, but he just made things worse.

After an hour or so, another vampire came in and asked Oscar to step outside. Oscar didn't return for about fifteen minutes. When he came back, he looked at Bubba. "Time to go."

Bubba didn't want to go, but Earl and Oscar put their heavy gloves on and got him by the arms. They frog-marched him out the door and tumbled him into the back of a golf cart that Oscar had parked there.

"Home, James," Earl said, settling into the front seat as Oscar got behind the wheel. The golf cart's motor whined as Oscar drove to the mansion. Bubba was jostled around in the back, but he didn't fall out.

Oscar stopped at a back door of the mansion, and he and Earl got Bubba out of the cart and onto his feet.

"This is gonna be your big night," Oscar said as they half walked, half dragged Bubba inside.

They went through a kitchen and a long hallway into a large room where a gathering of vampires and fangbangers awaited them. Vampires and humans alike began to applaud when Bubba entered. At first he was puzzled, but not for long. He remembered that people had once applauded him like that long ago. He generally didn't like remembering things like that, but this time it didn't bother him for some reason, maybe because the pain from the silver mesh that encased him was so great.

Looking around the room as best he could, Bubba noticed a big cross in the middle of it. He didn't think the place was a church, but maybe he'd been brought into some kind of religious service. The melodies of a couple of old songs floated to the top of his consciousness: "Peace in the Valley" and "Crying in the Chapel." Remembering the songs didn't bother him the way it usually did, just as the memory of being applauded hadn't.

He heard someone say, "You know, he looks familiar." People were always saying that around Bubba.

The red-haired man who'd looked at Bubba in the garage came over to where Oscar and Earl held him.

"You've trespassed on my property," the man said. "Do you have any idea who I am?"

"Nope," Bubba managed to say.

"Russell Edgington is my name. I'm the King of Mississippi. Does that mean anything to you?"

"Nope," Bubba said. Being the King of Mississippi didn't mean squat to him. He could tell Edgington something about being a king if he wanted to, which he didn't, but again the thought of it didn't bother him. Bubba attributed it to the pain, which was squeezing pretty much everything else out of his head.

"Very well," Edgington said. "Maybe it will mean something to you later. Do you know Bill Compton?"

"Yeah," Bubba said.

Edgington looked a little surprised at the admission. "Did you know he was here?"

"Yeah."

Again Edgington looked surprised. "Did you help him escape today?"

Bubba always took things literally. He was practically incapable of lying, but he knew he hadn't had a hand in Bill's escape. So he said, "Nope."

"Do you know how he escaped?"

"Nope."

Edgington now looked more frustrated than surprised. "We'll see about that." He turned to Earl and Oscar. "Put him on the cross."

The two vampires pulled Bubba over to the cross. An excited buzz went through the crowd. Bubba knew that sound. He'd heard it many times. They were anticipating a big show, and he was the star. He wasn't quite sure just what the show was, however, and the way he was feeling, he wasn't going to be able to do much about it.

Two more vampires joined Oscar and Earl, and working together they managed to hoist Bubba up against the cross. It wasn't easy, as Bubba was a bit hefty. Oscar and Earl held him in place while the other two vampires freed his arms from the mesh. Bubba struggled weakly, but he was too weakened to bother the vampires. They tied his wrists to the crosspieces with silver chains. When they were sure his arms were secure, Oscar and Earl released them and freed his lower legs. Bubba gave a feeble kick at Oscar, who grabbed both his feet. He and Earl crossed the feet at the ankles, and the others chained his ankles to the wood with more silver.

"Check him," Edgington said.

The crowd watched expectantly as a vampire came forward with a silver knife. It had a wooden handle, but the vampire still wore heavy gloves. He didn't waste any time. He stabbed Bubba in the stomach.

Bubba howled and strained against the chains that held him, but he was tied securely and couldn't pull loose.

The vampire with the knife looked at Edgington, who nodded. "Bring in the drainers," he said.

Two men were led into the room. Both of them wore overalls, heavily scuffed work boots, and blue denim shirts. Their faces were pale and drawn underneath several days' growth of whiskers. They'd been caught only a half hour earlier, and they were plainly frightened.

"You don't have anything to worry about," Edgington told them. "This should be a dream come true for you. A vampire to drain at your leisure, and when that's done, you'll be released." He turned to Betty Joe, who'd walked up beside him. "Where are their implements?"

Betty Joe made a gesture, and a vampire brought in a canvas bag that he handed to one of the men.

"You can have every drop you can drain," Edgington said to the drainers. "All we ask is that you take your time. Let us enjoy the experience."

The two men looked at each other. Vampire blood was literally worth its weight in gold to humans, even if the vampire wasn't top quality. Being a drainer meant being willing to risk your life to get the blood. They couldn't believe it was being offered to them for the taking.

"I promise you," Edgington said, "that you will be free to leave here with as many vials of blood as you can drain. If you know who I am, you know my word is good."

"It's not that we don't trust you," one of the men said. "It's just that—"

Edgington smiled. "It's just that you don't trust me. And I don't blame you. However, I'm telling you the truth. Now get to it, or you're going to be very sorry."

The thought of what Edgington could do to them seemed to encourage the men to get busy. They removed knives and vials from the bags and moved toward Bubba.

"Remember," Edgington said. "Slowly. Don't start with the larger veins. Think small."

The men approached Bubba, who knew what was coming but who could do nothing about it. The chains weren't going to drop off magically. All he could do was take what was coming. For the first time in many years, he was afraid. He didn't like the feeling, not one bit.

The murmurs of the crowd grew in volume as the vampires' excitement grew. The fangbangers were excited, too, but for different reasons. Some vampires' fangs had extruded.

The drainers stepped up and looked Bubba over. He tried to spit at them, but found that his mouth was dry.

In the normal course of things, with a helpless vampire at their mercy, the drainers would have gone for the carotid or the femoral arteries, but they followed Edgington's orders. One of them cut into an ulnar artery on Bubba's left wrist, while the other held a vial to catch the blood. Bubba wrenched his arm and tried to make it hard for them, but the chains held him too tightly.

Betty Joe Pickard's face was a study in avidity, and she twitched away angrily when someone touched her shoulder.

"Sorry, ma'am," one of Russell's servants said. "There's a phone call for you."

"Not now," Betty Joe said.

"It's someone called Sookie Stackhouse. She said to tell you she's the one who saved your life last night and that she has to talk to you right now."

A cheer burst from the audience as the blood started to flow from Bubba's vein and drop into the vial.

"Damn," Betty Joe said. "Just when things were getting good."

She turned and followed the servant to the phone, picking it up in her gloved hand. After she'd expressed her displeasure to Sookie for being interrupted, she allowed Sookie to get a word in. Sookie explained her situation and said, "I am supposed to tell you that the vampire you have there, he's the real thing."

"You're shitting me, right?"

"Absolutely not." Sookie told her the circumstances of how Bubba had been brought over. "Don't call him by his real name. It upsets him, and he gets out of control. Call him Bubba. And for goodness' sake don't hurt him."

"But we've already . . . Hold on."

Betty Joe ran back to the living room, her heels clicking on the tiled floor, and found Edgington watching as the drainers worked.

"We need to talk," she said.

"Not now."

"Now. Definitely now." She took hold of Edgington's arm and pulled him away and into the hall. "That man we have up there, he's the real thing."

Edgington stared at her. "He can't be."

"Yes, he can." She told him what had happened. "We have to get him down."

"There might be trouble."

"You're the king. You can handle it."

Edgington thought it over. "Very well. But I'm not entirely con-vinced. He'll have to prove himself. If he's real, we should keep him."

"Just don't call him by his real name," Betty Joe said, and she returned to the phone.

"We got him down in time. Would it be all right if he stayed and sang for us?"

Sookie told Eric, who was standing by. He said, "Very well. They can ask, but they can't insist. You know how he gets if he doesn't want to. They won't like him if that happens."

Sookie relayed the message.

"We might want to keep him," Betty Joe said, "if he's the real thing."

Sookie gave the phone to someone, not saying who it was, and some-one with a British accent spoke to Betty Joe. He explained that Bubba was a sacred trust of the Louisiana vampires, and he'd better be allowed to leave. Otherwise there would be certain unspecified consequences.

Betty Joe didn't want to cause any trouble for Edgington, so she agreed to persuade him to allow Bubba to leave. That was too bad. If Bubba was the real thing, he'd be fun to have around. On the other hand, if he wasn't the real thing, if he was just some impersonator, it would go hard with him. Very hard.

-4-

Bubba didn't know what was going on, but he knew it looked good for him. Edgington came in and announced that the crucifixion was over. There was a lot of hubbub when he said it, but the redheaded vampire explained that there would be other, better, entertainment, so things calmed down. Oscar and Earl led the drainers away. They weren't happy at first, either, but since they were allowed to keep the little blood they'd drawn, they didn't put up any argument. Bubba figured they knew better than to do that.

A couple of vampires removed the chains and mesh from Bubba.

Bubba felt better instantly, the cuts on his wrist already healing. Relief surged through him, and he dropped down from the cross, striking a martial arts pose as his feet hit the floor.

"Any of you sumbitches lays a hand on me's gonna be sorry," he said.

Edgington walked toward him, arms raised, palms out. "Nobody's going to harm you. This has all been a terrible mistake. We didn't realize that, like me, you are royalty."

"I ain't like you," Bubba said.

Edgington dropped his arms to his sides. "I'm sure that's true. For one thing, I don't sing. Nobody can sing like you do. I was wondering if you might treat us to a song."

Normally a request like that would rile Bubba up, but the memories he'd had of his past in the last hours hadn't bothered him at all for whatever reason, and the thought of singing didn't, either. Maybe it was relief that was working on him now. Bubba didn't do much self-analysis, so he didn't know, or care. He dropped his pose and looked down at his clothes, which were shabby and dirty. He ran a hand through his hair, which hadn't been washed in a while, much less styled.

"I don't know about that," he said. "I'm not really dressed right."

A young-looking vampire leaned forward and whispered in Edgington's ear. Edgington nodded, and the vampire spoke to Bubba.

"I'm Talbot," he said, "and I think a new wardrobe can be arranged. If you'll follow me, I'll see what we can do."

Bubba wasn't too sure about that, but he figured it wouldn't hurt. He reckoned he could handle Talbot or anybody else in that room. Put a few karate moves on them, and they'd be down for the count.

"Come along," Talbot said. He gestured to someone else. "My friend Felix and I will fix you right up."

Another young-looking vampire joined them, and Talbot led the way out of the room. Bubba got a lot of curious and eager stares, but he was used to that. Or he had been at one time. These days it usually bothered him, though not now. First the fear and then the feeling of relief that had come over him had taken away the bother.

Talbot and Felix led Bubba to a second-floor bedroom that was tastefully decorated with scarlet wall hangings, a chandelier, and elaborate sconces. The king-sized bed was covered with a furry red bedspread, and there was a dressing table nearby. It was a lot different from the room where Bubba had left Mr. Eric and Miss Sookie. He approved.

"Nice room," he said.

"It's mine," Talbot said. "I'm glad you like it. The bathroom's right over there. You get cleaned up while we lay out some clothes."

Bubba went into the bathroom. It had black granite countertops and gold fixtures. The walk-in shower, also granite, was huge. Bubba shucked off his clothes and turned on the water in the shower. When it was just right, he got under the stream and luxuriated in it for a few minutes. On a little shelf sat a bottle of fancy shampoo and some good-smelling soap. Bubba took the time to wash his hair and get really clean.

When he emerged from the shower, he found a thick towel and a fluffy white robe. He dried off and put on the robe. On the counter lay a hair dryer that was already plugged in. Bubba dried his hair.

He went into the bedroom, where Talbot and Felix stood beside the bed. Laid out on the furry bedspread were some clean red boxers, a red jumpsuit sparkling with rhinestones, and a wide white belt with a huge gold buckle. A pair of black half boots sat beside the bed.

"I think you'll find that everything fits," Talbot said.

Bubba grinned. "You boys sure been TCB."

Talbot looked at Felix, who shrugged.

"Takin' care of business," Bubba said. "It's a motto I heard somewhere."

Talbot nodded. "It's a good one. Do you want us to step outside while you try on the outfit?"

"Naw, you can stay in. Just turn your backs." Bubba undid the belt of the robe. "No peekin', now."

"We wouldn't dream of it," Talbot said. "Would we, Felix?"

"Us?" Felix said. "Never, ever, cross our hearts."

"All right, then. Gimme a minute."

They turned their backs. Bubba dropped the robe and reached for the jumpsuit. He thought he saw Felix sneaking a peek, but he couldn't be sure. He didn't say anything, just slipped into the boxers and tried on the jumpsuit. It was just right. He found a pair of socks in the half boots. He pulled on the socks and then sat on the bed to put on the boots. Not a perfect fit, but they'd do. He stood up and spread his arms wide.

"You can turn around now, fellas."

Felix and Talbot swiveled to look at him.

"You look marvelous," Felix said.

"He looks better in it than you do, even," Talbot said.

Felix looked hurt.

"Just kidding," Talbot said, giving Bubba a critical look. "His hair's a mess."

"We can fix that," Felix said. "Sit right over here, Bubba."

He went to the dressing table and pulled out a stool. Bubba sat down, and Felix and Oscar went to work. It didn't take them long to get his hair gelled and styled into a modified duck's ass.

"What do you think?" Oscar said.

Bubba looked into the mirror and admired himself. "I still got it. I damn sure do."

"Do you feel like singing, Bubba?"

Bubba thought about it. Maybe it wouldn't be so bad to sing for a bunch of folks again. He was feeling better than he had in a long time.

"You got a guitar around here anywhere?" he said.

"We can get one," Talbot said. "Felix, go tell Jack to fetch his guitar."

"Hold on," Bubba said. "I'm kinda hard on guitars. I break a lotta strings." He touched the big buckle on his wide belt. "These buckles tend to scratch 'em up, too."

"Jack won't mind," Talbot said. "He'll be honored."

"Okay," Bubba said, "but remember I warned you."

"Go on, Felix," Talbot said. "We'll meet you downstairs."

-5-

Bubba heard the hum of conversation as he followed Talbot down the stairs and along the hallway, but when he entered the room where the big wood cross still stood, the voices trailed off. People turned to look and stopped talking the instant they saw him. Soon there was complete silence as the vampires and fangbangers stared at him.

Felix came up behind him and handed him a guitar. Bubba put the strap over his neck and settled the guitar until he had it just right. He strummed a couple of chords. Russell Edgington brought a microphone and set it in front of Bubba.

"The amplifier isn't state of the art, I'm afraid," he said, "but it will work well enough."

Bubba cleared his throat and said, "Hi, ever'body."

One of the fangbangers screamed, "It's him! It's him!"

The vampire standing beside her shushed her. Edgington said, "Everyone's looking forward to hearing you sing."

"Well, I guess I could give it a try," Bubba said. "My throat's kinda dry, though."

Edgington waved a hand at the room. "Pick anyone."

Bubba looked around the room. "I like somethin' a little different if it's all the same to you. You wouldn't happen to have a cat around, would ya?"

Edgington looked at him. "A cat? Really?"

Bubba looked back. "Yeah. A cat."

"No cats. I'm sorry."

"Shoot."

"What about TrueBlood?"

"I guess if that's all you got, it'll have to do."

Edgington snapped his fingers, and in seconds someone handed him a bottle of TrueBlood, which he gave to Bubba. Bubba took a couple of swallows, then drained the bottle and smacked his lips.

"Did that help?" Edgington asked.

"We'll see," Bubba said.

He struck another chord and then began strumming a rhythm, striking the strings hard. He cleared his throat and sped up the strumming. He felt something moving in him, something that he hadn't felt in . . . He didn't know how long it had been. The feeling had been building in him for a while now, ever since he got unchained.

"Sing it!" someone yelled, and Bubba did. He sang "Mystery Train" and "That's All Right, Mama" and "My Baby Left Me."

He swiveled his hips. People screamed. He grinned, remembering how it had felt when people had screamed for him at other times, in other places. More people screamed, and his grin grew wider. He launched into "Heartbreak Hotel."

Betty Joe stood by Edgington and whispered in his ear. "It's like pure hot gold is pouring from his throat."

"Don't swoon," Edgington said.

"You just don't know," she said. "You just don't know."

Bubba segued into some slower numbers, a sultry "One Night" followed by "Love Me Tender." Then he launched into "Good Rockin' Tonight."

"I'll say there is," Betty Joe murmured.

Bubba was enjoying himself, something rare for him. He found himself wishing he had a bass player. And maybe a few backup singers. But he didn't, so he sang "Don't Be Cruel" without them.

After that number, Bubba stopped and looked around. The room was hushed. He stood quietly for a second before slipping the guitar strap off his neck. When he did that, everyone began to applaud. The noise crescendoed. It echoed off the walls and floor, and it sounded as if there were a thousand people there instead of only seventy or eighty. Bubba grinned and handed the guitar to Talbot.

"Tell Jack I said thank yew," he said. "I hope I didn't hurt it much."

"Oh, my, no. You've made it into a sacred object."

"I need to go," Bubba said. "I gotta get back to where I belong."

Edgington was suddenly beside him. "You can't just leave us like this. Stay awhile."

"Can't do it. Bubba's gotta leave the buildin'. I know the way out."

Edgington put a hand on Bubba's arm and started to speak, but Betty Joe came up and said, "I promised we'd let him leave. We have to honor that promise."

"We do?" Edgington said.

"You know we do."

Edgington dropped his hand. "Very well, Bubba. You may go."

"You can keep the suit, too," Felix said. "I want to dream of you wearing it."

"Thank yew," Bubba said. "Thank you ver' much."

He turned and slipped away.

When he was outside in the cool night, Bubba took a deep breath and let it out slowly. He took a few steps with a little swagger, the way he had long ago. It had been a long time since he'd had so much fun. The evening had started out bad, but it had ended real well.

Bubba felt changed somehow. He felt good. He felt as if things were going to be different from now on, at least for a while. He didn't know how or why, and he didn't care. He just knew it was a pleasure to experience what had happened.

There was just one thing he needed to make his night complete. There had already been a little bit of magic, so maybe he could find a cat on the way back to Bon Temps.

It could happen.

WHAT A DREAM I HAD

NANCY HOLDER

Alcide Herveaux, werewolf and member of the Long Tooth pack, has always carried a torch for Sookie. Alcide famously has a disastrous history with women. Though he and Sookie had chemistry, Sookie had to kill Alcide's murderous ex, Debbie Pelt. After that, Alcide's love Maria-Star Cooper was murdered. Then her replacement, Annabelle, was unfaithful. Maybe this pattern of bad luck began with Alcide's prom date, Emmaline Ravel. You be the judge.

●━●━●━●━●━●━

NOW . . .

"That best friend must still be dying, Alcide," Dale the bartender said. "Third night in a row you been in here."

"Someone's dying, but he's no friend of mine," Alcide muttered.

Dale put down Alcide's first shot of the evening—what had once been an occasional ritual was becoming more customary—and Alcide threw it back. The bourbon was as hot going down as the slap that still burned his cheek. Dale placed another shot on the shiny varnished oak bar without being asked.

"You have any regrets in life?" Alcide asked Dale. The bartender grunted. And Alcide quirked a half grin. "I'm buying, if you need to lighten your load."

Behind Dale, the ornate engraved mirror caught a slice of light as someone came in from the steamy Louisiana rain. Idly, Alcide glanced into the glass.

He froze with his second shot of bourbon raised halfway to his mouth. And as he absorbed the shock of what—*who*—he was seeing, the hard, cynical part of his mind spun lemon-sour thoughts: *A dead girl walks into a bar . . .*

But his heart broke into a million pieces all over again, and his very soul whispered, *Em. Oh, Em.*

Oh, Em.

A LIFETIME AGO . . .

Oh, Em. Ma belle.

Alcide was buzzing like a live wire. Emmaline Ravel was a spun-sugar princess in her pink prom dress, rosebud pink she said it was called, her blond curls just rushing down the sides of her face and over her bare shoulders like a waterfall, and she smelled so good, like honeysuckle and roses with a little dash of Old Overholt rye on her breath. They were Cajun kids and of course they'd spiked up the punch at their big fancy *fais do-do.* The guys had been merciless to him, laying bets that he'd get laid tonight, because what sweet little girl could resist Alcide Herveaux in a damn tuxedo? With that mop of curly hair and those big green eyes? Him with his little rosebud boutonniere Emmaline had bought him to match her dress, all liquored up and horny as hell?

He'd taken her to the prom in his daddy's Camaro. Steak, dancing, waiting, waiting, waiting. Now that the prom was over, Alcide and Emmaline had finally pulled up at the brand-new construction site his daddy had done the survey for. Alcide was about to unlock the foreman's motor home with the keys lent to him by his friend Roger, who worked for the construction company.

The motor home was like a real house, far fancier than the more modest Airstreams at most of the other jobs. This was going to be a long job and one of the principals owned an RV lot, so they got the foreman a nice place to stay. Front door, back door, kitchen, And a *bedroom.* Which, for Alcide, meant *Score!* It was someplace nice for a nice girl. Also, uninhabited. Roger had told Alcide that the foreman

hadn't moved in because the valuable equipment and material he would
guard at night had not yet been delivered.

That morning, Alcide had put fresh sheets on the bed and had
almost brought a vase of flowers but he didn't want to look like he'd
planned it that carefully, even though he had thought of little else since
he'd asked Em to go to prom. There was no damn way he could take
Emmaline to a fancy hotel like the other guys were doing with their
dates; someone was sure to talk and if his packmaster Boyd Lescaux
found out, there would be hell to pay. Hot-blooded Alcide had been
specifically warned off human girls. Maybe other packs had human
friends who knew about werewolves, and they even had human babies,
but their packmaster said anybody in his pack who changed in front of
a non-pack human would sign their own death warrant and the
human's, too. He did not hold to mingling, would have none of this
crap of people intermarrying. Wolves were for wolves, period, no matter if you had a firstborn Were or what. Lescaux's word was law and
those who broke it knew it, and he'd just as soon kill a mouthy, horny
teenaged boy as run free on a full-moon night.

But Emmaline wasn't just any human girl; she was Alcide's girl.
And she had a crappy daddy named Zachary Ravel who smacked her
around. Ravel subcontracted for several of the larger, statewide construction companies, and he was well-off. But Ravel was a bad man and
a worse drinker and Alcide would seriously have loved to kill him. Em
had no *maman* anymore and she had bruises all the time and Alcide
just wanted . . . He wanted . . . He didn't know exactly what he wanted,
except to make life good for her. In the pack, mating meant marking
and he wanted to extend his protection to her. But he was the worst
thing that could happen to her. He told himself that a million times
while he was getting the prom tickets and buying the tux and keeping it
all on the down-low from Lescaux—thinking he was crazy but he was
crazy in love and that had to matter, didn't it?

So here they were, like newlyweds when the guy carries the girl over
the threshold, and he knew she knew why he had driven her there, and
that she wanted him as much as he wanted her.

His guilt was exactly equal to his lust. He began to think that if he did this he was a pig and he had better just take her bowling with the Baptist kids at their virginal little after-prom instead of acting exactly like the animal he was.

He had his hand on the front door and she was shyly looking down at the ground, and he would never know if he would have opened that door to have sex with her or not. Because the next thing that happened was a gunshot from inside.

He threw himself around her as her eyes widened and her cry was muffled by his hand on her mouth. She wasn't used to violence, but werewolves live and die violently. Then he heard a moan and he thought the voice sounded familiar. Em was stunned enough not to realize that he was tearing the door off the hinges—or he hoped she was—and he flew inside to find Delano Bouchard flat on his back just off the kitchen beside a tipped-over desk chair, with blood gushing like a broken water main from his chest.

Delano was the town's head building inspector. Alcide's daddy had dealings with him all the time, survey matters. Alcide's father liked him well enough, said he was tough but fair. Now he looked to be dying.

"Go get help," Alcide yelled to Emmaline, but she was rooted in the splintered doorway, wheezing in terror.

"Lost . . . my nerve," Bouchard whispered. In his right hand there was a gun. Alcide was so stunned he almost lost his balance as he flattened both his hands over the horrible geyser of warm blood. Bouchard had shot himself.

"Desk," Bouchard ground out. His eyelids and chest were both fluttering. "Note. Take it. Let 'em know."

"Oh, God, oh, my God." Em sobbed wildly, unable to look away. Makeup ran down her face in trails of black and blue and silver.

Alcide picked up the landline. Wasn't hooked up. He pulled out his phone. No bars. He already knew she didn't own a cell phone.

"Chère, go get help," Alcide said desperately. He looked at the desk and saw an empty bottle of Jack Daniels and a yellow piece of paper from a legal pad with CONFESSION written at the top; below, a paragraph of precisely hand-printed words in blue ink, and at the bottom, the man's signature, which Alcide had seen on dozens of building inspection forms. There were blood spatters on it but the gush had mostly missed it.

"*Note,*" Bouchard insisted.

Alcide grabbed it. His hand was blood-scarlet, and now the paper was smeared with it, too.

A truck engine roared close; the motor died and doors opened and slammed; footsteps crunched the same gravel path Alcide and Emmaline had walked up to the motor home. The Camaro was parked behind some magnolia trees, well out of sight.

Bouchard's spasming hand wrapped around Alcide's fingers. His grip was weak. His eyes were bugging out of their sockets. Alcide had seen terror like this a few times before—during executions of werewolves. Boyd Lescaux killed wolves for things other packmasters didn't even bother with.

"Kill me before he . . . gets here," Bouchard begged Alcide. "Please."

Then the inspector was dead, the fire of life extinguished from his eyes. His hand slid to the floor and flopped into the spreading pool of blood.

Alcide lunged toward Emmaline and grabbed her forearm. He spotted another door—back door—just behind the desk. One hand clutching the piece of paper, the other dragging his panicking girl, Alcide got himself and Em the hell out of the trailer. She was panting and crying and he scooped her up in his arms and ran.

Ropes of Spanish moss brushed his face. He was listening hard for more gunfire, or men coming after them. He got into the trees and set her down, then unfolded the bloody, crumpled paper and in the moonlight read:

CONFESSION

> *I, Delano Everett Bouchard, took a bribe from Zachary Ravel in return for signing off on his subcontracted fram-*

ing work on Stillwater Project #13-721. But I cannot let that stand. A second inspection will reveal that the building is unsafe, and should be undertaken immediately. I have warned Ravel that I plan to recant, and he has warned me that he will strip the skin from my bones and shoot out my eyeballs if I do. I do not have the courage to see if he will make good on that threat, nor to drag my family's name through the mud in a court trial. I am sorry.

I am of sound mind and body.

Delano Everett Bouchard

Oh, my God, that's her daddy, Alcide thought. Then the trailer exploded and Emmaline was so startled that she lost her footing and crashed to the ground. Instinctively he threw himself on top of her and began to growl, looking back toward the orange-and-yellow flames and thick, oily smoke roiling up toward the moon and blotting it out like a river of blood. The trailer was ablaze, white-hot and untouchable.

Metal screeched and another explosion shook the ground. A hickory tree beside the trailer went up like a roman candle. The grass sizzled. He smelled gasoline and burning flesh.

Was that her daddy in the truck, coming to kill Bouchard just like he promised? Did he set that fire with his filthy, murdering hands?

Alcide got up and took Em's wrist. She stumbled and staggered and turned back to look, like Lot's wife in the Bible. She was wheezing and trying to scream and he wheeled her around and then he heard . . . He didn't exactly *hear*, but he *knew* . . .

Werewolf.

Close.

Alcide's heart hammered. Every sense ratcheted up to high alert. Warning of danger. Urging him to action. His bones began to ache and his blood to heat. His face tingled, his fingernail beds stung. He began to shake.

Oh, God, I'm going to change, he realized and he fought it down because if she saw, and *another* Were saw that she saw . . . Boyd Lescaux would kill them both.

No, no, no no no.

More trees caught fire, flames whooshing toward the moon. Reflected flames danced on shaking leaves. Pools of rainwater shimmered. Em was hunched over gasping, fragmenting into panic. That gave him a couple of seconds to try to force the change to stop. Then she straightened and looked right at him.

No!

The horror on her mud-caked face; her crazed, earsplitting screams. She scrabbled away from him, shrieking, making sounds he had never heard anyone make before. Falling and stumbling and bolting, flinging herself out of his reach.

He thought of the werewolf in the woods and ran after her, holding out his hands. Hair and claws and smoke and fiery death. He changed and ran, howling in rage.

The flames came after him; the town talked about that fire for years. He ran searching, still howling. He would have stayed in there and cooked if it meant he could find his Em. But she was like some ghost, vanished into the swamp, and when the sun rose he knew he had to face that she was gone. Not dead, he begged, and he prayed as he had never prayed before or since. He staggered for hours, and then he fell to his knees, clenched his fists, weeping.

Delano Everett Bouchard and his damned confession must be ashes. Everything burned away.

He thought hard about that confession, trying to concoct a story so he could tell his daddy about the bad inspection. But a werewolf had been out by the trailer and Alcide had no idea who it was or if he—or she—had seen either him or Em. He was so scared for her he spent too long trying to figure out how to tell his daddy about the confession without telling him how he knew about it. He was afraid he'd trip up. He didn't know if she was still alive to protect, but there was no way he would take any chances.

And because of his cowardice, that building did collapse, and three people were severely injured. Eighteen, and he had blood on his hands, and his sweet Em was nowhere to be seen.

A week later, Zachary Ravel told Marie-Louise Crissertary, the social worker who visited him, that his sixteen-year-old daughter, Emmaline, had probably run off to find her whore of a mother, whom, contrary to public opinion, he had not murdered and buried on his soybean acreage. Then he told Miz Crissertary he would shoot *her* and it would be legal if she didn't stay the hell away from him.

A year passed, two, three, five. Alcide searched every square inch of Shreveport for Emmaline. Tried to be discreet, but worry made him aggressive.

NOW . . .

"Em," Alcide said in the bar, as she stood uncertainly before him. Though he'd had fair warning—had seen her reflection in the bar mirror before they came face-to-face—he couldn't conceal his shock. She looked old and gaunt. Some kind of disease sallowed her skin. Her dirty, wet clothes hung on her as if she were a little girl playing dress-up in a garbage dump.

He slid off the stool and took a step toward her. She took one back. Then her eyes shifted from him to the two empty shot glasses on the bar, and the vacant seat beside his. She moved painfully toward it and climbed on, lowering a cheap boho bag to the floor. She kept her gaze fixed on her leathery hands.

"Two more," Alcide told Dale as he sat gingerly beside her. He was dying to wrap his arms around her. But she, it seemed, was dying of something else. He took off his black leather jacket and settled it around her shoulders and she tried to smile in thanks.

Her shot glass full of bourbon didn't touch the varnished wood; her hand darted forward like a rattlesnake and she snatched the drink from Dale and gulped it down. Her head dipped as if her skull weighed too much for her creased, crepey neck.

"Alcide."

"Oh, *chère*," he said, reaching for her, and she shrank away again.

"I got word. That he's dying." Her voice vibrated with a hundred different kinds of pain. A tear dripped off the end of her nose. Another followed, and she didn't wipe it away. Her cheeks were sunken, and she looked like a heroin addict. Maybe she was a heroin addict.

He said to Dale, "We're going to a booth. Please ask Jane Anne to bring us two steaks, rare, and baked potatoes."

Em didn't protest when he gently took her forearm and helped her off the bar stool. She was as hollow-boned as a duck. He could almost hear her joints cracking as he walked her to the back of the bar and helped her slide over the burgundy leather, as if she were his grandmother instead of a girl he had once loved. Still loved, he realized.

He sat across from her and splayed his hands on the table to watch her body language for signals. She didn't sit back. She hunched over, and the pointer finger of her right hand almost brushed his left. But not quite.

"Who sent you word?" he asked.

"The person I wrote to," she said, then clamped her mouth shut. "I think I'll keep her out of this." She looked down at the varnish. "He dead yet?"

"Nope."

"I don't know how I feel about that."

I do, Alcide thought. He hated her daddy as much as he hated his former packmaster Boyd Lescaux. Colonel Flood had challenged him, and Flood had won. The reign of terror was over. But with the knowledge that Em's daddy was dying, all the misery had rushed over Alcide like a flash fire. And so he had spent three nights in a row at Dale's, pouring bourbon on the flames.

"Where did you go?" he said quietly.

"I don't even remember." She pulled out a pack of cigarettes. He got out his lighter and flicked it on. She blinked as if she'd forgotten that people did things like that, lit cigarettes for each other.

"I was homeless for a while. I never told anyone my real name. I just couldn't get over it. I got put away. They told me they'd pay for an operation to make me better," she said, raking her fingers through sopping, tangled hair that was more gray than blond. "Didn't help. Electroshock. Drugs. Then I wound up on the streets again. Then y'all showed the world what you were. Y'all and them vampires. Right there on the TV. I was sure nobody else was seeing it. That it meant I should just give up." She raised her chin. "I thought about, you know, tying up loose ends." Her hands were shaking. "He beat me, Alcide. And I swear to *God* he killed my mama and buried her in our field."

"*Oui, chère,*" he said. Everybody believed that Ravel had killed his wife. Soon he would be dead, and Alcide was sure he'd go straight to hell.

Em stared at him. Her eyes were yellow and bloodshot. A tear cut a channel through the grime.

"I lost my whole life because you never told me what you were."

His heart truly ached. It was like frozen lead in his chest. "I wanted to tell you. But it would have meant bad things for both of us."

"I figured." But accusation shaded her words. As if to say, *You should have told me anyway.*

"He's suffering," she said, accepting the light, drawing in the smoke. "My daddy. He's dying in pain."

"Good," he said flatly.

She exhaled and smoke wreathed her head.

"I read about that building collapse. Or maybe I saw it on TV." Her face clouded. "Was it . . . Mr. Bouchard's?"

He had planned to lie to spare her any further pain, but instead he nodded. They sat without speaking. Their food came. She was three bites away from polishing off her steak when she huffed and muttered, "Oh, shit. I forgot that I've gone vegetarian."

Alcide said, "I was supposed to stay away from you in high school. From human girls. That's why I didn't take you someplace nicer after the prom."

"Oh." Her voice contained a multitude of emotions. She tapped her cigarette ash onto her plate with trembling fingers. She pressed her forehead against the ends of her fingers and wearily rubbed, as if she had a headache.

"You got a place to stay?"

She shook her head. "I haven't for years and years," she said. "I've been sleeping in alleys. Thumbing around. I saw you come here a couple of nights ago. So I stuck around here. Working up my nerve. I was going to get cleaned up . . ." She covered her face. "I'm so ashamed for you to see me like this."

"I did this to you." He was stricken.

"You were the best thing that ever happened to me, until you were the worst. In between . . . there was always Daddy."

"Let me get you out of here," he said.

She nodded, her head nearly bobbing against her chest. "I'm so tired."

He paid the bill and they left. He helped her into his truck and they drove away. He thought about taking her to a beautiful five-star hotel, the kind he had wanted to take her to the night of the prom. His mind spun ahead to her sliding into a hot bubble bath and soaking the grime and misery away. Saw her getting the works at the beauty parlor. New clothes. A job at the company, something simple to start, like filing paperwork.

Then he brought himself back to reality and parked in front of a modest but not trashy motel. He saw her shoulders go down, relax a little. He'd made the right call. She wasn't ready for much more than this.

He paid for the room and got the key. Em sat down tentatively on the bed with her bag on her lap. He was willing to bet that was all she had.

She reached into her satchel and pulled out a plastic baggie. Tattered bits of blood-spattered notebook paper were pressed inside the filmy pouch like dried flowers in a diary. It was Bouchard's confession.

He was speechless.

"I thought that burned up in the fire."

"It didn't," she said simply. Maybe she'd taken it when he was changing. He had no idea.

"I came back to make it right," she said, lifting up the baggie. "I want to make it public. I want to do it before he dies. I want people to hate him."

Don't you worry—they already do, Alcide thought.

"Of course, Em," he said. "We'll do it however you want."

Then suddenly he knew it was all right to sit beside her on the bed. Their hips touched and a heavy sob convulsed out of her and he put his arms around her. She turned on one bony hip and pressed her face into his chest and wept like she must have wept when her *maman* disappeared and her boyfriend turned into a hallucination and she had nowhere to go but down way too deep.

"You led me on. You made me think you loved me," she said brokenly. "When all along—"

He stroked her hair. She cried and cried and when she was spent, he pursed his mouth to bestow a kiss on the crown of her head, a gesture she could not see.

"I was a kid, Em. Part of me hoped that it would be enough if I loved you. That we would get to have what we wanted because we were in love."

"*Romeo and Juliet* was assigned reading in the ninth grade, Alcide Herveaux," she mumbled, and they both actually chuckled.

"You know me. Never much for school."

Silence fell on them. He wondered if she wanted him to leave.

"Who set the trailer on fire?" she asked.

"I don't know, but I've always assumed your daddy paid for the matches," he said bluntly.

"How can people be like that?" Her voice was tiny and fragile. Shell-shocked. "How can my own kin be like that?"

"How can I be a werewolf?"

He held her chastely. There was no desire in him, and he could tell she didn't feel any, either. She only needed holding.

"Did you get married? Do you have kids?" she asked.

He told the truth. "I've got someone."

"I'm glad." She took a breath. "I'm relieved." She broke away from him and crossed her arms. "I'm dirty and I stink."

"No. You smell like roses and magnolias," he told her.

"Will you stay while I take a shower? Then will you take me to see Daddy?"

"Of course." It was ten at night. But he would have taken her anywhere in the whole wide world no matter what time it was.

Em came out of the bathroom damp from the shower and back in her dirty clothes. She had pulled her hair into a ponytail, and when she caught him studying her, she averted her face, as if in shame.

They got in his truck and they drove out to the plantation home where she had grown up. For all of his being a criminal and an abusive asshole, Zachary Ravel had been a successful businessman. Em drummed her fingers on her knees, and it began to rain again. They didn't talk on the drive, but when they turned onto the road that had once been lined with perfectly trimmed hedges, Em blurted out, "Shit!"

The hedges were either dead or overgrown. Peeling paint curled off the steepled entrance of the house and the columns of the porte cochere were covered with graffiti.

"What happened? Did he get caught?" Em asked Alcide.

"Someone was bleeding him dry. That's all I've been able to figure out." He took a deep breath. "I've been on a death watch myself. I came out here a few times to ask him if he'd seen you. I hoped there'd been a miracle and you'd survived the fire, gotten in touch with him. He just laughed in my face."

When they stopped, he gave her a flashlight and she turned it on, leading the way to the front door. All the lights were out. She rapped twice on the door, hard.

Nothing.

She wrapped her hand around the knob, but Alcide caught her wrist.

"Mr. Ravel?" he shouted.

There was a long silence, and then he tried the door himself. It was locked. They went around to the side of the large house, all of it in terrible disrepair, windows broken, bricks pitted, to the side door, and then to the kitchen, the entrance blocked with mustard plants and rotting cardboard boxes. This time Alcide forced the door and Em trained the flashlight over cabinets and a stovetop strewn with cobwebs and dried leaves.

"Oh, God, Alcide, what if he's dead in here?" she whispered.

"Mr. Ravel?" Alcide called again. "It's Alcide Herveaux."

Em opened the kitchen door to reveal a flight of stairs, and they climbed up. Em moved softly, but Alcide made noise. He didn't want to surprise anybody. This was Louisiana, and homeowners could shoot intruders with impunity.

He didn't know the layout of the house, so he followed Em down a hall to where a sliver of light glowed beneath the door and Alcide heard coughing on the other side. As they drew nearer, Em did, too, and she stiffened; this time he didn't stop her when she reached to open the door.

Zachary Ravel sat not in his bed but on a ratty recliner with a tattered blanket pulled over his lap. A little calico kitten nestled in the crook of his elbow. There was a bottle of Jack balanced on the arm of the chair and he had been reading a book.

"Holy shit." The book dropped to the floor. He half rose; the kitten protested. "Jesus."

"Hi, Daddy," Em said, as stiff and cold as any corpse.

He blinked. "God, I thought you were your mother."

"You're not going where she is," Em snapped.

Alcide looked around the room. There were delivery boxes with canned goods and a box of fresh kitty litter. Beside the bed, the litter box was clean and there was dry cat food in a clean white porcelain dish and a matching bowl of water. Someone had been doing for him, or had been up until very recently. Maybe he'd been able to order things on a computer, take in the deliveries himself. All Alcide knew was that folks were talking in town that he was dying. He didn't know how they knew. But the gossip had put him in mind of Em.

And that had sent him to Dale's bar three nights in a row.

"Someone got you," Em said, and Alcide heard the hurt and the fury. "Blackmailed you or cheated you. Beat you at your own game and took you down."

"You look like hell," he replied, looking her up and down with a strange, clouded smirk. "No one took me down. I went there on my own accord."

Then he cocked his head at Alcide and said, "It was me in the woods that night, Herveaux. Me and a packmate of yours. Jeraud." He crooked a smile. "Told me he'd tell Boyd Lescaux all about you and my Em unless I paid. And paid. And paid. Left me enough to get by on, but in this country, you get sick, you may as well shoot yourself as find the money for the medical bills."

Em's eyes were enormous, her brows raised, mouth slack. She stared at her father without moving a muscle, as if she had been turned to stone merely by looking at him.

"So, it's all gone, and I did it for you." He regarded her, and his expression did not soften. "I saw you run out of that fire. I knew you'd made it."

Alcide blinked. *"And you never told me?"*

The old man choked out a rheumy laugh and fell to coughing. "I never did," he said evilly. "I let you twist in the wind, you goddamned freak."

Em swayed and Alcide put his arm around her to keep her from falling down. The night he'd shifted had been a life-changing shock for her. Here were two more, one for each of them.

If I had known, he thought. But would he have followed her? He'd been afraid to tell his father about the confession. Such a coward. Would he have risked everything to go after Em?

I would have.

"I'm a bad man," her father said. "A wife beater and a murderer. I know I lost my temper around you, Em, and you deserved better than me. And I let you go too easy. But . . ." He coughed again. "I let you go."

Alcide watched years of torment move across her face. They didn't leave. When you went through life the way she had, you kept all your belongings that you could manage to hold on to. Here was more weight for her to carry: more terrible secrets. Misguided love.

Maybe. Maybe it was love.

He thought about the bloody pieces of the confession. He wondered what she would do now.

The kitten hopped off Zachary's recliner and cautiously approached. It looked up at Alcide and fell over its own feet as it zigzagged to the cat food and began to nibble.

I would have gone to her, Alcide thought again. *Left my pack, everything.* He closed his eyes tightly. He was shaking.

"Will you come to see me before I die?" Em's daddy asked. His voice was papery; he wouldn't last long.

Alcide waited for her answer. He saw the pretty girl in the rosebud-pink dress, curly blond hair running all down her shoulders like a waterfall. He clenched his hands, waiting for that girl to show herself again, after all these years of hiding inside another skin.

"Come to see you?" she repeated. Then she smiled bitterly. "I just did."

He spared you, Alcide thought.

But for the first time since she had walked into that bar, Emmaline Ravel walked straight and proud, right out of her father's life.

Into something better, chère, he thought, as he caught up with her. *Into your* own *life.*

They drove back to the motel, and this time, she stopped him at the door. She rubbed her mouth with the back of her hand, reached up on tiptoe, and kissed him softly.

"Thank you, Alcide," she said as she opened the door. When he swallowed hard, she cupped his chin. "I won't be back."

He moved her hand and pressed it over his heart. *You never left,* he thought, but did not say. *Never, Em.*

As if he had spoken aloud, she said, "I know."

Then she smiled, and she was *there,* he saw her, he did, really, and life was about to unfold before her. When you're eighteen, there's a magic carpet that flies you to the moon on the first night of the rest of your undiscovered life.

He smiled back. For a moment, she hovered. And then very gently, very gracefully, she shut the door.

ANOTHER DEAD FAIRY

MIRANDA JAMES

My friend Miranda James has always admired Claude Crane, fairy and stripper, first introduced in the story "Fairy Dust." Miranda's story takes place a couple of weeks after the events in "Fairy Dust." On a rainy night in Monroe, Louisiana, Claude's cousin Seamus O'Flaherty disappears not long before he's due onstage at Hooligans. Claude and Claudine have to work fast to uncover the truth about his disappearance—and possible murder.

Only the killer heard the fairy scream in agony when he died.

Rain pounded the roof at Hooligans while the sparse crowd at the front of the house whooped it up. Thanks to the threat of widespread flooding, only six women had straggled in for Ladies' Night. Claude Crane focused on finishing his routine. The lustful gazes of half a dozen rowdy women were better than no attention at all, though he was used to hearing the roar of a frenzied crowd.

Claude paused at the edge of the stage to allow groping hands to stuff money in his thong. He graced the woman who brandished a twenty with a slow smile that promised hours of wicked pleasures. When she tucked the bill into the thong, he wiggled his ass and she screamed ecstatically. He smiled and moved lithely backward, bowed, and slipped quickly from the stage.

Barry Barber was up next, and then Seamus O'Flaherty would join Claude for one final number. Barry's music started, and he strutted onstage in his cop gear. The women were already chanting, "Take it off."

Claude padded off to the men's dressing room to change. He was glad to find the space empty. His cousin Seamus usually lingered there, admiring himself in the mirror and waiting to chat. He was considering having his ears surgically altered the way Claude had done, but he couldn't seem to make a decision. Instead he kept pestering Claude at every opportunity with one question after another.

Relieved to be spared yet another inquisition, Claude put away his cowboy outfit and pulled out the pirate gear he wore in the finale. He dressed quickly and brushed his long, dark hair before wrapping a brightly colored scarf around his head. He stopped to admire his ears. No one looking at them would ever suspect he was a fairy and not human. He clipped a large gold hoop to his left ear and watched it dangle. He stared at his reflection in approval. He was far better-looking than the blond Seamus, even though Seamus was taller and slightly better built.

He passed by the office on his way back to the stage. Claudine sat behind the desk, staring at a computer screen as she prepared for a meeting. The club's female strippers were there to discuss some grievance, and that was Claudine's responsibility. When they took over the club from its previous owner, Rita Child, they'd decided Claudine would handle personnel matters, and Claude would oversee the artistic side of things. If necessary Claudine could use a little magic to settle any problems and keep the women happy and eager to continue working at Hooligans.

Thoughts of Rita irritated him. She hadn't surrendered the club willingly, but that was part of the bargain they had made with her. The other part of the bargain—well, they still had plenty of time to track her down and settle unfinished business.

Claude paused just offstage and glanced around, trying to locate Seamus while Barry strutted one more time around the stage. He spotted Jeff Puckett, his former boyfriend and the club's bouncer, near the front of the house. Jeff stood chatting with a big bear of a guy named Marlon Eccles, who was dating Velva Gillon, one of the female strippers. The trio of dancers occupied a table nearby, sipping at drinks while they watched Barry perform. Claude supposed they wanted to see the show before they tackled Claudine.

He felt another presence near him. He made a quarter turn to his right. Seamus stood there, his expression a sorrowful smile.

"Why aren't you in costume?" Claude snapped. "Barry's almost done, and we have to go on next." Sometimes, he thought, Seamus didn't take his job seriously. He seemed to think the twins, as his closest relatives, should overlook his lack of dedication.

"I will not dance tonight," Seamus said. "I came to bid you farewell, *mo chol ceathrair*, for I am now dead. *Slán*."

The image faded.

Stunned, Claude wondered when it had happened. He had seen Seamus about an hour before when he first arrived at Hooligans but not since. Fairies rarely died of natural causes, except extreme old age. Surely if Seamus had been ill he would have told them.

Claude realized with a start that Barry was coming offstage. The music for his number with Seamus would start in a few seconds.

Barry glanced around. "Where's Seamus? Aren't you two doing the finale together?"

"Not tonight." Claude had to think fast. He had to do this number, or the audience would get restless, but he also needed to speak to Claudine as quickly as possible. "Go tell Claudine I have to talk to her the moment I finish onstage."

Barry started to protest, but one look at Claude's expression warned him to shut up and do as he was told. He scurried off.

The music started, and Claude began to dance. The women might wonder why he was alone onstage, but they would be satisfied with a solo once he used his magic to charm them into forgetting that there was supposed to be another man with him. Instead he convinced them he was the only man they wanted to see as he moved seductively through the routine. Their eyes never left him, and the noise rolled around him.

At the end he collected multiple bills from each of the six, including another twenty from the woman who had given him one earlier. He made his bows as the lights dimmed, and he slipped off the stage when the bartender switched the sound system to automated music.

Claudine was waiting for him in the hallway door. "What do you need me for so urgently?"

"Seamus is dead." Claude clutched his costume to his chest. "He appeared to me while Barry was dancing."

"I spoke to him about an hour ago." Claudine frowned. "He was not ill that I could tell. He would have complained and wanted special attention like a child does. What could have happened to him?"

"Perhaps someone killed him." Claude was thinking of their sister Claudette's murder only a few weeks before. He motioned for his twin to accompany him. "Perhaps we should retrieve Sookie and have her read minds again to discover who is responsible."

Claudine followed him into the dressing room. "I doubt we can. The water is rising all over Monroe, and everyone is going to be stuck here overnight as it is."

"She was useful when we had to find out who murdered Claudette." Claude quickly dressed in his regular clothes. "But we are every bit as intelligent as a human, even if we cannot read their minds. We can handle this ourselves." He thought of all those television cop shows Jeff liked and that he had watched to please his boyfriend. Surely he could recall enough of the cops' techniques to finger the perp in this case. He felt pleased that he recalled the jargon.

"I suppose." Claudine regarded him pensively. "Where should we start?"

"With Jeff," Claude said after a moment's thought. "You get him, and I'll wait in the office."

A couple of minutes later Jeff entered the office, with Claudine on his heels. Jeff smiled tentatively at Claude but sat obediently when Claude pointed to a chair. Once again, Claude thought about restarting his relationship with the tall, muscular bouncer. His late sister had interfered when they dated before—she'd insisted that Claude should find a more worthy lover.

"What's up?" Jeff glanced back and forth between the twins who now stood before him. His narrow hazel eyes focused on Claude, who easily read the yearning in them. Jeff had frequently told Claude how gorgeous he was. Maybe Claudette had been wrong. He would have to think about that later.

Claudine spoke first, her tone sharp. "Have you seen Seamus tonight?"

Jeff stared at her blankly for a moment. "Yeah, sure. He was out in the bar earlier, talking to Marlon and flirting with the ladies before the show started. You know how he is."

The twins exchanged glances. Seamus couldn't keep his pants zipped, as the humans would say, and he bedded any attractive female, customer or employee, that he could. Then he moved on to his next conquest. Claudine had warned him about messing around with women at Hooligans, but Seamus had laughed in derision.

"They're not going to cause any trouble," he had told her smugly. "If they start to, I'll make them forget I ever fucked them. End of story."

What if one of them hadn't forgotten, and she was angry enough to kill when he brushed her off?

"How long ago was this?" Claude asked.

Jeff looked at his watch. "Maybe thirty, forty minutes ago."

"And that was the last time you saw him?" Claudine picked up a pad and pen from the desk and jotted something down.

"Yeah," Jeff said. "I went back to the door to see if anybody else was coming in, but it was raining so bad by then, I figured that was it for the night. I hung around, though, until about ten minutes ago when I came back into the bar and started talking to Marlon and the ladies."

While Claudine made notes, Claude asked, "What did you think of Seamus?"

Jeff shrugged. "He's okay, I guess. Doesn't have much time for me." He glanced away.

Claude knew that gesture meant Jeff wasn't telling the complete truth. They had been together long enough that Claude could read his ex-lover's body language. "Did he do anything to bother you? Say something nasty?" Seamus had a sharp tongue and used it indiscriminately.

"He ragged on me because he found out you and me used to be

together." Jeff's expression betrayed his hurt, mixed with anger. "Kept going on about how I was too ugly to make a hot guy like you happy and that's why you dumped me."

Claude didn't like seeing Jeff upset. He loved Jeff in his way. He approached his former lover and laid a hand on his shoulder. Jeff twitched slightly, as if the touch hurt him. "Jeff, look at me." Claude waited until Jeff's gaze fixed on his. Then he used a bit of magic to erase the hurt from Jeff's memory. Jeff smiled vaguely, and Claude stepped back, ignoring Claudine's glare.

"Why all these questions about Seamus?" Jeff said after a moment. "Are you going to fire him?"

"He's dead," Claudine told him, and Jeff's head jerked back.

"Dead? What do you mean?" He stared at Claude, his eyes suddenly wild. "He didn't look sick to me. And if somebody offed the jerk, it wasn't me."

Beside him, Claude heard his sister mumbling, which was her way of using her power to cloud human minds. Jeff's expression smoothed out, and he stood. "Guess I'd better go keep an eye on the door." He ambled out of the office.

"He didn't do it." Claude was convinced of that. Jeff hadn't cared for Seamus, and Claude hadn't much, either, when it came right down to it. But Jeff wasn't a killer.

"No, he probably didn't." Claudine looked at her pad in her hands. "What should we do now?"

"Check the men's dressing room," Claude said after a brief reflection. "Perhaps we can find a clue of some kind to what really happened to Seamus." He strode from the office, and Claudine followed.

The twins spent several minutes searching the small room. Claude found Seamus's costumes on their hangers in the closet but not his street clothes. Seamus was never messy and had always hung up his garments when he changed. Claudine searched the small chest of drawers the men shared but found only spare thongs and underwear, along with a few toiletries.

Claude sorted through the contents of the wastebasket but found only discarded tissues and the small cotton balls they used when removing makeup. He set the wastebasket down and glanced around the room. Where else should he look?

He eyed the small sofa bed that occupied a corner. He took the cushions off and set them aside. Claudine grasped the nylon cord to pull out the mattress, and as the mattress unfolded, they saw a sparkly substance.

Claude stared at the scattering of fairy dust. "The killer probably didn't know that Seamus would appear to us after death, nor that he would leave something behind."

"And since he died on the bed, that probably means he was having sex when he died." Claudine frowned.

"Having sex wouldn't kill him, or else he'd have died long ago," Claude said.

"Of course not," Claudine snapped. "You know what it had to be." There was only one thing that could kill a fairy that quickly—lemon juice, one of the few weaknesses a fairy had. "With the storm and the flooding, the killer couldn't get far."

"Nobody left the building after Seamus was last seen, so the killer must still be here, and it must be a woman because Seamus never had sex with men. Since none of the customers would have been able to come backstage without being seen, the killer is either Velva, Lula Ann, or Artemisia." Claude nodded, pleased with his logic. "Let's get them into the office and question them, and I'll ask Jeff to search their dressing room while they're with us."

"What is he going to look for, besides lemon juice?" Claudine asked. "I wouldn't count on him finding anything. But I suppose if he does find lemon juice, at least it won't hurt him."

Claude said, "Jeff really is smarter than you think. You underestimate him, just as Claudette did. I will tell him to look for lemon juice, of course, but also to look for anything odd."

Claudine didn't appear convinced but did not argue further as they moved to the office. "You wait here, and I'll bring them back. I'll send Jeff first."

Claude pulled an extra chair behind the desk and sat. Jeff appeared a minute later.

"Claudine said you want me to do something?" He smiled happily, and Claude returned the smile briefly.

"I want you to search the women's dressing room for us," he said. "I can't explain why now, but see if you can find anything with lemon juice on it, or anything that might have contained it recently. Also, anything you think might shed light on Seamus's death."

Jeff nodded. "Sure, I can do that. Kinda like they do in the cop shows. Should I get some plastic gloves from the kitchen?" He looked excited by his task.

Claude shook his head. "They won't be necessary." There was no need to worry about compromising evidence, since the local police would not be involved.

"Okay, then." Jeff shrugged. "I'll be thorough."

Moments later, Claudine returned, herding the three female strippers ahead of her. Marlon Eccles trailed behind. There were only two empty chairs, and Velva Gillon and Lula Ann Sheffield, the blonde and the redhead, claimed them. Velva dropped her handbag by her chair. That left Velva's boyfriend and Artemisia Jackson, the third stripper, on their feet. Marlon stood behind Velva, one large hand on her shoulder, and glared at Claudine. Claude wondered whether the man, large as he was, realized that Claudine was strong enough to disembowel him in five seconds flat.

Velva, always the mouthy one, spoke first. "What the hell is going on here? We wanted a friendly meeting to discuss a few things, and you hustled us in here like a bunch of kids going to the principal's office." She patted her heavily lacquered head.

Lula Ann giggled. "Chill out, Velva. I bet you got sent to the principal's office a lot, all those years ago when you was in school."

Velva glowered at Lula Ann's little sally, but before she could reply, the third stripper spoke.

"Can we get on with this?" Artemisia's sultry voice betrayed the black woman's annoyance. "I have a paper to write."

Velva flashed Artemisia a look of loathing. "You're always throwing it up to me and Red about how you're going to college." She mimicked the other woman's throaty tones. "*I have a paper to write.* Lord, you surely do piss me the hell off."

"Shut up." Claudine didn't raise her voice, but the women and Marlon started. Velva's expression grew sullen, and she leaned against Marlon.

Claude whispered, low enough that only his sister could hear, "I've got this." He had thought of the tactic he wanted to use. He spoke in normal tones. "Seamus has disappeared." He tried to gauge the reaction from the four humans, but he detected no unusual expression, only what he read as curiosity.

"Probably ran off with some skank from the audience." Velva laughed. "He couldn't keep it in his pants if his life depended on it."

Lula Ann snorted. "You oughta know, hon."

"I ain't no skank, and I ain't never done nothing with Seamus." Velva grabbed a handful of Lula's hair and yanked hard. The wig flew off. Velva might have thought Lula Ann would be upset, but the woman just smirked as she patted the short black hair now revealed. Marlon put both hands on Velva's shoulders and held her back. Lula Ann plucked her wig away from Velva and put it in her lap.

"Au contraire, Velva." Artemisia smiled. "That means 'I beg to differ with you.' The first night Seamus came to see us perform, I heard the two of you going at it in the guys' dressing room after the second set."

Marlon's deep voice startled the humans. "Velva, what the hell were you doing fooling around with that asshole?" His hands tightened around his girlfriend's neck, and Claude noted that Velva started to get red in the face. She reached up and grabbed Marlon's hands and wrenched them from her neck.

"It was only one time," she said after she caught her breath. She twisted in her chair to stare up at her boyfriend. "I swear to you. I don't even know what came over me. He ain't my type, you know that, Marlon. I like 'em big and burly and tattooed."

Claude couldn't tell by Marlon's wooden expression whether he was satisfied with Velva's claims, but the man folded his arms across his chest and stepped back to lean against the wall. Velva looked stricken and huddled in her chair.

"You appear to be unhappy with the news that Velva had sex with Seamus." Claude watched the big man closely. "Did you know about this before now?"

Marlon eyed his interrogator with what Claude assumed was contempt. "If I had, you can bet Seamus would've disappeared before now. I'd have beat the crap out of him and left him in the Dumpster." He laughed. "Guess he decided to run off before I got hold of him."

Claude and Claudine exchanged a quick glance. She shrugged slightly, and Claude reckoned that Marlon was telling the truth. He probably would have tried to beat Seamus up, but he would have been surprised at the outcome of such an attempt.

Claude focused on the women as he continued. "Is the men's dressing room one of Seamus's accustomed trysting spots?"

"If you mean he liked to get it on in there, then yeah, it sure was, even though that dang sofa ain't too comfortable," Lula Ann said. "He got me in there once, and I have to tell you, he sure knew what he was doing." She sighed. "Only problem was, he was a onetime kind of guy."

"Did that distress you?" Claude asked. "Did you perhaps want more from Seamus?"

Lula Ann shrugged. "Wouldn't have minded, but there's plenty of guys out there that know how to hit the right spot." She batted her eyelashes at Claude. "I bet you do, don't you, hon?"

Claude regarded her. He had occasionally dallied with women, but he much preferred men. Lula Ann didn't interest him as a potential sexual partner, so he decided to ignore her attempt at flirtation.

He focused on Artemisia. "How about you? Did Seamus succeed with you?"

She stared coolly back at him. "No."

Claudine nudged her brother and tilted her head in the direction of the door. Claude spotted Jeff hovering there.

"Excuse me a moment." He went out into the hallway and pulled Jeff a few steps away from the door. "What did you discover?"

"First thing is this." Jeff pulled a small atomizer bottle from his jacket pocket and held it up for Claude to examine. "There's lemon juice in it. Not much. Have a smell."

Claude shuddered and took a step back. "No, thank you. I'm allergic." He stared at the bottle—nondescript plastic with no markings on it. "Where did you find it?"

"Stuffed in one of the drawers of the makeup table." Jeff shrugged. "All kinds of crap in there. Could belong to any one of them, I reckon."

Claude continued to stare at the bottle. Had the killer brought the lemon juice for the sole purpose of killing Seamus, or did it have another use?

"Do women use lemon juice for anything?" he asked.

Jeff laughed. "My cousin Odette tried it when she was about thirteen. Said somebody told her you could get rid of freckles by putting it on them. Like bleach, maybe."

"Did it work?"

"I guess it did, at least a bit. Her freckles kinda faded, long as she stayed out of the sun. Still uses it, I think, to make her skin look tighter and younger."

Claude considered this information. Of the three women, which was most likely to use lemon juice as a beauty treatment?

He discounted Artemisia on the grounds of skin color, and that left him with Lula Ann and Velva. Neither of them had freckles that he could remember, but Velva was in her midforties, while Lula Ann was probably a decade younger. Either one of them could be using it on her skin.

"I need something to wrap the bottle in," Claude said. "I don't want to get any of the lemon juice on me."

"I got you," Jeff said as he pulled out a handkerchief. "Clean, so it should do the trick." He wrapped the bottle and handed it to Claude, who held it gingerly.

"Did you find anything else?" he asked.

"Yeah," Jeff said. "There's one more thing. Well, two things, actually." He waited for Claude's nod before he continued. "First off, I heard what Artemisia said when you asked her about Seamus. She's lying. I saw her and Seamus coming out of the dressing room together one night last week, and the way Seamus was smirking, I knew he'd just screwed her."

"Thank you for telling me." Claude did not like it that Artemisia had lied to him. He had always thought of her as honest. She was smart and a hard worker to boot. "What was the other thing?"

"This." Jeff reached into his jacket pocket, pulled out a small photograph, and handed it to Claude.

Claude recognized the former owner of the club, Rita Child, immediately. It was one of those glamour shots, with Rita smirking at the camera.

"Look on the back," Jeff said.

Claude turned it over. He recognized Rita's handwriting as well. She had scrawled, *Don't I look hot, cuz?*

"Where did you find this?"

"In the same drawer as the bottle," Jeff said. "So I guess either Lula Ann or Velva is related to Rita. Never heard either of them mention it, though."

Claude could have enlightened him as to why Rita's cousin wouldn't claim kinship publicly—or at least in Hooligans—but Jeff had no need of that information.

Claude considered the implications of the photograph and the relationship to the former owner it revealed. Of the three women, only Velva was new to the club. In fact, she had shown up looking for work not long after Rita signed over the club to him and Claudine and then disappeared.

"You've done well, Jeff." Claude yielded to an impulse and kissed him. Jeff, though obviously surprised, returned the kiss with enthusiasm.

The two broke apart. "You go on back to the front of the house and keep an eye on things," Claude said. "Claudine and I will wrap this up, and I'll see you later."

"Sure thing." Jeff grinned as he strode down the hall.

Claude reentered the silent office and took his seat behind the desk, then passed the photograph to Claudine surreptitiously. She glanced down at it. Claude did not wait to see her reaction as he placed the handkerchief-encased bottle on the desk in front of him.

He had one piece of business he wanted resolved before he confronted Velva. He regarded Artemisia with an intent gaze. Artemisia frowned back at him.

"You lied to us," Claude said. "You, too, had sex with Seamus."

Artemisia grimaced. "I guess Jeff saw us after all. He told you, didn't he?" When Claude didn't respond, she continued, "Well, so what if I did? I can't work and study all the time, can I?"

"Not so high and mighty now, are you?" Velva glared at Artemisia. "You're just like the rest of us."

"Hardly. I didn't cheat on a boyfriend when I screwed Seamus."

Velva leaped out of her chair and started for Artemisia, but before she could take more than a step, Claudine was around the desk with one hand on the blonde's shoulder. Velva winced with pain as Claudine forced her back down into her chair.

Marlon stepped forward, as if to intervene, but stopped uncertainly when Claude moved from behind the desk to stand between him and Velva. Claudine mumbled, and the tension in Marlon's face eased.

"I gotta go." He smiled. "See y'all later." He walked out. Velva tried to get up to follow him and called for him to come back, but Claudine held her in her chair. Velva whimpered.

Claudine looked at Artemisia and Lula Ann and mumbled again. The faces of the two women went slack.

"Really enjoyed the discussion," Artemisia said. "See y'all later."

Lula Ann smiled and nodded as she followed Artemisia from the room. Claudine shut the door behind them and leaned against it. Claude resumed his place behind the desk.

Velva jerked her head back and forth between the twins. "What the hell is going on? Why did they all leave?"

Claude smiled. "We have no further need of them, you see. I have figured out who murdered Seamus."

"M-m-murdered? What do you mean?"

"Why did you do it, Velva?"

"I don't know what you're talking about." Velva's expression hardened. "What reason would I have to kill Seamus? You've gone completely off your rocker."

She started to stand but Claudine shoved her back into the chair. Velva yelped and squirmed. Claudine held firm until the woman stopped moving.

"Why don't you tell us a little about your family?" Claude leaned forward. He watched as she tensed at the word *family*. "We really don't know that much about you."

Velva glared at him. "Why the hell do you want to know about my family? They're none of your damn business."

Claude nodded at his twin. Claudine stepped forward and held the photograph of Rita Child in front of the stripper.

Velva's hand trembled as she accepted the photo. "Who's this supposed to be?" The attempted bravado in her voice only convinced Claude further that he was right.

"That's your cousin Rita. She used to own the bar before my sister and I took it over."

Velva didn't respond.

"Claudine and I—and our sister Claudette—got to know Rita pretty well, although I don't remember her ever mentioning you."

"Maybe because I don't know who the hell she is." Velva gave a strained laugh. "And she don't know me from Adam, either."

Claude glanced at the gaudy handbag on the floor by Velva's chair. He nodded to his sister, and Claudine picked it up to hand to him.

"So if I open this, I won't find anything to connect you to Cousin Rita?" Claude grasped the bag, ready to pull it open and dump its contents on the desk.

Velva jumped up and tried to jerk the bag out of his hands. Claudine grabbed her by the neck, and Velva sputtered as her airway constricted. Claudine shoved her down in the chair, but this time she kept her hand on Velva's neck. The stripper breathed hard, her expression one of panic.

Claude opened the bag and emptied it. Loose tissues, tubes of lipstick, keys, coins, wrapped pieces of candy, a pack of gum, and other items clattered on the desk. Claude set the bag aside and surveyed the jumble.

"I bet this might tell us something." He picked up Velva's cell phone. The stripper moaned.

Claude played with the phone, a model similar to the one Jeff had. He noticed that Velva had a new text message. He clicked on the icon and read it.

He looked up at Velva. "Interesting. You say you don't know Rita Child, but here she is, sending you text messages." He smiled, and Velva shrank back in fear.

"Here's what Rita has to say, Claudine. *One down two to go.*" He scrolled backward through the conversation. "Here's a little tidbit from you to Rita. *Lemon juice worked like you said.* Then there is a smiley face. *Wish it worked on my freckles like it did on the fairy.*"

Velva squealed as Claudine's grip on her neck tightened once again. She started babbling, "Please don't kill me," over and over.

"Did Rita ever tell you how she knew about us?" Claude asked when Velva's breath gave out and she stopped talking.

The stripper nodded weakly, and Claudine loosened her grip. Velva rubbed her neck. Her voice was hoarse when she spoke. "She spied on you. Had the dressing rooms bugged. Heard all kinds of shit about you fucking fairies."

Claudine shared a glance with her twin. They had wondered how Rita knew enough about them and their weaknesses in order to use lemon juice to kill Claudette. They hadn't taken time to question her when she admitted to the murder, simply told her to run for her life. Thus far she had managed to elude them. Perhaps Velva's phone would be useful in their hunt, and they could deliver justice to Rita as well.

"One more question, and then we will pass judgment." Claude picked up Jeff's handkerchief and unrolled the spray bottle, letting it drop on the desk. "You sprayed Seamus with juice from this bottle. Why did you do it on the sofa bed?"

Velva shuddered. "I said that Marlon wanted to watch him and me having sex. He liked that. Thought it was funny. I told him to open up the bed and get ready and Marlon would come along in a few minutes and catch us going at it."

"Then what happened?"

"He, well, he laid back on the bed and looked up at me, and I squirted him right in that stupid smirking face of his." Velva glanced fearfully back at Claudine, then at Claude.

"Did you enjoy the screams as he died?"

"No," she whispered. She gazed at Claude, obviously terrified. "What are you going to do? Call the police?"

Claudine placed a hand on her shoulder, and Velva started.

"No," Claudine said, smiling down at her, showing her teeth.

Claude came around the desk to join them. "No, Claudine and I will settle this ourselves."

After Rita killed their sister, they'd given her a chance to live in return for her signing the bar over to them—if she could hide from them for a full year, they would not kill her. They would not make the same mistake with Velva. And when the flooding receded, they would hunt down Rita.

The storm raged outside, but only the fairies heard the killer scream in agony as she died.

THE BAT-SIGNAL

SUZANNE MCLEOD

Suzanne McLeod's story combines characters who never met in the books. Luna Garza, shapeshifting werebat and undercover operative for the Dallas shifters, is on a flying visit to Bon Temps to look for a missing teen. She receives unexpected help from Sookie's telepathic cousin, Hunter Savoy, and his father, Remy. This story takes place between *Deadlocked* and *Dead Ever After*.

Luna swooped across Merlotte's mostly empty parking lot, the humidity in the early afternoon air leaving sticky, uncomfortable moisture trails along the thin membranes of her wings. A pinprick of color lit up on her mental radar, and she darted left, snagging a bug out of the air. Her nose twitched at the enticing scent of fried food wafting from the bar until the smell of stale beer, rising like a wraith from the Dumpster near the back door, curdled her appetite. There were times when having a bat's sensitive snout wasn't an advantage.

And there were times when it was. Like now as she glided over the roof of the trailer situated at the back of the bar, and her snout told her there was no one home. Hadn't been for a couple of days, maybe three, going by the way the scent of its shifter occupant was nearly as stale as the Dumpster's old-beer smell.

Which meant today's mission was a bust.

Luna hadn't really expected it to be anything else. After all, Sam hadn't answered her e-mails or texts. So he was more likely off having fun as his other-natured self. Collies, or whatever animal Sam had chosen to shift into this full moon, don't do so well with phones or computers. Of course, something could've happened to him, but then the local media would've picked up on a disappearing bar owner, shapeshifter or not. The same way the news was full of the runaway boy she and everyone else in the Dallas-area twoey coalition were looking for.

Besides, Bon Temps was way down the list of possible places the boy might head for. Far as they knew, he'd never been here, had no friends or relatives here. It had only made it on the list of places to search because Sam had been in the news a few times, and he was, like a score of other shifters, kinda high profile.

But really, for a teenage boy who'd spent his first fourteen years in Fort Worth, to head for somewhere as rural as Bon Temps and look for a shapeshifter he didn't know was as likely as Luna flying to the moon, despite being named for it. No, Dallas was where the boy had last been seen heading for. Dallas was where they'd discovered, according to the children's home files, that he had a great-uncle. And Dallas was where the coalition was concentrating the search.

Luna knew Dallas like the back of her wings, and she could've searched the city as fast as, if not faster than, any other twoey. But when the call for help went out to all the coalition members and she'd volunteered as usual (she couldn't sit on the sidelines if a twoey was in trouble, not like some), she'd been given the "safe" job. Oh, the Dallas packmaster—who'd taken the lead on this one, as he managed to do most times—had said it was because she and Sam were acquainted, but she'd known that for the excuse it was.

Damn werewolves with their delusions of superiority.

She snapped at a passing bug, tiny teeth crunching down.

Just because she was small as a woman, and even smaller as a bat, didn't mean she wasn't as capable as any of the larger, hairier, four-legged two-natured. She was so over the packmaster treating her as if she were made of spun glass; even her most exciting undercover job spying on the Fellowship of the Sun had been posing as an office worker/helper. Which had been nearly as boring as actually being one. Until

Sookie Stackhouse had turned up. Things had gotten way more exciting then, and the Fellowship members had gotten their asses kicked.

Of course, now that the weres and shifters had clawed their way out of the closet and shown the world that vamps weren't the only supes, even Luna's undercover work had dried up. She needed to do something more with her life. Something that meant something. Something worthwhile.

Catching a runaway werewolf who'd attacked an adult and another teenager, and maybe killed the teen (the doctors weren't hopeful the boy would regain consciousness), before the world found out and started pointing their shotguns at the first shifter they thought they'd seen, would be a good start on that *something*.

Frustration dipped Luna's wings as she flew toward the tree-crowded end of the parking lot, heading back to her car. Maybe she should pay Merlotte's a visit, in person, as it were. Sookie might be working. It would be good to see her again, catch up on some gossip, and while Luna couldn't tell her exactly what she was doing here in Bon Temps, Sookie was a telepath and a barmaid: two things that upped the odds she might've heard something useful.

And hey, while they were chatting, there was always food to eat, and now that Luna was far enough away from the icky Dumpster, she was hungry again. She snagged another bug and was trying to think up a good enough reason to explain why she was passing through when the back door of the bar swung open. A man, holding the hand of a boy of around five, came out.

"Y'all take care now, Remy," a breezy female voice called from inside. "Sorry I wasn't any help finding Sookie for you."

Sookie isn't here. Disappointment filled Luna. Even hungry as she was, the idea of a meal wasn't so good now with no chance of a friendly chat.

The man said a polite "Thank you, ma'am."

He sounded as disappointed as Luna felt. Then the door was yanked shut, leaving him and the boy standing by the smelly Dumpster as if they'd been put out with the trash. They looked at each other, the man's face worried as if he were wondering what to do next, the boy's brows drawn in a frown that looked too old for his childish face.

Luna circled, the fact they were looking for Sookie intriguing her. She swooped back, keeping high above their heads. Fly too close to humans (and the man and boy had to be human to stay that close to the stinking Dumpster), especially in daylight, and they got silly ideas about rabies and/or using her for target practice.

Not that the man looked like he had a gun, but better safe than shot. In fact, he looked easy on the eyes, good-looking in a rugged sort of way with wide-spaced eyes, a big nose, and a cute-dimpled jaw that stuck out. His thick, blond-brown hair was long enough to brush the collar of his flannel shirt, which, like his jeans, was worn but clean and showed off his muscular build. He was obviously no office flunky but worked hard at some manual job. The boy's clothes, corduroy pants and a bright blue sweatshirt with a picture of a cartoon dog, were newer, his hair was darker, and his young face promised to be even more handsome than his dad's. *He's going to be a heartbreaker when he's older,* Luna thought.

"She wasn't really sorry, Dad."

The boy had whispered, but despite that, Luna's sharp ears picked his words out as clear as if he'd been shouting. Curious, she dived closer.

"Shhh, son." The man, Remy, darted a nervous glance around. "Remember what we talked about."

"But, Dad, she was thinking rude things about how she didn't have time to talk about Aunt Sookie and wishing we would just get out of her hair already!"

Aunt Sookie? Surprise made Luna's dive steeper than she meant, and she almost tangled in the man's thick hair before swooping up to perch on the roof of the bar. She hooked her claws into the wooden overhang, furled her wings tight about her, and hung there, listening and watching.

Remy hunkered down in front of his boy with that patient exasperated look good parents get when they're about to lay down a rule for about the millionth time. "It doesn't matter what folks are thinking, Hunter, you don't get to say anything about it unless they say it out loud, remember?"

Hunter's chin dropped contritely. "Yeah, Dad. I know. Stuff in others' heads is private."

"That's right, son." Remy gave him a sad smile. "We aren't supposed to talk about it, 'less they do first."

Luna put two and two together.

Sookie was a telepath. The boy was a relative of Sookie's. It didn't take much to do the math and work out that he was a telepath, too. Woo-ee. Luna let that bombshell settle in, thinking how hard and terrifying life must be for a kid to hear all the crap adults thought about. Or really hear anyone's thoughts at all. Like *hers*. Though all her flying about and thinking hadn't seemed to catch the boy's attention. So far . . .

Luna narrowed her piercing bat eyes at the boy and mentally asked, *"Can you hear me, Hunter?"*

Hunter's head jerked and he looked around as if she'd actually spoken out loud.

"You hearing someone, son?" Remy asked, his tone alert and anxious.

Hunter nodded, and his dad jumped up from his crouch, his hand on the boy's shoulder pushing the child behind his legs protectively, and did his own scan of the parking lot and the trees bordering its outskirts. Regret filled Luna that while her little experiment had gotten an interesting result, she'd scared them both.

Which, now that she thought about it, wasn't such a surprise. She knew Sookie was always being made to use her mind reading to "help" the vamps and the weres, and Luna knew firsthand how quick Sookie's "helping" could go bad. The first time she'd met her, Luna's car had been totaled, and poor Sookie had ended up with a trip to the emergency room. And that wasn't Sookie's only hospital visit, according to what Luna had heard on the shifter grapevine. With experiences like Sookie's, it was only sensible that Hunter's dad wanted to keep his son's ability a secret.

Luna stayed quiet and still, trying not to think directly at the boy, not wanting to frighten him or his father again. She'd wait till they left, then check out Merlotte's for any gossip about the runaway. She probably wouldn't find anything, but she didn't want to leave any stone unturned.

Remy made sure there was no one about, even looking up, which not many humans did (not that he saw her, hanging in the shadows of the eaves as she was), before he took Hunter's hand in a firm grip and walked them toward a faded blue pickup truck as fast as the boy's legs could go without running. The truck, like the man's clothes, had seen better days but was clean and well cared for.

Remy hoisted his son up in the cab and settled him in a booster seat.

"It wasn't like an ordinary person's voice, Dad. It was more snarly." Hunter's whisper pricked Luna's ears. It sounded like the boy could tell the difference between hearing a shifter's and a human's thoughts.

Remy's quiet words floated up. "Was it like the other voice? The one you heard crying. The one we were going to tell Aunt Sookie about?"

"Yeah. Only this one wasn't scared, Dad."

"Is the voice still here?" Remy said, lifting his head out of the truck and glancing around, looking pretty scared himself.

A moment's silence, then, "I'm not hearing it anymore, Dad."

"Good." Remy's mouth thinned in determination. "Let's see if Aunt Sookie's at home, sport. Maybe she's doing work in her yard and forgot to bring her cell with her, and that's why she's not answering." He jogged around to the driver's side and jumped in. The engine roared to life.

Luna unfurled her wings, excitement and concern racing through her. The boy had heard another voice. One like Luna's. Did that mean he'd heard another werebat's voice? Not that there were many werebats in Louisiana; Luna knew of only one other, and she lived down in New Orleans and was old enough she wasn't going to be flying around this far from her home turf. Or maybe all shifter voices "sounded" the same in Hunter's head? So it could just be another were of some sort he'd heard. A were who was frightened and needed help. Could it be the runaway they were all searching for? Possible but doubtful. Whoever it was, he or she was in trouble. Which was all Luna needed to know. She was going to find the other twoey and help.

But to do that she needed to catch up with Remy and Hunter and get them to tell her where the boy had heard the voice.

Luna released her claws' hold on the roof and dived fast across the parking lot to the far corner where her silver Subaru was parked, almost hidden beneath a tangle of overhanging trees. She did a quick check around to make sure no one was watching, then swooped in through the half-open driver's window and burrowed into the clothes she'd left draped over the car's fabric seat. (Fabric seats made clothes-burrowing a less slippery affair.) She breathed in the citrus scent of her perfume, using it to anchor the image of her other nature in her mind, and made the decision to be human. A sharp burst of static filled her mind, and a second later her perception of the world shifted, and she was sitting behind the steering wheel with most of her clothes where they were meant to be.

She hastily adjusted her bra beneath the gypsy-style embroidered blouse (changes inside her clothes always played havoc with the fit of the lacy underwear she loved to wear), wriggled more comfortably into her jeans, pulled her socks up, and scooted her feet into her sneakers. Other weres might think a bat was only good for checking out dead ends and doing "safe" undercover work, but she was one of the few who was small enough, and had practiced enough, that she could shift without doing a bad Hulk-clothes-splitting impression, or ending up naked as a newly born babe.

She checked her cell—no news on the runaway—and started the car. She took the same turn out of the parking lot as Remy's pickup. There was no sign of the truck on the road but she knew the route they'd take, and they'd only gotten a few minutes' start on her so catching them was going to be as easy as snagging a bug. Plus she had a good idea where Sookie's house was in relation to Merlotte's thanks to an in-depth Google Maps search; the satellite view made it way easier to recognize new locations if she ever needed to do a flyover. Her planning and preparation was something else that made her a good tracker, one as good as, if not better than, those werewolves with their supposedly superior noses. Not only was her snout nearly as sensitive as theirs, but she didn't need to have it stuck to the ground, and she could cover as much distance or more, and see things they couldn't, when she was in the air.

Holding on to her mental satellite image, she drove along, tongue absently worrying at something stuck in her teeth—a wing off that last bug she'd crunched—she planned how she was going to persuade the protective Remy to let her talk to his telepathic son. She caught sight of the pickup ahead and decided that playing it straight was her best chance. Remy looked like a decent guy and obviously wanted to help the owner of the scared voice his son had heard, so appealing to his good nature should do the trick.

About four miles along the road the pickup turned just as Luna expected. She kept a respectful distance as she tailed it down a tidy gravel drive bordered by dense woods. The drive was long, and she was starting to wonder if they would ever reach the end, when it opened out into a wide clearing. At its center was a comfortable-looking two-story house with a tin roof and steps leading up to a broad wooden porch. There was a small painted shed to one side, lots of flower beds filled with cheerful, colorful blooms, and a lawn chair on the grass that looked as if it were just waiting for someone to rush out of the house and soak up the late-afternoon fall sunshine.

Luna parked a bit away from Remy's pickup, which he'd turned so it faced anyone arriving. She jumped out, taking a good lungful of air. Her bat snout might be supersensitive, but (bad pun aside) her human nose wasn't anything to sniff at, either. Despite the waiting lawn chair, Sookie wasn't home, and, like Sam's trailer back at Merlotte's, no one had been in the house for a good couple of days. Luna briefly wondered if the pair were off somewhere together, then remembered that last she'd seen Sookie, she'd told Luna she was hitched up with the big blond Viking deader, Eric. And she'd heard Sam was still seeing that insane Were, Jannalynn.

Luna's feet crunched on the gravel as she walked slowly toward the truck. It had a shiny bull bar attached to the front; those things could do some damage if they hit you. Hell, the pickup alone would. And judging by the way Remy was eyeing her suspiciously through the windshield, he'd considered that, and had parked the truck front-facing deliberately. *Smart guy.* She held her hands out at her sides so she didn't spook him any more than tailing him here had already.

Remy stuck his head out the pickup's window, a deep frown on his face. "You lost or something, ma'am? That why you followed me down here, on private property?"

"I'm Luna Garza, a friend of Sookie's," she said, offering him a placating smile as she stopped half a dozen feet away. "I know you and your son are relatives of hers, and I was hoping we could chat for a minute."

Remy's frown got deeper as he gave her a good once-over. She kept the smile on her face, hoping that the sight of a tiny, smiling Hispanic woman with big eyes and a mass of curly brown hair would reassure him she wasn't dangerous. Oh, and if her size didn't reassure him, there was always her freckles (which she'd learned to love a long time ago). No one ever expected folk with freckles to be evil. Which, of course, she wasn't.

But Remy obviously wasn't the trust-the-small-woman-with-freckles type. He jerked his head toward the house. "We're just on our way to visit with Sookie," he said. "If you're her friend, then we can chat with her."

"Okay," Luna said, "but she's not at home."

"How do you know?" he said.

Luna poked her sneaker into the gravel. "Stones are noisy," she said. "I think Sookie'd have heard us and come out of the house by now if she were here, don't you?"

Remy gave a reluctant nod.

"And I can tell with this." Luna tapped the side of her nose. "I'm a shifter."

Shock and fear rounded Remy's eyes. He moved his hand below the truck's window. "I got a gun, lady. And just so you know, it's loaded with silver bullets."

Luna's gut twisted. She backed up a few steps, raising her hands, her thoughts whirling in panic.

Getting shot with silver, coupled with getting shot just for being what she was, was her worst nightmare. And not just hers; most weres worried about it, especially as the law wasn't exactly clear on what rights they had now that the world knew they existed. Hell, Luna had heard Sam's stepdad had shot Sam's mom when she'd told him she was a shapeshifter. (Luckily, the bullet hadn't been silver.) Sam's mom hadn't been the only one to get hurt; there'd been plenty others.

Even a couple of the Dallas werewolves she knew had run into trouble. One had told his boss, who'd freaking whipped out a dinky pistol and plugged the Were straight in his chest. (He'd healed up and been right as rain, apart from the whole losing-his-job thing.) The other hadn't been so lucky. He'd been killed by his own daughter (the twoey had married a straight human and had kept his other nature a secret from his family, something Luna thought was asking for a crapload of trouble, though nothing that deserved him ending up shot dead).

And the latest was the runaway they were all searching for. Poor kid was an orphan and had been in a children's home since he was two. He hadn't known he was a Were until he hit puberty, had gone all werewolf at his first full moon night before last, and had been shot by one of the counselors. The man had caught him attacking another boy. The counselor was in the hospital with a mauled and broken arm, and sadly the other kid was in a coma, though not from the injuries from the werewolf attack, but from the bullet in his chest. The report said the counselor's gun had gone off accidentally a second time when the werewolf had turned on him.

Thankfully, so far, there were enough vamps and weres in the local police that while the incident had made the news, the fact that the teen-ager was a Were had been kept out of it. And if the Dallas packmaster had his way, he was going to make sure that particular furry pile of dirty laundry never got aired. As soon as the runaway was found, the packmaster was going to deal with him in the old way.

Luna didn't think it was right, but with folks so riled up about shifters just existing, trying to get the teen Were a fair trial would likely only lead to more deaths. No sensible, decent person wanted to feed the sort of violence and hatred that had dogged the Weres since they'd gone public.

Thinking of sensible and decent people, Luna hoped her initial impression about Remy was right. Especially as, while she'd been men-tally feeding her very own scary being-held-at-gunpoint nightmare, he seemed to be holding his own Mexican standoff and waiting for her to do something. As was Hunter, whom she could see peeking over his dad's shoulder, his face watchful and curious.

"Do you really want to shoot me in front of your kid?" Luna said, pleased her voice was calm and didn't betray the fear roiling inside her. "Just because I'm different?"

"I'm only gonna shoot you if you shift to wolf, ma'am," Remy said flatly, "same way I'd do if you was anyone trying to hurt us. Nothing to do with you being different."

"I'm not planning on hurting you. Or the boy," Luna said, frantically trying to think of a way to convince him. An idea hit her. It was a bit sneaky, and risky, but if it worked, Remy would know she knew Hunter's secret (hopefully he wouldn't then shoot her on the spot) and it would save them all a lot of time. Time they needed if she was going to get them to tell her where to find the frightened shifter Hunter had heard.

She thought very clearly at the boy. *I turn into a bat, Hunter. And I want to help the other person like me you heard, who was scared and crying.*

Hunter's eyes went saucer-round. "Dad!" He tugged on Remy's shirtsleeve. "She's a bat woman. She just told me. She wants to help the other voice. The one I heard."

Remy shushed Hunter as a mix of emotions flashed across his face; fear, anger, exasperation, indecision, and finally resolve. Luna could see he was going to protect his son's secret no matter what. The glare he fixed on her confirmed it.

"You planning on telling anyone, ma'am?" he demanded.

She shook her head. "Nope, not my business. And Sookie's my friend. Plus I'm not the sort of lowlife who'd rat out a child. Kids are innocents and should be protected. I give you my word that his secret is safe with me."

Remy glanced at Hunter with a hesitant expression. "She sound all right to you, son?" He tapped his son's head gently. "In there?"

"She was scared when you told her you had a gun, Dad," the boy said, sounding way older than his five years.

"She still scared?" Remy asked.

"A bit," Hunter replied.

Luna nodded in agreement. No way did she want to be shot.

"What about you, son?" Remy asked. "Anything in her head frighten you?"

"No, sir," Hunter told him, again with more assurance than his age warranted. It made Luna wonder exactly what horrible thoughts he'd heard in the past.

Remy's shoulders sagged in resignation, and he gave Luna his full attention again. "What do you want from us, ma'am?"

"Is it okay if I put my hands down?" she asked. Her own shoulders were tense and tight from being held at gunpoint.

"Sure," Remy said, with a shrug. "I haven't got a gun anyway." He popped open the truck's door and showed her his empty hands. "Don't think they're the right kind of thing to have around children."

Luna blinked, astounded, then burst out laughing as relief coursed through her. "Well, you freaking fooled me," she said, shaking her head as she rubbed her arms to get the stiffness out of them.

One side of Remy's mouth twitched up in response. "Yeah, well, I meant to, ma'am," he said. Then his expression turned curious. "You really turn into a bat, Ms. Luna?"

"I do." Luna grinned. "Want to see?"

"Yes!" Hunter shouted, and clambered over his father to leap out of the truck, excitement lighting his face.

Remy got out behind him, placed a gentle admonishing hand on his son's shoulder, and said, "Son, mind your manners."

"Sorry, Dad," Hunter told him without taking his gaze off Luna. "Yes, please, Ms. Luna," he said, "I'd be very happy to see you change into a bat."

"Then I'd be very happy to show you, Mr. Hunter," Luna replied, grinning wider. "After I have, maybe you and your dad could show me where you heard that voice?"

Hunter looked up at Remy, his face echoing Luna's question. Remy gave a broad smile, one that carried a whole world of relief. "We'd be very happy to do that."

Luna nodded, boosted herself onto the hood of her car, and concentrated on her bat image. She caught the flare of sharp static in her mind—

And then, as her clothes fell in a heap, she flew, wings beating hard to lift her tiny body from the short dive. Finally, she caught a warm updraft that lifted her up through the heavy air, and, as she soared higher and higher, Hunter's delighted squeals lit up the bright blue sky around her like fireworks on the Fourth of July.

Swooping back down, she saw the little boy jumping and waving his arms, laughing. Remy stood beside him, gazing up at her as she dived and darted through the air, a bemused expression on his face as if the world had suddenly become a stranger and more wondrous place. Luna looped the loop, and gave herself over to the sheer, heart-thudding exhilaration of being alive, and flying.

Hours later, Luna pulled onto the shoulder of a deserted potholed parish road and parked behind Remy's pickup. Remy and his son didn't live in Bon Temps but Red Ditch, which was even more rural and was, Luna realized now that she was here, a perfect place for a runaway shifter to hide out in.

She got out and stopped for a moment, breathing in the scents and sounds and sights of the bayou that stretched out in all directions as far as she could see, until it merged into the gray sky of dusk. The smell of green growing things, undercut with the sweetness of decay where the rotting vegetation enriched the peaty water. A slight saltiness on the back of her tongue. The quiet rustles, squeaks, chomps, and tiny splashes of myriad lives going about the business of living. Even the soft hoot of an owl couldn't dim her enjoyment. Maybe to someone else the place might feel uninhabited and desolate, even spooky, but she loved the way the landscape hid nearly all signs of human habitation, loved the expanse of earth in all its uninhibited beauty. And her other nature was eager to answer the call of the moon, to stretch her wings, and take to the night.

"*Soon,*" Luna promised herself, wondering why, when there were places like this, she'd lived in cities nearly all her life.

She picked her way along the crumbling shoulder, taking care not to slip and fall into the water-filled ditch that ran alongside it, and joined Remy where he was standing by the pickup's open door.

Hunter was inside, strapped into his booster seat, head lolling back, mouth open as he slept. Poor kid was worn slap out, and she hated that they were going to wake him up soon. But he'd had a good meal, as they all had, at a cute mom-and-pop restaurant. Food was a necessity for a five-year-old who'd had a long day, and for a father who was trying his best to protect his boy, and for a werebat who had a night of search-and-rescue flying ahead of her.

Plus the time they'd spent eating had given a local garage the chance to mount the huge halogen headlights now fixed on the bull bar on the front of Remy's truck. (Luna had paid for the meal and the lights; working for the twoey coalition, even if she got stuck with the "safe" jobs, still came with perks.)

She waved at the bayou and, keeping her voice low so as not to wake Hunter, said, "This is where he heard the crying voice, right?"

Remy nodded. "We drove up and down the road a way, making sure, and here's where he heard it strongest. He knew it weren't a human, like we told you, and that's when we decided to go get Sookie."

"You manage to get hold of her yet?" Luna asked.

Remy shook his head. "Still getting her voice mail," he said glumly. "Same as the last hundred times I called her."

Disappointment itched at Luna. The search would've been so much easier with Sookie. She could've helped listen and locate the Were in trouble. And with Sookie on board, Luna could've called in more searchers from the nearest werewolf pack. But she couldn't do that and keep Hunter's ability a secret. So that meant only the three of them could be here to put their "war plan" into action.

A loud, heavy splash made her jump. "What's that?" she said, peering in the direction of the sound.

"That's a gator off to find his supper," Remy said, way too calmly for Luna's comfort. "There's a good few in the bayou, enough that you can get a hunting license here in the season, but no one sees them much. Most gators are shy of humans. Bobcats are the same. The black bears are a bit more curious, but if you shout at them they usually go away. Unless there's food, of course. Though we don't get many bears round this way, so there's nothing to worry about."

She was going to be searching for a twoey hiding out in swamp full of freaking alligators, big cats, and bears! The bayou didn't look so enticing now. Good thing none of those critters could fly. Which, she reassured herself, made them less of a worry than that owl she heard earlier. Of course, she wasn't the only bat around, so the owl had plenty of options for its dinner.

Luna took a steadying breath, buoyed up by that thought. "So," she said, "time we got started."

"Reckon it is," Remy agreed. He leaned into the cab and gently shook Hunter awake. The little boy groaned and yawned, then, as he saw where he was, popped wide-awake, eyes shining with anticipation. With his father's help he quickly unbuckled and climbed out of his seat to jump from the truck. Remy picked him up and sat him safely on top of the hood.

"You ready, son?" he asked.

"Sure am, sir," Hunter replied smartly, grinning as he squeezed his eyes tight shut. He cocked his head as if he were listening. Which he was. Though Luna had spent enough time with the boy by now to know he didn't need all the dramatics to hear other folks' thoughts. Not even hers. But she was glad it had turned into a game for him; poor kid had enough to deal with without getting traumatized by all this.

Hunter made a low "ahh-ahh" sound and stuck his arm straight out, pointing left into the twilight. "He's over there," he said, then opened his eyes. "He's not crying anymore but he's really, really sad."

"Can you tell how far away he is, sport?" Remy asked.

"I think he's about as far away as Ms. Luna went when we played the game."

Luna had come up with the game during their "war council" (Hunter's enthusiastic description of their initial chat on how they were going to find the shifter). She'd flown around Sookie's house, and the woods, even the nearby cemetery, and thought directly at Hunter to tell him where she was, so she could work out at what distance he stopped hearing her. The kid was smart so it hadn't taken them too long to discover Hunter could hear her right to the end of Sookie's long drive.

Which meant that the shifter was about two miles away—the length of Sookie's drive—in the direction Hunter had pointed.

Of course, that still left Luna with a lot of ground to cover, but she could fly as high as ten thousand feet and cover forty-odd miles in a night (which was the same height as and a bit more than the distance of the Mexican free-tailed bat her other nature was closest to), so she had a good chance of finding the sad werewolf.

The sun set with its usual suddenness, and a swath of bright stars and the fat one-day-past-full moon lit the night sky, calling her to shift and fly!

"Thanks so much, Mr. Hunter," Luna said. "That's going to be a big help."

The little boy smiled at her, pleased. Then his face fell and he said, "He thinks his best friend's dead, Ms. Luna. That's why he's so sad."

Luna's heart thudded. The teen the runaway werewolf had attacked at the children's home had been his best pal. This had to be him. For a minute indecision warred in her. Should she let the Dallas packmaster know? Call for help? No, she'd promised not to betray Hunter's secret. She'd find this sad Were first, make sure he really was the runaway, and as soon as Hunter was safely out of the picture, then she'd call for help.

"My turn," Luna said, and headed for her car.

She slid into the seat and rechecked the details of the runaway on her phone. Better to know them and not need them. She shifted to her batself, then crawled out of her clothes and into Remy's waiting palms. His big hands were warm and slightly damp with sweat and smelled of the lavender soap the restaurant had provided in the restrooms. Luna's little bat heart skipped an anxious beat as he carefully lifted her as high as he could. When they'd been planning this, she'd decided that asking Remy to literally hold her life in his hands was one way to show him he could trust her with his son's secret. And of course, the higher up she was, the easier it was to launch into flight.

Her trust was rewarded and seconds later she was zooming out in the direction Hunter had pointed.

"Cold?" she thought at him.

The huge halogen headlights bolted to Remy's pickup flashed brightly twice, lighting up the night about her. *Cold.*

Luna squeaked with success. They had two-way communication! And the halogens were so bright she'd be able to see them for miles. Unlike their afternoon "game," Luna wasn't going to have to fly back every time she thought at Hunter to see if he'd actually heard her. And the amazing thing was that the halogens had been Hunter's idea. Well, not the halogens as such, but he'd said that as she was a bat, they should get a giant torch so he could signal to the nontelepathic Luna, like they did with Batman.

And so the halogens became the Bat-Signal (without the bat cutout, though Hunter had taken some convincing by Remy that they didn't need one). Of course, the next problem was how Hunter could tell Luna if she was getting close to the other were, and again Hunter came up trumps, saying they could use clues, like in the game. *Hot. Warm. Cold.*

A few minutes' flight later, Luna thought at Hunter again, "Cold?"

The Bat-Signal flashed twice. *Cold.*

She still wasn't close enough, but she estimated she was only a quarter of a mile out over the bayou. She flew on, the night alive with hisses and croaks and rustles and splashes. The air swarming with buzzing insects, all of them bright spots of color on her mental radar. She flapped over thick clumps of leafy trees here, sparse skeletal ones there, seeing the fat face of the moon reflected again and again in the brackish water of the sluggish creeks, and huge lily pads floating like mini islands on the still-watered ponds.

"Cold?" Luna thought.

Cold.

She spied a small spotted frog on a lily leaf and just barely stopped her automatic dive; dinner already seemed a long time ago. Then she glimpsed a sinuous gray length marked with black, winding its way toward the pad. Its ripple rocked the frog's raft, there was a snap of teeth, and the tasty snack was gone. She turned her attention back to the search.

"Warm?" Luna asked.

Cold.

Not close enough.

Another stream.

Another reflection of the moon.

Lots more trees.

She was nearly at the two-mile limit. "Warm?" she thought.

Three flashes. *Warm*, the Bat-Signal confirmed.

She snapped up a passing bug to celebrate and flew faster.

Below her a lake opened out. Cypress trees draped in ghostly Spanish moss rose out of the water like a scattering of dark towers. More giant lily pads covered the surface, and here and there among them floated a solitary log. A round shape—a turtle the size of a dinner plate—swam almost silently through the water. A nearby log moved suddenly, surging through the water, one end yawning wide—it crunched down on the turtle, twisting and rolling and foaming the lake surface.

The lake was obviously alligator central. The runaway werewolf wasn't going to be down there. And the distant shore was too far out-side Hunter's range.

She swooped back to the nearest bank.

"Hot?" she thought.

Three flashes. *Warm.*

Maybe Hunter's range out here in the sticks was longer than they'd thought. She flew back out over the lake, heading for the far bank.

"Warm?" Luna asked, soaring higher to see the answer.

Four flashes lit up the Bat-Signal. *Hot!*

Hot! But she was only halfway there. Below her was nothing but the lake.

"Hot?" she asked, double-checking.

Hot, confirmed the Bat-Signal.

The Were *was* down there, but down there was nothing but freak-ing water. It didn't take a genius to realize he wasn't going to be pad-dling around as a werewolf, not in the middle of a lake full of lily pads and silently floating log-impersonators. That was a surefire way to end up as gator chow.

So where was he?

"Looking," Luna thought.

A single flash from the Bat-Signal. *Okay.*

Flying over the moon-silvered water in ever-widening circles, she put her sensitive snout and mental radar on full alert. And got a hit as she passed over a cluster of cypress trees.

She swooped down and around their bulbous bases, zipping through the stalagmite-like knees sticking out of the water. The base of one large tree had split, forming a dark watery cave. Her nose told her the werewolf was in there. Though how he'd gotten safely out here past all those gators was a mystery.

She landed on the nearest tree where two branches split about six feet above the lake, dug her claws in, and shifted. A moment later she was squashed securely in the V, feet braced against the rough, stringy bark. A sting on her butt let her know a nasty little bug had taken retri-bution for all of its pals she'd munched.

She grabbed some handfuls of moss to protect her modesty, not that she was prudish, but talking to a stranger, especially a teenager, while nude could be distracting for all involved. Fixing her gaze on the tree cave, she cupped her hands and hollered. "Jimmy, I'm Luna Garza. I'm a werebat, and I'm here to help you. So get your furry ass out here."

A hush fell over the bayou for a breath, and then the buzzes, rustles, and splashes rushed back in like shocked whispers as if the local inhabitants had suddenly noticed a human had appeared.

"Hurry up," she shouted again. "We ain't got all night, y'know."

The tree cave stayed dark and silent. Had her nose got it wrong?

She sent a mental question: "Still hot?"

Four flashes from the Bat-Signal lit up the distant sky. *Hot!*

Freaking werewolf was ignoring her.

"You've got five minutes," Luna called, "before I fly out of here." Then acting on a hunch, she added, "Your friend Gordon is still alive."

Before the echo of her voice faded, water rippled and something crawled slowly out of the tree cave and clawed its way up onto the thick-spread base of the cypress.

It didn't look like a wolf. Its head and body were rounded, not pointed. Its fur, even slick and shadowed by the water, was mottled with dark patches. Its tail was wrong, too: short and stubby. And were those tufts on its ears?

Just as Luna was wondering what in freaking hell had happened to the poor Were, it hit her why the animal looked so wrong.

She wasn't looking at a wolf, as she'd been expecting, but a huge bobcat.

The twoey was a freaking shifter.

Well, that explained why he'd bypassed Dallas and headed for Bon Temps. He really had been looking for Sam.

The air around the bobcat shimmered, and a scrawny teenage boy took its place. He shook, then sat huddled on the tree's sloping trunk, skinny arms wrapped around his drawn-up knees, eyeing her with patent distrust. She recognized his thin, dark face, his black tight-cropped curls, currently dotted with water drops that glinted like diamonds in the light of the moon. Definitely the runaway, Jimmy.

"Gordy ain't dead?" Jimmy's question was rusty, as if he hadn't used his voice much recently. Or he'd been crying. Which, of course, he had been.

"He isn't," Luna replied gently. "The shot didn't kill him." Then because she wasn't about to sugarcoat things, she added, "But he's in a coma. The docs aren't sure if he'll pull through."

A mix of grief and anger crossed Jimmy's face. "If he dies, it's Mr. Nicholson's fault." He said it in a sullen croak, like he didn't expect Luna to believe him but he had to say it anyway.

It sounded as if there was a story to be told, and truths to be sifted—especially considering how fast and easy Jimmy had changed from bobcat to human; shapeshifting didn't look as new to him as the police report said—but other things needed to be dealt with first.

Luna directed a quick thought at Hunter. "Found him."

The Bat-Signal flashed, *Okay.* Then after a brief lull, it flashed six times: code for *Good-bye and good luck.* Remy and Hunter were going home.

"Good-bye and good luck to you, too," Luna thought with a pang of sadness. She'd probably never see the brave little boy or his protective dad again. Then she leaned forward and fixed the teen with a stern look.

"Did you attack Gordon?" she asked.

"Course not!" Jimmy's head jerked up in affront. "Gordy's my best friend."

"The police report said he had bite marks on his throat," Luna said, eyebrows raised in silent question.

"Well, yeah." Jimmy looked embarrassed. "I bit him. Gordy wanted to be a werewolf like me."

Of course he did. Never mind that Jimmy wasn't a werewolf but a shifter, so he couldn't bite anyone and change them. The teen was an orphan; he didn't know any better.

"So," Luna said, keeping the exasperation out of her words. "If Gordy wanted to get bit, and you weren't attacking him, how did things end up with Mr. Nicholson shooting at you?"

Jimmy sniffed loudly. "Like you'd believe me. Or care."

Teenagers! "Instead of having fun in Dallas with my friends," Luna said evenly, "I'm sitting in a tree, in the middle of a gator-infested lake, in a swamp, talking to you. I think that counts as me caring, don't you?"

Jimmy frowned. "Suppose so."

"Glad to hear it," Luna said. "And as for believing you, I won't know if I do until you've told me what happened. Why don't you start with something easy like how you got out here?"

"I swam. Cats can swim, y'know." His tone suggested it was a stupid question, which Luna admitted it probably was. Though how he'd managed not to end up as gator chow . . .

"Fair enough," she said. "Why don't you tell me how you found out you were a shifter and take it from there?"

Jimmy wriggled about a bit, then let out a deep sigh.

"First time," he said slowly, and then his words rushed out, eager to tell his story now that he had an audience, "I turned into a hamster like the classroom pet." His face screwed up in disgust. "I knew I was a were 'cause I'd seen them come out on the TV, but I thought that was it, and I was stuck turning into something small and useless every full moon. Then next time I turned into a cat like the one at the home. That's when me and Gordy worked out that I was changing into the animal I looked at before the moon rose. So we found a picture of a wolf, and it worked!" He grinned. "Werewolves are the best."

Of course they are, Luna thought, *if you suffer from delusions of superiority.* Like every werewolf she knew. And small didn't mean useless! She clamped down on her irritation; Jimmy didn't know any better. But he could learn, if he got the chance. He and his pal had been smart to work out the mechanics of shapeshifting without any help.

"So Gordy wanted to be like me," Jimmy carried on. "Once we found out I could be a wolf, anyway. No one bothers you when you're strong and tough. But that stupid Mr. Nicholson was always on our backs, and when he saw my wolf, he didn't even shout or nothing, just pointed his gun at me. Gordy threw himself in front, and took the bullet." He shuddered. "It must've hurt bad 'cause Gordy screamed an' then he made this funny gurgling sound and Mr. Nicholson was going to shoot again . . ." Jimmy trailed off, staring down at the dark water.

"So you went for the gun," Luna finished softly. *Brave kid.*

"Yeah," he muttered, then raised his head and stared straight at her. "Is Mr. Nicholson okay?"

Luna could hear the fear hanging on his question the same way she could see the thick Spanish moss dripping off the tree.

"His arm's tore up," she replied matter-of-factly. "And you broke a couple of bones. He's gonna have a scar or two, but he'll live." Which was good, more than the idiot man deserved after shooting at a couple of innocent kids, just because one was two-natured.

"I knew I hadn't hurt him bad," Jimmy said, his face twisting with frustration. "I was careful. I just want to know if he's gonna turn into a werewolf? Now I've bit him?"

Luna shook her head. "He can't," she said. "You're not a werewolf, Jimmy. You're a shapeshifter. Shapeshifters are born, not bitten."

"But it said on the Internet this guy got bit by a werewolf and he turned into a wolfman."

"That's something that only happens with weres, Jimmy," Luna replied. "Not shapeshifters."

"Oh." Jimmy's face fell. "But that means Gordy won't be a werewolf."

"No, he won't," Luna agreed. "But isn't it more important that he gets better?"

He nodded, chin dropping sadly to rest on his knees. A couple of seconds later he muttered, "Good thing Mr. Nicholson won't turn into a werewolf, either. He don't deserve to be one."

And you don't deserve what's happened to you, Luna thought.

"C'mon," she said, "you can't stay here. Those gators are going to start thinking about their empty bellies soon. How about we both head for somewhere more comfortable?"

The teen half sniffed, half sneered. "What for? It ain't like going back's gonna change anything. Now I've attacked Mr. Nicholson and they all know what I am, they'll lock me up and throw away the key. I might as well stay here. None of the other animals will bother me if I stick to shifting into a bobcat."

The twoey coalition, especially with the packmaster throwing his weight around even though the young shapeshifter wasn't technically his responsibility, would do more than lock him up, Luna thought, her heart heavy. And for a moment she wondered if life in the bayou was better than none at all. Except that Jimmy was just a kid, and he hadn't done anything wrong. Why should he have to pay for someone else's stupidity? Only how to persuade him to come with her?

She pondered for a moment, then made a show of looking around, and said, "Spending your life as a bobcat isn't going to change anything, either. I expect it'll be pretty boring, too. No computer games, no Internet, no TV, no movies, no music. Though, of course, it'll liven up during hunting season." She grinned. "Bet you'll make a pretty fur coat one day."

He blinked at her, horror widening his eyes. "Fur coat?"

"Yeah, that's what they use bobcat skins for," she said cheerfully. "They'll probably stuff your head and mount it on a wall, too."

She saw his Adam's apple bob as he swallowed.

"If you come with me, Jimmy," she said softly, "I'll help you."

As she spoke, something inside her clicked into place. And she knew she was going to do exactly that. She was going to go to the coalition and make them do the right thing by this runaway shapeshifter. And not just them, but the rest of the world, too. Even if it meant fighting for the rest of her life. Just because weres and shifters were different, it didn't mean they were any less human. And it didn't mean they shouldn't have rights. Luna fixed Jimmy with a serious look. "That's a promise."

He stared at her, suspicion, skepticism, and hope warring in his eyes. "Okay," he said finally, and cautiously. "I guess you helping me's got to be better than being a fur coat."

Luna grinned, and said, "Hey, bobcats can't fly. Think you can change into a bat, Jimmy?"

Ten days later Hunter received a short letter sent to his aunt Sookie's address. The envelope had a New Orleans postmark but no return address—secrets needed to be kept, after all.

Dear Mr. Hunter,

I am writing to thank you, and to let you know what happened to the sad boy. You were very brave and smart, and his rescue would have been very different, and difficult, without you.

Well, he is no longer sad, as his best friend was not dead as he thought but only hurt. And now the friend has made a full recovery.

As for the boy who was sad, he is now living with an old friend of mine in New Orleans, who is going to make sure he does not get into any more trouble, and where I am sure he will be very happy.

Please could you let your dad know, and tell him a huge thank-you, too.

Love and best wishes,
Batwoman

THE SUN, THE MOON, AND THE STARS

DANA CAMERON

Dana Cameron was always a Pam fan. She wanted to see more of her past, which I only hint at in the books. Dana decided to start with Eric's creation of Pam as a vampire, weaving that into her own story about why Pam loves being a vampire and the trouble that enjoyment—and Pam's nature—get her into.

The day I died was the day I'd never anticipated. Not in the sense of every oblivious mortal, ignoring what inevitably must find us all. It was the day I felt something, profoundly.

I blame the artists. The men, most especially. They taunt us with ideas of freedom, and fail to tell us that it exists only in their prose, their pictures, their verse. I vowed I would give up the sun, the moon, and the stars for that kind of freedom. When I sneaked out to visit my darling, I thought myself daring, a tragic heroine. After that night, I understood I had been living a mummified existence, bound by corsetry and social niceties.

Before, I did not know myself, with my "wild" ways, to be alive but immured.

And yet if I hadn't been trying to live, to feel, as the poets claim we must, I never would have drawn my master's attention. If I hadn't tried to leave the drab, mortal path I was confined to, I would never have died and discovered true life.

I remember shadows from Before. A shadowy existence, shadows between our garden and that of our neighbors'. I thought that place was Elysium: It housed my closest friend and, occasionally, her cousin, my love. But mine was nothing but a weak imitation of life, soon to be snuffed out entirely, a feeble gesture at something more than a muffled existence. A young lady's fanciful imagination that her tentative efforts to trammel convention were real, meaningful. Potent.

Then came a series of shocks, too many things wrong all at once. That stranger waiting just outside my garden gate, as he'd waited in the chilly winter churchyard in past weeks.

Watching me.

"I have news, from—" He nodded at our neighbor's house, where my love was no doubt writing poetry to me at that moment.

His words puzzled me. "I've only just left—"

"He has a plan for the two of you to be together, and it demands urgency. We are too visible here." He followed me through the garden. "You should ask me in."

I was dazzled. The stranger was blond, an Adonis. Something not quite the gentleman about him, and yet I did not hesitate.

"Please, come in." I opened the door, took off my cape, and—

One strong hand at my back, the other brushed against my cheek, and a thrill as he pulled me to him. I expected a kiss, but his hand swept over my hair, pushing my head so that I could feel his mouth on the soft skin above the lace of my collar and below my ear.

The touch of his cold lips against my neck and my knees went weak. He bit me.

I opened my mouth—was it to scream or moan?—and before a noise could come out, I felt the pain.

Sharp teeth sheared through my flesh like scalpels. Blood—my blood—rushed into his mouth. The life was drawn from me by his lips.

And still beyond all that, beyond death, I felt a thumb across my nipple.

It was the most intense thing I'd ever experienced in my life. Shock, fear, suffering, arousal in a moment. The sensation was more than the sum of my parts; I felt my whole body alive at his touch. Primal experiences that no lady should have known, until the wedding night and childbirth.

I'm not certain how we arrived in my room, but he settled me onto my bed and raised his left wrist to his mouth. I saw a flash of white, white teeth, so long, so sharp. His jaw worked; I heard the gentle growling, a dog with a bone, and then the ripping of flesh.

A sharp scent caught me. Rich, dark, earthy, a metallic edge. My body, my being, contracted with need for it. All my earlier thoughts of the physical element of romance, those utterly chaste kisses tinged with hope and illusion, fled in the face of that longing.

That was real need. Real life.

I knew instantly what to do. I grabbed his wrist, drew it to my mouth. I latched on as surely as any babe to its nurse. My teeth sank into his flesh and I guided his blood over my tongue. The dryness that threatened to consume me tightened to an ache, as if resisting the offered nourishment, and then . . .

It began to burn, as if I were being devoured from the inside out. I could no more stop the flow of blood than I could scream with the pain it brought. As I kept sucking, the wildfire devoured me, and all I knew was that if I perished at that instant, I would die craving more blood. A slave to my own torment, a willing victim to a terrible pleasure.

I was a fool, was nearly my last thought. *So wrong. This was what I sought, this commingling of fear, lust, life. And death.*

Even as all the fires of hell seemed to consume me, I was grateful and remembered my manners.

"Thank y—"

Night. Again. I woke to bitter cold and blinding light.

"Sally, why are the windows open? It's—"

But my voice didn't work; my lips cracked as I tried to form the words.

I reached for the water pitcher; my hand hit something slippery and softly resistant, too close to me.

My fingers floated along the cloth. A shiver from my fingertips up my arm, until it felt as if my entire body registered what I felt: satin. I wasn't in my bed. I was in a lidless box.

I realized it was a coffin.

The light was starlight. I was staring up at the stars. My eyes focused slowly, aching as if there were too much for them to take in. There was too much beauty in the night. The silver music of the stars, the brilliance of the sandy soil as it trickled from the earthen walls that surrounded me. It pattered on my sleeve, making a noise as quiet and as fleeting as mice.

Soil and satin, two things that ordinarily I would keep far apart. But with the shrill fairness of the stars above, the glorious pulse of the dark city around me, the cacophony of worms and voles beneath . . . it was just one more note.

I wanted to cry out in amazement, but I was as parched as the desert. A small noise escaped, barely a croak, but even that was gratifying to me.

The dryness of my mouth triggered something. A terrible hunger seized me, a thirst so awful it was as though I were filled with coal dust and cobwebs. I struggled to sit up, the movement only underscoring the misery of my desiccated body.

"All will be well."

Cold blue eyes, nameless but not unfamiliar, appeared, another constellation in the firmament. A sudden movement, quicker than even I could follow with my newly sharpened eyes, then strong arms around me and a rush of frigid air. My preserver took me from the grave with as little effort as if he'd scooped up a kitten. Just as easily, he cradled me in his lap.

"—you." The effort of finishing my last mortal sentence made my throat ache. "I am so—"

"Here."

He offered me his wrist again, and finally, his blood quenched my tortured throat. I began to relax, began to feel . . . more than alive. Sure-minded. Free.

He taunted me a little, as if he could tell the worst was past, and moved as if he'd take his wrist from me.

I clung to his arm, my fingers powerful, my mouth still demanding.

He laughed and relented. "Slowly, now, Miss Ravenscroft. Another moment, only. I did not bring you to life only to abandon it myself."

I let his blood roll over my lips, felt it spill over and caress my cheek, as if I were savoring the juice from a stolen peach. I swallowed the last mouthful greedily as he firmly took his arm from me. I could make no complaint. I had never enjoyed food so well, never felt it nourish me so completely. So perfectly.

Now that the blood was gone—I wondered if my next mouthful would taste as lovely—I could smell him. Masculine, faintly of horse, laundry soap, and blood—perhaps even some from the laundress who'd washed that shirt. More distinctly I sensed power and lust.

"I do admire a young lady with an appetite," he said, helping me to sit. A politeness, only; I felt more vital than I ever had. "I am Eric Northman. I will teach you about your new life and I shall protect you as my own. In return, I expect your obedience in all things."

It was a better bargain than any lady in my acquaintance had ever been offered, and far more honest. I did not hesitate. "Oh, yes, please!"

A present to seal our compact: He gestured and a gaunt street Arab with a vacant look on her face stumbled to our side, obeying the same will that had compelled me to allow a strange man into my father's house. Her rags were redolent of the perfume of the East End slums. She wordlessly stretched her dirty neck out in front of me.

"Drink," was all my master said. He didn't need to say more; the hunger I felt instructed me. The stink of her poverty was sharp but secondary to the entrancing rhythm of the pulse in her neck. It called me, the answer to my killing thirst.

A new and peculiar spasm in my mouth: I felt my teeth lengthening, becoming sharper. A throbbing in my entire person seemed to match the pulse at her throat that filled my ears.

I rose to my knees and clutched her by the shoulders. Without a second thought, or even a first, I bit down hard on her neck, felt the skin puncture and rend under my fangs. Her tiny whimper was a sweet counterpoint to the thumping in her veins, her weak resistance enthralling, as her blood filled me. The most delectable flavors rolled over my tongue like my favorite dinner: roast pork and savory pudding and dark red wine all together. I sucked harder, the tear in her skin wider than my greedy mouth could cover, and the blood sluiced down my chin and neck. The heat of the lost blood warmed and thrilled me as it soaked into my silk dress and my tumbled-down hair.

I felt myself refreshed to the point of ecstasy as existence vacated her forever.

I cast the small body away from me, useless now, an empty foul thing. My strength was greater than I realized. She arced through the air, to land, a broken doll, on a monument of an angel nearby. I licked at my lips and chin in a very unladylike fashion.

I half stood. "More!" The more I ate, the more I desired, and I craved other things, too, though I could not have put a name to them.

"You are wonderful!" My master, Eric, laughed. "There will be more, I promise you. But what if I told you there was something even better than feeding?"

"There cannot be." There was not even a twinge, as there might have been Before, at such greediness. Every sermon I'd ever heard against the sins of the flesh had been burned out of me. I yearned for more.

"There is."

Eric raised me to my feet, placed my hand on the front of his trousers. The satisfaction I'd felt in drinking from the urchin diminished beside what I experienced now. The talk of love and eternal passion that—I could not even remember the name of my friend's cousin—had promised me, was pretty, hollow, gilt-tin words, now banished by an irresistible yearning. Eric's face was stunningly beautiful, pale, and hungry as mine, and those blue eyes burned still.

"Yes! Oh, yes, please!"

Then the naughty Miss Ravenscroft, whose previous noteworthy transgressions were only silly declarations and clumsy, stolen kisses from a boy whose name she couldn't remember, truly became the vampire Pamela. No thoughts but my own satisfaction troubled me, and as I hauled up my skirts and petticoats, Eric lifted me to sit on the edge of a monument. An instant later, I felt him slam inside me, and I knew he was right. This was nearly the match of feeding, but in a way I had never experienced. I wrapped my legs around him, locking my ankles behind his back, and felt his being—no pulse, no heart—merge with mine. The blood he shared with me now linked us in a divine knot, sharing each other's pleasure.

Even as I moaned my climax—only dimly aware of the chilly London air, the cooling corpse of my first meal nearby—I felt a pain that threatened to eradicate me. It grew and grew and I panicked. As the spiraling agony threatened to swallow me, I was certain I was entering hell.

More than a hundred years later, I *am* in hell.

I wake, remembering with longing my happy dream of sex with Eric. And now . . .

I'm facedown in a pile of blankets. My head feels as if it's lined with silver as shiny black millipedes with leaden feet tap-dance inside my skull. The pain threatens to shatter me, and it's only after a bit that I realize I was dreaming of my making. My most treasured memory, the night my life After began, came to console me. Given my circumstances, I'm worried that this may be the night my After life ends.

Finally, someone turns off the damn klaxon alarm, and my head reverberates with its dying echoes. Agony, as if I've been sunbathing, but I don't smell smoke, don't feel flames. I'm awake, so it must be night.

I've been poisoned, captured, but I can't remember anything.

I burrow deeper into the blankets despite the fact that they reek of mothballs and mildew.

A grating noise—a door opening. I wish my head would just explode and be done with it. I must get up *now*, because I know I am in the worst kind of trouble.

I'm still trying to pull myself up when I hear the voice. Of any in the world, it's the last one I want. It fills me with dread.

"Pam Ravenscroft. I'm sure you remember me."

I can't see past his motorcycle boots, but I remember flaming red hair and, incongruously, a scatter of freckles.

"Of course, Morgan," I mutter to the damp cement floor. "I keep a scrapbook of degenerate monsters. You're my prize."

Not my best retort, but I've a head full of silver filings I can't account for.

"Well, you put up quite a fight, though I'm not sure what tipped you off. Exactly how old are you, that you can smell trouble like that?"

Idiot. Never ask a lady her age. If she's human, she'll lie and say younger. If she's vampire, she'll lie and say older and more powerful. "As old as sin itself, and twice as sexy. Where's Eric?"

"Unaware of my intentions. For the moment."

"Good. He'll be on his guard and you'll shortly be a puddle of guts."

"I think not. He suspects nothing." Morgan stoops and shows me my phone. "He imagines you've secured the perimeter of the 'Out-of-the-Coffin Day' anniversary dinner party and are meeting Lily for a private celebration. I owe him a lot of money and don't want to pay him, so I'm going to make it look like human fang-haters when I kill him. I can be as gruesome as I want and still have people believe it's a human attack."

Simple math, if you're a vampire. Plus, Morgan is a pervert, so "gruesome" would only be the start of it.

I must escape and warn Eric, but—

Morgan might have been reading my mind. "That silver will be in your system for a couple of hours. By the time you can sit up straight, I'll be solvent and Northman will be dead."

"Eric shit bigger things than you when he was human."

He laughs. "Maybe I'll keep you around as a pet. Or I could feed you to Lily. You disappointed her so terribly, that would be a thing to see."

Oh, hell. Lily. I slump. Years ago, Morgan killed Lily's maker and took her as his own, treating her vilely.

Morgan laughs again and leaves.

I give him a few minutes to get out and then manage to sit. I'm not as sick as he thought; I don't think they got the full dose into me, but I'm still feeling rough.

I must do something, so I go for the low-hanging fruit. "Hey! Hey!" I bang on the door.

A vamp so green you can still smell the dirt on him opens up the peephole. "Shut up in there!"

"Unless I get something to eat, this silver will kill me. You don't want that."

Instead of telling me, *Yeah, he does*, he says the most wonderful thing in the world.

"Huh?"

Oh, thank you, fates. "If I die, Eric will sense my death. He'll know something's up." I try to look pathetic. It's not hard.

He actually bites his lip, he's trying so hard to think. I've seen more wit in Bubba sizing up a three-legged tabby for dinner.

"Get me a bottle of TrueBlood." I hate the stuff; it tastes like a Barbie smells. "If you don't want Morgan's plan to fail."

The door shuts. I'm alone with my worry.

It opens again shortly, and I can't believe my luck. I raise my hand weakly, then let it fall back, as if exhausted.

The little idiot actually comes in. I wait until I can almost see where his pimples used to be, before he was made, then spring up. I grab his arm and yank down, seizing the back of his head, which abruptly meets my knee. Then, since I still appreciate the housewifely virtue of "waste not, want not," I drain him dry.

His body collapses into a pile of nasty black gunk that will require a squeegee to clean up. I toss back the TrueBlood as well; I'll need every bit of strength I have to get through the night alive.

I know the house. It doesn't take me long to find my way out.

There's one other guard, and he's bigger and meaner than the puppy I ate downstairs, but I'm warmed up and feeling feisty. Once he's returned to primordial ooze, I take his phone and car keys, and then his car.

Eric's not answering. He's probably so far underground the cement is blocking the signal.

As I drive, I wonder. I may not actually be as old as sin, but I'm not being vain when I consider that the junior varsity shouldn't have been left to guard someone like me. It seemed far too easy to—

Oh. I get it. The A-squad is reserved for taking Eric out.

Shitballs.

I gun the engine and race hell-for-leather toward the party. I can't concentrate on a plan. The only thing in my mind is seeing Lily right before the silver-filled hypodermic needle hit my neck.

I loved the twenties. I *roared* through them. Jazz and gin and shoes made to dance in. Beaded dresses, no more than scraps of silk but so heavy, so sensual, they might have been designed with a vampire's heightened senses in mind. Feeding at that time was like ripping open an expensive box of chocolates. After years of thousands of tiny jet buttons and yards of wool, it was easier than tearing the plastic off a Twinkie and twice as sweet.

I met Lily while I was hunting on New Year's Eve. The woods of the Scottish highlands in 1926 were as pretty as a picture as I tracked two partygoers who'd sneaked off for a chilly game of slap-and-tickle.

The stink of their fear as I chased them was sauce on game, lemon in tea, whiskey on cake. My stomach wasn't actually growling, but the idea was amusing. Every time I ate, it was as if I were rediscovering the act, finding some nuance revealed, some ecstasy not yet explored. Terror, exhaustion, and confusion added indefinably exquisite layers to taste. Maybe we lacked the need for other mortal organs, but vampire senses and appetites were enhanced to joy almost beyond bearing.

My hunger lent lightness to my step and wings to my feet. I'd cast off my dainty dancing slippers, rather than lose them—I've always taken care of my nice things—and gave in to the chase so quickly, I made no tracks on the snow.

The pair were weighed down with their meaty mortal bodies, their fear, and their clumsy will to live. They had no concept of what living was. Despite their every pretense at decadence, this would be the most lively night of their lives. It would be my gift to them.

A faint rustle, a skitter of ice pellets across the crust of snow. A rabbit? Some bird stirring?

My pace slowed as I warily tried to identify the source of the noise.

Another vampire, a stranger. There might be additional violence before the evening was through.

Best not to anticipate. It could as easily be happy violence as angry. Either would please me.

Like a breath, the rustling was gone. My fellow hunter had gone ahead, like a lioness circling around prey.

A shriek in a clearing ahead of me. The other vampire had appeared out of nowhere. She set down a lantern on a stump.

The light showed a man who'd been stopped by a slight woman, apparently in her late twenties, her black hair in a fashionable shingle, ornamented with sparkling jewels and graceful white feathers. The beads of the fringe on her dress were green on white silk, and the way they swayed reminded me of windblown pine boughs.

Her mouth was perfectly formed, a Cupid's bow in scarlet that matched her nails. I had not seen such pallid perfection in skin since meeting Eric. Her features hinted at a delightful mix of Asian and European ancestry.

"Shall we share?" Her voice matched any Bloomsbury bluestocking, educated and precise. "Or shall we fight over them? You found them, but *I* stopped them."

"What do you mean, share?" The big man had found his balls again. It was now clear that he believed he'd been chased by devils, who turned out to be two flappers from a New Year's party. "Get away from me, you thieving tarts!"

"I do not tolerate interruptions!" she snapped. "Sit down and be quiet!"

Under her glamour, he sat down on a log, quite ignoring the thick layer of snow on it.

His companion was a slight thing, shivering with fear and cold; her thin dress was garish red and cheap. She should have taken a lesson from me; my dress was far nicer and the deep rose red suited my complexion. "He has money," she said. "Take it, let us go!"

"Now, now," I said, chiding her. "Money is a good and useful thing, but it is not all, my dear. Sit down."

She sat down on the log beside her beau, trembling, her eyes glazed with terror. A small nosegay of red carnations fell from her hand.

"So, what is it to be?" Lily asked me.

I was quite fascinated by her. "What are your plans this evening?"

She affected casualness. "I had nothing particular in mind."

All thoughts about meeting Eric for hunting and a late dinner had fled. It was the first time I'd ever found anyone who could distract me from him. "Perhaps we could share these, and then find some diverting way to see in the New Year together?"

She clapped her hands. "*C'est tres agréable!* Shall we start with the big one? Let the little one stew a bit, save her for pudding?"

"My thoughts precisely." I held out a hand. "I am Pam Ravenscroft."

She shook. "Lily Macintosh."

"A pleasure."

"I hope so." She clapped her hands again, and said, "You! Big 'un!"

The man roused from his dullness, and without another word, Lily clawed the collar down from the man's shirt and tore into his throat. His face was a mask of horror and ultimate torment, but he was helpless to resist.

I took a moment to admire the reflections of Lily's beads against the hard snow, the spatter of blood in the flickering lamplight, and the eager way her head bobbed as she fed.

And, oooh! She liked nice things, too; her dress was by Worth!

The big man fell, a slave to weakness and gravity. I saw the blood flowing still, heard the faint flutter of his still-beating heart, and took his wrist before she could drain him entirely.

He tasted of rare roast beef, Yorkshire pudding, a reasonable Bordeaux, followed by champagne . . .

Nothing like good traditional British fare in winter, shared by lamplight.

Lily's appetite was as great as mine. She licked the tears from the sobbing girl's cheeks, and I couldn't resist doing the same.

Sublime.

Lily grabbed a meager wrist and I took the carotid. Even though we dug in with all the gusto of schoolgirls sharing a chocolate sundae, I realized I was no longer hungry for blood.

Lily stared at me from across the body of the girl, who was dying but far from gone.

My new friend reached over, removed a drop of blood from my lip with a finger. Popped it in her own mouth with a mischievous grin.

I moved the hair behind her ears, wiped a smear of blood from her chin.

Lily stood and hooked her thumbs under the straps of her dress. The weight of the beads pulled the silk down as quickly as any stage curtain. Besides her shoes, she wore nothing but the most charming camiknickers.

I undressed instantly and we embraced. Our bodies weren't much warmer than the snow. The girl watched us make love, helpless to escape, as her blood slowly seeped out and colored the snow around her.

After, we stirred only when daylight was nigh. The girl had finally died, but I didn't begrudge the waste of food or my wrinkled, damp dress, for Lily was quite simply the cat's meow. She was delicate and fierce at the same time, and her body was delicious, with a superb rump and delightful little breasts.

In a giddy mood, besotted with my new friend, I plucked three red carnations from the fallen nosegay and set them on the remains of our dessert.

Lily cocked her head. "According to my grandmother, that means . . . fascination and love."

I was taken aback she understood me. "You know the language of flowers?"

"She called it *hanakotoba*. My grandmother was Japanese. She taught me years ago, before I was turned." She looked me straight in the eye. "That is the same flower I would have chosen. For you."

"You are delectable!" I exclaimed. "We must meet again."

"We were clearly made for each other," she agreed. "So I shall make a point of it." Stooping, she took two carnations from the corpse, tucked one in my bosom and the other behind her ear.

I sang as I made my way back to Eric.

Lily and I met again over the years, never for long, but renewing our affection and passion every time. Eventually I learned that she'd sold her human life to her maker, Frederick, her servitude in return for the payment of her father's gambling debts.

"My father had three choices: Be killed, turn my little sister Rose out as a whore, or sell me to Frederick. It was not a difficult choice: Rose is everything to me. To protect her, I would undertake far worse than turning vampire."

As always, I marveled at how human affection survived the transformation and even grew with the intensity of vampire feeling. I admired Lily for it.

But then Morgan had killed Frederick and taken Lily as his own. He made her swear an oath to obey him for a number of years, but each time her term was nearly up, he found another reason for her to swear again. I suspected Morgan arranged more of Lily's father's gambling debts so as to torment Lily for his own amusement. I thanked heaven and hell for Eric, for he was as decent a master as one could ask for. More than giving him my obedience, I was thankful for Eric.

"My word is everything to me," Lily said, late one night in Paris. A prostitute lay drained at the foot of our bed. "But almost . . . I would run away from Morgan. I would break my oath. Almost, I would, Pam, for you."

"And almost I would leave Eric for you," I said. It was untrue, of course, but she was well worth the compliment. I nuzzled her neck and nibbled her ear. "Merely say the word, and I'll help you escape."

"Pam," she said sternly, giving me a little shake. "I made a promise. My sister's safety depends on it."

"My apologies, Lily," I said. "I understand."

We nestled together as the sun rose, but secretly, I considered how short a mortal's life was, and that when Rose died, Lily and I might be together.

I park a block from the front of the party venue—an establishment with huge underground rooms to accommodate vampire events. I don't want them to recognize the car and wonder what the guard from the house is doing here. There is a raincoat in the backseat of the stolen car, and I pull it on to cover most of the blood, a temporary solution until the odor betrays me.

The place is crawling with the dignitaries' guards. I recognize a lot of them but don't remember seeing them on the way in. There are far more of Morgan's people, and I wonder who else Morgan owes money to.

I need to find another way in. I circle around to the service entrance in the back. The security is looser here, which makes no sense.

Until I see who's running the show—no one would cross him. I walk purposefully toward my potential ally. There's a slim chance, but I might make it past him.

But will I make it out again? As I approach the entrance and the big man with the clipboard, I remember that hypodermic earlier, and how I failed Lily so badly so long ago. She's in on it, has to be. No love for me, and none for my master—she has everything to gain by helping Morgan and, as much as she dislikes him, she'll never turn on him.

I gather up my courage, for Eric's sake. I owed him all. I once had said, with a mortal girl's silly bravado, that I would give the sun, the moon, and the stars for true freedom. With Eric, I'd only had to give up the sun.

The last I'd heard from Lily was in 1955. I'd been cleaning my house when she called, nearly hysterical.

Another gambling debt: Her father was old, but not too frail to find a bookie. His debtors wanted an exorbitant amount of interest, and Morgan, again, had offered help.

"You got the money from him . . . by promising another fifty years of service?" I said. "But . . . I have some money and I could ask Eric—" Though I didn't think he would give me the cash, I thought he might loan it to me. With interest, of course, but never with such unreasonable demands as Morgan.

Again, the thought crossed my mind that Morgan might be using Lily's family to torture her.

"It was the only way. And Morgan insisted I find someone else to deliver the payment. Pam, I'm asking you. Will you save my sister?"

I had promised to meet Eric in two days, but I was closer to the Chicago suburb than Lily was. "I'm on my way."

"Thank you, Pam. If anything happens to Rose—"

"It won't. I swear."

"Go now, my darling! Come back to me with good news!"

I ran to my car without even changing from my jeans into a skirt. I drove like the demon I am but had miscalculated the distance to the town I intended to spend the day in. My skin began to tighten as I raced the coming dawn, but the city limits were still ahead of me. I considered digging myself a hole in the ground, but I saw an abandoned barn. I pulled my Thunderbird into it and there was a distinct smell of burning bacon when I finally put myself into the trunk, pulling the door down just shy of locking. My skin felt as though I'd had a blistering sunburn as I pulled a blanket over me.

June days are hellishly long.

I drove dangerously far the next night with the gas gauge needle pinning *E*. Relieved when I saw a service station, I cursed the slowness with which the tank filled.

Halfway between the gas station and my goal, disaster. A tire blew out.

It was a bad puncture, possibly made by a piece of ragged metal from my day in that rubbish-filled barn.

I changed the tire, rather than running the rest of the way. I might need the T-Bird to escape.

I got to the rendezvous, a small house in the suburbs, with a minute to spare. The race across country, the fear, the happiness I'd bring to Lily, the rush of triumph—my emotions were so heightened they bordered on the erotic.

Then I noticed the door hanging open, not even latched, let alone locked.

I sniffed tentatively and dread replaced my fleeting sense of victory.

I was too late. If I was a minute early, the gangsters had been thirty minutes early. They'd gotten bored, perhaps, or didn't believe Lily would come.

Maybe, now that he had fifty more years of service from her, Morgan had finally decided to remove this distraction from Lily's life.

The headless corpses of Rose and her father were in the living room. I reached out to rearrange the soaking, bloodied dress of the girl, place her head closer to the top of her neck, for the sake of decency.

I left, following the trail of the killers. I had little time, with two pressing demands on me: the coming day and my meeting with Eric. But if I'd failed to save Lily's family, I could still act on her behalf.

"Hey, you! Hey, stop!"

I'm almost to the guy with the clipboard when I hear the voice behind me. It's the type of voice usually followed by chambered rounds or drawn stakes.

I rush forward, waving. "Quinn! So, *so* sorry I'm late!"

He recognizes me and dismisses the guard. He's frowning in a way that still means mine is a slim chance.

"You have to help me."

"Oh, yeah?" The bald weretiger gives me a glance meant to wither. "Listen, Pam, why aren't you inside? Through the front door, with the other vampires?"

"There's a trap, for Eric. I don't trust a note, and he'll need my help to escape from Morgan—who owes Eric money. I can't go in through the front because they'll recognize me."

Quinn shakes his head. "I have a reputation to maintain, professional discretion. And I don't like your boss." He makes a face at my blood-soaked outfit under the raincoat. "I don't like *you*."

I go straight for his soft spot. "If I don't get out, and Eric with me, the first one Morgan will go after is Sookie Stackhouse. You know how useful she is to vampires."

He growls. I must admit his warning makes me go all gooey inside, which helps focus my nerves. I have no idea what I'll do when I get in. Eric might sense I am in trouble, but he won't know that the danger comes from Morgan.

"Morgan's a sadist; there's no way you'd want him near Sookie." Then I apply the coup de grâce. "You don't want these fuckers to get one over on you, either. Using your event as cover."

"No one screws around with my business." He looks me up and down. "And no one, but no one, messes with Sookie if I can help it. Okay. But you can't just go onstage like that. And they all have props; you need one, too. It's a parade of costumed blood donors; Missy must have seen a movie about the elaborate displays at court banquets. A show of grotesques before dinner—it's not as shocking as Missy thinks, but it's a way to get you in."

"Well?" I can barely keep from tapping my foot. "We don't have time to waste."

"All I have left is a chimp and he's not feeling well." A smirk crosses that pretty face. "I hate to think what he'd do if he smelled vamp up close, in his state."

"A chimp isn't enough," I say, biting my lip. "I need to bring the house down, literally. We need more impact, I need all eyes on me until the last moment. And enough cover for me and Eric to get away." Inspiration strikes and I look up at Quinn. "I need a tiger."

"*No way.*"

"Not even for Sookie?"

He pauses. I hold my breath, metaphorically speaking.

Quinn finally sighs. "Fuck it. Okay."

I'm starting to like this idea; I've always had a certain flair for entertaining. "Do you have a leash?"

His shaved head flushes dark and he says through gritted teeth, "I'm not going to let *anyone* put a *leash* on me!"

I shrug. "Fine, but you're going to have to do something spectacular when I get out there. You *do* have a reputation to live up to." Even though I think what he is doing is tacky, a higher-end version of serving sushi on a naked woman. *Honestly.* If I'm going to diddle my food, I want to do it in private.

He nods.

It isn't fair; he's only a man, after all. There are only so many routes you need to try: offer to protect what he desires or appeal to his ego.

Quinn starts stripping. When he gets down to his boxers, I pause to enjoy the rest of the show.

I'll give this to Sookie; the little sun-sucker and I have our differences, but I admire her taste in man-flesh.

I'm enjoying the view of Quinn naked when he says, "And now you. You can't go out there looking like that."

I frown and look down. The weretiger had a point. The raincoat is filthy, my twinset is torn, and I am blood-soaked down to my capris. I didn't have time to change after checking the security, so at least my lovely dress was spared. But then I see the full extent of the ruin and curse: Fucking Morgan owes me a new pair of driving mocs! That's it: I'm officially going to kill him myself.

"Fine, give me anything. Just make it quick."

"The only thing that will fit you is . . ." A sly look crosses his face.

He pulls the dress off the rack and hands me a bag of accessories to match. The bag is marked *Wonderland/Alice.*

"Oh, *hells* to the no." The bane of my life Before . . . there was no way I'd sully my life After with *that.*

"Come on. I've seen the Morticia drag you wear at Fangtasia. You're not bothered by that."

"Strictly a marketing device. Eric's orders. This—" I shake my head.

"It's either that"—he nods at the hateful costume—"or—"

"I'll go naked."

"You said you need to make a big impression. This is bigger than naked."

I snatch the garments from him, snarling. "Fuck you, tiger."

He grins at me. "Fuck you, vampire."

I saw Lily only twice after my catastrophic failure. The first was when I told her what had happened. She went as close to catatonic as I'd ever seen in a vampire. The grief came off her in waves, but I watched her go carefully about her duties as usual, managing the motel she ran for Morgan, checking the security, giving orders to his day man. I explained what happened, how I was late and the enforcers early. I didn't mention my suspicions about Morgan.

"But they paid, I assure you," I said, putting a hand on hers. "I followed them home. I slaughtered their children while their wives watched, letting the women know their men were responsible. Then I killed them all, too. The one with no family, I followed to the construction site they used as a cover and knocked him unconscious. I nailed him to the studs of a new wall. When he woke up, I told him he had fifteen minutes. If he could pull his hands and feet and ears from the nails, I'd let him go. He failed, but that was only because I'd used an epoxy underneath him first. I had only a short time before I had to meet Eric, but I made them suffer as much as I could."

She looked up with an unreadable expression in her eyes. I had never seen anything like it in a human, vampire, were, or animal. She opened her mouth to speak, but Morgan came in.

"Visiting hours are over. Back to work, Lily."

"You're a real prick, you know?" I stood up, furious and foolish enough to take him on. I might not win, but he'd know he'd been in a battle.

"In fifty more years, Lily can call her time her own."

"You have a lot to learn about your responsibilities as her master. It goes both ways, Morgan."

"Time for you to run along now, Miss Ravenscroft. Your huffing and puffing and strutting do not impress me, and Northman wouldn't like it if you forced me to rebuke you in a permanent fashion. Take your cheap sentiment and be gone."

"Not cheap. Not sentiment. I gave my word."

Lily looked up. "Go now, Pam." She stood suddenly, almost faster than I could see, and was holding the door open. "You're not making things better by being here."

I sent purple hyacinths, white poppies, and crimson roses to her. In my Victorian world, it meant, "I am sorry. Be consoled in mourning."

I hadn't seen her again until tonight, when she betrayed me.

There is torchlight everywhere as we enter the staging area, the better to set the air of fantasy Quinn has set up. Our hostess, Missy Van Pelt, was making a dramatic point about how hard she was, because fire is one of our few vulnerabilities. My eyes adjust quickly and I can see the layout: The small backstage area leads to an arena where the other meals are displayed. The rest were already out there. Just ahead of me I saw identical twins with an orangutan, all in matching harlequin; a pixieish fairy—not one of those big, evil fuckers, but fluttery, like Tinkerbell— with a poodle on a leash, and in *its* mouth was another leash, holding a submissive in full bondage gear, complete with a full mask and ball gag.

I admire a skillful *tableau vivant* and don't mind ostentation. I pride myself on setting a nice table. Anyone can serve blood in the skull of an enemy; it's been done to death. Yawn. *Much* more attractive to have the top of the skull carved into a proper cup, and then add a nice stem.

All this is pretty enough, but lacks a certain *je ne sais quoi*, and I tell the tiger so. I begin to describe the ball I attended in—

He responds with a growl only I can hear. I can feel it as well, and it is a memorable moment. I admire animal pelts—one could hardly live for decades with Eric and not develop a taste for furs, a little touch of the barbaric. But I have never ridden a tiger in what could only be described as a too-short skirt and petticoat, a garter belt, and not much more in the way of underthings. Those big back muscles between my thighs, the pacing gait, is inspiring. The rumble of his protest adds an unexpected extra vibration. It's been years since I've been surprised by anything so carnal.

"Ooh, you great, nasty pussy. Do that again!" I whisper, wriggling around. "Growl again!"

Any life is too short, I say. Take your pleasures while you can.

Quinn turns and snaps at me, which inspires another frisson. The look in his eyes is sobering, and I get the impression that if he could, he'd say, *I will dump your skinny blond ass right now if you don't shut up.*

"My apologies, Quinn." I lean down and whisper to him. "We're here for work, and you're doing me a favor. It's just that going into battle makes me a little—" I dig my fingers into the soft fur behind the tufted ears on his massive head and growl back at him.

Another snap of those giant teeth, and I collect my capricious thoughts. "Right. It's showtime."

We are preceded by a half dozen doxies in eighteenth-century dress; there are gory bandages across their white faces, as if they've been blinded. They carry matching white Persian cats. And suddenly I am the main event. Main course. Vampires like shiny and tawdry, and we get bored quickly; hence the display. The only thing left on Quinn's rack that would fit me was a short pink dress and a blue pinafore, meant for a living "doll" who hadn't shown up. I'd been told over and over, in three different centuries, that I resemble the Tenniel drawings of Lewis Carroll's Alice. Through the looking glass, indeed—an hour ago, I was bashing out the brains of two flunkies. Now my hair, pulled back with a headband, is brushed to a gleaming gold that cascades down my shoulders. The abbreviated petticoat flares prettily out at my knees, giving tantalizing glimpses of striped stockings and boots. And as I ride in on the back of the tiger, I have to admit, it's a nicely aesthetic moment. I would have chosen to have it rendered by Burne-Jones, or perhaps Maxfield Parrish, but—

But they are dead and I have killing to do.

"Go quickly and smoothly, please, Quinn. Two circuits of the arena, and on the second, I'll strike."

Quinn chuffs quietly, and I sense his big golden eyes picking out Missy and her progeny; he'll want to know what they knew about using his event as an ambush.

I stand on the tiger's back, finding my balance easily enough. A slight "ooh" from the crowd tells me I am making the picture I wanted. I keep my face pretty and blank, all the while projecting my worry and excitement to Eric.

Out of the corner of my eye, I see him carefully set down his blood and lean back as if enjoying the spectacle.

Good. He understands something isn't right and will watch for a cue.

As we pass the halfway mark in our circuits, I throw my head and arms back, the picture of rapturous abandon. The audience tenses, waiting for what I'll bring next.

Quinn picks up the pace, but I have the trick of it now. As we pass the last torch, I grab it. Before anyone has the chance to gasp, I spring from the tiger's back, screaming.

"Eric! Beware Morgan!"

I'm quite certain that the poor human Happy Meals are terribly confused. It must be a bit of a blur to everyone but us vampires.

It's a shame they should miss any of it. I am wonderful.

As I swing the torch at Morgan, who is outraged to see me free, Lily is instantly there.

Lily is what I most fear. Most crave.

Time stops while I drink her in.

She is tricked out in black leather slashed with scarlet. Her dark hair is streaked with cobalt blue, razor-cut, asymmetrical. She's a blur of midnight colors and I approve.

I don't much approve of the fucking katana she's flashing, though.

I'm sure it's an ancient masterpiece and probably was given a name—Lily still likes nice things—and that some believe it would be a privilege to die by its blade.

Only one of us can walk away alive. She won't break her word to Morgan and I must protect Eric. As much as I don't want to kill Lily, I don't want to die, either. A good, honorable death someday, defending Eric, perhaps, but right now I'm not done living. Not by a long shot.

I'm more than spoiling for a fight now and thankful that I might save Eric. There's a growing sadness that I will have to kill my darling to do it.

The choice is made. No time for regret. If I must kill Lily, I shall make it a masterpiece.

Time starts up again.

I can't change my trajectory, but I can change my target. I adjust my swing so that I catch Lily in the gut with the torch.

The leather keeps her from burning but it doesn't protect her from the blow, which is so great it tears the torch from my hands. She screams and sprawls on the floor of the arena; her sword sings as it flies from her grasp. She leaps back up at me, hissing, her face contorted.

I dive into a roll, snatch up the katana. She grabs my shoulders. Even as I swing around to slam my elbow into her face, I hear her whisper, "Pam, my darling."

I know how fierce Lily is, how loyal and passionate. I don't expect tenderness, so I won't fall for it. She punches me, hard, in the neck. I stagger back, but her face is a mask of blood.

It would take only one swing—

My eyes might be blurred with bloody tears, but my hearing is as acute as ever. She shrieks, and it carries over the mayhem and confusion in the audience. "You can try, Pam Ravenscroft, but I'll kill you as quickly as I snuffed out that little bitch in Scotland!"

The words race through my brain. The girl in Scotland died slowly, watching helplessly while we fucked in the snow. Lily is giving me a signal.

One of the reasons I am so fond of Sookie Stackhouse is that despite her ridiculous refusal to let Eric turn her, she makes the most of her opportunities. It's a quality we share, and it's what attracted me to Lily close to a century ago.

Go.

I step forward, and Lily does, too. It feels as if we are both moving in slow motion. While she would never break her word to Morgan, Lily might well engineer a situation where someone else must kill him. And while it might make sense for Morgan to bring his best troops with him, only Lily could have arranged such runts to guard me and given me a too-small dose of silver. If Morgan succeeds, Lily will get more power as his fortunes improve; if he fails, she'll be free of him, one way or another.

I have to decide how much I can trust my instincts. Trust her love.

I bring the sword down. It bites deep into her shoulder. I hear it cleave through muscle and bone.

It's a magnificent blade; the balance is perfection. I don't take her head, but it looks as if I'm fighting for my life. Even if I'm wrong about her, Lily won't be able to follow me.

She collapses. When I see the faint smile on her face and her hand twitch, I know for sure. I follow the direction she indicates, out through the confusion; the animals are yowling and scattering, the vampires fighting, and the orangutan is shitting all over the place as it bites the guy in the gimp suit. I need to get out front, because Eric and Morgan have disappeared and that's where they'll be heading.

I find something unexpected at the top of the stairs off the arena. Scarcely believing that I correctly interpreted Lily's plans, I pull the tarp from it. Something small and light falls as I do.

Underneath the tarp is a gleaming red motorcycle.

I bend down to retrieve what has fallen. A sprig of bluebell tied up with a stem of lavender. Gratitude and faith, in the language of flowers.

This is a gift, a fast exit for me and Eric. This is Lily's good-bye.

I tuck the flowers into my pinafore and start the bike. It thunders to life, as beautiful and deadly as Lily herself.

As I reach the front of the venue, the crotch rocket swerves dangerously. I fight to keep from ditching, feeling my fangs poking out. It's almost as exciting as a tiger between my legs.

Chaos: I see Quinn, still a tiger, batting combatants apart. I see Eric tangled with Morgan.

I love to watch Eric fight; you can see his Viking heritage in his berserker glee. Eric is my everything: sun, moon, and stars.

Lily is the perfect reflection of my joy in being a vampire.

But I'm the one who should kill Morgan.

Eric lands a crushing blow—he's using a stanchion to beat the shit out of Morgan—and draws back for another.

"He's mine!" I shout. Eric cocks his head at my costume and my demand, then nods graciously. He steps back and pulls out his phone.

I stand and raise Lily's sword.

I swing, screaming her name.

I let the blade have its way now. When it strikes, Morgan's battered and bloodied head comes off cleanly, suspended in the air a fraction of a second before it goes to goo.

I hear a click, somewhere beyond the roar of the engine, the screaming.

Eric has taken a picture of me as I kill Morgan. A blood-streaked, katana-wielding Alice wreaking vengeance astride a Ducati.

I adore Eric. He has as much an eye for a moment as I do. As much a taste for retribution, too.

But my inattention means I lose control over the motorcycle. I vault away, before it crashes into a wall and bursts into flame. You have to admire such a grand finale to the party.

I tumble and roll. I'm careful to protect the katana, because when the dust settles, and Morgan's treachery is revealed, Lily will be gone, fleeing the memory of her ill use by Morgan. But someday she might seek me out, and if she does, she will certainly want the sword back.

Until she claims it, however, her katana—like her heart—belongs to me.

WIDOWER'S WALK

MARYJANICE DAVIDSON

MaryJanice Davidson was always an Eric appreciator; he's the man with the plan. Her story "Widower's Walk" takes place 201 years after the events of *Dead Ever After.* Eric is nursing a drink and musing over life, death, the state of the world, and the repercussions of love and sacrifice. Since he's a multitasker, he's going to flirt with yet another waitress . . . and keep an eye on the assassin targeting Sookie's descendants.

When is a betrayal not a betrayal?
When it's not a betrayal.

He's been here before, except he hasn't. Two hundred one years ago, Louisiana was a different place, which stands to follow as it was also a different time. The bar was here, but now it's called Were About. There are still waitresses here, but instead of leaving tips on tables customers use the datpads to send credits wherever the waitress *(petcash, savings, WorldTax, 401K, direct-to-IRS)* wants them. There are blond waitresses here with big eyes and sweet smiles, but they aren't Sookie. There are bad people here.

Of course.

Eric Northman waits for a waitress (not for the first time) and ponders the nature of change. It would be difficult not to, since everywhere he looks he is reminded. *Whoever wrote "The more things change, the more they stay the same,"* he thinks, *had a brain tumor. Because the more things change, the more things change. Even the youngsters can see it.*

Louisiana, as a starting point. Because first it was known for its mound complexes and status as a de rigueur Native American paradise and then it was known for the bow-and-arrow welcome that hostile tribes gave the Spanish (perhaps they saw their future once Europeans hit the shore?) and then the French got their claws in and hung on until it became Slavery Central and then England spanked the French and took some of Louisiana as a penalty/prize and Spain snatched the rest, which only increased the slave population (Louisiana by now being, essentially, the Walmart of slavery), and then Napoleon more or less declared, "You know what France would like back? Louisiana. Cough it up, bitches," but then changed his mind and sold it to the United States, which knew the deal of the century when they got it and never once had buyer's remorse.

And then things settled down but not really and Louisiana was known for exporting sugar and cotton and a bunch of rich guys decided to secede ("Um, if there's no slavery, who's gonna build levees? Besides us? Which, obviously, is not acceptable. Who's ready to throw a secession soiree?"), which did not work out *at all*, and then the whole Reconstruction thing happened and the slaves were free and the supplanted planters took it pretty well (except for the KKK, the White League, and, um, the Colfax Massacre)—okay, *pretty well* might be an exaggeration—and then the state was known for the rabid discouragement of African Americans registering to vote and then it was known for a sizable section of the population moving to California and then it was known for civil rights and then it was known for the Hurricane Katrina clusterfuck and then it was known for its seafood export (until they lost New Orleans to the hurricane that made Katrina look like a spring breeze) and then it was known for its petrochemical industries and now it isn't.

Now Louisiana is primarily known for (1) tech and (2) paranormal inhabitants. And Eric isn't there for a computer upgrade.

Shaking his head, he thinks, *I have been spending too much time in the Wikipedia archives.*

He considers the cars and trucks in the parking lot, and the fact that at least four-fifths of them are solar-powered or electric. It's still legal to own and operate gasoline-fueled engines, but only for so many hours a week, only for specific jobs (for example, farm equipment), and it's generally understood that even those will be phased out within twenty years.

Which is fine with him. He knew electric cars would kill petroleum-fueled *anything* back in 1995, for God's sake, and planned (and invested) accordingly. It was all well and good to be proved right, and it was even better to get rich doing so. Besides, it's much easier to make mischief when you have the checkbook (not that anyone used those anymore) to back it up.

"Hi, welcome to Were About."

"How too cute," he replies, almost-but-not-quite bored. She's cute, too. Blond, but then, he has a thing for them. "TrueBlood, please, straight." No ice, God forbid, no cinnamon sprinkle, no salted rim. After fixing the ozone dilemma and developing the prostate cancer vaccine, as far as Eric was concerned the greatest accomplishment over the past few centuries has been engineering TrueBlood as a palatable drink. The downside to that? People who weren't vampires now drank it, which caused all sorts of trouble. "Passing" was becoming a problem. Not since the dark days of the *Twilight* franchise had it been so trendy to be dead.

The waitress walked away, hips rolling beneath her uniform, and he watched for a second and then decided, *No, too small. And too blond.* She didn't have to come over to take his order; he didn't have to speak to place it; this wasn't the twentieth century. It was all done by Net, like everything else. But Were About prided itself on being quaint. No, that wasn't right. Retro, was that the word?

Retro, ha. The new Louisiana, on the surface of things, could almost pass for the old, except for the fact that for the first time in an age the state doesn't have a vampire king, but a human queen: thirty-two-year-old Adele Merlotte, of the famed and formidable Stackhouse-Merlotte clan.

Eric smiles in spite of himself and glances down at the table. Head-lines and a stock stream flick past, as well as inane "news" about whatever celebrity delivered a baby, got married, or was torn apart by a shrieking mob the night before. And supe news, of course, always. Which vampire was running for reelection, which shifter was stepping down, which norm came out about not actually being a supe (would that be coming out about coming out?), et cetera, et cetera, boring boring boring. He can get more details by tapping the table but doesn't bother. It just reinforces what he already finds hilarious: Humanity was so busy worrying about vampires, they never saw the shifters coming.

Even now, so many years later, Eric was vague on all the details of the Great Reveal but had nothing but admiration for the endgame. The shifters' decision—to wait a few years after the vampires revealed themselves before doing the same—paid gigantic dividends in the long run, as constant infighting forced alliances that had never before been considered. As when vampires came out, things were chaotic and violent for the first few years. Lots of "you never told me you were one of *those*" and "well, you never told me you were one of *those*" and "but some of my best friends are shifters, I am *not* an anti-wereite!"

Humanity ultimately decided the undead were the bigger problem and behaved accordingly, because when you gave them two choices, humanity invariably picked wrong. Which eventually put shifters into the enviable position of being kingmakers. Literally.

All that to say that after a century of conflict, the vamps were (kind of) humbled, humans were (sort of) grateful the dust was settling, and shifters controlled the White House and several states. Even more interesting, sociologically speaking, humans who came from shifter families were accorded the same respect as their fuzzy brethren. Your parents and older brother are shifters, but you aren't? Run for Congress.

Hilarious! The very best kind of irony. And all that most of the vampires could do was wait and watch. The ones who stuck their necks out lost them. The ones who stayed out of it . . . well . . . speaking of Bill Compton

(was I?)

he had been so busy playing *The King and I* with anyone but Sookie, he almost didn't notice the trouble until it was too late, which is what

Eric would expect from a man who didn't notice the Civil War until he was in it. By then Compton was King of Louisiana, of course, which saved him. Or perhaps his computers saved him; Eric could not make himself care.

Suddenly it was trendy to be a were or a shifter, and if you were uncool enough to be a garden-variety human without so much as a shifter cousin to claim, you made were friends, got yourself a were boyfriend or girlfriend, went to shifter bars. And when a Were eventually became president things *really* changed, and not with the glacial slowness normally clogging government progress. These days that particular political post was more ceremonial than anything—like the kings and queens of England before the Windsors ruined it for everyone—but still much loved by the sentimental. And no entity spins so well as politicians. Before long humans were wondering why it had taken the weres so long to get into gear. Eric admires this finest, most brilliant way to triumph: when the losers are glad you came. Sometimes he wonders if the entire nation succumbed to Stockholm syndrome.

Cute Little Blond Waitress returns with his drink and gives him a big smile along with an alarming number of extra napkins *(does she think I'll drool?)* and implores him to zap her if he needs *anything*, anything at *all*.

Eyeing his drink, and not troubling himself to watch her hips on the exit, Eric ponders the fact that not only have many things changed, but some came as a surprise, some he indirectly manipulated, and some he brought about full-on in front of the world. He thinks of Appius for the first time in a long while, the way the man would study Eric as if he could know him if he simply looked long enough.

Your thoughts are like wheels inside wheels; there is always something going on in there. Then his maker would tap Eric's forehead, hard, and let loose a long, cheery laugh.

When Eric thinks of Appius, it's usually about the laugh.

Wheels inside wheels, yes. Vampires worrying about humans worrying about weres worrying about fairies, and who could have predicted that the supe situation would implode at the worst possible time for Castro? And who could have guessed that in her attempt to undo the damage, Freyda, his wife and queen, would also suffer true death?

Well. *Eric* could have, if anyone

(Sookie)

had troubled themselves to ask. *Always have an exit.* That was something else about him Appius often saw and shrugged off.

Queens who rise quickly are to be loved and feared and, above all, aware that a fast rise can be followed by a dizzying fall. Poor Freyda. Right to the end, she had had no idea what she had signed on for. Sometimes he thinks about her face when the knowledge that true death was something that could *actually happen* to her hit her like a boulder, that it couldn't be flirted away or bribed or ignored, he thinks of her eyes and how they got big, so big *("I don't—I can't—Eric . . . why?")* and he laughs and he laughs.

When is a trap not a trap? When it's your *trap.*

So things had worked out more or less according to plan, no thanks to anyone but him, and he had too much pride to dash to Stackhouse Central the moment he was free. So he waited—and not just until what would have been the end of the contract. He tacked on another year for no other reason than to prove to himself that he could. Because pride might goeth before a fall, but sometimes pride is all you have

(the thing they can't take; the thing you can't ever ever ever LET THEM TAKE)

and you protect it the way a dragon guards treasure.

". . . would have sold my soul to the devil for a shot at that man!"

"Please, you would have sold your soul just to look."

He shrugs off the customer chatter that flows around him like a polluted river. He thinks, *Anticlimax.* He thinks, *Who would have thought the devil would be such a bore?* He thinks, *Keep your soul, leave the devil out of it, and invest in Martian water shuttles instead.*

He remembers a throwaway line from, of all things, Stephen King's *Christine.* A horror classic, required reading for the last hundred years along with literary giants Edgar Allan Poe, Dave Barry, and Janet Evanovich, and the line that caught his attention, *seized* his attention, had come from a willful, unpleasant character, a woman so used to domi-nating her loved ones that she had forgotten what losing felt like.

The character's self-realization had slammed into his brain and he'd nearly dropped the paperback; he had instantly recognized himself in a woman who had never existed, a character thought up by a long-dead resident of the state of Maine.

"And if her own family thought she was hard sometimes, it was because they didn't understand that when you went through Hell you came out baked by the fire. And when you had to burn to have your own way, you always wanted to have it."

(No, he couldn't relate to that. At all.)

(He bought a Plymouth Fury to honor the book, if not the hero's mother, and keeps it in an underground garage outside Tulsa. Tulsa itself is also underground since the EF5 tornadoes of 2100.)

So Eric is a widower, and that is fine, he is a king *sans* queen and that is fine, too, and he has money, which is good, and power, which is better. In short, he has everything he set out to gain for himself, and his fear, his "you know what happens to people when they get everything they want" fretting, was unfounded because he discovered that getting (almost) everything you want is *wonderful*. Even better than his wildest imaginings. And so he has no regrets.

Well. Almost. One regret, perhaps, one blond regret, but regret is irrelevant even if the lady herself never was, and—

Ah.

Finally.

Eric watches a family come into the bar; they don't know it, but they're there for him and he for them. It's a chattering, charismatic group; any one of them could fill a room by themselves. He watches them and thinks of his one almost-regret; several have her eyes.

The problem with living without the person you can't live without is eventually realizing you can *live without them.*

While he waited out the supe situation he'd set in motion to make him a widower (and, it must be said, a tidy bundle of cash and a secure power base), he had missed Sookie Stackhouse, oh yes. *Missed*, in fact, scarcely covered it. He missed her, and speculated about her, and wished her well, and wondered if Sam Merlotte had the vaguest idea of his good fortune (doubtful), and was pissed at her.

How could she . . . ? Why would she . . . ? Most of all, worst of all, why would I . . . ? For all those years, why would I . . . ?

But as the years slid by and her name popped up now and again in national news (to his delight, and her displeasure, because being in the news interfered with Operation Housewife), and then the names of her children and of their children and their children's children, the ache became longing, longing became nostalgia, nostalgia became fondness, and after a while he could see the funny side of it.

A *long* while.

Now here they are, her many descendants, a riotous, charming group, and he has no trouble picking up the snippets of conversation they drop so casually. They talk the way people do when they know they're in a safe place. They talk as if everyone knows them, ergo no one means them harm. They talk like even if something bad happens, it's fixable.

They are so young it would hurt, if he allowed it.

So he is here, good, and they are here, also good, but now comes the tedious part . . .

"She'll scorch us, she's exactly like her mom who's exactly like *her* mom! We'll try the spin and she'll scorch us so dry!"

. . . deciphering slang.

There was keeping up with slang so as not to stand out more than necessary, and then there was an utter refusal to sound like an ass. Until *toast* was no longer a synonym for *fucked up*, he was out. He's heard of hysterical blindness; he cultivates hysterical deafness.

They are a mixed group of young men and women, blonds and brunettes and one redhead; he estimates their ages between fourteen and nineteen. They are well-spoken and polite, noisy and good-natured. He knows without conscious thought that at a party, people gravitate to them and don't know why. The children do know, and never question it. He thinks again that any one of them can fill a room by themselves.

"Come on, we've all heard the stories and the 'rents are right. You don't, nope, can't, you *can't* picture the horror," the redhead was saying, voice high with glee, "when you bring someone home because you like 'em enough to get horizontal—"

"Oh, yuck," one of the younger ones interrupts. "That's all you think about. And talk about. Double yuck."

"Shut up, Sam—and there's your *caliente* great-great-grandma running around braless in a white dress—"

"How old is that white dress?" another one yelped. "We've all seen pictures. She wore it all the time." This in a tone of restrained affection.

"My theory: She had a closet full of them."

"Talking, still talking here, still have the floor and still talking and anyway, assuming your would-be horizontal bang buddy *wasn't* starstruck, even though they all were, they always were and they always lied about it—"

Another family member—this one small and dark-haired and dark-eyed and positively elfin—singsonged, "I've neeever met a faaaaairy before," to the groans of everyone else at the table.

"That's another tall tale they keep handing down—come on. Most of them didn't even know she was fairy. Barely fairy, at that."

"Well, there was plenty of stuff they did know. 'Did you reeeally catch your grandma's killer and figure out how to make lumpless gravy like you were Nancy Drew if Nancy used to be a waitress? Didja? Didja?' Followed by, *always* followed by, 'No, I'd love to stay and drink gallons of sweet tea and listen to you talk about the good old days and hear how you palled around with *the* Eric Northman. Wonderful white dress, by the way.'"

At the mention of his name Eric almost spills his drink. He's not sure if he's pleased or appalled that Sookie turned him into a bedtime story for her progeny.

"Uh-huh, and while all that's going on, our grandma's grandma would quietly step back out to the porch so she could throw up in her mouth a little," the eldest finishes, equal parts triumphant and horror-struck. She has to raise her voice to be heard over the chorus of giggles. "Because back in the way back, that was a fourth date at Casa Stackhouse-Merlotte, also known as the House of Pain."

Eric does not quite snigger, though it's a near thing. There is nothing funnier than pampered young adults babbling about houses of pain as if they understand the concept. It reminds him of Goth angst, shortly before the Goths grew up and began the destruction of the Republican Party, then stepped back and let their children finish the job. *Goth* is now a synonym for *sabotage*, which is a tremendous improvement over when it was a synonym for *black-clad angsty douchebag*.

I'm dating myself. Nobody says douchebag *anymore.* He tries to care. He fails.

If nothing else, it was interesting to hear confirmation of what he suspected even before his "marriage" to Freyda: Sookie's intent hadn't been just to live and die in Bon Temps; she meant to stake, defend, and keep a claim, and not just for herself, but for her family, down and down through the generations. Eric swallows a laugh, thinking of the old saying: *If you can't join them, beat them.* Bon Temps held Sookie in contempt for years; now her descendants hold Bon Temps. And the rest of the state. Heh.

But the slang, dear God, *the slang.* Good things were *ice* or *cupcake*, bad things were *armpit* or *blade*, boring things were *allday* or *flick.* At least *like* was back to being used properly instead of as a maddening verbal tic.

"—like?"

"Pardon?"

The waitress is smiling down at him. He'd been so lost in thought he hadn't noticed her approach, which is shameful, really; he knows better. Her corn-fed good looks are somewhat marginalized by her *Ask about my finger-lickin' ribs!* hat. "Just checking back again, seeing if there was anything else you'd like."

Properly used! The pure joy of it nearly left him dizzy. "Like?"

"Prefer?" She licks her lips in what he assumes she thinks is a subtle signal of carnal intention. Or perhaps her lips are chapped; his interest level is the same either way. "Desire?"

"I would *prefer* you continue using *like* as a modifier as opposed to a vocalized pause." Since she just stands there, blinking, he adds, "And another glass of TrueBlood."

She vamooses again, allowing him another few seconds of eavesdropping . . .

"Quit complaining; it doesn't matter what Gram *looked* like. She never jumped any of the 'rents' 'rents' boyfriends. Or girlfriends, for no other reason than who hangs with a fetus by choice?"

"It's true," another striking blonde in the collection of striking blondes adds. "She'd only hang with a fetus if she lost a bet. A really big one."

"Twenty is not a fetus," another one corrects, voice light and tart, like lemonade.

"Comparably speaking, twenty was absolutely a fetus. I mean, come on. She lived for a long time."

"Um . . . anybody remember when she was born?"

"Nineteen sixty-nine?"

"That's the moon landing," another sibling corrects, fond and exasperated. "Not the Gram landing."

"Damn. We should know this. At least one of us should know all the sordid weirdness of the matriarch's sordid past when she was running around in white dresses being sordid. We need to appoint one of us—"

"I nominate anyone but me."

"—to be the unofficial family historian."

"Oh, yawn. Pass."

"You pass on everything; could you maybe step up just once?"

"Shush up."

"*You* shush up."

"Make me."

"I will! Right after I order some apps. I can't be the only one who wants chicken wings, right?"

"Better get two baskets."

"I'm getting two for *me*. Any of you other hogs want some, order them yourselves. After we remember how old our gram's gram's gram's gram is."

"I don't think you used enough *grams*."

. . . which reassures Eric that the family sees nothing, knows nothing, suspects nothing.

Good.

He sips and thinks that everyone got what they wished for, with all that entailed. Sookie wanted sunbathing and babies and Merlotte, probably in that order, so his darling had chosen to live in a swamp and have puppies with a sentient Labradoodle, or whatever the hell Sam Merlotte decided to be that month. Gone now, of course, like

(his no not his never his not for a long long time)

Sookie, she to the heaven she so unwaveringly knew awaited her and Sam to wherever the souls of Labradoodles go. Eric is sure Sookie mourned, but Merlotte's children remained, and his grandchildren, et cetera, et cetera, ad nauseam, and that would have been enough for her; she would have died happy knowing her line would go on and on.

Like Eric goes on and on and will after true death. Merlotte is not the only sire to ensure his line continues. He has Pam and he has Karin, and through them many others, and soon he will have a nation.

It had been his maker's will that Eric and Freyda marry to consolidate power and eventually take the United States. (Well. The first part was all Appius, to be sure. Eric might have tacked on the second as an addendum.) And he had been fine with that plan, once he tweaked it, because—oh, yes, there's always something—he had always known he wouldn't need Freyda to take the States. He only needed the more powerful supes to be looking the other way when he made his move, which worked out nicely, but only for him. The Stackhouse-Merlottes can have their swamp, and welcome to it. He'll take more. He always takes more.

He wonders when his plan-within-a-plan finally became clear to Sookie. If she kept up with the news, she would have realized in less than a decade that things had never been so cut-and-dried as they'd appeared. He wonders if she regrets giving him up—or letting him be handed over.

I won't ever settle for settling.

He is always amused by those who insist that having a good choice and a bad choice means having no choices. In the end, it *is* a choice, everything is, good and bad, and crying otherwise is for children. He is many things, but he has not been a child since William of Normandy walked the earth.

You've got no choice . . . There's no choice . . . You have to . . . You must . . . You will . . . No. Eric has been forced, it's true, but he always, *always* has choices. Forced to be with Appius, and then Freyda. Forced to speak to people he would never have spoken to otherwise; forced to touch and be touched by people he would never have touched otherwise. Well. They are gone and he remains. And like Merlotte, he has ensured his line regardless.

Pam Ravenscroft and Karin Slaughter. His marriage/prison term with Freyda horrified Pam, because for all her morbid sense of humor and lethal charm, she values Eric's happiness above all things. Pam had been so young when he married the queen—less than two hundred years old—that she still hadn't picked up the knack of seeing the long con. She caught on after she'd been the Area Five sheriff for a decade. Karin, always more sanguine about such things, so pragmatic as to seem detached, caught on about a week after the wedding took place.

Even better, his darlings were instrumental in Castro's downfall. Karin had taken note of everyone, *everyone* who sought Sookie for any reason, every single night for a year. By the year's end Sookie was used to having her around, and Karin offered to keep watch indefinitely, so Eric always knew who was in Bon Temps and why, and from there it was a simple matter to—

There we are.

He spots the other person he is there to see, another stranger who has no idea Eric Northman is in his future, however briefly; the idiots on the Council have sent a hard case to Were About. Said hard case is there to observe his targets, a flock of oblivious magpies all too busy bitching about unreasonable grandparents and great-grandparents, and also the sorry state of implant holos, whatever the hell those are ("You've never experienced *Gone with the Wind* until you've seen it projected inside your own head") to realize they are in the crosshairs.

How will the killer do it? Something in their food? Their drinks? A traffic accident? A home invasion gone wrong? Is he there for one of them or all of them? Will he order the ribs and, if so, try to kill one of Sookie's line with barbecue sauce under his fingernails?

For some reason, Eric finds that last thought borderline repulsive— and it takes a lot to repulse him.

Whatever the hard case's plan, for now he is there to observe, and it's a hilarious irony that he has no idea he, in turn, is being watched. Well. It's not as if Eric has come to Were About for the fine cuisine and—

"That was just so completely icy I could have *shit*!"

—stimulating conversation.

He stands, he follows the hard case, he kills the would-be assassin in the men's room. Stupid bastard never heard him come up, probably never heard the crunch of his C2 and C3 vertebrae disintegrating under Eric's fingers and really? This guy (who dresses like an accountant but has the hands of a lumberjack, a good trick since there haven't been lumberjacks for decades) is the best they can do? Who sends a norm to kill a Stackhouse-Merlotte? To kill a flock of Stackhouse-Merlottes? This was hardly worth getting out of bed for.

Who are you kidding, Northman? You couldn't see her, *so you arranged for the next best thing. The killer-who-wasn't was superfluous, just like the TrueBlood you had no interest in ordering, much less drinking.*

Well, yes, yes to all of it but it hardly matters at this point. Sookie's protection had been part and parcel of that long-ago wedding contract and it's interesting to see how that has evolved. Perhaps it is now difficult to find assassins not affiliated with vampires or shifters; perhaps the average freelance assassin has zero interest in messing with any or all Stackhouse-Merlottes. Perhaps the hard case is indicative of murder-for-hire's shallow labor pool.

That is . . . hilarious.

Inwardly chortling, Eric is in a rush now, slinging the body over one shoulder and zipping to the Dumpster outside. Not as dangerous as it would seem; the kitchen and waitstaff are so busy handling the dinner rush they likely wouldn't notice if he'd set the corpse on fire and heaved it onto the grill.

("Order up! Wait, what? This is not on the menu. Are you people *trying* to get the board of health to shut us down? Again? Get the corpse off the grill!")

As it is, the body will quickly be found (but not so quickly as to inconvenience him) and a good thing, too; a message no one receives isn't much of a message. And the corpse will be more effective than a sternly worded note, to wit: *DEAR SHITHEADS, ALL STACKHOUSE-MERLOTTE SPAWN ARE OFF-LIMITS OR I WILL FEED YOU YOUR OWN SEVERED HEAD. LOVE, ERIC NORTHMAN.*

He returns to his table, prepared to settle the bill and rebuff the waitress's advances and—what was the other thing? Oh. Right. Flee the scene of his murder du jour.

"Okay, sir, so do you want—"

Ah! There she is. "I'm a widower who is off waitresses who have a smidge of fairy and are alternately brave and idiotic, determined and wishy-washy, loving and spiteful."

The waitress blinks at him slowly, like an owl. "Okay, I really only wanted to know if you needed anything else. And I don't have a smidge of fairy. Are those even a real thing?"

He shrugs.

"Aw, cripes," she mutters as she moves away, low enough so most customers wouldn't have heard. "I always get these guys. Always."

He snickers to himself and then: the first genuine surprise in decades.

"Hi."

"Hello." It is one of the Merlotte magpies, the eldest boy. Eric is impressed and annoyed. He should have heard him coming.

"I'm sorry to disturb your meal—" A pointed glance at the glass brimming with TrueBlood. "You look familiar. Have we met?"

"No." Not for the first time, Eric is thankful to be one of the supes who keep themselves out of the media spotlight. The boy will not recognize him, unless Sookie handed out pictures along with her bedtime stories.

"Maybe you knew my Gram?"

Or perhaps he *will* recognize Eric. The boy (who doubtless considers himself a man but he's surely not old enough to drink) is polite and unafraid. Sookie's eyes, Merlotte's hair and build. Courteous but not fawning; an excellent balance and Eric is (a little) impressed in spite of himself.

"Maybe I did know your Gram," he replies, pointedly using the past tense. "We were . . . friends."

"Want to give me a name, so I can pass on your howdy to the rest of the family?"

"No." Pass on his howdy? Ugh. Not even on a dare.

"Give me a name anyway." Still polite, still not afraid. Steel behind the smiling eyes. Courage to spare, perhaps not so much intelligence. Even without the eyes, he would know one of her blood. "Or how about I give you one?"

"As you like."

"It's Eric Northman."

"What a coincidence," he mock-gasps. "That's *my* name."

"Mmmm. Mine's Jason."

"Oh. Sorry."

"What?"

"Nothing." Poor thing, named for a Hotshot wedding survivor and fairy werepanther almost intelligent enough to remember to put pants on his human form. God, the humanity.

Jason stares thoughtfully down at Eric, then flicks a glance back at the table of his relatives. The oldest three are watching them. The younger ones are more interested in a FreeVee-versus-implant-holo argument, and wolfing down the bowls of peanuts and popcorn that stand for hors d'oeuvres at Were About. This is very well, since the concentrated attention of four Stackhouse-Merlottes is . . . unsettling. For a moment Eric experiences an emotion he hasn't felt in decades; for a moment, he fears them.

Well. Afraid or not, he must speed things up; there *is* a corpse in the Dumpster, after all, and he has miles to go before he et cetera. So he comes right out with it.

"Yes."

Jason blinks and doesn't speak right away. His confused *not sure what's going on but will blunder through anyway* expression exactly mirrors that of his great-great-great-great-great-great-uncle and namesake. "Sorry?"

"You're about to ask me if I am just passing through. Yes, I am. Then you'll ask me if I've ever been here before so you can recommend some hideous local B and B. I will laugh in derision and you'll puff up like a toad, which will make me laugh harder, and you'll swear at me and I'll get a cramp from all the laughing and you'll make a vague threat and then you'll stomp back to your family while convincing yourself that our encounter went exactly as you planned and later will mention to your grandparents what an arrogant ass I am and they will concur."

"So I don't actually have to be here for this conversation."

Eric laughs; he can't help it. It's kind of glorious. "No."

He is so intrigued by the boy he almost doesn't notice the waitress is there again, not to pester Eric but to tease Jason. "You just go sit down with the rest of those reprobates. I'll get your orders in a minute. Stop bothering my customers."

"Thank you," Eric tells her. "I felt quite bullied and vulnerable, but now that you're here I feel much safer." He pauses. "Hold me?"

She rolls her eyes—he's deflected her flirting too often for her to think he's truly interested—and as she walks away he hears her muttering, "Sunday rush, *hate* the Sunday rush."

There is a pause that is almost awkward—the boy has not left but is preparing to, and Eric decides to risk a quick query. "If you'll permit an old friend of the family an impertinent question—"

"The way I heard the stories, *impertinent* is sort of your middle name."

"Oh?"

A shrug. "Your rep kind of precedes you."

"I literally have a ten-dollar bill for every time someone has said that to me over the years."

"And you're eating here?" Jason doesn't have to glance around the restaurant to make his point. The place isn't a dive, certainly, but yes, Eric could certainly afford a finer meal. Several of them. "Except I'm betting you're not here for the food."

"Nonsense. I love finger-lickin' ribs," he replies with a straight face. "You didn't know that about me, did you?"

"Nope. Good trick, since you don't eat. Right?"

"Right. And it doesn't matter what I'm here for. Because you can ride on a reputation, or it can ride you or run you over like a dog in the street. But still: It's *your* ride. And I'll stop now, because I can practically hear your neurons shutting down." Eric knows he looks young, knows he is conventionally handsome, and knows that most people who are aware of his true nature treat him based on how he looks, not how old they know him to be. It is a tremendous advantage at times to not be treated as a doddering elder relative who may or may not wet his pants while waiting for a nursing home volunteer to fetch him pudding.

But that wouldn't apply to any of Sookie's family. They would know better than most that the outside doesn't matter, maybe never mattered. They will treat someone they see as an old man . . . like an old man, and never mind how he looks or what he wears. So Jason, like most young people, is half listening to Eric's well-meant advice while no doubt thinking about whatever teenage idiots ponder as he waits for their conversation to be over.

"My neurons are none of your business," Jason snaps, but he softens it with a smile.

"Getting back to my impertinent question"—Eric hears the boy's not-quite-inaudible sigh but lets it pass—"is she happy?"

"Who? Her?" He jerks a thumb to the left, toward the kitchen. "The waitress?"

"Sookie." *Shit. Should not have used the present tense.* It was a luxury he should never have indulged. When he craved her the most, when he missed Sookie the most, it had been easier to think of her as apart from him, not dead. But that led to grammatical inaccuracy, among other things. Sookie was gone, but a part of her was stashed safely away in his mind, and she is always smiling, there, she is always happy to see him, there.

"Which one?" Jason asks.

Ye gods, there were multiple Sookies now at large in the universe? How fertile had the woman been? *Let's see, if each generation named at least one girl child after Sookie, that would . . .* Horrified, he stops doing the math.

"Mr. Northman? Which one?"

"Your—" For a moment, he fears his lips won't form the words. "Your, uh, great-great-great-great-great-grandmother, I think."

"Oh . . . Super Great Grammy Gram."

He is appalled and does not hide it. "That's what you call her?"

"No, we call her G-Cubed."

Dear God. "Yes, that one, was she happy?"

The boy thinks it over, and Eric gives him a few marks for it. A platitude doesn't come rushing out of his mouth as it would from almost anyone else. He wants Eric gone but will not say just anything to bring that about. "Yeah, I think so. Or at least not *un*happy. From the stories I heard, anyway." He shrugs with the fond blankness of a boy who loves his elderly relatives and tolerates stories about long-dead ancestors while remaining confident he himself will never be old, because that sort of thing only happens to Other People. "She loved her house and her family and her town. I don't think there's anything else. Or if there was . . ." Another shrug. ". . . she never said."

"A happy ending, then." He's surprised and pleased to hear no bitterness in his tone. Perhaps this errand wasn't sentimental and silly. Or at least not *just* sentimental and silly.

"Sure."

He studies the boy and thinks of the girl in the white dress, the one who is long dead and the one who lives in the lockbox of his mind, always young, always happy, always wanting him. *I loved you and I hated you and I missed you and then I realized I would always love you and, in the end, they're just words and they change nothing and you reaped what you sowed, my darling, but if it's what you wanted I suppose I can be happy for you.*

"Thanks for answering my questions," Jason says at last and oh, right. They are having a conversation. Best get to it, then. Or end it. Yes, that was better.

"Thank you for answering mine."

"Nice talking to you."

"Was it?"

Jason Stackhouse-Merlotte shrugs and wanders back to his family. Their heads come together like a flock of charismatic pigeons squabbling over peanuts in the park, and he feels their regard and, better, their dismissal

(silly children, a rookie move, really, but I've got no time to show you your mistakes)

and he knows he's got maybe another five minutes before the body is discovered. He drains his drink, pops a fifteen percent tip into the waitress's account via the table tab (the tables remind him of the iPads of old, except larger and with remarkably greasy screens), and heads out the door.

He passes the table

(don't do it)

unsure if he's relieved or annoyed when none of them look up

(do not do this)

and pauses, ten feet from the door and the rest of his life.

(Really? You're really doing this?)

"You can love a parent while disliking the decisions they made for you," he informs them, part of his brain wondering why he is bothering. With any of it. Is he talking to them or just using them to remind himself of a few home truths? "You can love them even as you pull away from them. You won't ever be rid of them. Even in death—perhaps especially not in death."

Jason looks up. They all look up. Bred to politeness by their elders, none of them say what they are thinking.

"Uh . . . okay. Thanks for that, I guess, mysterious weirdo."

"Eric," the redhead corrects. "Jason *just* told us. God, if it's not about food or sex you're really not interested, are you?"

"That's exactly right. So anyway, thanks, mysterious weirdo who knew G-Cubed and whose name is Eric."

All right, one of them says what they are thinking. Eric has to bite his lip to stifle the smile.

"Sookie," Jason says by way of mild reproof.

"Sorry," This Younger Sookie says, not seeming at all remorseful.

"And his name is *Mr. Northman*," Jason reminds the rest of the table. "Like I started to tell you, he was a friend of G-Cubed."

"Sorry?" This Younger Sookie tries again, sounding the smallest bit remorseful.

"I don't think you are," Eric replies, and gives them a real smile, and moves past them to the door, "but that's fine."

"Um, okay." And then, the last thing he hears before the door shuts between him and a throng of Stackhouse-Merlottes: "Well, that *was* mysterious. You gotta admit."

He feels good, and he thinks he even knows why. Returning had been bittersweet, but he'd been afraid the bitter would outweigh the sweet, and it hadn't. He feels satisfied and curiously pleased. He's seen evidence of Sookie's post-Eric life and it hasn't broken him. It hasn't even bent him. He can move on to the next phase of his life knowing he has tied up loose ends.

Perhaps he will marry again. It would be novel to marry without tricking the other party or being forced himself. How . . . how does a marriage like that even work? When you can just tell the other person the truth all the time? Perhaps charts are made. Or something. Chore charts? Lovemaking charts? Since everything can be out in the open from the beginning, there would be lots of time to plan spousal activities. So definitely charts of some kind would be involved. Maybe? He honestly has no idea; the whole thing is baffling.

A strange thing to suddenly be happy about, but it is quite something to realize that even at his age, there is still unexplored territory, things he has yet to experience.

He gets in his personal vehicle—no driver today, unnecessary for so many reasons—and pulls out of the lot to find whatever awaits him.

His future.

CONTRIBUTORS

Rachel Caine is the *New York Times*, *USA Today*, and internationally best-selling author of more than forty novels in urban fantasy, romantic suspense, and young adult. She's probably best known for her Morganville Vampires novels and has been a proud Sookie fan(atic) from the start. Her most recent novel is the YA Romeo and Juliet novel *Prince of Shadows*. Visit Rachel online at rachelcaine.com, facebook.com/RachelCaineFanPage, and twitter.com/rachelcaine.

Dana Cameron can't help mixing a little history into her fiction. Drawing from her expertise in archaeology, Dana's work (including several Fangborn stories) has won multiple Agatha, Anthony, and Macavity awards, and earned an Edgar® Award nomination. Her first two Fangborn novels, *Seven Kinds of Hell* (2013) and *Pack of Strays* (2014), were published by 47North. Dana lives in Massachusetts with her husband and benevolent feline overlords. For more information, visit danacameron.com.

Bill Crider is a former college English teacher and the author of more than fifty published novels and an equal number of short stories. He's won two Anthony Awards and a Derringer Award, and he's been nominated for the Shamus and the Edgar® awards. His latest novel in the Sheriff Dan Rhodes series is *Compound Murder*. Check out his homepage at billcrider.com, or take a look at his peculiar blog at billcrider.blogspot.com.

New York Times bestselling author **MaryJanice Davidson** is a former model and medical test subject. Her books are available in fifteen countries, and she frequently speaks to book clubs ("I don't know why my books sell"), writer's groups ("Seriously. No idea"), and World War II veterans ("Thanks for driving Hitler to suicide!"). She lives with her family and dogs in St. Paul, Minnesota, and her latest book, *Undead and Unwary*, came out in July 2014. She loves hearing from readers and can be reached at contactmjd@comcast .net or via her website at maryjanicedavidson.net.

Leigh Evans was born in Montreal, Quebec, but now lives in southern Ontario with her husband. She's raised two kids, mothered three dogs, and herded a few cats. Other than that, her life was fairly routine until she hit middle age. Some women get tattoos. Leigh decided to write a book about a half-Fae, half-Were girl who's a magnet for trouble. The first Mystwalker novel was released as *The Trouble with Fate* in 2012. Second and third books have quickly followed: *The Thing about Weres* and *The Problem with Promises*. At the age most people start thinking about retirement, Leigh has found her career slinging words and pummeling plots. A little tardy, but then again, her mum always said she was a late bloomer.

Christopher Golden is the *New York Times* bestselling author of such novels as *Of Saints and Shadows*, *Strangewood*, and *Snowblind*. He has cowritten three illustrated novels with Mike Mignola, the first of which, *Baltimore, or, The Steadfast Tin Soldier and the Vampire*, was the launching pad for the Eisner Award–nominated comic book series *Baltimore*. The first volume in his graphic novel trilogy collaboration with Charlaine Harris, *Cemetery Girl*, was released in January 2014. Golden was born and raised in Massachusetts, where he still lives with his family. His original novels have been published in more than fourteen languages in countries around the world. Please visit him at christophergolden.com.

Nancy Holder is the *New York Times* bestselling author of the Wicked Saga (written with Debbie Viguié) and the recipient of five Bram Stoker Awards for her supernatural fiction. She received a Scribe Award for *Saving Grace: Tough Love*, based on the TV show of the same name. She is known for writing "tie-in" material for such universes as Buffy the Vampire Slayer,

Teen Wolf, Beauty and the Beast, Sherlock Holmes, Nancy Drew, and many others. Next up is *FutureDaze2: Reprise*, an anthology of young adult short science fiction, which she coedited with Erin Underwood. She was a guest of honor at the World Horror Convention in May 2014. Find her at twitter .com/nancyholder and facebook.com/nancyholderfans.

Miranda James is the bestselling alter ego of Dean James, author of mystery fiction and nonfiction. He has won the Agatha and Macavity awards for Best Nonfiction and has been twice nominated for the Edgar® Award for Best Critical/Biographical Work. As Miranda, he is the creator of the Cat in the Stacks series featuring librarian Charlie Harris and his Maine Coon cat, Diesel. The latest in the series, *The Silence of the Library*, was both a *New York Times* and *USA Today* bestseller.

Jonathan Maberry is a *New York Times* bestselling author, four-time Bram Stoker Award winner, and freelancer for Marvel Comics, IDW, and Dark Horse Comics. His novels include *Extinction Machine, Fire & Ash*, and *Patient Zero*. His award-winning teen novel *Rot & Ruin* is now in development for film. He is the editor of *V-Wars*, an award-winning vampire anthology series that is also in development as a comic from IDW, and *Out of Tune*, a forthcoming dark fantasy anthology. Since 1978 he's sold more than 1,200 magazine feature articles, 3,000 columns, plays, greeting cards, song lyrics, and poetry. He teaches Experimental Writing for Teens, is the founder of the Writers Coffeehouse, and is a cofounder of The Liars Club. Jonathan is a frequent keynote speaker and guest of honor at genre conventions and writers' conferences, often speaking on the craft and business of writing, the publishing industry, social media, and other topics. He's a member of the Mystery Writers of America, International Thriller Writers, the Horror Writers Association, and the International Association of Media Tie-In Writers. Jonathan lives in Del Mar, California, with his wife, Sara Jo, and a fierce little dog named Rosie. For more information, please visit jonathanmaberry.com.

Jeffrey J. Mariotte is the award-winning author of more than forty-five novels, including supernatural thrillers *Season of the Wolf, Missing White Girl,*

River Runs Red, and *Cold Black Hearts*, and, as Jeff Mariotte, *The Slab*, the Dark Vengeance teen horror quartet, and others. He also writes comic books, including the long-running horror/Western comic book series *Desperadoes* and the original graphic novel *Zombie Cop*. He has worked in virtually every aspect of publishing and is a co-owner of the specialty bookstore Mysterious Galaxy in San Diego. He lives in southeastern Arizona on the Flying M Ranch. For more information, please visit jeffmariotte.com.

Seanan McGuire writes things. It's surprisingly difficult to make her stop, which is why she has two ongoing urban fantasy series and a pseudonym (Mira Grant) under which she writes science fiction and medical thrillers. When not writing things, she travels a lot, spends too much time in Disney Parks, and watches horror movies with her three abnormally large blue cats.

Suzanne McLeod is the author of the Spellcrackers.com urban fantasy series about magic, mayhem, and murder—with dangerous faeries, seductive vampires, bureaucratic witches, eccentric goblins, and rock-solid trolls! *The Shifting Price of Prey*—#4—is her latest book. Suzanne has been a cocktail waitress, dance group roadie, and retail manager before becoming a writer. She was born in London (her favorite city and home to Spellcrackers.com) and now lives on the sunny (sometimes) South Coast of England, with Mr Mc and Bella the Hound, and they share their garden with a small colony of pipistrelle bats!

Nicole Peeler writes urban fantasy for Orbit Books and, in her spare time, is an assistant professor at Seton Hill University, where she teaches in their MFA in Writing Popular Fiction. Having recently finished the final book of her award-winning Jane True series, she is looking forward to the upcoming publication of *Jinn and Juice*, the first book in a series about a cursed jinni living in Pittsburgh. Nicole also lives in Pittsburgh, although she's neither cursed nor a jinni. Please visit her at nicolepeeler.com for more information on her books, or on Facebook for pictures of her sandwiches.

Leigh Perry is Toni L. P. Kelner in disguise, or maybe vice versa. As Leigh, she writes the Family Skeleton Mysteries. *A Skeleton in the Family*, the first, came out in September 2013, and *The Skeleton Takes a Bow* in September 2014. As Toni, she's the coeditor of *New York Times* bestselling anthologies with Charlaine Harris. (Obviously, this is their most recent.) She's also the author of the "Where Are They Now?" Mysteries and the Laura Fleming series (all of which are available as eBooks and audiobooks), and is an Agatha Award winner for short fiction. Though she has published a number of stories as Toni, this one is her first as Leigh. Leigh/Toni lives just north of Boston with her husband and fellow author, Stephen P. Kelner, Jr., their two daughters, and two guinea pigs. On the Web, she's found at leighperryauthor.com.

Jeanne C. Stein is the bestselling author of the urban fantasy series the Anna Strong, Vampire Chronicles. Her award-winning series has been picked up in three foreign countries and her short stories published in collections in the United States and the United Kingdom. Her newest book, *Blood Bond*, was released in August 2013. She also writes under the name S. J. Harper with San Diego author Samantha Sommersby, and the first book in their new series, *Fallen*, was released in October 2013. She has been a fan of Charlaine Harris and Sookie ever since a special lunch in San Diego when Charlaine offered encouragement and friendship to a writer just embarking on a publishing journey of her own.